TO LOVE A QUEEN

A PAWN'S GAME TRILOGY
BOOK ONE

TO LOVE A QUEEN

JENNIFER MEINKING

Published by

Soul Splash Press

Cover and Interior Design: Nick Zelinger, NZGraphics.com
Editors: Jen Zelinger, TwinOwlsAuthors.com,
D'Anne Frazier, WebOpter Associates

ISBN: 978-1-7337076-4-0 (print)
ISBN: 978-1-7337076-5-7 (e-book)

Library of Congress Control Number: 2022904405

First Edition

Printed in the United States of America

To Colin, my oldest son, who never hesitates to ask if I'm okay and always seems to know before I do when I'm not … Thank you for all the ways you have stepped up as you grow into the man you were meant to be. I cried with joy the day you were born, and sixteen years later, I still consider it a privilege to be your mother.

To Amanda Branch, who has been a lifeline during some of the most difficult trials I have faced during the writing of this book … Thank you for the countless hours you have spent listening, engaging, investigating, and growing with me as I explored the depth of this material.

And finally, to all the women out there who have borne the scarlet letter … This book is for you. May others listen to *your* stories with compassion and understanding—truly hearing your struggles, your joys, and your pain. Your value is beyond measure, for you have loved much.

1

A stab of anxiety pricked her.

Though no one had spoken, something within—some faint whispering—had suggested the guest of honor would arrive any moment. When the banquet hall doors flew open yet again, she did not look, despite the fluttering in her stomach. The sensation leaped into her throat as the announcement of his name hovered on the air, then vanished. She forced herself to take several deep, even breaths. Keeping her face serene and unaffected, she slowly turned her gaze toward the splendid figure approaching in his full dress uniform.

Years of military service had given him a powerful yet lithe physique, which the other women eyed with obvious appreciation. As their giggles and whispers echoed in her ears, she resisted the temptation to crane her neck and gawk at him as they did. As always, he paid the tittering beauties little heed and strode confidently to take his place behind the last of the soldiers who had formed a line to pay their respects to the ruling monarchs of Asgard.

As the line moved forward, she discreetly stole glances at him but did not meet his eyes. She had not seen him since he left for Muspelheim weeks ago. The separation had brought an agonizing uncertainty that plagued her whenever she analyzed every moment, every look, and every word that had passed between them in the past. But as soon as he stood before her, all doubts fled, driven away by the familiarity in his smile. A feverish warmth washed over her, rendering it difficult for her to breathe normally.

"My queen," he murmured as he bowed respectfully, the velvet resonance of his voice sending shivers up her spine.

His strong, straight-edged nose and chiseled cheekbones formed one of the handsomest faces she had ever seen. The strands of premature silver that peppered his rich brown hair and well-groomed, trim beard only added to his charm. But her appreciation of his good looks had been purely aesthetic until she had gotten to know him.

"You honor us with your presence, General Vidar," she returned, gracefully dipping her head. "I thank you for your service to Asgard and to your king."

"The honor is mine to stand before you. All service I have given is both my duty and my pleasure, Queen Frigga," he responded eagerly, then bowed again as she acknowledged him with a nod and a warm smile.

Acutely aware of how many eyes were upon the two of them, Frigga closed her own briefly, resisting the urge to scratch at the scarlet jewels rubbing against her throat. Though she had been the queen of Asgard for centuries, she had never quite gotten used to the feeling of wearing the heavily jeweled chokers her husband seemed to prefer. Was it her nervousness that had made her skin itch suddenly? She told herself to maintain her composure and forced her eyes open again, but the general had moved on to pay his respects to King Odin, who stood next to her on the slightly elevated dais in the beautifully decorated banquet hall.

Frigga proudly surveyed her handiwork as the general spoke with the king. As a tribute to their victories in the fire realm, she had chosen an abundance of red silk, which flowed through golden clasps at every window and puddled on the marble floor. But the tall, misshapen lump of red cloth tucked away between two columns drew the most interest from the banquet attendees. A surge of excitement welled up inside her as she imagined the general's reaction when the draped fabric would be removed to reveal the gift she had commissioned for him—a two-headed wolf statue carved from alabaster, which King Odin would present to General Vidar as a token of Asgard's gratitude.

The king's husky voice sounded throughout the banquet hall as he addressed Vidar's special detachment of highly trained soldiers known as the Valiants, who now stood at attention with their general. Every one of the thirty men had accepted the invitation to join their commander at this banquet held in his honor. Quite a few of the foot soldiers in Vidar's charge were also in attendance, including Crown Prince Baldur and his best friend, Hod, the youngest son of the keeper of the gates. The two of them listened to the king speak with gleaming eyes, for they both aspired to join Vidar's elite group themselves.

Slightly bored with the ceremony, the queen allowed her eyes to flit to the two-headed wolves engraved on each Valiant's breastplate, tracing them in her mind. Vidar had chosen the emblem when he first started the group three hundred years ago. He had once held Frigga spellbound with the inspiration for this symbol—an old, haunting story he had heard as a boy. The riveting legend detailed how a giant wolf named Fenrir had terrorized Asgard until a brave soldier cleaved his head in two, which then transformed into separate heads, making the beast even more formidable. Rather than take on this strengthened foe, the soldier used his wits and patience to trick the wolf into devouring itself. Though parts of the retelling had made Frigga shudder, she shared Vidar's philosophical insights and sympathy when he explained his interest in the wolf. This common depth of thought was one of the initial attractions she had experienced toward the general, who now bowed gracefully in acceptance of the king's final words before dismissing his soldiers to enjoy the revelries of the evening.

A crowd of eager women almost immediately surrounded Vidar, blocking Frigga's view. He gently extracted himself and made his way over to the royal table, where he took his seat in the place of honor at King Odin's right hand. As the soothing notes of flute and lyre floated through the air, the other Asgardians filled their plates at the buffet tables while the servants set the meal before those seated with the king.

Frigga picked at her plate in silence, barely noticing the food as she arranged her face into the regal expression expected of her rank. Though the king had given her the deep red gown she wore, which brought out the red sheen in her blonde curls, he had not given her so much as a second glance or kind word. Vidar, on the other hand, could not hide the golden glow of admiration in his hazel eyes whenever he looked at the queen.

Pleased as she was by what she saw, Frigga marveled at how one such as he could desire a woman like her. Most of the time, she felt trapped in her own palace, nothing but King Odin's castaway. But Vidar made her feel alive again.

As the meal drew to a close, the king still paid no attention to his queen, engrossed as he was in his lengthy conversation with the general. Since Odin's distraction had become a common occurrence during the lengthy war on Muspelheim, Frigga told herself not to allow her husband's indifference to overly bother her. Instead, she comforted herself with what she had hidden inside the gift Odin would bestow upon the honored general at the end of the festivities.

In the brief lull after dessert, Frigga joined a group of married noblewomen who gossiped with each other under the red silk billowing in the summer evening breeze from the balcony.

"Queen Frigga, that dress is most becoming," gushed Lady Ithunna as she adjusted her own purple gown, which brought a pleasing sheen to her raven hair. "I've been admiring you all night."

"You look lovely yourself, Lady Ithunna. And thank you," Frigga responded. "The king gave it to me before he left for Muspelheim since he knew he would not be here for our anniversary."

Ithunna sighed dreamily, her slate gray eyes sparkling like wet river stones. "I wish Bragi doted on me the way King Odin dotes on you."

"Oh, come now. Surely, he must," Frigga responded casually. Inwardly, she snorted, *You wouldn't say that if you knew how unhappy we are.*

But since she had to maintain appearances, she never spoke of her heartache to any of the noblewomen.

"Oh, I suppose he does in his own way," Ithunna giggled. "Sometimes, he writes me sonnets during the king's war councils."

"Ithunna, don't say things like that in front of the queen," chided Lady Annette, a feisty noblewoman with wavy blonde hair and magnetic eyes that reminded Frigga of the South Sea, Annette's birthplace.

"Why not? You would," Ithunna grumbled.

"Of course I would," Annette retorted. "If Berg wrote me sonnets, I'd want the whole realm to know. You, on the other hand, would very much care if the council knew that about Bragi. And so would he."

Ithunna drew her eyebrows together and scowled at Annette, who merely smirked knowingly.

"The king won't hear a word from me, Lady Ithunna," Frigga laughed, delighted by the playful banter, which bespoke their comfort and friendship with each other. "How is Lord Berg recovering from his injuries, Lady Annette?"

"Oh, he's been a beast," Annette answered, the laughter in her voice showing she was not truly serious. "But he's healing well. Between visiting him at the House of the Healers and caring for little Sigyn, I haven't had a moment's rest."

A pang of grief shot through Frigga, for Annette's adorable daughter always reminded the queen of the flaxen-haired baby girl she had only held in her arms for a few hours after birth. Sigyn's sweet nature often made Frigga wonder what life would have been like if the child had not died. Despite this reminder of her loss, she enjoyed the little girl's company, especially since Sigyn was between the ages of Frigga's two youngest sons, who were as rambunctious as most boys in their primary years.

"Doesn't Sigyn go with you to the House?" Lady Gladys inquired innocently, blinking her large violet eyes as she absentmindedly twirled a strand of her light brown hair around her finger.

The noblewoman had been silent up to that point, which surprised Frigga since she usually had more to say. Had something been distracting her? It seemed she had just registered the conversation.

"Berg doesn't want her to see him like this, so she sits out in the hallway," Annette lamented. "It makes it quite difficult to focus on my husband when I'm worrying about her."

"Why don't the two of you stay here at the palace for a few days, Lady Annette?" Frigga offered, eager for another chance to spend time with the young girl. "While you visit Lord Berg at the House, Sigyn can play with Loki and Thor in the gardens after their morning lessons."

"She's a saint!" exclaimed Gladys as Annette eagerly accepted the offer. "But what about that delicious General Vidar? He's the guest of honor. Why aren't we talking about him?"

Frigga bristled as she noted a mischievous gleam in the pretty noblewoman's eyes, but she stuffed the resentful feeling down. After all, most women found Vidar attractive. Besides, Gladys was married.

So are you! Frigga scolded herself.

"I simply cannot understand how he's still single," Ithunna remarked. "He's almost as handsome as Bragi. And the single ladies adore him."

"Almost? Ithunna, you are a hopeless romantic," Annette scoffed. "Someone's bound to catch his eye sooner or later. Don't you agree, Queen Frigga?"

"Of course! It's only a matter of time," Frigga said casually, almost flippantly. "I shouldn't wonder if he takes a fancy to your sister, Lady Annette. She's grown quite lovely."

"Who, Brynhilde?" Annette hooted. "She wouldn't notice him if he tripped in front of her! She's joined the healers, you know. That's all she cares about."

"You're far too hard on her, Annette," scolded Gladys. "The healers have done wonders for your husband … and mine."

"Was Lord Trebent hurt in battle?" Frigga inquired with surprise, suddenly noticing the nobleman across the room, sporting a cast and a sling.

"No, that silly man fell down the stairs yesterday," Gladys informed her. "He comes through an entire war unscathed, then breaks his arm in his own home within hours of returning."

The women all laughed quietly. Frigga relaxed as she picked up on the fondness in Gladys's tone and the tenderness in her eyes when Trebent smiled at her from where he stood talking with several other soldiers. Perhaps her husband's condition distracted her and not some hidden attraction to Vidar.

Gladys continued, "Regardless, you shouldn't look on the healers with such disdain, Annette. It's an honorable profession. Why, the queen is practically a healer herself!"

"Oh, I simply know a thing or two about herbs and comfort," Frigga brushed aside the praise. She paused thoughtfully. "But if I were not the queen, I might enjoy that line of work."

"You're Vanir," Annette pointed out with a wry smile. "If you'd stayed on Vanaheim, you probably would have become the exact opposite of a healer."

"What does that mean?" Frigga laughed.

"You know," Annette said in a conspiratorial tone as she gently nudged the queen. "A warrior."

"One of the Idisi?" Gladys breathed with excitement.

"Not likely," Frigga snorted. "Lady Freya and I had a falling out."

"Over King Odin," Annette laughed. "If he had married her instead of you, I imagine you would have made those warrior women better than Freya ever did."

"Annette! Now who's saying scandalous things in front of the queen!" Ithunna shushed her. "Why in the nine realms would Queen Frigga choose that life over King Odin?"

"I'm not saying she should have," Annette hastened to explain. "I wouldn't want anyone else as our queen. But I think she should have opportunities to use her talents."

"Which ones?" Gladys asked curiously.

Frigga peered at Lady Annette, who winked at her. Few people knew how gifted Frigga was with the sword. She did not purposely hide her abilities, but not many people seemed interested in what the queen could do outside of her duties to manage banquets, decorate, assist Odin in arbitration, and raise the princes. Annette only knew because she had seen Frigga use a sword once, many years ago. Was Annette pushing her to reveal her skills?

Before Frigga could answer Gladys, Ithunna suddenly gasped and gestured toward General Vidar, who was speaking with a pretty red-haired noblewoman. The girl giggled at whatever he had said and laid her hand possessively on his arm.

"Maybe it's finally happening, girls!" Ithunna exclaimed. "We'll marry off that handsome rogue soon enough."

"That's Lord Gunnar's daughter," Gladys observed. "I've forgotten her name, but she just came into womanhood. Quite beautifully, I might add."

Frigga watched the two with an expression of detached interest, hiding the pang of jealousy that shot through her. She told herself Vidar only spoke with the young lady to ward off any suspicions of his interest in the queen. While the other women whispered to each other over this new development, Frigga remembered a time when she had been completely oblivious to Vidar's attraction to her, focused as she had been on the unraveling marriage she had tried to salvage so many times. As if he knew she was watching, Vidar glanced at her briefly and winked so subtly, no one else could possibly have seen it. But she knew he meant to reassure her that his heart still belonged to her. Instantly, she felt as if she were back in the library where he had first offered her his friendship upon finding her crying by herself. Though it had happened years ago, she remembered it as if it were yesterday.

"My queen, are you injured?"

She had not seen or heard her husband's most trusted advisor and highest-ranking general enter the library. But now, General Vidar knelt before her with great concern all over his noble face.

"I'm fine," she choked out as she tried to wipe her face with the sleeve of her cobalt blue day dress.

To her shock, he took her hands and shook his head. "No, you aren't. And you haven't been for quite some time now."

The gentleness in his rough-looking fingers surprised her, and she found she had no desire to pull away. Something inside her sprang to life—something she thought had died beyond revival. She felt utterly relaxed in his presence.

"Forgive me, my queen, for being so forward, but I see you are in great distress," he said quietly. "Perhaps I can help?"

"How?" she asked somewhat warily, uncertain of his intentions.

"I can listen," Vidar suggested. "I have kept a great many secrets. I could be a friend to you."

"My husband certainly trusts you," Frigga acknowledged. She frowned, though she still did not remove her hands from his, comforted as she was by their warmth. "But what grieves me concerns my husband. So I do not think—"

"I saw him storm into his main office twenty minutes ago," he interrupted softly. "Things are not happy between you, are they?"

She merely stared at him sadly, allowing all of her pain to show in her eyes.

He winced as if he could feel her agony. "Odin is a fool," he muttered.

She gasped and tore her hands from his grasp. "You must not say such things."

"Do not misunderstand me, my queen," Vidar hurried to say. "I am loyal to my king. I believe you already know how we grew up together and fought together under his father.

And I was there when King Borr died an untimely death. We are like brothers."

"Yes, I know," Frigga stated. "And you were there for his coronation." She paused and looked down as tears filled her eyes again. "And for our wedding day."

"There never was a more beautiful bride," he murmured.

She raised her eyes to his. "I think perhaps Odin might disagree."

"Doesn't he tell you how beautiful you are?" Vidar asked in surprise.

Frigga did not miss his use of the present tense, but she simply replied, "He barely speaks to me at all these days. And when he does, we only argue."

"As I said, Odin is a fool," Vidar repeated, standing suddenly. "I won't stand by and watch him lose the best thing that's ever happened to him because of his stubbornness and pride."

Frigga blinked twice at Vidar's words. "Please, General. I appreciate your fervor, but there's nothing you can do. You'll only anger him further."

"King Odin will heed me," Vidar declared confidently. "I know how he has shamed you. And it must never happen again."

She paled, and her hands shook. "What do you mean?"

He knelt in front of her again and took her shaking hands. "Frigga," he said gently. He had never dared to address her without her title until that moment. "Odin told me of Baldur's mother after Borr died. And Loki's mother after your daughter died." He shook his head. "He has never handled grief well, but I know he regrets what he has done."

Frigga sat there in silence, acutely feeling the shame of her straying husband. She could not look the general in the eyes for she had thought no one knew of the king's indiscretions, which still pained her. No matter how hard she had tried in the past, it seemed to her that Odin had simply chosen to stop loving her. And so she had resorted to such scorn and disrespect in private, he avoided her company whenever possible. Deep inside, she believed herself to be at fault for his affairs. If she had been more willing to share his bed, more beautiful, less flawed—

"Don't torture yourself," Vidar interrupted her thoughts as if he were reading her mind.

But she told herself he could not have. As a gifted mind reader herself, she would have known immediately if he had even attempted it.

He took her hands again and continued, "You did not deserve this shame. It was his choice and his alone. I've never seen anyone handle what you have with such grace."

"What am I going to do?" she asked weakly. "I have no friends here. My life is nothing but a farce, and I grow weary of pretending."

"You have one now," Vidar said, squeezing her hands slightly. "I am your friend and ally. I will speak with Odin. And things will change for the better."

But things had not improved where Odin was concerned. Vidar's attempts to influence the king had fallen on deaf ears. As her marriage continued to crumble, Frigga's one comfort over the years was the beautiful friendship that had developed from that encounter.

"Frigga, didn't you hear me?" Odin's irritated voice interrupted her reverie.

She breathed a sigh of relief when she saw she had been staring off into the distance and no longer at Vidar, who had moved to another part of the room.

"No, I did not. My apologies, my king," Frigga replied with a disarming smile. "I'm afraid I was lost in thought."

"It's time to present our gift," he repeated in a gentler tone. "Would you join me for the presentation?"

"Yes, of course. If you wish," Frigga agreed, taking her husband's arm.

"It was your idea, after all," Odin offered, almost kindly. He paused, then said, "And a fine idea it was."

"Thank you, my king," she responded shyly, surprised at his abrupt change in attitude.

Together, they walked to the concealed gift. And though Odin gave another eloquent speech, Frigga did not hear a word of it. She stood there with a warm smile frozen on her face as she daydreamed about the last time she had seen the general, when he had found her walking alone among the rose bushes in the palace gardens the day he left for Muspelheim.

"How do you fare today, my queen?" he asked gallantly.

"It's a good day," she replied, her heart fluttering in his presence as it often did lately. *"Especially now. I didn't expect to see you today."*

"The king noticed you were out here alone," Vidar informed her. *"You know you're supposed to have a guard with you."*

"Oh, is that why you're here?" she asked with disappointment, for she had hoped he had come to see her.

"I volunteered to come collect you," he declared cheekily.

"Is that so?" She hid her smile with a pink rose, allowing its sweet scent to fill her nostrils. "Baldur was with me until only a few minutes ago, or so I thought. I didn't see the need to call a guard."

"It's protocol, my queen," Vidar reminded her. "Outside their homes, all noblewomen are to be accompanied by a guard or the equivalent."

"I know," Frigga sighed. "I cannot leave the princes. They're still down in the grove, getting into who knows what kind of trouble."

"Maybe we should investigate," he chuckled. "I doubt Odin will mind if you continue enjoying the sun a little while longer —as long as you're with me."

"He really does trust you, doesn't he?" she asked softly.

He grinned and looked at the ground.

She frowned suddenly. "Why does Odin care if I walk in the gardens alone when his attitude toward me remains unchanged?"

Vidar's face lost its grin. "Apologies, Frigga. I wasn't entirely truthful with you. Odin doesn't know you're out here. He's closeted with the war council. I spotted you from the window and decided to secure your safety personally."

"Why did you lie?" she asked flatly as she turned down the path that led to the grove of golden apple trees where Baldur had taken Thor and Loki to play.

"I didn't want to hurt you," he responded simply. "I feel I already have by giving you hope that Odin might love you again."

"I no longer care if Odin loves me or not," she declared flippantly. "I've resigned myself to this life."

"You speak as though nothing gives you joy," he observed.

"I have my sons," she said defiantly.

"Nothing else?" he asked sadly.

She stopped in the middle of the path and stared at him. "Why, Vidar, what troubles you? You're not yourself today."

"The conflict on Muspelheim has intensified," he told her. "I'm not supposed to tell you this, but we're leaving in a few hours."

"Who's we?" she demanded, dread filling her heart.

"I'm taking the Valiants and the entire Seventh Corps," he answered gravely, "which means Baldur and Hod are going too."

"No, not Baldur!" she exclaimed. "He's not ready!"

"He's ready, Frigga," Vidar contested. "He's been waiting for this day for a long time. In fact, after we return, I'll start training him to become a Valiant. It's what he wants. You know this."

"I know," she whispered. "But what if he doesn't return?"

"He will return," Vidar assured her. "The king won't let any harm come to his heir. He's going as well. Lord Bragi will act in his stead since Lord Berg is going with Odin."

"Odin is going?" Feeling faint, she reached out her hand and grasped Vidar's arm. "Then the situation is dire!"

"It is. But I won't let any harm come to him either," he promised her, patting her hand gently. "I've sworn an oath to give my life for his."

"No, no, you cannot!" she cried, forgetting herself in her dismay as she bunched his sleeve up in her fist. "Promise me you won't!"

Vidar regarded her strangely. "Promise you I won't what?"

Tears poured out of her eyes before she could stop them. "Promise me you won't give your life for his!"

"You would ask me to break my oath?" he asked quietly. "Why? I've left for battle many times before now. And you've never reacted like this."

She turned away from him, fighting the emotion threatening to drown her where she stood. "Forgive me, Vidar. I won't ask you to break your oath."

"You haven't answered the question," he pointed out quietly.

"What question?" she muttered.

She felt his hands grasp her shoulders to gently turn her to face him, but she refused to look at him. She felt as if he could see right through her.

"Frigga, please tell me why," he pleaded.

She sighed. "Just make sure all three of you return. And Hod too. Gjallar has already lost his wife. Losing his youngest son would be too much grief to bear."

"I'm not concerned with the keeper of the gates just now. If my friendship means anything to you—"

"No, Vidar," she interrupted him, furtively glancing toward the palace. "I must not speak of what your friendship means to me. Or why I said what I should not have said."

"Then I will speak, in case I do not return," he declared, lifting her chin with one finger to make her look at him. She shook her head, but he spoke anyway, his voice low and intimate. "You are more precious to me than anything or anyone."

She tried to interrupt him, to stop him from saying what hovered in the air between them and what she had suspected for some time now. No one at the palace could possibly see them, even from the windows, but she sensed everything was about to change.

He pressed on, ignoring her attempts to silence him. "I would swear fealty to you and you alone, regardless of the consequences."

"And what of Odin?" she whispered, though her heart thrilled within her. "What of your fealty to him?"

"If Odin is going to continue to disregard the priceless treasure he has, then he deserves to lose it," he declared fiercely.

"What are you saying?" she gasped in spite of herself.

Too much had already been said. But since he had opened his soul to her, she could not bear to watch him leave for battle without some conclusion to the matter.

"I've loved you long before that day in the library, my queen," he confessed. "But when you put such faith in me, I told myself only your happiness mattered and dedicated myself to saving your marriage. I've failed you in that, but perhaps—"

"No, you've never failed me," she protested, cutting him off. "You made my situation bearable. You gave me a reason to live again."

"I would do more than that, Frigga," Vidar said softly, his eyes glowing with that soft golden light she had come to understand. "I would give all I have simply for the chance to make you happy. Even my life."

"Vidar, you must not talk that way," Frigga sighed. "Nothing can change. What you speak of means serious consequences for us both, though I wish I were free to return your sentiment."

"Then I am content," he replied, smiling at her with hope shining in his eyes. "Perhaps you will be free someday."

"You cannot waste your life waiting for that possibility," she contested. "There are many women who would be happy to—"

"I will have no other," he stated firmly. "And if all I can have is to simply be in your presence, I will gladly accept that."

"Odin should learn from your example," Frigga murmured. "He is not content with one woman, despite the laws of his land, but you are willing to commit yourself to a life of celibacy because of one woman you cannot have."

"Odin is used to taking what he wants," Vidar remarked with a shrug. "I never was that kind of man."

"You are a man of honor," Frigga acknowledged.

"So is he, deep down," Vidar insisted. "He's just a little lost right now."

She laughed. "And here you are, still defending him and fighting for him."

He grinned sheepishly. "What can I say? I love him … almost as much as I love you."

She placed one finger over his mouth, though her heart rejoiced at his words. "Don't make such declarations out here. Someone might hear you. And then where would we be?"

And sure enough, just after she stepped away from Vidar, Baldur came around the bend of the path followed by his much smaller brothers, who bore several scratches and bruises on their arms and legs. Though too far away to have overheard, Baldur eyed both his mother and the general warily as they moved to meet the three boys in the path.

Frigga had the uncomfortable sense that her oldest son knew more than he let on, but she pushed the feeling aside to demand, "What have you boys been doing?"

"Climbing trees," boasted Thor, eyeing his younger brother with disdain. "Loki fell. Then I fell because I tried to save him."

"You did not, Thor!" Baldur growled as he smacked the back of Thor's head. "You fell because you were acting like an idiot."

Loki snickered, his green eyes flaring as they always did when he was happy, just like his birth mother's used to before she withered away and died from sorrow. Frigga felt a pang of sadness, for Laufey had been her only friend until Vidar. But she brushed it aside as she always did when those memories threatened to break free from where she had banished them—to protect the boy as well as herself.

"They're fine, Mother," Baldur insisted, no doubt sensing her shift in emotions, an ability with which he had been born. "Nothing a little Asgardian ointment won't cure." Then he addressed Vidar, "How goes the war, General?"

"You'll be called up in a few hours," Vidar informed him, grinning at the young man's visible excitement.

"Hod too?" Baldur asked.

"Yes, Hod too," Vidar affirmed, chuckling slightly.

"I'd better go tell him!" Baldur exclaimed, grasping his thick black hair with both hands as his dark eyes gleamed.

"No, you stay with your mother," Vidar commanded, affectionately tousling the hair of both of the smaller boys as he spoke. "She shouldn't be walking around out here alone. And I must take my leave."

Frigga snapped back to the present as she realized the king had finished his speech.

"Thank you, my king," Vidar proclaimed as he strode forward to accept the two-headed wolf statue, which had apparently been revealed while she was lost in her reverie. "Your gift pleases me greatly."

"Queen Frigga commissioned it," Odin corrected him. "I only paid for it."

"The queen honors me," Vidar said respectfully, bowing slightly.

She acknowledged him with a nod.

Realizing the brief ceremony had ended, the gathered Asgardians broke into pairs as the gentle roll of the goatskin drums signaled the start of a warrior dance. Rather than join her frolicking subjects, Frigga watched with delight as Vidar explored the alabaster statue with his long fingers, almost in rhythm with the popular Asgardian song the court musicians played. He seemed to be murmuring to himself over the cold bristling fur and realistic fangs of the stone creature, which appeared to be gathering for a spring. The sculptor had perfectly captured the one detail she knew Vidar would appreciate above all—the heartbreaking intensity of panicked, wounded eyes in one wolf's head in stark contrast to the fierce, bloodthirsty expression of the other head.

As the dance ended and another began, Lord Bragi and Lady Ithunna approached the king to speak with him. Frigga used the opportunity to step up to the statue and place her hand on the saddest-looking head.

"Do you like it?" she asked Vidar, who still stood gazing at it.

"It's perfect, my queen," he murmured, placing his own hand on the savage-looking head, just as she had hoped he would.

Frigga longed to slip her hand over his, but she merely whispered, "When you're alone, reach that hand into the wolf's mouth."

Vidar looked at her with a puzzled expression but nodded. Satisfied he could find her hidden gift, she beckoned to two strong manservants who had been waiting for her signal to take the statue to Vidar's quarters in the palace.

As the music faded and the banquet drew to a close, Frigga rejoined the king and turned her attention to cheerfully bidding their guests goodnight.

When only she, Odin, and the servants remained in the hall, she turned to her husband with a bright smile. "Are you ready to retire, my king?"

"I have some matters of state to attend to with Lord Bragi," Odin informed her. He paused, an unreadable look in those gray eyes of his that used to weaken her at the knees. He added, "If that pleases the queen, that is."

Frigga stared at him. He had not asked her to approve his plans in so long, she did not know what to do.

"I could postpone with Bragi until tomorrow morning," he offered.

"Oh no, that's not necessary," Frigga hurriedly reassured him. "How long will you be closeted?"

"Several hours at least," he sighed. "We have much to discuss. Will you be alright?"

Frigga blinked, her heart tugging at the concern in his voice. What had prompted such a change? How was it that the slightest sign of compassion in him felt like rain on thirsty, dry ground? Something passed between them—something old and yet new, something familiar and yet strange. But just as quickly, the root of bitterness in her soul choked out whatever tiny seedling had sprung in her heart.

"I have no reason to think otherwise," she answered coldly. "I fare just fine in your frequent absences."

She fancied she saw a flash of pain in his eyes, but when he only nodded, she left him standing in the banquet hall. Once inside the royal chambers she shared with the king, she removed her jewels and changed from her red gown into a simpler dark blue dress. She wrapped herself in refracted light to make herself invisible, one of the skills she had inherited and learned how to expertly wield from her now-deceased mother.

Once hidden, Frigga hurried to the secret room where Laufey had birthed Loki, manipulating the light to hide the opening and closing of each door as she muffled the sounds, another of her naturally born abilities.

A measure of dread tempered her excitement, for neither Frigga nor Odin had set foot inside Laufey's old room since her death. But if Vidar had found the hand-written note and the key she had stashed deep within the open mouth of the savage wolf's head, he should already be inside waiting for her.

Frigga placed her hand on the doorknob and found it unlocked. She pocketed her own key, took a deep breath to calm her pounding heart, and banished any lingering images that might threaten to burst through the protective wall she had built around the memories of Loki's birth mother.

She stepped inside. The motion activated the sensors, flooding the dark room with light.

It was empty.

2

Frigga fought the rising dismay and confusion she felt, quickly adjusting the settings to dim the lights, which she feared might draw attention to the hidden room despite the heavy drapes and remote location. The hygienic air filters, which were installed in every palace room, hummed above her, softening the lonely silence.

She stared blankly at the vague shapes of several pieces of furniture in the room, wondering if she had set herself up for heartache. She took a few steps toward the curtained window, then suddenly remembered she was still holding her invisibility.

As soon as she dropped her illusion, Vidar swooped in from behind her and enveloped her in his arms. Immensely relieved, she turned into him and silently allowed him to hold her, basking in his warmth. He had never held her like that, even when she had cried in his presence, and she wanted to stay there for as long as she could.

"How I've missed you, my queen," he finally murmured. "You have no idea how happy you've made me."

"Where were you hiding?" she teased, reluctantly stepping away from him.

"Behind that chair over there," he admitted, pointing to the worn piece of furniture near the wall.

"I thought you didn't find my note or chose not to come," she chided playfully.

"I thought I should play it safe when I heard someone at the door," he explained.

"Who else do you know who can go invisible?" she chuckled.

"No one. I just didn't want to take any risks," he told her somewhat sheepishly. He looked around him at the humble setting. "Doesn't Odin ever use this room?"

"No, and he won't ever again," she declared. "He's closeted with Bragi for several hours, so we have some time."

"Time for what?" he asked with a shy smile as he nervously tugged at his right earlobe.

Despite the dim light, she clearly saw the golden glow light up his hazel eyes again. He had left his sword behind and changed out of his uniform. The thin cotton tunic and simple breeches he wore accented his muscle definition. She gulped and looked away. After seeing the slight change in Odin, she knew she could not go through with the real reason she had wanted to meet Vidar in secret. Thankfully, he was none the wiser, though she imagined he had likely hoped for the same.

"To talk," she clarified with a resigned sigh as she sat down on the slightly dusty settee. "I want to hear how you've fared these last few weeks."

"All I care to say is that I've stayed warm and alive all those nights on the battlefield because of you," he stated as he sat beside her.

She blushed, then asked smartly, "Isn't Muspelheim hot?"

"Yes, there's an abundance of volcanoes and fire," Vidar explained. "Oh, and tar pits. It's blistering hot during the day, but it can get cold at night."

"What are fire giants like?" she asked shyly.

He chuckled. "Are you going to force me to talk about this?"

"I'm not forcing you to do anything," she declared, tossing her thick mane of reddish gold curls arrogantly.

He reached out to feel one of her tresses, his eyes smoldering as the hair slid silkily over his hand. "You could. I would do anything you asked."

"Vidar, please," she gasped, trembling slightly.

"Forgive me, my queen," he murmured as he dropped his hand. He took a deep breath, then answered her previous question. "Fire giants are similar to the Jotuns in a way. Just like the ice giants, they are taller than we are by about twelve to eighteen inches respectively. But their skin tones range from a dusky gray to midnight black. Oh, and their eyes are unusually large. They burn like flames."

"Their eyes or their bodies?" she asked playfully.

"Their eyes," he chuckled. "If they weren't so tall with such terrifying eyes, they wouldn't look so different from us."

"How do they fight?" she asked.

"Ferociously," he mused, his eyes darkening slightly. "And they ride dragons that breathe fire. But please, Frigga, I didn't come here to relive the horrors of war. Let's talk about something else."

"I wanted to ask if something happened between you and Odin," she voiced with some trepidation. "He was almost kind to me tonight after you left."

"Nothing I can think of," Vidar admitted. "Maybe all of my pleas about how he treats you made some difference." He stood abruptly. "I should go back to my own room."

"Why?" she protested. "I just got here."

He sighed deeply. "Frigga, I cannot rein in how I feel about you now that I've let it out. I thought you wanted … Never mind. It's not safe for me to be alone with you."

"I feel safe with you," she contested. "And I know you are a man of extraordinary discipline." She stood and approached him, drawing as near as she dared. "You would never compromise my honor."

He shut his eyes tightly. "Are you testing me, my queen? Because if you knew—"

"You said you would do anything for me … that you'd be content to simply be with me," she interrupted. "All I ask is for you to keep your word."

"As you wish, my queen," he agreed, his voice clipped as he tried to banish the emotion from his face.

Then he groaned and pulled her to himself as if he could not help it. She nestled against his chest, feeling cherished and wanted, a sensation she had dearly missed. A deep longing filled her soul, coupled with an almost crippling guilt. She did not want to think about the last time Odin had held her like that—on a cold, lifeless day almost two hundred years ago when grief unlike anything she had ever experienced almost took her life. She shut the memory down, unwilling to spoil her time with Vidar.

She lifted her head and met his eyes, then whispered, "Tell me what you're thinking."

He lowered his gaze to her mouth and gently caressed her cheek with his thumb. "I'm asking myself if there's any harm in one kiss."

"Just one?" she whispered, feeling as if her throat would close from the thought of it.

"Just one," he murmured as he closed his eyes and leaned toward her.

She almost gave in, but she turned her head just in time so his lips brushed against her cheek. "Oh, Vidar, we cannot. We both know it wouldn't be just one kiss." Her voice broke and tears filled her eyes when she saw the embarrassment on his face. "This was foolish of me. I don't know what I was thinking. I'm … I'm so sorry."

"Please don't cry," he begged her. "I shouldn't have pushed you."

But she could not stop the tears. His tender admonition made her feel even worse.

"It's not fair," she sobbed, not caring how childish she sounded. "I'm married to an unfaithful man who doesn't love me, who just happens to be the king! There is no escape."

Vidar simply held her during her fit, but she could feel how tense he was and knew she had caused him pain. He wiped away several of her tears after she quieted herself.

"Even if we cannot be together now, I will never stop hoping, never stop loving you," Vidar proclaimed. "But if Odin decides to be a proper husband, I will step away for the sake of your happiness."

As starved as she was for affection and love, Frigga mustered every ounce of her self-respect to keep from pouncing on him when he spoke those words. Instead, the only indulgence she permitted herself was to silently cup his cheek with one hand. She smiled weakly at him, then turned to leave.

"Tomorrow night, same time?" he called after her.

"Yes," she said automatically, then immediately shook her head. "I mean no … well … yes, if you promise we'll only talk."

"I promise," he agreed.

When she reached the royal chambers, Frigga changed into a nightgown and climbed into her side of the bed, acutely aware of the cold, empty space beside her. She curled up into a ball and sobbed herself to sleep.

The king accidentally woke her when he returned to their room, but she stayed as far from him as she could, pretending to be sound asleep. When he also maintained his distance, she wished she had Baldur's gift of reading someone's emotions. She toyed with an urge to read Odin's mind, yet another skill she had been born with and honed since her youth. But since he could also read minds by touching someone's forehead, he would know if she attempted it and might even examine her thoughts. Unwilling to risk that, she slipped back into an uneasy sleep.

When she awoke the next morning, the king had already left but for some reason had drawn the drapes. She nestled in their four-poster bed, watching the rays of the early sun filter through the windows and dance across the lush golden brown rugs splayed out on the white marble floor.

A sudden gust of wind fluttered the rich crimson valances, causing the sunlight to spill onto the delicately embroidered pillows stacked against the headboard. Delighted by this little performance, she eased herself out of bed to embrace the day. Just as she reached for the doorknob of their bathroom, Odin opened it from the other side and walked out.

"Odin!" Frigga exclaimed, jumping back slightly. "I thought you were gone."

"I don't have anywhere to be this morning," he stated. "It's quite lovely outside. Would you care for breakfast in the garden?"

She eyed him suspiciously. "Well, Odin? What do you want?"

"What makes you think I want anything?" he asked innocently. "The war is finally over. I'd like to spend some time with my queen."

"Do you honestly think you can ignore me for years, then turn on a little charm and expect things to be the way they were?" she huffed, folding her arms across her chest.

Anger transformed his face almost instantly at her sharp tone. "Why do you have to be so difficult, Frigga?"

"*I'm* difficult?" she repeated incredulously. "Well, you've got a nerve!"

"I'm trying to do something nice—"

"For once," she interrupted haughtily.

"And you throw it in my face!" he finished hotly. "Why should I bother?"

"You usually don't!" she shot back. Then she turned away from him so he would not see the tears pricking at the corners of her eyes.

"Don't turn your back on *me*, wife!" he commanded so forcefully, she whirled around to face him.

"Do you enjoy inflicting pain on me, *husband*?" she seethed, unable to stop the hot tears from streaming down her cheeks.

"No, of course not." His broad shoulders, which she had once admired, slumped in defeat. "Frigga, I don't understand why you're always so angry with me."

She looked away.

"Everyone respects me but you," he pointed out indignantly.

"No one else knows what I know," she whispered.

"After all these years, you still haven't forgiven me?" Odin asked flatly.

"I forgave you for Athena," she countered. "But I don't know if I can ever forgive you for Laufey."

"You said you did," he accused.

"I thought I had," she defended herself.

"So you lied?" Odin scoffed.

"Even if I did, I learned from the best," she spouted, folding her arms as she peered at him haughtily.

He shrank back, masking his face so as not to reveal how her words stung him. But she knew and felt a twisted sense of pleasure that she had managed to wound him. She expected him to lash out at her or storm from the room. But he merely regarded her with those stormy gray eyes she had once loved. She shuddered, imagining he could look into her soul and see her secrets. Feeling exposed and unnatural, she dropped her own eyes to stare at the ground.

Finally, when it seemed the seconds stretched on for a thousand lifetimes, he spoke. "You truly loved Laufey, didn't you?"

"I'm the only one who did," she replied softly, too quickly. "You abandoned her."

"What else could I have done, Frigga?" he demanded. "Tell me. What?"

"I don't know," she retorted, having no idea what to say.

"The law forbids bigamy," he continued. "And—"

She snorted. "The law forbids adultery too, even for the king, but that didn't stop you. I would have been stripped of my title and cast away if I had done what you did. But you've gotten away with it completely. I sometimes wonder how many mistresses you've entertained."

"The mothers of my sons and no more," he growled.

She blinked in surprise. But unwilling to back down, she spat, "Are there more sons you must reveal to me?"

"No, Frigga," he responded slowly. "I have explained this, but I simply cannot seem to get through to you. I succumbed to Athena's seduction after my father's death, then never touched her again."

"I know," she whispered. "And she hated you for that."

He began to pace the floor, ignoring her comment. "And Laufey was nothing more than a foolish fling after Thora—"

"Do not speak the name of our daughter," Frigga interrupted coldly. "I grieved alone while—"

Odin abruptly stopped pacing. "Do you think I did not grieve?" he growled, glaring at her as the muscles in his forearms flexed from balling his hands into fists.

"You carelessly sowed your seed where you never should have," she flung at him.

He winced at her words. "No, I never should have."

Undeterred by his uncharacteristic show of regret, she

added, "Laufey died because of your carelessness. And if she had lived, she would likely hate you as Athena did."

"And you, Frigga?" Odin asked quietly. "Do you also hate me?"

Tears filled her eyes again. She did not know what she felt, but it was not hatred. She did not want to feel anything toward Odin at all. She preferred the numbness of the past few years to whatever emotions surged through her at that moment.

But Frigga was not a woman who could lie easily, and so she answered truthfully, "No, Odin. I do not hate you. But Laufey's blood is on your hands. And if nothing changes, mine will be as well."

And with those words, she fled from the room. Odin did not attempt to stop her. She turned back only for a second to see him rapidly blinking and staring at the floor. Disturbed by this rare sight of vulnerability in her husband and appalled by her words, she quickly shut the door and hurried to the family dining room to join her sons for breakfast. Odin did not appear, and Frigga went about her day as if nothing had happened.

When Lady Annette brought Sigyn to the library as they had discussed, Frigga felt relieved for something to focus on besides lessons, her heartache, and the confusion fogging up her mind. She wanted to ask Annette about their conversation at the banquet, but the noblewoman hurried off too quickly to return to her injured husband.

"Well, Sigyn, what would you like to do today?" Frigga asked the young girl, who stared after her mother, then focused her innocent blue eyes on the queen.

"Whatever the princes are doing is fine with me, my queen," Sigyn murmured shyly. "I can read if they still have lessons."

The blonde girl smiled at both of the boys flanking their mother, but her gaze lingered longest on Loki. The black-haired boy grimaced and pretended to be interested in the pattern of the floor covering he stood on, tracing it with his shoe. Thor, on the other hand, rolled his bright blue eyes and groaned at the possibility of returning to their lessons.

"The weather is nice today, don't you think?" Frigga asked Sigyn as if she were an adult. The child nodded, her eyes lighting up as Frigga continued, "What if we let the princes play hooky this afternoon? Can I trust you to keep them out of trouble, darling?"

"Oh yes, my queen!" Sigyn burst out excitedly.

Loki leaned forward to flash his towheaded brother an impish grin. "Race you to the gardens, Thor!"

"Not so fast, young man," Frigga chided as she grabbed him before he could dash away. "Put your books away and remember your manners. You can race all afternoon if you wish."

Both princes eagerly obeyed, containing themselves until they reached the grassy knoll where Frigga usually settled while her children played. Despite the unresolved conflict with her husband, she genuinely enjoyed watching their antics, even joining them for a few races as the sun blazed its trail across the western sky. Though fairly fit herself, she could not match their energy and eventually returned to her spot until one of the guards informed her the evening meal was ready to be served.

After dinner, Frigga spent some time reading with Loki and Sigyn in the library while Thor played games with Baldur. Much to the children's delight, Frigga let them stay up later than usual, for she dreaded facing Odin again.

After she bid her sons and her temporary charge goodnight, she reluctantly retired to the royal chambers. She slowly opened the door and peered inside.

Empty.

Relief flooded her, mingled with a surprising disappointment. Memories of their happiness in their first centuries of marriage tickled at the back of her mind, but she shoved them aside. She stood at their balcony for a while gazing out over the steady lights and gleaming alabaster spires of Asgard as she waded through formless thoughts and emotions, completely unaware of her surroundings.

She came to herself suddenly and realized Odin stood silently beside her. She stiffened, uncertain of what to expect.

"I've just been to see Lord Berg," he informed her awkwardly, placing his hands behind his back.

"And how does he fare?" she asked cautiously.

"He fares well," Odin replied, matching her formal tone. "He will be released to his family in a few more days."

"That will make Annette happy," Frigga remarked.

"Yes. I expect it will," Odin acknowledged, offering her a tentative smile. "It was kind of you to help her with Sigyn."

"It's no trouble," Frigga replied, returning his smile. "Sigyn is a delightful child. She certainly seems fond of Loki."

He chuckled. "I cannot imagine anyone not being fond of Loki."

In spite of herself, Frigga laughed and turned toward him. When he reached out one hand to move a lock of hair away from her face, she resisted the sudden urge to collapse into his arms and stepped back slightly.

"It's nice to hear you laugh," he said softly, dropping his hand as if she had slapped it away.

She told herself she did not care how her subtle movement had wounded him. *He deserves it, doesn't he?* she thought. Aloud, she said, "It's been a while."

He frowned. "Frigga, about what you said earlier—"

"Let's not speak of that," she interrupted him. She forced herself to step closer to him and placed her hand on his arm. "Please?"

"As you wish," he conceded. She felt the muscles in his arm relax at her touch and heard relief in his voice as he stated, "I suppose we'd better go to bed. I'm leaving first thing tomorrow for Muspelheim to discuss the peace treaty."

"How long will you be gone?" she asked.

"Only a few days," he answered. "Will you see me off?"

"Of course," she affirmed, smiling demurely.

She accepted Odin's polite kiss goodnight, then lay awake listening for his breathing to change. When she was certain he had fallen asleep, she crept out of the royal chambers and hurried to Laufey's old room.

Just a few minutes later, the waiting general wrapped her up in the comfort of his embrace.

But when she raised her face to his, he stepped back and reminded her, "I promised you we would only talk tonight, my queen."

"And what if I release you from that promise, General?" she whispered suggestively.

He squeezed his eyes shut and took a deep breath, then opened them again as he slowly exhaled. "No, I would still keep my word."

She smiled, feeling a little disappointed. "A man of honor, as always."

"How could I love you if I lacked honor?" he returned. "Now sit with me and tell me how you fare."

She obeyed and filled him in on the lighter matters of the day, finishing with, "And the king leaves for Muspelheim tomorrow."

"Yes, I know," Vidar announced.

"Are you going with him?" she asked with dismay.

"No, he's only taking Lord Shronner and General Tyr with him," Vidar replied. "He does not wish to send the wrong message to the fire giants."

"Then the king goes unprotected," she sighed.

"Odin can see to himself," Vidar reassured her. "And Shronner and Tyr will defend him if necessary. Lord Bragi will oversee matters here again." He grinned as he told her his next news. "The king personally asked me to attend to you and the princes while he is gone."

"He did?" she gasped. "Has he ever done that before?"

"No, but he must have a reason," he said with a shrug. "He did seem unusually quiet today."

"We argued this morning," she admitted. "I said some rather ugly things to him, and he actually showed some emotion other than anger."

"You see, Frigga? He does care," Vidar announced

triumphantly. He shifted away from her slightly. "Perhaps there is hope for the two of you yet."

"Perhaps," she murmured, staring at him in confusion. "But wouldn't that leave you heartbroken?"

He put his arm around her and drew her to himself. "I thrust a dagger into my heart years ago when I first began to love you," he told her. "I'll take the pain to see you happy again."

"You say that a lot, Vidar," she pointed out.

"That doesn't make it any less true."

She buried her face in his shoulder, and they sat like that for a while in silence, clinging to each other.

"I'd better go back before Odin notices I'm gone," she finally said, extracting herself from his arms. "Tomorrow will be easier without him around."

"Until tomorrow, my queen," Vidar said softly, daring to stroke her cheek with one knuckle.

She grabbed his hand and kissed it, then rushed out of the room. She slept fitfully that night as the man woven throughout her dreams changed faces from Odin to Vidar and back again until he disappeared entirely.

Relief flooded her when morning came. After an early breakfast, she accompanied the three princes to say goodbye to their father. With a tremendous sense of guilt, she wondered what her life might be like if Odin never returned. But when she considered her sons, she knew how they would grieve the father they adored, and so she put such thoughts out of her mind.

Shortly after Odin's departure, Vidar joined them in the library, quietly observing as Frigga taught the two younger boys about the nine realms connected through the intergalactic pathways collectively called Yggdrasil, or the World Tree. Asgardians accessed the other realms through the Bifröst Bridge, which had been built from black ore that shimmered with mysterious multi-colored light.

Though this was their favorite subject, Frigga still found teaching them both to be more of a challenge than schooling Baldur had been. The crown prince now studied independently, preparing for the rite of passage that would usher him into society as a mature man. Though still a century away, Frigga dreaded letting him go. But as she moved from astronomy into training the younger boys to control the gifts they were born with to influence their environment, she comforted herself with the reality of how much Thor and Loki still needed her. Thor had caused more than one mishap in his struggle to learn balance with his ability to control the weather. And Loki's unquenchable thirst for mischief combined with Thor's temper made their brotherly scuffles far more intense than Frigga could handle at times.

Despite this, Frigga persevered and continued to teach the youngest princes as many subjects as she could, choosing not to employ most of the gifted tutors available to the royal family. But since math was not her strong suit, she gladly relinquished the boys to Mimir for that subject. The renowned scholar and math tutor happened to be Odin's uncle on his mother's side. He lived at the palace now that his wife had died and his two sons had relocated to Midgard, a realm on a lower plane.

When the gray-haired, wizened intellectual arrived to teach for his regularly scheduled hour before lunch, Vidar sauntered over to where Frigga sat on her favorite cushioned chaise lounge.

"The queen amazes me with her abilities," he complimented her.

"Which ones?" she asked lightly, pleased by his words.

She patted the seat beside her. He gingerly sat down but maintained a respectable distance.

"You certainly are intelligent, my queen. I enjoy listening to you teach. But I've not been privileged to see you use your gifts to such an extent," he informed her. He brought his voice to a whisper so the tutor would not overhear. "Except invisibility."

She flashed him a smile, then stood. And because he knew the protocol required of him regarding the queen, Vidar leaped to his feet as well.

So the math tutor *would* overhear, she announced, "I should check on Baldur to ensure he has stayed focused on his own studies this morning. General Vidar, would you kindly accompany me?"

"Of course, my queen," he murmured, bowing slightly. "I am at your disposal however you need me."

Mimir glanced at the two of them briefly but returned his attention to assisting Thor through a particularly difficult problem. Loki had already solved a page of his own and sat waiting for the tutor to check his work. The black-haired boy fidgeted in his seat and gazed longingly at the window, where a brightly colored songbird had just alighted.

"Mind your tutor, Loki," Frigga admonished him. "If you behave yourself until I return, we'll go to the gardens after lunch again."

His green eyes, so like Laufey's, lit up in response to her suggestion. He nodded and buried his nose in his math book.

General Vidar held the door open for Frigga, then quietly closed it behind them. "Are we really going to Baldur's room?" he whispered.

"Of course," she answered in surprise. "Everyone knows you've been assigned to us, which does afford us some freedom. But by day, we must observe decorum. We can talk as we walk."

"Tell me about your abilities," he prompted as he matched her stride. "You've attended enough rites of passage to know most Asgardians only have one gift, though we can have many skills. But I've always wondered why all of you Vanir have at least two gifts."

"The Vanir descended from the same bloodline as Asgardians and Midgardians," she explained. "But somewhere in the genetic code, a split occurred. The Vanir grew stronger in mind and multiplied their abilities through blood transfers until they became ingrained in our genetics."

"Fascinating," he breathed, casting an admiring glance on her that she sensed encompassed more than her looks.

"The humans, on the other hand, became weaker, losing longevity and any abilities they may have had at one time," she continued.

"Yes, my grandfather said Midgardians lived for hundreds of years in his day," Vidar replied. "I've even heard of one who lived for just shy of a thousand years. Methuselah, I believe his name was. But conditions on their planet have changed. Now, their years are shortened to a mere one hundred, far less in most cases. They age much differently than we do."

"Yes, I know," Frigga responded. "Aging every year you're alive sounds frightful to me, though more logical than how we age."

"Do you mean to tell me it doesn't make much sense to you that we only take nine months in the womb and two years for infancy, just as humans do, then everything slows down for years through childhood?" Vidar challenged playfully.

"Exactly!" she laughed. "And then speeds up again for the transitionary years, only to slow down yet again."

"Throw into the mix that girls develop into mature women so much faster than boys, and we make even more sense," Vidar shot back. "Humans might not live long, but they have it easier in some ways."

"You visit the human realm quite frequently for my husband, do you not?" Frigga asked curiously. When he nodded, she sighed wistfully. "I've never been there. I'd like to visit someday, though I have never understood why some Asgardians prefer Midgard to here."

"It has its merits," Vidar answered lightly. "There are many beautiful places on Midgard. But why do you say 'human realm' like that?"

"Like what?" she asked innocently.

"With disdain," he answered gently. "The Midgardians that I've interacted with are quite charming. I like them."

"Are the rumors about their appearance and weakness not true?" she probed quietly.

"They are physically weaker individually," he confirmed. "But they don't look very different from us, although some are much shorter. I have no idea why our annals have pictured them with stringy hair and all that nonsense. I've yet to meet one like that."

"You said they are weaker individually. Are they stronger together?" she asked as they neared Baldur's door.

"Incredibly so. I'd even call them unstoppable when they are of one mind," he affirmed. "The Greeks, for example, drove out the Olympians. Then Alexander the Great, who was both Macedonian and Greek, almost succeeded in global domination. He was a powerful leader in his time. I met him once, and I've studied some of his battle methods."

Frigga felt a painful twinge in her heart when he mentioned the Olympians. Athena's people. Baldur's people, though he did not know he had not been birthed by Frigga. But she found herself strangely drawn to Vidar's descriptions of humans and wondered at her own interest.

Vidar continued, "Sadly, Midgardians rarely are of one mind. I've never seen a planet so rife with conflict. They fight each other over their beliefs, their pantheons, who owns what land, and even their different skin tones."

"They fight each other based on their skin color?" Frigga gasped. "How absurd!"

"Indeed," Vidar agreed. "But don't think too badly of them. They are also capable of incredible generosity, kindness, and love."

"They are?" Frigga queried, feeling confused and ashamed. "Perhaps I've been too harsh in how I've viewed them."

Vidar smiled lovingly at her. "I admire your willingness to learn a new perspective." She blushed at his praise as he expounded, "Too many Asgardians have their own prejudices. And I'm certain the Vanir do as well."

Frigga sighed, remembering the taunting songs of several children she had witnessed teasing a dwarf slave when she was a mere girl. "Yes, they do. Especially toward the lowest realms."

"Perhaps you can tell me more about that," Vidar suggested. "And speaking of your people, I would like to know more about your Vanir gifts."

Since no one was in the hallway, she dared to lean into him just for a second as she whispered, "Tonight."

Vidar grinned at her, then knocked on Baldur's door.

"Enter at your own risk," Baldur called back good-naturedly.

The general opened the door for the queen but remained outside as she swept into Baldur's room, where her oldest son sat reading at his desk.

"What have you been up to this morning, Baldur?" she asked him.

"I'm studying Asgardian history, Mother," he answered as he used his finger to hold his place. "This book is really interesting. I'd like to get back to it."

"As you wish," she chuckled. "I'm glad to see you so focused. After all, in a mere hundred years, you'll be a legal adult. And someday, the king of Asgard."

"Let's not rush things, Mother. That's still a long way away," Baldur chuckled.

"When you've lived as long as I have, dear boy, one hundred years can seem like the blink of an eye," she laughed.

"I'll be a Valiant first," Baldur told her. "The general says I can start my training after Father gets back."

"Oh really? How exciting!" Frigga said, hiding a slight frown as she reminded herself to be supportive. "I'll see you at lunch then?"

"Yes, of course," he muttered distractedly, already engrossed in his history book again.

She smiled to herself, delighted to see him applying himself to his studies. It grieved her that Thor, her only biological son, had shown an aversion to reading, one of her favorite pastimes. But Baldur did not mind books, and Loki was proving to be a voracious reader.

She quietly closed the door on her studious oldest son and rejoined the general, who stood at attention in the hallway. Several servants walked by him. One of the maids eyed the general's physique with a lustful look in her eyes and gave him a seductive little wave. He merely dipped his head respectfully at the woman. Frigga frowned, tempted to have her dismissed for her boldness. But without any real reason other than pure jealousy, she felt it unwise to risk the questions that might arise from such a move.

After they had put enough distance between them and the servants, Frigga remarked, "That maid certainly was a pretty thing, wasn't she?"

He chuckled. "There are many pretty women." He looked around carefully to ensure no one could overhear, then whispered, "There is only one you, my queen."

Satisfied with his answer, she smiled serenely as they returned to the library, where the math tutor gave a good report for both boys before he left for the day.

"Now you must take us to the gardens after lunch, Mother," Thor prodded as Loki chimed in his agreement.

"Must I?" Frigga teased, laughing when the boys clamored for her to keep her promise.

"They might riot if you don't," the general warned playfully.

"It seems my hands are tied," she quipped. "Shall we ask General Vidar to join us, boys?"

"Doesn't he have to?" Thor asked dryly.

"Thor, don't be rude," Frigga chided.

"Yeah, Thor," Loki taunted. "Don't worry, General. You can play with me!"

"Thank you, young prince," Vidar said with a generous bow. "It would be an honor."

"I didn't say he couldn't come," Thor grumbled.

"And what about me?" interjected another voice.

"Baldur!" both boys cried in unison as they charged their older brother, nearly knocking him over.

Baldur laughed delightedly. "Alright, you two rascals. Let's get some lunch."

Frigga exchanged a smile with Vidar as they all traipsed to the family dining room. Baldur and Loki seemed to enjoy the general's company at least, although Loki never could get his name right. Tired of Thor's teasing every time he messed it up, Loki had resorted to calling Vidar only by his rank.

After lunch, Lady Annette brought Sigyn out to meet them in the gardens, then left to attend to Lord Berg. The small blonde girl stayed close to the queen while Baldur and the younger boys chased each other around the bushes.

"Don't you want to play, Sigyn?" Frigga asked gently.

"No thank you, my queen," she answered sweetly. "Sometimes I like to just watch them."

"So do I, dear girl," she chuckled. Her eyes lingered on the fit form of the general as he joined her sons in their wild game. "So do I."

3

"Do you have other gifts besides manipulating light and sound?" Vidar asked Frigga after they had chatted for a while. "Or is it just the two?"

Being with each other all day had relieved some of the tension between them, lending to a far more relaxed atmosphere when they met in secret that night.

She glanced at him shyly, then decided to divulge what few people knew. "I can also read minds and influence thoughts."

His eyes widened. "Have you ever done that to me?"

"No, Vidar," she said softly. "I never do it without permission."

He reached for her hands. "Then I give you my permission."

"Why would you do that?" she gasped, shrinking away from him slightly.

"Because it's another part of me I can give you," he replied with intensity. "You already own my heart."

"I … I cannot," she stammered, pulling her hands away. "Please don't ask me. I'm not ready for something like that."

He smiled softly. "I'll leave it open ended. Just warn me before you do it."

"I promise," she murmured.

"Does Thor share that ability?" Vidar asked.

"No, but Loki does," she confirmed. "I just haven't told him yet."

"How do you know, but he doesn't?"

"He accidentally entered my mind right after he was born," she answered.

"But how did you know that?" Vidar pressed.

"I saw my own thoughts through him," Frigga explained. "I had to gently push him out to protect him. Beyond the first few days after birth, most gifts stay dormant during the childhood years, and mind gifts are the last to make themselves known. So he shouldn't be aware of it for a while yet."

"So, if you read my mind, would I know what you see?" he asked.

"Yes, unless you were wholly focused on something else … or mentally weak," she replied. "And you, my dear general, are not mentally weak."

He chuckled as if pleased by her compliment. "Can you teach me how to lock my mind?"

"I can try," she agreed. "But I'm too tired to start tonight."

"We'll have plenty of time another night," Vidar assured her. "It will give me something to focus on besides …"

"Besides what?" she asked when he trailed off.

"I'll leave that for when you're ready to read my mind," he said. Then he raised his eyebrows as if a thought had just occurred to him. "How does Loki have your gifts when he's not your biological son?"

Frigga dropped her eyes and stared at her hands. "Did Odin tell you who his mother was?"

"No, only that Loki came from a careless fling after Thor's twin died," he replied. "I have no doubt he only told me because I already knew about the affair with Zeus's daughter."

"That's all he said?" Frigga pressed him.

"He expressed more regret than I had ever seen him show before," Vidar mused. "I dared not ask questions. And he swore me to secrecy after he confided in me. I haven't told a soul but you. And that's only because you already know."

"I haven't spoken of what happened to anyone since it happened, except briefly to Odin here and there," Frigga murmured.

"Would it help you to talk about it?" Vidar asked. "I'll listen."

"Maybe," she agreed. "But I'm afraid of what will happen if I unlock those memories."

"You have to teach me how to lock and unlock memories too," he declared.

She laughed, then closed her eyes and breathed deeply. She toyed around the walls encapsulating the painful memories, then sent a mental probe to touch one of them. She winced, recoiling in fear. Instinctively, she grabbed both of Vidar's hands and squeezed as she eased into the mental space where Laufey's memory lived, though it occasionally tried to break free. The general shifted to put one arm around her, allowing her to squeeze his other hand with both of hers.

His nearness gave her courage, and eyes tightly shut, she began to speak the memories aloud as if she told a story. "After Thora died, I fell apart. Odin could not handle my grief, so he withdrew. He buried himself in his duties as king, so I thought. I sank into a deep darkness, alone. I was aware he was visiting other realms, but I did not care why. The grief was so great, I could barely manage caring for my remaining baby. Thor, of course."

"Didn't you have servants to help?" Vidar asked curiously.

"Yes, of course. But I'd lost one child already, so I couldn't bear to let Thor or Baldur out of my sight," Frigga explained, opening her eyes before easing back into her story. "I couldn't rest even when Odin suggested it, and he resented that all my energy went to Thor."

"Did he say that?" Vidar asked quietly.

She nodded. "Among other painful things. But I freely admit that I completely disregarded his physical need for me. Since he never pushed me in that arena, I believed he respected my need for space. After several months of this, dawn suddenly broke in my heart. I felt I could live again. I reunited with Odin and conceived another child."

"I remember when your pregnancy was announced at court," Vidar said softly. "Everyone rejoiced, including me, because you seemed so happy."

"I was, but it didn't turn out how I hoped," she sighed. "I wasn't very far along when Odin brought me to this very room one stormy night. An unusually small giantess with bright green eyes and blue skin sat shivering where I'm sitting now."

"A Jotun!" Vidar gasped. "I always assumed Loki's mother was some unnamed common woman who died or gave up her rights to him."

Frigga's eyes flitted to Vidar's face. Seeing no judgment or fear there, she continued, "Yes, she was a Jotun. Her name was

Laufey. She looked nothing like I expected. She was actually quite beautiful … and utterly terrified. At first, I was afraid of her too. But then Odin told me she had been cast out by her people because of her size and her condition."

"Pregnant with Odin's child," Vidar spoke ironically.

"Yes, but neither of them told me who the father was," Frigga countered.

"You didn't know?" Vidar pressed, his tone laced with scorn.

For a moment, Frigga keenly felt all the shame she had tortured herself with in the past for not seeing what seemed so obvious to him. "The thought never occurred to me," she murmured, her eyes downcast. "But you're right. I should have known."

"No, he should have told you," Vidar said, anger creeping into this voice.

"Well, he didn't," Frigga sighed. "He left Laufey entirely in my charge and never showed any interest in her or even visited her."

"I thought he was better than that," Vidar muttered.

"Maybe he would have treated her differently had she been one of us," Frigga mused. "You know how people from higher realms view Jotuns."

"Yes, I do," Vidar responded, almost as though he had not registered her comment, deep as his anger was with Odin. "Is that why you had to hide her?"

"Yes, even from the palace staff. I brought her all her meals, changed the bedding, cleaned the room, and took care of her when she got sick. And since I was pregnant too, we bonded quickly."

"Odin allowed you to do all of that work in your condition?" Vidar asked indignantly. "No wonder you miscarried."

"Did Odin tell you that?" Frigga asked quietly.

"Everyone knew you were pregnant," Vidar replied. "But I knew the child born was not the child you carried. I assumed you had lost yours. Odin never corrected me."

"Probably because that was true from a certain point of view. And I did the work because I felt I had no choice," Frigga answered flatly. "One of the healers warned me that I was showing signs of fatigue and told me to rest. But I knew Laufey had no one else, so I ignored her advice. I didn't even tell Odin when she fell into a deep depression. He never did seem to care when I updated him as her pregnancy progressed. I never understood that, especially since I thought he rescued her out of a sense of charity."

Vidar snorted derisively.

"I know. I was a fool," Frigga sighed.

"No, you trusted him, as a wife should," Vidar reassured her. "Stop looking for ways to blame yourself."

Frigga nodded, flashing him a thankful smile before returning to her story. "During the last two months of her pregnancy, Laufey seemed to have lost the will to live entirely. Sometimes I could get her to walk in the gardens with me. I would keep her invisible, of course. At one point, she told me I was her only bright spot and the most precious person in her life."

"I can understand that," Vidar interjected. "You exude kindness, Frigga."

She smiled again as hot tears pricked at the corners of her eyes. "Thank you, Vidar. Anyway, I became so worried about her, I brought the healer who oversaw my pregnancy to her room without telling Odin. She discovered Laufey was suffering from severe anemia and needed a blood transfusion. She advised me against donating my own blood because of the risk to my child, but once again, I didn't listen. In my mind, there was no one else, and I would not let Laufey and her child die. So I swore the healer to secrecy and escorted her out. I did the transfusion myself."

"Then what happened?" Vidar asked apprehensively, clearly riveted by her tale.

"She rallied, but I grew weaker. Several weeks later, I delivered my child prematurely—a stillborn son. Laufey blamed herself but did her best to comfort me through my grief. But I blamed myself. I felt I had killed my own child because of my stubbornness and my circumstances."

"And where was Odin?" Vidar asked sharply.

"Who knows?" she remarked bitterly. "On some trip somewhere. The healer helped me wrap my son's body with a blend of herbs to preserve him until Odin's return—"

"The Egyptians on Midgard do something like that," Vidar interrupted. "Do the Vanir as well?"

"Only if we must delay the funeral pyre for whatever reason. I wanted to wait until Odin could participate, so I did not announce the loss. Laufey went into labor four days later," Frigga continued. "I had been staying with her despite not being healed myself. And since Odin had given me strict instructions to notify him when she was ready to birth, I sent word to Gjallar to summon the king."

"Did Gjallar know why?"

"No, I used a code word Odin gave me. And Gjallar was only told that code meant absolute urgency. He asked no further questions," Frigga answered. "After I returned to her, Laufey begged me not to leave her again. When Odin arrived, she went into hysterics as soon as she saw him. She could not even coherently speak, so I asked him to leave."

"Did he?"

"No, he refused," Frigga stated. "I was too distracted to fight him on it, but he at least allowed me to hide him. It was hours of brutal labor, and there was nothing I could do to ease her distress because I couldn't shut down the pain signals to her brain. And the herbs we tried weren't working either. Finally, Odin pulled me aside and said the healer had told him we must calm her down. I had already been using much of my own power to quiet her screams. It took both of our mind gifts to settle her down."

"Odin has a mind gift?" Vidar blurted out in an injured tone. "He never told me that."

"He has even more power to change thoughts and memories than I do," she answered.

"All these years of friendship and he never once told me he has two gifts," Vidar grumbled. "And he's even one of the few people who know that I do too."

"You do?" she gasped.

"And now you know," Vidar bantered.

"But I don't!" she protested. "What are they?"

He raised an eyebrow at her. "Did Odin ever tell you tales of our boyhood?"

"No, he never has," she said. "Were you little terrors?"

"That's one way of putting it. Remind me to tell you some time." He chuckled as if at some fond memory. Then he frowned. "I cannot understand why Odin has never told me he has a mind gift."

"Probably because of how dangerous it is. He believes respect taken by force is not true respect, so he rarely uses it," she informed him. "He's also hinted that Borr's overuse of the same gift is what led to his premature death."

Vidar raised his eyebrows. "Does he also ask permission before reading someone's mind?"

"I don't know," she admitted. "But unlike with my gift, you wouldn't likely know if he's ever used it on you."

"Now I have another reason to learn how to lock my mind," Vidar observed.

"I will teach you one of these nights. I promise."

"And I'll tell you about my gifts. But I want to know what happened next in your story. How did the two of you work together to calm Laufey down?" Vidar prompted.

"I eased her panic enough for Odin to alleviate some of the pain. Then he gave her the strength and will to bring forth her son," Frigga answered, looking toward the bed as she remembered. "Loki was absolutely perfect. Odin showed no reaction, but I wept with joy. I was so busy admiring the baby's beauty, I did not register how much he looked like Odin or how little like a Jotun. Her vivid green eyes were all he had inherited from his mother. We didn't find out until later that I had passed my gifts to him through the blood I gave Laufey."

"I didn't know that was possible," Vidar breathed.

"I did, but I didn't even think of it at the time," she admitted. "Loki's gifts are even stronger than mine because he has the genetic codes of three races. And since Jotuns don't come into their powers until much later in life, he may have abilities we don't even know about yet."

"When did you find out Loki was Odin's son?" Vidar asked.

"Right after his birth. Odin had stepped out of the room to speak with the healer out of Laufey's hearing. She tried to suckle the babe, but she was too weak. Since I had just birthed a stillborn myself, I was able to nurse the child. When she looked over to see me smiling down at her baby at my breast, the ghost of an answering smile came over her face. She could barely speak, but she managed to say, 'As it should be,'" Frigga recounted sadly. "When Odin returned to the room, no longer hidden, Laufey pulled herself up with the last of her strength and looked him straight in the eyes. She told him to love me and only me, to which he had no response. He simply looked at me with those stormy gray eyes of his. Then she named the boy Loki, which means something like 'lock' or 'cage' in her language. Almost in the same breath, she asked me to forgive her but died before I could ask her why."

Vidar sucked in a sharp gust of air. "Then what?"

Frigga blinked away tears as the shame over her husband's choices washed over her again. "Odin stood there in shock after her life left her body, then muttered, 'What have I done?' Then he told me the full truth about meeting her several days after Thora died and drowning his own sorrow in her embrace."

"What did you do?" Vidar asked quietly.

"I held myself together for the sake of little Loki, but something inside me died. We placed our dead son with her body and burned their funeral pyre in secret to send their souls to Valhalla."

"Did he have a name?" Vidar asked.

"Odin never told you?" Frigga queried.

"No, and I never pressed him," Vidar answered. "You don't have to tell me."

"He wanted to name him after you," Frigga told him hesitantly. "But because of what he had done, he forfeited his right to name him at all. So I named him Váli."

"I'm honored that he thought to name him after me but relieved he didn't," Vidar said quietly. "If he had, my name would only bring you pain."

Frigga blinked away tears at the tenderness in his voice and found herself unable to speak.

"What happened next?" he prodded gently.

"We announced Loki's birth as if he were the son I lost," Frigga said sadly. "I told Odin I forgave him when he asked it of me, but I must have deceived myself. I cried every night for months on end. Things haven't been right between us since."

"I wondered why you never had any more children," Vidar mused. "Do you no longer share Odin's bed?"

"What a question!" she responded with a forced laugh.

"Apologies, my queen," he murmured quickly. "That was not my place."

"I'm not offended," Frigga reassured him. "After I lost my son, the healer said it was likely I'd never bear another child. She's been proven correct, it seems."

"My deepest sympathies," Vidar said softly, squeezing her shoulder slightly.

"I am content with the sons I have," she informed him. "I no longer wish to bear any more of Odin's offspring."

Vidar fell silent as he tightened his arm around her. Frigga breathed deeply of his comfort and the relief that had accompanied sharing Laufey's story with him.

"Does anyone else know what you just told me besides Odin and the healer?" he asked.

"No one else. And the healer died seventy years ago," Frigga replied. "She took her secrets with her to Valhalla."

"I am honored that you trust me so," Vidar whispered, turning her toward him and enveloping her with both arms.

She nestled into him, wishing she could spend the rest of her life as protected and cherished as he made her feel. It was only when Frigga feared she might fall asleep in his arms that she bid him good night.

She slept soundly, without confusing dreams. Confiding in Vidar had produced a powerful healing effect in her heart. And as each day of Odin's absence passed with the general by her side, Frigga felt happier than she had in years. She laughed more freely at the antics of the younger boys and showed more interest in everything around her. When Sigyn returned to her family after Lord Berg's release from the House of the Healers, Frigga dearly missed the girl but comforted herself with Annette's promise to bring the child on her next visit. And so, the rest of them spent their time as they usually did, settling into an almost lazy routine. And at night, Vidar regaled her with tales of his exploits with Odin when they were boys. The general even showed her how he could gather water from the air, which the boy Odin would send flying on the wind into buildings or even people from time to time. The two friends had never caused any real damage, but King Borr had had to discipline them more than once. His stories reminded her of her youngest two sons, who often used their gifts together in their play.

After several days, Baldur approached Frigga late in the afternoon. "Mother, may I ask you something?"

Vidar stood nearby, absentmindedly polishing his sword, while Thor and Loki played near the garden pond. Baldur had grown more agitated as the days passed since Odin left, but Frigga could not figure out what was bothering him.

"Of course, my son," Frigga answered, laying aside her needlework.

"Privately?" Baldur prompted, glancing at the general.

"General, would you stay here with Thor and Loki?" she asked sweetly. "Baldur and I are going for a little walk."

"As you wish, my queen," Vidar responded, bowing respectfully.

Frigga took her son's arm and looked up at him, marveling at how big he had grown. But then, the Olympians were taller than Asgardians with a much denser muscle structure. They were very similar in appearance to the elves of Alfheim but without the pointed ears and able to pass as human almost as easily as Asgardians and Vanir. They had even settled on Midgard until the humans had driven them back to Olympus some time ago. Even after that, Zeus, their king, had walked Midgard in disguise with Odin many times before Frigga knew either of them. She knew they had been close, but since the scandal over Athena, Odin and Zeus had not spoken or had anything to do with one another. The only way Odin had avoided war was by taking responsibility for Baldur when Zeus threatened to kill the child as well as paying a sizable dividend to the Olympian monarch for agreeing to part ways permanently. It was the strangest peace treaty Frigga had ever seen, but the Olympians had always done things differently. And that had been the end of it.

"What are you thinking about, Mother?" Baldur asked.

"Oh, I was thinking of you when you were a baby," she chuckled. "You've grown so much. I'm quite proud of you, you know."

"Thank you," he murmured.

"What did you want to ask me, Baldur?" Frigga prompted. "We're alone now."

"Do you know when Father is coming back?" Baldur asked.

"Soon, I would imagine," she replied, trying not to frown at the reminder that her happiness might end as soon as Odin returned. "He's already been gone longer than he expected."

"Did you notice how sad he was before he left?" Baldur prodded.

Frigga looked at him with concern. She knew her oldest son could feel the emotions of other people without even touching them. If Baldur sensed sadness in his father, perhaps something had changed in the king.

"I'm ashamed to say I didn't. Something did seem different, but I couldn't determine what," Frigga admitted. "You were with him on Muspelheim. Did something happen?"

"We fought long and hard," Baldur mused. "But most of the time, I was with General Vidar, not Father. I cannot say anything really stood out to me. And it was only after the celebration upon our return that I sensed his sadness."

"Why, whatever could it be?" Frigga queried innocently, ignoring her increasing discomfort. She tightened the mental locks of her mind to prevent him from reading any more than her surface emotions. "Can you pinpoint when you noticed it?"

"A little during the banquet but mostly the next morning," Baldur thought aloud.

"We did have an argument that morning," she said thoughtfully. "Could that be it?"

"Perhaps," Baldur answered. "Father asked me to report to him before lunch that day to give my account of the last battle. And then he asked me my opinion of General Vidar. He's never done that before."

"That's very strange," Frigga said slowly. Inside, she fought a rising panic as she thought, *Odin knows! But how?*

She had no idea what Baldur had sensed in the general and felt nervous her oldest son might also suspect something.

"But he trusts the general, doesn't he?" Baldur prodded. "Why else would he command Vidar to stay with us instead of assigning someone of lesser rank?"

"Of course he trusts the general," Frigga replied. "They've been friends since boyhood. What did you tell your father when he asked?"

"I told him that the general is my friend and a gifted warrior," Baldur stated confidently. "And that I respect him."

Frigga silently breathed a sigh of relief. "I will speak with your father when he returns. It's most likely his sadness was over the harsh words between us before he left. Whatever his reasons for asking you about Vidar, I'm quite certain they were unrelated."

Baldur nodded, seeming relieved himself. "That's good because I cannot bear the thought that the general might not be trustworthy. He's my closest friend besides Hod."

"You needn't worry about that," Frigga reassured her son. "I know beyond a shadow of doubt that the general is loyal to your father and to Asgard."

"I feel the same," Baldur said with a broad grin. "And I trust your judgment, maybe even more so than Father's."

She laughed with delight. "You'd best not let your father hear you say so!"

He laughed with her. Then they turned back the way they had come to rejoin Vidar, Thor, and Loki.

Baldur had relaxed considerably and eagerly asked the general to fence with him in the time they had before dinner would be served. Frigga, Thor, and Loki watched the two of them try to best each other. Frigga quite enjoyed their display of strength and prowess, for she had loved swordplay since she was a small child. And as was the custom on Vanaheim, her father had given her the proper instruction right alongside her brother, who was now the king of that realm. Frigga had even shown Baldur a thing or two, which was what Lady Annette had witnessed before Odin and Vidar had taken over his training in that department.

I still need to ask Annette why she brought up my abilities at the banquet, Frigga thought.

"Your skill grows by the day, my prince," Vidar praised Baldur, wiping some sweat off his brow. "Shall we call it a draw?"

When Baldur nodded, Loki shyly asked the general, "Would you teach me how to fence?"

"Your brother hasn't taught you yet?" Vidar asked the boy, throwing a rebuking glance at the crown prince. "What about your father?"

"Baldur is too busy," Loki complained. "And Father is never around."

Frigga hid her consternation at the boy's request. She had not even known Loki was interested in such things.

"Very well, young prince," Vidar agreed graciously. "I'll show you a few moves tomorrow. Prince Thor, would you care to join us?"

Thor made a face. "I like axes better."

"It wouldn't hurt to learn how to wield more than one weapon, Thor," Frigga admonished him gently.

"Fine," Thor grumbled. "I guess it's a good idea." Then his face brightened. "You are very good with your sword, General. If you teach me, maybe I'll be the best."

Loki rolled his eyes. Baldur raised an eyebrow at Thor as Frigga snickered into her hand. The boy was as arrogant as his father and just as strangely lovable. As they all went inside for dinner, Frigga walked with the general.

"That was kind of you to agree to teach them," Frigga said.

"I'll enjoy it," Vidar responded. A wistfulness crept into his voice as he added, "Odin has some fine sons."

She glanced up at him, but his expression was unreadable. She made a mental note to ask him about it when they met that night.

After dinner, Baldur took Thor and Loki horseback riding. Since Frigga did not want to go, Vidar stayed behind. No one so much as gave them a sideways glance as they walked together to the library to read until the boys returned.

"Shall I stand guard outside?" Vidar offered.

"Is that really necessary?" Frigga asked, her eyes sparkling at him. "I assumed you'd join me."

"I was hoping you'd say that," he murmured as he held the door open for her, grinning at her with that golden glow in his eyes that she had come to look for in their moments together.

Even though they were alone in the library, Vidar maintained his distance while Frigga selected a book. She looked up a few times to see him gazing at her with the same wistfulness she had heard in his voice. Finally, she set the book down and crossed over to where he stood.

"Any sign of the boys?" she asked, peering out the window.

"Not yet," he answered. "I expect they'll stay out until dark."

"Why don't you come talk with me then?" Frigga suggested. "I cannot focus on my reading when you're over here staring at me like that."

"Apologies, my queen," Vidar said with a slight bow. "Perhaps I should wait outside after all."

"Don't be silly," Frigga protested.

"We should not grow careless, Frigga," he whispered. "What if we're discovered? What if Odin finds out?"

"He might already know," she said quietly.

Vidar's eyes widened in alarm. "How?"

"I was going to wait to tell you until tonight," Frigga told him. "There is much for us to talk about."

Vidar cocked his head. "Why not tell me now?"

"What if someone comes in here or overhears?" Frigga whispered. "Didn't you just say we shouldn't be careless?"

He sighed. "You're right. But I don't see how I can wait. What if Odin returns tonight?"

Frigga paled considerably. "Do you think he will?"

"He told me he expected to return before now," Vidar pointed out. "It's entirely possible."

"Then I *will* tell you now," she conceded. "In case we cannot meet tonight."

As a precaution, she sent an illusion of the general into the hallway to stand guard. Then she quickly filled him in on her conversation with Baldur.

"I don't think you can assume he knows from that, though I can see why you would think so," Vidar mused as he relaxed noticeably. "Odin charges everything head-on. Why wouldn't he confront one of us if he knew?"

"Maybe he will," Frigga suggested. "I think we should be ready for it."

"That's wise," Vidar agreed.

"And perhaps we should stop meeting in secret," Frigga added sadly.

A flash of pain crossed Vidar's face, and for just a moment, Frigga regretted the last few days of her life. Vidar made her so happy, she had given little thought to the effect their budding relationship might be having on him. And she suddenly realized the snare she had unwittingly laid for herself. It seemed love had been offered to her, then snatched away like fresh meat dangled in front of hungry dogs to make them fight each other. And the grief her realization brought shook her to her core. She turned away from him to hide her sorrow, but as well as he knew her now, he saw it.

"Frigga," he whispered as he pulled her just past the window and into his arms.

He had never before dared to show such intimacy out in the open. The shock of it rooted her to where she stood. She almost lost hold of the illusion she had cast of the general as he clung to her as if his very life depended on her.

"I-I'll think of something," she stammered, quite unwilling to give him up and return to her miserable life with Odin.

"Maybe he doesn't know," Vidar responded, letting her go almost as quickly as he had embraced her. "Maybe nothing has to change."

"Vidar, I'm afraid for you," she said quietly.

"For me?"

"Am I harming you by continuing like this?" she asked. When he shook his head, she insisted, "I am not free to give you all you desire, and I wonder how long you'll settle for this strange relationship we have."

He drew near her again and lifted her chin so she would look at him. "Don't talk like that, my queen. I am your friend, and only your happiness matters. Whatever pain I bear is worth the sweetness of what we've shared."

He bent his head down and brushed his lips against her cheek. Distracted as she was by maintaining the illusion in the hallway, she almost turned her mouth to his but stopped herself in time. She brought the illusion back into the library since no one had even passed by in the time the fake general stood out there.

He smirked when he noticed the illusion of the door opening, then saw himself enter and vanish. "Did you cast an illusion of me, my queen?"

"Yes, just to be safe," Frigga answered. "But I simply cannot focus when you say and do things like that."

"I don't think an illusion was necessary. I doubt anyone would question us for being in the library together," Vidar chuckled. "It's hardly the place for a romantic rendezvous, although I still maintain we shouldn't be careless. Someone could still come in here."

Frigga nodded, then cocked her head. "You mention my happiness quite a bit. But what of your happiness, Vidar?"

"I am happy," he insisted. "Especially knowing Baldur thinks so highly of me. I'm very fond of him. Of all your sons, actually. Even Thor."

"Even Thor?" Frigga repeated indignantly.

"Don't get upset," Vidar chuckled. "I sense the boy does not fully trust me, but he's a fine lad nonetheless."

"That reminds me. You called all of my sons fine earlier," Frigga remembered aloud. "But you sounded sad. Wistful."

He looked down and stepped away.

"Vidar, you say you are my friend. Then speak the truth to me," she prodded. "What troubles you?"

"How can I speak of my one regret?" he asked so quietly, she was not certain if she had heard correctly.

"What regret?" she inquired softly.

"Frigga, I don't want to tell you this," he admitted. "But if you are calling my friendship into question—"

"No, never," she protested. "I simply want you to be able to confide in me the way you've allowed me to confide in you."

"I don't want you to misunderstand me," he said slowly, reluctantly.

She placed her hand on his arm. "Please give me the chance to understand. Do you trust me as I trust you?"

He regarded her solemnly with his hazel eyes that spoke to her in so many ways, like Odin's gray eyes once did.

Then he blurted out, "I regret that I will never be a father."

"Why will you never be a father?" she asked, trying her hardest not to make any assumptions.

His words came out in a quiet rush like a stream of water that had finally pushed its way past an obstruction. "You will never bear another child, and I could never love another. So I wish Odin's sons were mine. I wish I had married you before Odin could so he never would have hurt you the way he has. I … I covet his life … and you, whom he does not appreciate."

Utterly speechless, she gazed at him, sensing he had more to say.

He grasped his own hair with both hands and turned from her in his consternation. "He's like a brother to me, but I would beat him senseless if he ever subjected you to such misery again. And I am utterly powerless to love you like I want to or even to protect you from him. My only choice is to continue to push the two of you together and so push myself out. And after these last few days with you, I … don't know if I can."

"Then I have ruined you," she observed quietly. "Oh Vidar, I am so sorry."

"Don't, Frigga!" he groaned in frustration, though he kept his voice down. "This is exactly why I didn't want to tell you."

"Did you lie to me when you said you would step aside if Odin decided to be a good husband?" She despised herself for even asking, but she had to know.

He sighed. "No, Frigga, I don't lie to suit my own self interests. I meant every word of what I said when I said it, but things have changed."

"Have I turned you against him?" she asked fearfully.

"Not at all. I really do love and serve the king despite his glaring flaws," Vidar assured her. "But I love and serve the queen more. I truly desire to seek your happiness."

"You are contradicting yourself," Frigga pointed out.

"I know it," he chuckled, breaking the tension. "Would you like to know my second Asgardian gift, the one I keep hidden?"

She cocked her head, wondering why he had changed the subject.

"I have not changed the subject," he told her. When her eyes widened with shock, he said, "And I have not read your mind. Not really. My gift is somewhat like a mix of yours and Baldur's. My mother called it wisdom. I have an uncanny ability to understand almost anyone, even in their silence."

"That is a beautiful gift," Frigga murmured. "And no doubt what makes you such a good listener. But I can also see why you keep it to yourself."

"Yes, sometimes I feel it is also a curse. I usually distance myself from people. I must for my own sanity," Vidar told her. "There are only a handful of people I have allowed past my protective barrier. You and Odin are two of them. And that is why I am so conflicted. I know and understand and love you both, though I could throttle Odin for his stupidity, even as I understand his flawed reasoning."

"What can I do to help you, my dear general?" Frigga asked softly. "Should I cast you aside and pretend I do not care for you?"

To her surprise, he laughed bitterly. "That would not fool me. I wish I had an easy answer, but I don't. I have questioned the wisdom of spending so much time with you, but as much as I understand others, I often do not understand myself. I cannot make myself stop seeing you. But I do know one thing—if ever you were to ask me to part from you permanently, I fear I would die of a broken heart, as Laufey did."

"How did you know that's how Laufey died?" she gasped.

He shrugged. "It seemed obvious to me based on your story, even without my gift. I gathered that Laufey loved Odin, but she loved you more. As do I."

"Do not compare us to Odin and Laufey," Frigga pleaded. "Odin never loved her. He only used her. If it were not for my sons, I would smile in the face of Odin's wrath and run away with you this very minute!"

"Oh, my queen, you stir my soul with your words," he groaned. "What a wretched pair we make." He glanced out the window as he said this, which he had been doing off and on throughout the entire conversation. Then he informed her, "The princes are returning. We have but five minutes before we should go down to meet them."

"And how would you spend those minutes, General Vidar?" she asked shyly.

"Come with me, Queen Frigga," he said with a grin.

He pulled her into a small space behind a large bookshelf,

which effectively blocked any view someone might have upon walking into the library. Heart pounding, she allowed him to take her into his arms again. She laid her head against his chest and listened to his heart beat faster and faster. She looked up at him, and the intensity in his eyes left her stunned and breathless.

"I'm tempted to read your mind," she whispered.

"No, not now," he murmured. "The thoughts racing through my mind should not be there. I don't want you to see them."

"They no doubt match my own," she crooned, daring to link her hands behind his neck.

"I know. I can feel it." He shut his eyes and pressed his forehead against hers, then said, "We're out of time, my queen."

"Should we risk meeting tonight?" she asked hopefully, dropping her hands and stepping away from him.

"I'll meet you at half past midnight if Odin doesn't come," he promised.

And to her relief, Odin did not come that night or the next.

Things went on as they had in his absence with the addition of Vidar's fencing lessons with Thor and Loki, which Frigga greatly enjoyed watching.

After two more days, the king sent word through the keeper of the gates that complications had arisen to detain him for a week or more. Lady Ithunna was quite upset by this news since it meant Lord Bragi, who was running the kingdom in Odin's stead, could not return home. But Frigga had to expend serious effort to hide how ecstatic she was.

Day by day slipped by as Vidar tended the rich, fertile soil buried in the heart of the queen. And she blossomed like a rose under his care. She somehow managed to curb her desire for him physically, never allowing him to do more than hold her for a little while when they met at night. But even that action bonded her so strongly to Vidar, she responded quite coldly to Odin when he finally did return one evening, despite her admonition to herself to be kind to him. He showed no reaction to her response, and their bed seemed even more empty to her with him in it.

4

Frigga stood silently and regally in her place below the king as he seated himself on the throne to hear what grievances and legal matters had been delayed until his return. She felt Vidar watching her from where he stood but refused to look in his direction, lest she betray them. But she was so intent on her efforts to appear as she should, she heard almost nothing of the proceedings. Thankfully, Odin did not seek her opinion on even a single matter.

After lunch, the king beckoned to his queen.

"Frigga, there is a matter I must discuss with you," he said solemnly.

She trembled within herself but answered sweetly, "Of course, my king. Do you wish to retire to our chambers?"

He nodded, his expression unreadable. She meekly followed him to the royal suite, then sat gingerly on their bed, warily watching him pace the floor.

"I don't know how to say this, Frigga, so I'm just going to say it," he blurted out.

She braced herself inwardly but kept her face carefully masked.

"I've been thinking about our last argument a great deal during our time apart," he continued, kneeling in front of her.

"You were absolutely right. I've never been able to come to terms with your love for Laufey, especially since I never really loved her."

"I know that," she said coldly. "And, it seems, so did she. Eventually."

He lowered his head briefly. "I was even jealous of her for a time, which sounds terrible when I say it out loud. But I finally understand. You loved her because it is in your nature to love. What a cold, callous, selfish man I must be in your eyes." Frigga stared at him in shock, listening intently as he choked out, "I've already asked for your forgiveness, but today, I promise you I will never again betray you as long as I live."

Frigga began to shake, completely flabbergasted by this turn of events. "What's come over you, Odin? Why this sudden change?" She peered at him carefully as a thought occurred to her. "Are you dying?"

He shook his head. "Have I been that much of a beast for you to think I would only say such things if I thought I was dying?"

She had no idea what to say.

"Frigga," he whispered, cupping her face with both his hands. "How can I make this right?"

"I don't know," she muttered, fighting within herself.

Wanting to recoil from him and throw herself into his arms all at once, she did nothing when he pulled her forward to kiss her. Surprised at herself, she slowly relaxed and returned his kiss.

"I've missed you so much," he murmured against her mouth as if encouraged by her response.

Sensing he wanted more than that kiss, she pulled away and protested, "Odin, it's the middle of the day!"

"I don't care," he groaned softly, but with a tinge of defiance. "You are my wife, and I need you. It's been far too long."

She yanked herself away from his grasp and stood, deeply offended. "So! You reveal your true intentions, Odin Borrson. I'm the same as Athena, Laufey, or any other woman you say you *haven't* been with—just another female body to satisfy you."

Odin gaped at her, his face displaying emotions ranging from anger to deep sadness. She expected him to rage at her and prepared herself to flee from his wrath. He had never taken his anger out on her physically, but his tongue could be as sharp as a sword. They had flung many cruel words at each other over the years, and each wound he had formerly inflicted upon her seemed fresh and raw whenever he lost his temper again.

But Odin remained silent, appearing to be warring within himself.

Finally, he took one step toward her and said softly, "That isn't true, Frigga. But it doesn't matter how many times I say it. It's your choice whether to believe me or the lies you comfort yourself with." She opened her mouth to retort, but then he declared, "And I'd frankly like to know who has been satisfying you."

"What?" she exploded as shock and dismay flooded her. "I've never shared any man's bed but yours, Odin!"

He folded his arms across his chest. "Frigga, I know there's something going on between you and another man. And I have my suspicions as to who it is."

"I swear to you, O King, no man has compromised my honor," she huffed, thankful she could truthfully assert herself. "Why do you accuse me so? Because you are guilty yourself and cannot imagine it possible for someone to remain celibate?"

"I found this under your desk before the last banquet, by the wastebasket," Odin informed her, ignoring her accusation as he drew out a crumpled-up piece of paper from his tunic.

He held it out to her. She took it and surveyed it carefully, masking her reaction with light refraction. She had attempted to write the general three times before she settled on what to say in the note she had hidden in the wolf statue before she began meeting Vidar in secret. One of her crumpled notes must have fallen out of the wastebasket without her noticing.

She read aloud, "I have not ceased to think of you since you left. If you truly love me …" She looked up at the king. "The rest is scratched out, and it isn't signed."

"It's your handwriting, Frigga," Odin stated dryly.

"Is this why you ignored me at the banquet, even when I wore the dress you gave me for our anniversary?" she demanded, thrusting the paper back at him.

"Yes," he muttered as she angrily turned her back on him. "Now I think I know how you must have felt after my indiscretions. I couldn't even look at you. I just kept imagining some other man loving you, perhaps better than I ever have."

She suddenly felt an odd sense of compassion toward Odin and turned her face toward him slightly. "Then why did you begin to show courtesy toward me?"

"When?"

"Right before we presented our gift to …" She trailed off with a gasp and whirled around to look him full in the face, secretly proud of her act. "Why, Odin! Surely you don't believe that your wife and your most trusted advisor, your *best friend*—"

"Well? What of it?" Odin demanded, his body rigid as if he were bracing himself for an expected blow. "I know the two of you have become friends of sorts. And I saw you staring at him that night."

"If you suspected your dearest friend of such a thing, why did you entrust me and our sons to his care while you were gone?" she asked as innocently as she could muster.

"Because I wanted to see what you would do with freedom like that," Odin stated. "I had people watching you both."

"You are unbelievable," she muttered indignantly. "What people?"

"Baldur and a few of the palace staff," he answered curtly.

"You asked our *son* to spy on his own mother to catch me in adultery?" she gasped, her tone oddly stern in her aversion.

Odin grimaced. "I was desperate, Frigga. And I didn't tell Baldur why or what I wanted him to observe. I only asked him his opinion of the general before I left. And when I returned, I asked him several specific questions."

"And did you tell the staff your suspicions?" she asked coldly.

"No. If I was proven wrong, I didn't want to start any gossip about you," he admitted.

"Well, that's kind of you," she snorted sarcastically.

"I told two guards and the housekeeper to report anything that seemed amiss," Odin explained. "And I asked some questions about comings and goings when I returned."

"And what did they say?" she demanded hotly. "Did they tell you the general did his duty and nothing more? That he was the picture of respect and honor?"

"Actually, yes," Odin sighed. "And that has confused me greatly. If you've been sneaking around, you've covered your tracks quite well. Vidar was accounted for at all times, even at night. No one ever saw him leave his room once he retired." He narrowed his eyes and spoke as if to himself. "Unless you hid him … but you couldn't have done that if you were here and he was in his room. I thought perhaps you made yourself invisible and went to his room. Or met him some other place. But someone should have seen or heard his door open. You couldn't have timed everything to hide it all yourself. How could it be no one saw anything at all?"

Frigga silently wondered the same. *Vidar must have been very sly when he left his room*, she thought. *How was he not seen?*

Regardless, they had come incredibly close to being caught. This called for drastic measures—whatever it took to keep her husband from learning the truth.

Since she was a terrible liar, she decided to give him partial honesty. "Because there was nothing to see, Odin. Yes, the general has been a friend to me, but he has been your advocate and tried to help us heal our marriage."

"He has spoken to me about that multiple times over the years," Odin said warily. "But—"

"He has noticed what no one else has, but that does not mean I have such little self-respect to jump into bed with him," she interrupted as she glared defiantly at him. "If you still do not believe me, then read my memories."

It was a bold move on her part, but she knew what she was doing. Either Odin would turn down her offer or she would have the opportunity to manipulate his mind once he entered hers since he would be too focused on probing her mind to notice.

He blanched. "You know how I feel about that, Frigga. Your thoughts and memories are your own."

Frigga immediately felt a deep sense of shame that she had been willing to resort to changing his memories to hide her own wrongdoing.

"I'm glad you still feel that way, my husband," Frigga said softly.

Though she remained calm on the exterior, her heart roiled within her. Odin looked at her with such tenderness in his eyes, she felt every heartstring pulled back toward him. He had not looked at her like that in years. She marveled at herself over how she could be torn between these two men, who were so alike and yet so different. What Odin lacked and had denied her all these years, Vidar supplied eagerly. And though she craved the general's presence and kindness, she remembered a time when she had lived and breathed for Odin alone. Fragmented snatches of laughter, trust, and joy teased at the frayed edges of her earliest memories with him. If she had been happy with Odin at one time, who was to say she and Vidar might not eventually end up in this miserable place? And if she could fall in love with Vidar, could she fall in love with Odin again? Even though she spoke the truth that she had not compromised her honor with the general, deep in her heart, she knew their emotional bond would grieve her husband as much or perhaps more. As these thoughts coursed through her, she could not stop her tears. When they trickled out and streamed down her face, Odin stepped close to her and reached out to catch one.

"Are you telling me the truth?" he pressed as he searched her eyes. "There's nothing between you and Vidar?"

"There is friendship and mutual respect," she declared, hoping the partial truth would suffice.

"And did you write this letter?" he asked, waving it in the air.

She nodded.

"Why did you pretend you didn't?" he asked, standing so close to her, she could see shadows of emotion etched onto his face. "Who was it for?"

She fancied she saw the glimmer of actual tears. In all their years together, she had never seen Odin cry. But her shame and guilt over his trauma was not enough for her to put a stop to her meetings with Vidar. Her heart wanted what it wanted, so she thought of a deliciously wicked lie to steer him away from what was really happening.

She allowed her own tears to flow again. "I wrote it to you … to try to heal our marriage. I thought if we started over the way we did when you courted me, with letters and meetings in secret, perhaps we could …" She allowed her voice to fall to a whisper. " … fall in love again."

Frigga had never in her life lied so well. And she knew Odin would believe her precisely for that reason.

"Oh, Frigga," he sighed. Then he began to laugh with relief. "Frigga, my dear Frigga, I had no idea you cared that much." He grew sober again. "Why did you throw it away?"

"I threw *three* of them away … because they sounded so ridiculous," she answered truthfully, wringing her hands slightly. "I had no idea that one fell out. I didn't want you to know I wrote them. I felt foolish. And I was afraid you would reject me."

He drew her into his arms and held her tightly. As he stroked her hair, he murmured, "How have we gone so far astray?"

Frigga laid her head against his chest. A thousand memories rushed through her mind as she listened to his strong heartbeat. The power of nostalgia threatened to sweep her away, but she blocked it. How could she trust him again? She mustered the same effort she used to resist her physical attraction to Vidar and gently pushed away from Odin. Just as he was about to speak, the rap of a palace guard sounded on the door. Odin groaned, then moved to answer it.

"Forgive me, my king," the guard said, bowing before Odin. "An urgent matter requires your presence in the throne room."

"Very well," Odin sighed. "I'll be there shortly."

He closed the door, then returned to gently grasp Frigga's shoulders.

"Could we talk again tonight?" he asked her.

She nodded. And in a moment, he was gone.

She sank wearily into the comfort of their bed. She lay there for several minutes, trying to decipher her own thoughts and emotions. Unsure of what to do with herself, she went invisible, then slipped out into the hallway and hurried to Laufey's old room where she thought she could clear her mind. She quietly locked the door behind her and nearly jumped out of her skin in fright, for Vidar stood at the small window, peeking through the drapes.

"Vidar!" she gasped. "What are you doing here?"

His military training had made him so disciplined, he did nothing more than turn his head toward the sound of her voice.

"I've been wanting to come here during the day for a while now, but I haven't had a chance," he answered, beckoning to her. "Come look."

She joined him at the window. "What do you see?"

"Look through Laufey's eyes," he suggested.

"Odin and I used to walk the paths there after breakfast," she remembered, pointing toward the winding stone by the lilac bushes. "And back then, we would kiss in that pavilion there, thinking no one could see."

"How could she not see? No wonder she felt depressed, locked up here and cut off from her people," Vidar mused insightfully. "And if she tried to catch a glimpse of some beauty to get her through the day, she risked seeing the man she should not have loved and who only used her … happily loving his wife."

"That makes me incredibly sad," she whispered. "But it wasn't my fault she experienced such heartache."

He turned to face her. "No, of course it wasn't. I was only thinking of it because there were a few times I saw the two of you as well."

"Did that bring you pain?" she asked quietly. "You speak

as though you've experienced the same feelings Laufey must have."

"It brought me more joy than pain because I saw you were happy," Vidar answered. "But your misery seems to have returned with Odin. This morning, you seemed—"

"Never mind about this morning," Frigga shushed him. "There's something I must tell you."

He gave her his full attention as she recounted her confrontation with Odin. She did not tell him about her internal conflict, uncertain whether or not his gift would enable him to understand how confused she felt.

"And tonight, he wants to talk with me again," she finished.

"I see," he said quietly. "You are torn." He gazed at her solemnly. "And you won't be here tonight, will you? You'll be tending to him."

She blushed. "I don't know about *that.*"

"You are his wife," Vidar stated flatly. "I'd be an ignorant fool to deny what happens between a husband and wife."

"Well, in our case, it isn't a frequent occurrence," she admitted awkwardly. "In fact, I've kept him at bay for years."

"Years?" he exclaimed. "And he has been with no other women in all that time?"

"Do you think he's lying?" she asked, suddenly fearful and surprised at how much it still hurt her to think of Odin with another woman.

"No, not really," he said thoughtfully. "Maybe Odin has changed. If he is telling the truth, I'm impressed he's waited that long for you without straying."

"Why?" she asked curiously. She looked up at him shyly through her lashes. "Haven't you kept yourself from women?"

"I wish I could say I have, my queen," he answered, looking down at the worn rug on the floor. "Asgardian standards have changed since I was young. They are far more wholesome now." He shook his head sadly. "I have regrets … so many regrets."

Frigga regarded him silently, unsure of how to process this new information. She had naively assumed he had little experience with women, but his confident swagger and easy manner with the single noblewomen fit with this narrative rather than her assumptions.

"Then you are experienced," she said coldly.

"Yes and no," he responded quickly. "It's been a significant number of years for me too."

She blushed deeply. "Can we talk about something else?"

"Like what?"

"How did you come to me without being seen?" she asked.

"With this," he declared, showing her a small circular object that looked to her like a large black locket with no chain.

"What is that?" she breathed excitedly.

"It's my personal transport device," he explained. "It takes me anywhere I want to go within a realm. Watch."

He flipped open the lid. She gasped when a shimmer of multi-colored light flared, and Vidar disappeared. But just as quickly, he reappeared.

"Where did you go?" she demanded.

"Back to my room," he laughed.

"Was that Bifröst light?" she asked. "May I try it?"

"Yes, it has a small amount of Bifröst ore in it, but no, I

cannot let anyone else use this. I've sworn an oath to my order," he explained.

"What order?"

"I belong to a group of Asgardians who build Bifröst portals. The Order of the Sköll," he informed her.

"You named it after the fierce wolf from your story?" she gasped.

"It wasn't my choice," Vidar corrected. "The other members thought he was a better fit since we desire to see the suns of other realms."

"Ah yes, because he loved the sun. But you prefer the moon. As the wounded Hadi did," Frigga recalled.

"You remembered!" Vidar smiled tenderly at Frigga when she nodded proudly. "I do love the moon, especially Midgard's. Anyway, my order developed this technology within the last year."

"Does Odin know that?" Frigga asked, somewhat resentfully.

She knew that the Bifröst Bridge at Asgard's portal gate had been built millennia ago by Odin's great-grandfather. The strange black ore that made up its construct transported beings quickly and safely to other realms under Gjallar's watchful eye. But other Asgardians had built smaller, lesser-known portals during the king's wandering days. Odin had even commissioned a secret Bifröst portal to meet with her during their courtship. Had Vidar or his friends built it? And why was this the first she had heard of continued portal building?

"He knows about the order but not this device," Vidar answered quietly. "I am trusting you to keep this between us."

"But shouldn't he know about this technology?" Frigga asked suspiciously.

Though thrilled with Vidar's confidence in her, especially since she had long wished Odin would share such things, a sudden fear of potential treachery had hit her. She trusted the general but what of the other members of this order?

"All in good time," Vidar reassured her. "Several of us are testing them. We will present everything to him when we are certain there are no ill effects. I wish I could let you use mine, but you shouldn't even know about it."

"But it seems safe enough. And you said you'd do anything I ask," she pleaded.

"And you would never ask me to break an oath." He laughed when she pouted in disappointment. "Perhaps someday they'll let me give you one of your own."

"Perhaps someday you can take me with you to one of the places you've been," she countered playfully.

"I would like nothing more," Vidar admitted softly. "But back to how we were almost caught, I'm rather shocked you lied to Odin to protect me. I didn't think you had that in you."

"I didn't either," she lamented.

"I'm a little hurt he didn't come to me," he confessed.

"What would you have said if he had?" she asked quietly.

"I would have lied to protect you," he murmured as he brushed her cheek with his knuckles. "Now … since we won't see each other tonight, would you like to meet tomorrow afternoon?"

"No, it's too risky. I've pacified Odin for now, but I don't like how close he came to discovering us."

"Then when will we see each other again?" he asked as he laced his fingers with hers.

"We need to think of some way to communicate with each other that no one else would understand," she thought aloud.

"Or I'll simply come here every night and wait for you," he offered. "If you can come, we'll be together. If not, I'll try again the next night."

"You are so incredibly selfless, Vidar," she murmured. "I'll try to think of another solution so we don't have to do that for too long."

"I will too. Until we meet again, my queen," he whispered, lifting her hand to press it against his cheek. "I'd better report to my station before anyone notices my absence."

She nodded. When he vanished, she went to the window to look out at the gardens, imagining it through Laufey's eyes as Vidar had. But it made her so sad, she left to find out what her sons were doing. When a guard informed her they had gone fishing together, she decided to lose herself in a book in the library. She soon became immersed in the story, wandering into the deep recesses of imagination where time did not exist. She came to herself suddenly, feeling as though someone had tapped her on the forehead. But no one was in the room. She put it out of her mind as her stomach grumbled and growled at her, making her realize she had completely missed dinner. Surprised no one had looked into her whereabouts, she hurried to the kitchen to grab a snack, taking the book with her.

"The palace seems very empty tonight," she said offhandedly to the cook, who prepared her a plate.

"It was empty in the dining room too, my queen," the old woman chuckled, tucking several white hairs back into her starch white cap. "No one came for dinner."

"Where is everyone?" Frigga asked in confusion.

"I only know where they are not, my queen. And that is here," the cook replied with a clever glint of amusement in her wizened brown eyes.

Frigga laughed despite her growing worry. The cook grinned and curtsied, then turned her attention to chopping herbs for the morning selection of savories.

Returning to the last chapter in her story, Frigga had only taken a few absentminded bites of her food when Baldur burst into the kitchen, followed by his brothers. She looked up in time to see him grinning sheepishly at her where she sat at the large preparation table, munching on apple slices and crispy crackers spread with soft Asgardian cheese.

"Hello, Mother," he said cheerfully. "I didn't expect to see you here. Good book?"

"And where have you three been?" she demanded, holding her place with one finger.

"Loki took off after a stupid rabbit and got lost in the wilderness," Thor grumped. "We had to track him down."

Frigga gasped, noticing the youngest boy's nasty-looking scratches. "Did you fall into a briar patch, Loki?"

"Yes," the boy answered pitifully, his green eyes brimming with tears. "Baldur said there's some ointment in here."

"Baby," Thor muttered.

"Shut up, Thor!" Loki wailed.

When Thor stuck his tongue out at him, Loki threw himself at his slightly older brother. In seconds, the two of them were punching each other and wrestling on the kitchen floor. Frigga sighed, pushed aside her novel, and inserted herself into the fray to break them up, grabbing each boy by the ear. Baldur merely watched gleefully and nudged the equally amused cook as he helped himself to some bread.

"Owww!" the younger boys cried in unison.

"You sit there!" she commanded Thor, plopping him in a chair. Then she turned to Loki. "That is not how we handle conflict, young man!"

"Well, why not?" Loki protested. "Isn't that what Father and Baldur do when they go off to war? Pound the guy that made them mad?"

Annoyed when Baldur let loose a hoot of laughter, Frigga turned to him. "Why don't you try helping, Baldur?"

"What for?" he chuckled. "You're doing just fine."

Frigga rolled her eyes, then knelt in front of her youngest son. "Someday you'll understand the causes of war, Loki. But for now, you need to learn to ignore people who tease you. Bullies operate from a place of inadequacy." With that, she turned her glare upon Thor, who squirmed in his seat. "And you, Thor Odinson, have no right to taunt your brother. Frankly, you deserved to get punched in the mouth. I will not have that kind of behavior in my home. Is that clear?"

"Yes, Mother," Thor mumbled sheepishly.

"But whether he deserved it or not doesn't make what you did right, Loki," she admonished her youngest son.

"Yes, Mother," Loki sighed.

"Now tell me why you're upset with Loki, Thor," Frigga said gently.

She grabbed some Asgardian ointment to tend to Loki's scratches and Thor's split lip.

"Baldur told him to stay on the path, but he didn't listen," Thor said indignantly. "We left our gear to chase him down. We obviously found Loki, but by the time we got back to our fishing spot, some animal had gotten our fish. I wanted to show Father the big one I caught, but now it's gone."

"I understand why that upset you, Thor," Frigga affirmed him. "Loki, why didn't you listen to your brother? It's not like you to chase a rabbit."

"I saw a fox sneaking up on it while it was eating," he defended himself. "I tried to scare the fox off, but I accidentally scared the rabbit instead. When the fox went after it, I ran after them to get between them. The rabbit went down a hole, so the fox gave up. That's when I fell into the briar patch. I tried to find my way back, but Baldur and Thor found me first."

"And it's a very good thing they did," Frigga chided him. "Do you realize how foolish and dangerous that was?" When Loki hung his head, she hugged him. "That was a very kind thing to try to rescue the rabbit. But you must realize rabbits have their own ways to escape. And there are far nastier things in those woods than foxes."

"Yes, and they gobble up little boys," Baldur teased.

"Baldur, don't say such things," Frigga scolded him. She turned her attention back to Loki. "Next time, obey your brother and stay on the path."

"Yes, Mother," Loki agreed.

"Now, you two apologize to each other for fighting," Frigga said sternly.

Once they complied, she ensured they ate their dinner, then sent them all to bed so she could finally finish her book. By the time she dragged herself back to the royal chambers, she was so weary, she did not even register Odin's absence at first. And not knowing when he would return, she waited up as long as she could but slowly sank into the cushions piled on the settee near the window.

Frigga woke with a start in the middle of the night. Odin still had not returned. She climbed into the bed fully clothed and slept soundly until morning. Although used to Odin being gone, she wondered if he had been up all night. Perhaps he would appear at breakfast. She hummed as she changed into a fresh dress, fixed her hair, and opened the drapes. She chose a necklace to wear, one she thought would please his eyes. She looked briefly for the matching earrings, then suddenly remembered she had absent-mindedly removed them in Odin's main office months ago, during a long and boring cabinet meeting. She could not quite remember exactly where she had stashed them and hurried to the austere room to look.

Strangely, the door was unlocked. She turned the knob and opened the door quietly, peeking around to see if anyone was there.

At first, she saw nothing out of the ordinary. She stepped inside and closed the door behind her. The stillness felt like a thick blanket of air around her. She took a few steps toward the large table where Odin had last met with his cabinet, which included his nine generals and twelve war council members. She often attended strategy meetings as a figure-head but was never expected to contribute. Perhaps the nagging uneasiness she felt was due to the emptiness of the room and the knowledge that so many Asgardian soldiers had not returned from the Muspelheim conflict. Seven of the nine corps had been sent home to their families for respite, including Vidar's, but the generals staggered their leave time, as there was always much to do post-war. The room would be crowded again soon enough.

Behind the table stood Odin's bookcase of maps and war strategies where she thought she had left her earrings. But before she reached it, she saw a sudden flash of color out of the corner of her eye. She turned her head toward Odin's massive desk, where she immediately spotted the king face down on the floor.

5

A panicked scream rose in Frigga's throat as she rushed to her husband and shook him. He was still breathing, but he did not respond, even when she called his name.

She managed to flip him over and get his head into her lap as she shrieked, "Guards, to the king!"

After several agonizing seconds of trying to wake him, Frigga filled her lungs to scream for help again. Just then, General Vidar burst into the room, followed by three palace guards.

"Get a healer in here!" Vidar yelled at one of the other guards, who immediately rushed out of the room. Then the general knelt beside the queen and demanded, "What happened?"

"He never came to bed last night. I assumed he was still occupied with whatever called him away yesterday," Frigga sobbed, her pitch rising with hysteria. "I came to look for something just now and found him here like this. I don't know what's wrong with him. Why won't he wake up? How long has he been in here?"

"My queen, you must calm down," Vidar soothed her. "You're no good to him like this."

One of the healers arrived and took one look at Odin, then barked, "Get him to the House immediately. Time is of the essence! I pray we are not too late."

"Why? What's wrong with him?" Frigga cried.

"Not now, my queen," Vidar admonished her gently. "You need to get out of the way."

But Frigga would not let go of Odin. She knew she was impeding the healer's orders but could not move away from her husband. None of the guards dared address her or touch her. They looked at each other and at Vidar with uncertainty. He gently pulled Frigga back as he directed the guards to take Odin's arms and legs to lift him onto the electrically powered stretcher the healer had brought with him. She struggled against Vidar, not even knowing why, but he held her fast.

"You there! Accompany the king," Vidar commanded, pointing to the guard who had returned with the healer. "See that he is not harmed."

The younger man hastened to obey, marching after the stretcher as the healer guided it out of the office.

Vidar gestured to the others. "You two! Comb this room for anything you can find while I escort the queen to her chambers."

Frigga had stopped struggling by this point and merely sat defeated in a slump on the floor, silently sobbing. Vidar still had one arm around her to prevent her from moving.

She turned her face toward him and, in a much calmer voice, said, "Release me, General."

"Do you promise not to run after the king?" Vidar asked quietly, his tone tender and familiar.

The two remaining guards had already begun searching

Odin's office for any clues as to what had happened. They paused at the general's words. Frigga saw one of them raise his eyebrow at the other and immediately realized how suspicious it seemed for the general to respond that way.

She glared at Vidar haughtily and seethed, "How dare you refuse to obey a direct order! I am your queen. Unhand me!"

The two guards looked at each other again, then back at Vidar with concern. Vidar reluctantly released Frigga.

She stood, wiped her face, and smoothed out her dress. "Thank you for your concern, General, but I have sufficiently composed myself."

Vidar immediately rose to his feet as well. Silent questions mounted in his eyes. "How can I serve you, my queen? Where do you wish to go?"

"You may escort me to my room first and help me retrieve some things for myself and the king. Then you will take me to the House of the Healers," she instructed. "And I will hear no arguments on the matter. Is that clear?"

"Yes, my queen," he said with a bow. He turned to the guards. "Corporal, continue your work here. Private, report at once to Colonel Vale. Instruct him to double the guard, starting with the princes. Then return to assist the corporal or send another in your stead if the colonel has other work for you to do."

Both men nodded, striking their fists against their chests twice, as all Asgardian men did when showing deference to a superior. The private rushed out of the room as the corporal turned his attention back to the investigation.

Vidar escorted the queen to the royal chambers and stood

at attention while she gathered what she and the king would need while at the House of the Healers. She wondered if the general's silence was due to the expectations of his role or some other reason.

"I apologize for the way I addressed you in there," she said to him as she packed up a change of clothing for the king. "I didn't want any suspicion cast on you."

He regarded her with an unreadable gaze. "Suspicion of what, my queen?"

"Familiarity with me, of course," she replied as she grabbed an extra dress for herself. "Why are you acting so strangely?"

"I am greatly concerned for the king. Do you know what my men might find, my queen?" he asked quietly as he looked down at the floor.

"I haven't the faintest idea," she answered uneasily. She paused suddenly and drew near him. "Vidar, no one is here to listen. Speak plainly. Do you think I had something to do with this?"

"You were the first one on the scene, my queen," Vidar pointed out, glancing at her briefly. "And what lies between us is a viable motive."

Anger and hurt surged through Frigga, but she controlled her desire to lash out at him. "And you believe I am capable of such a thing?"

"Did you not suspect me?" he returned without answering her.

"No, it never even occurred to me," she retorted. "You have too much honor in you. And I'm grieved you don't view me the same. How could you think so lowly of me?"

"It is not that I thought lowly of you, Frigga," he responded slowly. He lowered his eyes again. "It is that I imagined your love for me and your unhappiness with Odin had driven you to do something you would never otherwise do."

"I have done nothing," she spouted. "I am not that foolish, Vidar! I realized some time ago that the death of the king would not free me to be with you. Not on Asgard. Besides, I couldn't possibly harm him. I … I …"

She could not finish her sentence, not to him. But he knew what she had not expressed.

"You still love him," Vidar finished for her. "Then your response was not an act?"

She shook her head. "Did your gift not tell you so?"

"If I don't want to believe something, I can deceive myself," he confessed. "And I haven't wanted to believe you still love the king because that means—"

She threw her arms around him. "Don't say it, Vidar."

He pushed her away and held her at arm's length, something he had not done since they started meeting in secret. "My queen, I believe it is time I stepped out of the way. I am content to be your friend."

"Well, I am not," she sputtered, shaking his hands off her arms so she could slip them around his waist. "Don't you dare push me away again. I might still love Odin, but I do not love you any less!"

He grinned down at her, then enveloped her in his embrace. "What are we going to do, Frigga? How is it we can both love the king and each other at the same time?"

"Perhaps we love each other because we both love the king," she suggested. "That's the only sense I can make of it."

He nodded. "Things may change now."

"How so?"

"We don't know what's happened to Odin or why," he explained. "You'll be with him at the House of the Healers. And I'll be here, finding out who tried to kill him … and may have succeeded for all we know."

"Don't say that!" Frigga gasped. "We'd better go to him."

She released him, then handed him the bag she had packed. She fixed her face, smoothed out her dress again, and sailed out the door with the general right behind her. Leaving things unresolved between them, she and Vidar walked together to the House of the Healers, which was not too far from the palace. Though the silence between them grew as they crossed the palace bridge and took the right fork toward the villages, Vidar's presence was more than enough.

As they drew near the serene alabaster building, the scent of the lavender plants lining the gravel path to the carved oaken doors calmed Frigga's mind, which prepared her to face whatever news awaited her inside. Vidar rapped his knuckles against the solid wood. A dark-haired woman in a crisp white gown answered and ushered them inside to where Eir, the head of the healer order, awaited them. As the queen and the general approached the youthful-looking healer, Frigga felt a stab of anxiety at the gravity in the woman's light brown eyes, a color that had never quite seemed to match her warm, honey-toned skin or sleek black hair. Though her features made her appear to be a slip of a girl just entering womanhood, those eyes of hers swirled with wisdom and depth that revealed her true age and reminded everyone of the stern competence with which she managed the House.

"The king has sustained an injury to his brain," Eir explained as she beckoned for them to follow her down the quiet, ivy-laden hallway. "His body has shut down so it may heal itself."

"Will it heal itself?" Frigga asked fearfully.

"It's entirely possible, my queen," Eir answered soothingly. "But much depends on him."

"Were there any signs of blunt trauma to his head?" General Vidar asked.

"No, the injury came from within," she stated.

"How do you know?" Vidar pressed.

"We've run several tests, including imaging scans of his brain," Eir expounded. "In layman's terms, he's had a stroke—the same thing that killed his father. Either Odin is much stronger than Borr or his injury was not as severe as it first appeared. Unfortunately, once a person has had a stroke, more can follow."

"What could possibly have caused him to have a stroke?" Frigga exclaimed. "He's as healthy as a horse."

"We haven't found a physical explanation," the healer admitted.

"Perhaps it was foul play?" Vidar asked.

"I don't see how that could be possible," she answered firmly. "No Asgardian has the power to rupture vessels in someone's brain, especially the king's. For now, we've taken over as many bodily functions as possible until he wakes on his own."

"When do you think he will wake?" the general asked.

"It's hard to say with this kind of thing. It could be hours. It could be years," Eir stated.

"Years!" Frigga almost shouted.

"Yes, my queen," Eir affirmed. "These things are quite unpredictable. But he might be able to hear you, even in this state. Perhaps you should speak to him. With so much to live for, he may yet recover."

"May I see him now?" Frigga asked.

"Of course," Eir agreed with a gracious nod. "He may look strange to you. We've hooked him up to several machines."

"I'm sure it's nothing I haven't seen," Frigga said bravely. "General, would you please accompany me?"

Vidar followed her into the room, where the gentle hum of Asgardian technology mingled with the soothing tones of silvery windchimes gently moving in a light breeze. From her past visits to recovering soldiers, Frigga knew the decor had been designed for relaxation, from the sheer white curtains to the periwinkle blue walls. She breathed deeply of the scent of lavender floating in through the high, open window, allowing it to calm her again as she gazed at the still form of her husband against the soft white pillows. He did indeed look strange, though she recognized the equipment. A double-pronged tube connected to his nostrils enhanced his breathing with fresh shots of oxygen every few seconds. A nutrient feed inserted in the largest vein of his right arm nourished and hydrated his body since he could not eat. There were electrical muscle stimulants on his arms and legs to prevent atrophy and pressure ulcers. One silver disc at his heart hummed as it monitored his heartbeat while a second one attached to his head monitored his brain activity.

"Would you like a chair, Your Majesty?" asked the slender young man who attended the king. "I was just about to check his pupils for light response."

"Why is that necessary?" Vidar asked.

"When we tested his eyes to see where the injury might be … in order to properly scan his brain, of course … we noticed his right eye did not respond as expected," Eir answered. "So we've been monitoring it."

"What does that mean?" Frigga asked fearfully.

"We cannot be certain yet, but the brain injury could have rendered him blind in that eye," Eir explained. When Frigga pressed her fingers to her forehead in distress, the healer hastened to add, "The left eye is fine though. He won't lose his sight entirely."

"Thank you, Eir," Frigga sighed. Then she addressed the orderly after the head healer left the room. "Do what you must. Then please leave me alone with him."

"I'll fetch you a chair," Vidar offered.

"Bring one for yourself as well, General," she instructed, projecting her words for Odin's benefit. "I'm certain he'll want to hear your voice."

"As you wish, my queen," he responded before ducking out to obey.

Frigga turned away as the orderly conducted his test. "Well?" she asked when he finished.

"No change, my queen," he said sadly. "I'll leave you now."

Frigga stepped close to the bed and grasped one of Odin's limp hands. "Odin, it's me, Frigga. If you can hear me, rest as long as you need, but please return to us. Your people need you." When no response of any kind came from him, she whispered in his ear, "I need you."

Feeling foolish, she fell silent. Vidar soon returned with both chairs. He placed one where she stood. She lowered herself into it carefully so she did not have to release her hold on the king's hand. Then the general set the other chair down on the opposite side of the king and grasped his other hand.

"Odin, Vidar is here," Frigga told her unconscious husband as she beckoned for the general to speak.

"My king, we have traveled many roads together," Vidar said, his voice breaking slightly. "Don't travel a road I cannot follow."

Then he too fell silent. The two of them sat like that in silence for over an hour, watching the slack and unresponsive face of the king. The subtle creaks from shifting their weight on the chairs were the only sounds to interrupt the hum of the machines. Frigga felt her eyelids growing heavy. She leaned forward more and more until she laid her head onto Odin's chest and closed her eyes.

The same orderly entered the room, waking her from a dreamless sleep. She sat up, bleary-eyed and feeling as though she had only dozed off for several seconds.

"You're back?" she asked the young man.

"Forgive me, my queen. We check vitals every four hours during the day," he informed her.

"Has it been that long?" she gasped.

"Yes, my queen," Vidar interjected. "You've been asleep for quite a while."

"Oh, how embarrassing," she muttered.

"It may have proved helpful," the orderly suggested as he surveyed the equipment. "His brain activity has improved as if he has been soothed. But I have a few other tests to run. Would the two of you care to step out for some refreshment?"

"I'm not leaving him," Frigga declared.

"You need to eat, my queen," Vidar protested.

"Then you go, and bring it here," she said curtly.

Vidar stood and bowed, releasing the king's hand. "I'll return shortly, my queen."

Frigga stepped back to allow the orderly to conduct his tests, not even bothering to absorb what he was doing. Vidar soon returned with a plate filled with bread and fruit. Frigga picked at the food at the general's insistence. When the orderly checked Odin's pupils again, Frigga watched this time, shuddering at how empty his eyes looked.

"I brought a change of clothes for him," Frigga informed the man, wanting to say something helpful.

"He won't need them until we release him," the orderly stated matter-of-factly. He gestured to the soft cotton shirt Odin wore, which had been left unbuttoned to expose his chest. "We use those so we can easily access the equipment but keep our charges comfortable. I'll close it up when I'm finished."

Frigga nodded. "What if he soils himself?"

"We've taken the proper precautions to avoid that," the orderly answered with a smile.

"I don't see any waste filters," Frigga pointed out, glancing again to see if she had missed any of the usual tubing or bags for that sort of thing.

"We used a less intrusive alternative for now," the orderly informed her. "The nutrients in his feed are very pure. His system won't have any solid waste for a while. Hopefully, he'll wake up before then. If not, we'll discuss long-term solutions with you."

She grimaced, too exhausted to inquire further and unable to bear the thought of seeing Odin like this for weeks, months, or even years. Panic coursed through her body. Her chest tightened, and she struggled to breathe.

"My queen, what's wrong?" Vidar asked in alarm, rushing to her side.

The orderly also rushed to the queen. She clutched at both men as her vision went dim. She heard someone barking orders above the sound of her gasping for breath. Then everything went black.

When she came to herself, she opened her eyes lazily, then sat straight up in a soft white bed. Someone sat in a chair by the door with his arms crossed and his head tipped back against the blue wall, sound asleep. At first, she thought the man was Odin. But remembering what had happened and looking closer, she realized it was Vidar. She threw off the downy white quilt and got out of the bed. When the floor creaked loudly, Vidar woke with a start and grabbed for his sword.

She plopped back down onto the mattress. "Please don't run me through, General."

He rubbed his eyes. "You're awake."

"So are you," she chuckled.

"I am now," he laughed. "I forgot where I was for a moment. How are you feeling?"

"Fine," she answered. "I must have fainted."

"You gave us quite a scare," he told her. "The healers are concerned your distress over the king's condition might hinder his care."

She scrambled out of bed again and headed straight for

the door. "I'm about to give them a tongue lashing they won't soon forget!"

Vidar stopped her. "Frigga, this won't help Odin."

"You heard the orderly!" she argued, trying to pull away from his grasp. "My presence helped him today."

"Yesterday," he corrected, gesturing to the star-studded sky visible from the window. "It's long after midnight."

"Oh no," she gasped. "Was I comatose?"

"No," he laughed. "You were just that tired. We can talk to Eir in the morning about letting you stay with Odin, but I'm under strict instructions to ensure that you eat and sleep."

"I've been asleep for hours," she protested.

"And now you shall eat," he said, leading her to another chair by a small table. "They left some nuts and fruit here for you. And they'll bring you breakfast in a few hours. If you eat this now, then sleep a little longer, I'm certain they'll give you another chance."

She obediently popped a handful of nuts into her mouth. She chewed thoughtfully and swallowed, then asked, "Have you been with me the whole time?"

"No," he admitted as he sat back down. "I went back to the palace to call off the investigation and ensure Bragi had everything under control, which, of course, he did. Then I checked on the princes. They're worried about you and their father but are otherwise fine."

"Thank you, Vidar," she murmured. Then she grabbed a few grapes. "Which room am I in?"

"Right next door to Odin. I've been in to see him a few times. Nothing has changed."

"They really won't let me in there until morning?" she whined.

He chuckled. "No, and neither will I."

She finished all the food they had left for her, then poured a glass of cold water from a white porcelain pitcher. She smirked at him. "I could persuade you, General."

"You could," he responded smartly as he linked his fingers behind his head and stretched out his long legs. "But I think I'd rather go back to sleep."

"Fine," she growled, climbing back into the bed. "I'll comply."

"Good girl," he murmured sleepily. "In case you're tempted to sneak by me, I always sleep with one eye open."

She laughed to herself, not bothering to point out she had just seen him asleep with both eyes shut. She snuggled into the pillows, unsure whether she wished more for Odin or Vidar to occupy the small space beside her. She faced the general, who had leaned his head against the wall again. She watched him until her eyes drifted shut. When she opened them again, sunlight streamed into the room. She saw the extra dress she had packed for herself laid out over the chair he had occupied but no general. She changed in the privacy of the small bathroom, then considered leaving the room to find someone to take her to the king.

But just as she moved to do so, an unfamiliar voice spoke from the open doorway. "Good morning, Your Majesty. How do you fare?"

An orderly bustled in, carrying a tray laden with honey cakes covered in strawberries and whipped cream. A vivid red rose stood proudly erect in a creamy white vase. She smiled when she saw it, wondering who had arranged for the extra touch of beauty.

"Well enough, thank you," she answered as she sat on the edge of the bed again. "Where is the general?"

"He's with the king," he responded happily as he approached. "He requested we send you the rose with your breakfast."

"The general did?" she gasped, surprised he would be so bold as to arrange even the smallest gift for her.

"No, of course not," the orderly chuckled as he set the tray down. "The king did."

"He's awake?" she cried, almost upsetting the tray in her haste to get out of bed. Though relieved the man seemed oblivious to her inquiry about the general, she felt she must get to her husband's side at that exact moment. "Why was I not informed?"

"A-apologies, Your Majesty," the orderly stammered. "I thought one of my superiors had already told you."

"And they likely thought someone else had," she muttered indignantly.

The general appeared at the door and addressed the orderly. "Were you not given instructions?"

"To deliver the rose with her breakfast?" the man replied with a confused look on his face.

"The other part," Vidar said in a hushed tone.

"No one told me anything else, General," the orderly explained. "I apologize if I have overstepped and said something I should not have."

General Vidar waved his hand to ease the man's obvious consternation. "No matter, we'll adjust," he reassured him. Then Vidar looked at Frigga and smiled. "Wait right here, my queen."

Something in his voice told her not to argue. She sat back down and started to eat, wondering if she would have to fight for her right to return to the king's recovery room.

A soft rustle sounded at the door. Frigga looked up to see Vidar firmly supporting the king as he stood in the doorway, sporting an eye patch that blended with his skin.

"Odin!" she cried as she rushed to him.

"Don't," Odin muttered thickly, trying to raise his hand to signal for her to stop.

Frigga sprang back, unsure of what to do or how to act. The right side of his mouth sagged slightly, and he seemed to be struggling to speak.

"He's still quite weak, my queen," Vidar explained. "But he wanted to surprise you." Then he addressed the king. "You've seen her. Now back to your room."

"Please let me come," Frigga begged with tears in her eyes.

Vidar nodded. Frigga approached slowly this time and took Odin's other arm to help him. She leaned her head on his shoulder as they slowly walked to the room next door, silently rejoicing over his improvement. Odin sighed as the two of them helped him ease back onto the bed. The orderly waiting in the room began to hook all of the equipment back up to the king.

"Is that necessary?" Frigga asked. "He's awake!"

"We need to monitor him in case he suffers another stroke," he said apologetically.

Odin muttered, "Wasn't … a …"

Vidar bent his head down to decipher the king's attempt to speak. Then he addressed the orderly. "The king says it was not a stroke."

The orderly glanced at the king. "We still have to monitor you, Your Majesty. But I will inform Eir. She will talk with you when you are able. For now, you must rest."

Odin moved his head forward slightly, which Frigga interpreted as a nod to acknowledge the man's words. The king shakily held one hand out to her. She sat beside him and grasped his hand firmly, holding it against her cheek.

"My king, was there foul play?" Vidar asked him.

Odin turned his head to the left, then slightly to the right.

"I assume that was a no?" Vidar prompted.

Odin dipped his head again in an attempt at a nod.

"Thank you, my king," Vidar responded. "We will speak more as you regain your strength. I'll give you two some privacy." He pointed to a spot just outside the door. "I'll be right there if you need me."

"Thank you, General," Frigga said graciously. When Vidar nodded and stepped out, she turned back to her husband. "Odin, you shouldn't have overdone it just now for me."

"Had … to … see you," he forced out, squeezing her hand.

"Shh, don't strain yourself," she murmured.

She leaned forward and kissed his forehead. He smiled weakly, then closed his left eye. Frigga looked fearfully at the orderly, who had just finished his tasks.

"He's only sleeping," the man assured her. "It will take him a few days before he's back to his old self again."

"Will he fully recover?"

"Eir will come in a little while," the orderly stated without answering. "She'll do a thorough check, then explain everything to you."

Frigga nodded, curbing her impatience. She watched Odin sleep until she felt she would fall asleep again herself, then quietly joined Vidar in the hallway.

"How is he?" Vidar asked.

"Sleeping," she answered. "When did he regain consciousness? How did I miss it?"

"Less than an hour before you woke up, my queen," he informed her. "I was with him when he came to himself. He spoke your name before he even opened his eyes."

As he said this, his hazel eyes filled with a deep pain. She knew he dare not speak candidly lest Odin overhear. Her own heart ached for Vidar even as it thrilled to hear her husband's first waking thought had been of her.

How long must I be caught in this agony I have brought upon myself? she thought. Aloud, she said, "Would you please send word for the princes to come see their father?"

"No!" Odin's voice sounded from inside the room.

Frigga whirled around to see him climbing out of the bed.

"Odin, you stubborn fool! Stay put!" she cried, rushing to his side as the general followed close on her heels. "You'll fall!"

"I may be a stubborn fool," he said quietly, "but I have no intention of falling."

"I'm certain you had no intention of collapsing in your office either," the general said wryly.

"I will admit I did not see that coming," Odin chuckled. "But I should have."

"I see you have your speech back," Frigga observed. "That must have been quite a nap."

"The king's brain is extraordinary," Eir interjected as she sailed into the room, her spotless white gown whispering faintly. "He is healing much faster than we expected."

"Hello there, Eir," the king said sheepishly. "I'll stay right here, shall I?"

"I think you'd better, Your Majesty," she declared. "I will strap you to that bed if I must. You may be the king, but you appointed me as the head of this order. And I will decide when you're ready to leave."

"Yes, my lady," he responded meekly.

"Now let me take a look at you," she said briskly.

She rolled up her sleeves and tucked a few stray black hairs away from her face and back into the tight bun at the back of her head. He obediently laid himself down and allowed her to peel back the patch to look into his damaged eye. The healer's movement blocked Frigga's view. Eir replaced the patch and peered into his other eye, then checked the equipment. Since she looked everything over in total silence, Frigga did not know what it all meant. Finally, Eir beckoned for the queen and the general to sit so she could address all three of them.

"My king, your orderly tells me you said you did not suffer a stroke, but all of my training says you did," she began. "Before I give you a chance to explain yourself, I will give you my official prognosis. Your brain function is excellent considering what you've been through. I believe you will make a full recovery within a matter of weeks, if not sooner."

"What about my eye?" Odin pressed.

"That remains to be seen. It may heal itself. It may not. We have some things we can do to help," she answered. "But they are risky. Again, it is possible it could resolve itself."

"What if it doesn't?" Odin asked quietly.

"What are the risks?" Frigga interjected almost at the same time.

Eir looked at the queen, then back at the king. "We could try growing new cells within the eye to replace the dead cells, but the growth healers are only just beginning to experiment with such methods. If the growth process is not carefully controlled, his eye could explode and kill him in seconds."

"We are not doing that," the king growled.

"Are there any other options?" Frigga prodded.

"Surgery," Eir stated. "But it is a risky, difficult process that might not even work."

"Why don't we wait a few days, then try the surgery?" Odin suggested.

"I agree. But we should revisit our options if there is no progress beyond a day or two. The longer we wait, the higher the risk," she informed him.

Odin looked at Frigga with his good eye. "The queen and I will discuss it later."

"As you wish, Your Majesty," Eir murmured. "Now I will listen to your theory on what you think happened to you."

"It's not a theory, Eir," Odin stated firmly. "I know what happened because I did it to myself."

"I'm listening," prompted the healer.

"I'd had a rough afternoon with matters of state that required my attention. I had promised my evening to the queen … and …" He looked at Frigga again as he trailed off. He swallowed hard, then spoke again. "Because of certain circumstances …" He trailed off again, then addressed the queen. "Please don't be upset, Frigga, but Eir knows about my mind gift. Vidar, I am sorry I never told you about it. Please keep what you are about to hear to yourself."

Vidar merely nodded. But Frigga narrowed her eyes, silently wondering why the king had told the healer such a secret and when.

Odin turned his attention back to Eir. "I used my mind gift in a manner I knew better than to use because of what happened to my father. As I said, I did it to myself."

"That's rather cryptic, Your Majesty. But I know better than to pry. And a surge of exerted mind power could certainly simulate a stroke," Eir mused. "Is that what happened to King Borr?"

"Yes, he overused his gift, against the advice of your predecessor," Odin said stiffly. "But I don't care to discuss it any further. The memories are difficult for me."

"Of course, my king," Eir soothed with a smooth bow. "It is important that you rest and not stress yourself. We will speak more later."

Frigga stared with concern at Odin. Why had he decided to use his gift to its full power and risk his own safety?

The general glanced at her, then back at Odin. "My king, before the healer joined us, you objected to something either I or the queen had said."

"Oh yes," Odin acknowledged. "I do not wish to have visitors, especially the princes."

"Why not?" Frigga protested. "Your sons are quite worried about you."

"I'd rather no one else see me this way," Odin said quietly. "And I won't be here long enough to justify visitors."

Frigga nodded. "I really should check on them. Do you

mind if I leave you to rest this afternoon, husband? I'll return to have dinner with you."

"That's fine. Vidar, would you accompany the queen?" Odin requested.

Concerned Odin might be testing them, Frigga answered before Vidar could. "I can return to the palace by myself, Odin. Surely you prefer to keep the general with you."

"Absolutely not," Odin and Vidar said in unison.

Frigga looked from one to the other and burst out laughing. Odin laughed with her, which was a welcome relief from all of the stress and drama of the last twenty-four hours.

Vidar only cracked a slight smile, then offered, "Why don't I take her back to the palace now, then arrange for a regular guard detail to escort her back and forth?"

"Excellent suggestion," Odin said, nodding with approval.

Frigga drew near the king and kissed him on the forehead, then followed Vidar out of the room. As they walked together back to the palace, the general remained silent.

"Vidar, you seem on edge," Frigga observed.

"Apologies, my queen," Vidar murmured.

He offered no explanation but kept his hand on his sword and his eyes straight ahead as he moved with the military grace Frigga had come to admire. Remembering how he had not laughed with her and the king, she decided to press him.

"Are you angry with me?" she said quietly.

"No," he said flatly.

"Then what's wrong?"

He finally glanced at her as they walked. "The king will likely lose that eye. And I feel responsible."

She gasped. "How do you know that?"

"I just have a feeling."

"Well, it's just a feeling. And there's no way this is your fault."

"Yes it is," he insisted. "In a way. I know something you do not."

"And you cannot tell me?" she asked, feeling hurt and worried.

"I shouldn't," he murmured. Then he took a deep breath and rushed through his words. "Because of my gift, I understood something deeper from what the king didn't say to Eir. Somehow, I gathered he was trying to do something for you … something to right an old wrong."

"But how is that your fault?"

"Because if he hadn't thought he was losing you to me, he never would have risked it," he sighed.

"But he believed me when I told him there's nothing between us," she reminded him.

"Not fully."

"I think you're wrong, Vidar," she contradicted him.

"After he woke up, he tried to tell me he planned to make things right with you," Vidar informed her.

"Now why would he say that if he still suspects you?" she challenged.

"As a warning," Vidar stated. "To let me know he's fighting for you."

"But—"

"Stop arguing with me, Frigga," Vidar half-laughed, half-scolded. "I hope you're right. Perhaps I'm being paranoid. But Odin has long believed people should be free as long as it doesn't threaten the common good. That's why he's a better king than Borr was. I thought he would address any suspicions toward us head-on because that's always been his way. But now I think he might be giving you the freedom to choose between us."

"Why would he do that? Am I so easily cast aside?" Frigga muttered. Then she snorted bitterly when she brought to mind Athena and Laufey. "Of course I am. I'm simply fooling myself that Odin could change."

"I think he has changed," Vidar said thoughtfully. "Something is different about him."

She sighed deeply. "Well, if you're right, I suppose we'd better be as careful as possible."

Vidar looked at her sharply. "Are you saying you wish to continue our relationship? I assumed … after all that's happened …"

"That I would choose him?" Frigga finished for him. "Vidar, I respect you and your gift, but I still think you're wrong. Those wonderful ideas of freedom do not apply to the queen. If I were to leave him or if he were to cast me aside, Vanaheim would no longer honor the alliance my father signed right before King Borr died. And that would most assuredly threaten the common good. No, my dear general, I am not free even to choose. I am caught between two men, two loves, two lives. And I fear that is where I must stay. For to sway in either direction would cause unbearable pain, not only for me but for others as well."

Vidar stiffened as Frigga said this. No one could possibly hear them, especially since Frigga kept the sound muffled. But they were drawing near the palace, where more people bustled about. Absolute propriety was necessary.

"It seems to me the path you must take is clear," Vidar stated, his face placid and void of emotion. "Perhaps we will have another opportunity to speak of this."

Frigga's heart ached to hear him speak so formally to her, but they were out of time. "Vidar, promise me you won't make any decisions about us until we can speak again."

His eyes softened as he looked at her briefly. "I promise."

6

Frigga spent a good amount of time with her sons, updating them on their father's condition. To protect Odin's dignity and her sons' feelings, she did not tell them their father desired no visitors, only that he needed to rest so he could return to the palace as soon as possible. After Vidar arranged for a guard escort to attend to her however she wished, he took his leave without anything more than a respectful bow. She dared not ask when she would see him again. But as she ate dinner with Odin in his recovery room, she truly missed the general. And, it seemed, so did the king.

"Where is Vidar, Frigga?" he asked quietly.

"I don't know, my king," she answered lightly. "I'm certain he'll be by to visit you soon."

"He is a loyal subject and friend. I feel quite ashamed of myself for ever believing he had designs on my queen," Odin sighed.

Frigga smiled to herself in triumph. *Vidar was wrong!* she thought with glee. Aloud, she lightly quipped, "We should conspire with Baldur to make the poor man fall in love with one of those noblewomen who adore him. He might be single for the rest of his life if someone doesn't intervene."

"Frigga! How could you suggest such a thing!" Odin exclaimed, his face twisting into a horrified expression.

"I was only joking!" Frigga giggled. "I would never do something like that, but it's funny to think about."

"Not to me, it isn't," Odin said sternly. Then he sighed. "Please close the door."

She looked at him in surprise. "Why, Odin, whatever is the matter?"

"I have something to tell you," he replied grimly. "Something I should have told you long ago."

A pronounced sense of dread rocked Frigga, making her feel queasy. She got up and closed the door, then returned to her chair by Odin's bed.

"The look on your face grieves me, my queen," Odin muttered.

"I'm expecting you to tell me about yet another woman," Frigga admitted stiffly. "Eir, perhaps? Is that why she knows of your mind gift?"

"I deserve that," Odin muttered. "But no, I have no interest in Eir, nor she in me. When I appointed her as head of this order, I told her about my gift in case something like this ever happened, but I did not tell her about my father at the time. She either did not recognize this for what it was or put on an act because I swore her to secrecy."

"Always secrecy with you, Odin," Frigga sighed.

Odin stared at his hands. "You are not making this any easier, Frigga."

"I'm sorry, Odin. I'll hold my tongue," she said in a kinder tone. "What do you need to tell me?"

"It's about when we first met. Do you remember?"

"Yes," she said softly. "What about it?"

"What do you remember?"

She chuckled. "Are you fishing for compliments, Odin?"

"No, I need to know," he said seriously.

"I remember going to the throne room with my father and several other single noblewomen to meet the dignitaries from Asgard," she reminisced. "I was wearing a simple yellow dress with a red sash."

"I love it when you wear red," Odin interjected.

She smiled even as she shook her head at him for the interruption, then continued, "All the talk of an alliance through marriage made me nervous, but my father assured me that even if one of the noblemen fancied me, it would be my choice. The first man I saw that night was King Borr. He frightened me."

Odin chuckled. "A common response. One he took pride in. But he was no threat to you."

"I know," Frigga acknowledged. "I had heard the story of your mother's death, but everyone knew he wasn't looking for another bride."

Odin looked down at his hands at the mention of his mother, of whom he rarely spoke. He had been a boy when she had died in a tragic accident that had also taken the lives of his younger twin brothers, Vili and Vé. So great was Borr's grief over the loss of Bestla and the toddlers, he had never taken another queen.

Feeling a surge of compassion for her husband, Frigga continued, "The noblemen with him didn't interest me in the slightest. Then I saw you."

"And?" Odin prompted, his face brightening somewhat.

"I thought you were quite handsome," she mused. "I didn't even know you were the crown prince at first. Lady Freya whispered that news to me just before they started the introductions. Of course, she was instantly smitten with you, but she couldn't get your attention at all."

"Of course not. I had already spotted you," Odin stated.

Frigga blushed. "She was terribly unhappy at the banquet that night. But I'm ashamed to say I did not care. You were so incredibly sweet and attentive to me … as if you only had eyes for me."

"I did only have eyes for you," Odin affirmed.

She smiled, feeling her heart soften toward him again. But she took a deep breath and continued, "After I got the letter you sent through my brother the next morning, I told my father I would consider your suit and no one else's. But he said nothing about it during the second assembly. He only asked for time to consider all the terms of the alliance. I was not permitted to speak, which was why I sent you my response through my brother."

"I was beyond pleased when Gylfi brought me that letter," Odin said, his tone intimate and filled with nostalgia. "I had heard more rumors about you and Freya's twin brother than I care to recount."

Frigga laughed. "Ah yes, Frey! I ended my relationship with him weeks before I met you. I did wonder at various points if I had made a mistake, especially when my father kept trying to persuade me to reconsider."

Odin snorted derisively. "He would have been a terrible fit for you."

"And that's your completely unbiased opinion?" she teased.

"Naturally," he returned with a becoming grin.

"Well, my father's behavior made no sense to me. He had seemed so in favor of it all at the banquet, but something changed," Frigga mused. "Thankfully, Gylfi was in favor of a match between us and saw the advantage of an alliance, which is why he hid our secret portal and our courtship from my father."

"Things seemed so much easier back then," Odin sighed. "Every moment apart was torture."

"And every moment together was pure joy," Frigga added softly. "So much has changed."

Odin shifted uncomfortably. "Do you remember what happened in the early morning after the banquet? Before your brother gave you my first letter?"

"There was nothing before that," she said, furrowing her brows. "I was just waking up when he knocked on my door to deliver it."

Odin swore under his breath, then muttered in frustration, "After all that, it didn't work."

"Such language, Odin!" Frigga scolded. "What didn't work?"

"I'll tell you in a moment," he said hurriedly. "What changed your father's mind about the alliance?"

"I've told you that part," she said warily. "Why do you want to hear it again?"

"Indulge me, please, Frigga?" the king pleaded, changing his position slightly.

She sighed, wondering where all of this was going, then rushed through her account since she had told him about it years ago. "Freya told me she asked her father to take her to

Asgard so she could see you again. Since I considered her a good friend, I told her about our secret courtship, trying to spare her a broken heart. She went straight to her father, who went straight to mine. And, of course, he flew into a rage because we went behind his back." She paused as she remembered her father's fury and the reason behind it. "One thing I never told you … he was convinced you dishonored me."

"But I didn't! I respected you too much," Odin protested indignantly.

"I tried to tell him that. But he didn't believe me and made me undergo a physical exam to prove I was still untouched."

"It's a good thing I didn't know about that," Odin seethed. "Why did he destroy the portal and send word to Asgard that there would be no alliance if he knew you were untouched?"

"Pride, pure and simple. You know how kings are, Odin."

"Ouch," he muttered.

Frigga smiled apologetically at him but did not retract her words. Instead, she continued with what Odin already knew. "When King Borr invited my father to Asgard to reconsider, I begged him to go. He sent word of the signing of the alliance at the same time as the news of King Borr's death. After your father's funeral, my father brought me your marriage proposal. He told me you were an honorable man and that he had made a mistake. Then I came to Asgard for our wedding. End of story."

"Have you ever wondered why my father's death was so close to Sigurd's decision to sign the alliance?" Odin asked quietly.

"Should I have?" Frigga asked warily, though she could guess his answer.

"My father forcibly changed your father's mind, then erased the memory. He believed what my father put into his head," Odin answered reluctantly. "He did it carefully so as not to damage Sigurd's brain. But he didn't look to his own, and the strain killed him, though not until a few days later. I have never forgiven myself."

Frigga stiffened at this revelation. "But why? Your father made his own choices."

"When Sigurd arrived on Asgard, he said he would only agree to an alliance if one of our noblemen married you or a Vanir noblewoman. He didn't want you to leave Vanaheim to marry me," Odin explained. "But my father knew I had my heart set on you and only you. He did what he did more for me than for Asgard. And I've never been able to fully tell you, though I've hinted at it several times."

"So you blamed yourself … and me?" she tentatively asked.

"No, never you," Odin objected.

"I don't know, Odin. Maybe you did subconsciously. Perhaps that's why you succumbed so easily to Athena," she suggested cautiously, looking at her hands rather than his face.

"I did not succumb to her easily! She'd been trying to seduce me for years," Odin corrected. "She would always tell me my son would sit on her father's throne someday."

"Which is why we've never told Baldur who he really is," she interjected. "I know that. I simply never understood how you could claim to love me like you did back then and still—"

"I thought you didn't want to know how it happened," Odin interrupted.

"I don't," Frigga confirmed. "But I wouldn't mind knowing why. Perhaps you can explain without too many details?"

"She caught me crying alone in the root cellar after the funeral," he answered. "No one had seen me cry since I was a boy."

"I've never even seen you cry," Frigga reminded him.

He ignored her comment and continued, "I had taken too much ale in my grief, though I wasn't drunk. I asked her to leave me alone and not speak of finding me there, but she wouldn't leave. She was strangely comforting—"

"That's no excuse," she whispered fiercely, not wanting to hear another word as a new surge of hurt pulsed through her.

He sighed. "I'm not making excuses. I'm simply explaining, as you asked."

"Fine, you've explained it," she snapped. Then she softened her tone. "But I did forgive you for it, so let's not speak of it anymore."

"Frigga, I must speak," he insisted, the urgency and vulnerability in his tone surprising her. "I thought Athena was beautiful, but I never respected her or trusted her. She was just another woman who threw herself at me because of my power and position. Freya was no different, which is why I refused to see her when she sought an audience with me."

"You're wrong about that," Frigga informed him. "Freya wasn't that shallow. And you might have been wrong about Athena too, though I didn't know her well at all. I think she loved you at first, then hated you for not loving her back. Even then, she could have utterly destroyed you, but she chose to leave us alone."

"You always have seen the best in everyone," Odin pointed out. "But it was respect for you and how you handled everything that made her so reasonable in the end, not any remaining fondness for me. Until that day when she confronted us and told us of Zeus's threat, she couldn't understand why I chose you over her."

"Why did you choose me over her?" Frigga continued to stare at her hands, afraid to look at him lest he see the turmoil in her soul.

"I knew there was something different about you from the moment I laid eyes on you," Odin answered. "I don't know how I knew. I just … did. When you looked at me with those calming blue eyes of yours, you saw *me*."

"I always have," she murmured. "I never cared about power or position. I certainly never thought I'd be a queen, nor did I want to be. I fought with myself for hours the night we met. I couldn't sleep until I had made my decision."

"What did you just say?" Odin spoke strangely, his tone low and heavy.

"Haven't I told you this?" Frigga asked in confusion as she looked up at him briefly.

"No, never," Odin said, staring at her with an unusual light in his good eye.

"I almost decided to go back to Frey like my father wanted. I liked him well enough, but you were something else altogether," she told him shyly, reaching for his hand. "I finally had to face the truth—I had already fallen for you."

"The night of the banquet?" he asked anxiously. "It wasn't my letter the next morning?"

"No, Odin," Frigga answered with slight irritation. She tried to pull her hand away, but he held it fast. "What exactly happened that morning that you think I should remember?"

"My father was the only person who knew this," Odin began, his voice slightly unsteady. "Frigga, that morning before you woke up, before I sent your brother with my first letter to you, I …" He took a deep breath and shut his eye, his confession escaping in a flurry of words. "I broke into your room and entered your mind to make you think you were in love with me."

"You did what?" she exclaimed, her voice reaching a pitch she rarely used. She yanked her hand from his grasp. "How … how could you?"

"I didn't think you'd love me any other way." Odin's voice broke and though he did not weep, Frigga saw the pain and regret on his face.

"Well, Odin Borrson, it just so happens you were wrong about that too!" she informed him indignantly.

"So it would seem from what you just told me," Odin replied. "If I had known you'd already decided, I never would have done it."

"It was wrong of you to do it, no matter your reasons!" she cried. "You … you violated me!"

"No!" Odin exclaimed forcefully. "Don't use that word. I manipulated you, but I've never violated you. Never! And I swore I would never enter your mind again. And I never have, not even when I tried to undo it. I've paid the price for my foolishness. All these years, I thought the only reason you loved me at all was because I made you believe you did."

"Odin, listen very carefully to me," Frigga said through clenched teeth. "I am beyond angry with you. And devastated that you would do something like that, even if it was so long ago. But you need to know something, to have your conscience eased somewhat. I have kept my mind locked at night since my mother taught me how as a very small child. I keep a decoy in my frontal lobe that automatically dumps any data accumulated through the night except for my strongest dreams."

"Do you mean to tell me I failed?" Odin gasped.

"Yes, Odin the Great, you failed miserably," she confirmed. She started to laugh. "And you almost fried your own brain trying to undo something that was never done in the first place. You honestly thought it would work remotely?"

Odin stared at her. "Why is that funny? I thought a little dark magic would do it."

She sobered instantly. "You're right. That's not funny at all. You know how I feel about the dark arts. That must have been the tap I felt on my forehead that night. Do you realize you could have hurt me instead of yourself?"

"No, I accounted for that just as my father did," Odin defended himself. He stared at his hands, clenching his jaw and furrowing his brow. "Now I don't even know if the spell would have worked. What a waste of energy."

"Foolish as it was, it does mean something to me that you tried to undo what you'd thought you'd done," Frigga admitted. "But Odin, how can I trust you now? You've lied to me over and over. You've been cruel and distant. Since we wed, you've manipulated and used me … and at least two other women."

"No more than that," he growled.

"Regardless, this is not the man I saw within the future king of Asgard, the man I chose to spend my life with … of my own volition, I might add! I saw honor and strength and kindness in you once," Frigga said sadly. "Where has that Odin gone?"

Odin hung his head in shame. "I wish I knew."

The sight wounded Frigga deeply. Not knowing how to respond, she threw herself across his lap, weeping as he sat there in the bed. He tentatively stroked her hair until she quieted herself.

She raised her head and looked at him through bleary, tear-stained eyes. "I don't know how much more I can take, Odin. I miss the man I *chose* to love. Please promise me you can find your way back somehow."

"I promise to try," he murmured. "Will … will you give me another chance? Will you forgive me for how I've treated you?"

She nodded, then grabbed his hand and pressed it against her cheek. "Be patient with me. I need time to come to terms with everything."

"I respect that," he offered. "I'm determined to earn your trust. Somehow."

"I think I should stay at the palace tonight," she said quietly. "I'll return in the morning."

When he nodded, she rose to her feet and opened the door. She took one last look at him before she called her escort to take her back to her room in the palace. She regretted her decision as soon as she took in the familiar surroundings. Everything reminded her of Odin. Unable to bear the thought of spending the entire night there alone, she made herself invisible and crept to Laufey's old room. At least she had pleasant memories there with Vidar.

She really should not have expected it to be empty, but she still felt a thrill mingled with a touch of dismay when she found the general there.

"Frigga!" he exclaimed, seeming just as surprised as she was. "What are you doing here?"

She could not stop the fresh flow of tears at the joy and kindness in his voice. "I'm s-sorry," she sobbed. "I cannot …"

Unable to finish her sentence, she collapsed onto Laufey's old bed. Vidar rushed to her side and gathered her into his arms.

"Is it the king? What's wrong?" he murmured.

She shook her head and wordlessly held her hand up to stop any more questions. He understood and held her silently until she felt ready to speak.

"I cannot sleep in the king's room," she finally choked out. "Too many memories."

"Why didn't you stay at the House of the Healers?" he asked gently. "I thought that's where you'd be."

"I cannot sleep there either," she sighed shakily, hiccupping slightly from her crying fit. "Odin told me something tonight …"

"Is it what I thought? Does he suspect?" Vidar guessed when she trailed off.

"No, I was right," she told him. "He said he's ashamed he ever thought you could have designs on me. But it brings me no pleasure to be right."

As she recounted her entire conversation with Odin, Vidar's face turned ashen, then red with anger.

"That is not the Odin I know! Does he have no honor?" he muttered.

Frigga suddenly felt a need to defend her husband. "But he asked me to forgive him. He didn't have to tell me. I never would have known. And he almost killed himself trying to make it right."

"How much more will you forgive, Frigga?" Vidar asked in frustration. "How much more will you tolerate?"

She looked down in consternation, having no answer.

"Forgive me, my queen," he murmured. He took both her hands and kissed them. "It grieves me deeply to see your suffering. I do not wish to cause you more pain."

"No. You comfort me, my dear general," Frigga soothed him.

He smiled and reached out to brush one knuckle against her cheek. "You cannot sleep here. If you oversleep and someone looks for you, you'll throw the entire palace into an uproar."

"Will you stay with me?" she pleaded. "You never oversleep."

"I might if you were lying next to me," he murmured. "I don't think I'd ever want to rise for fear it was only a dream."

Frigga blushed, pleased by his words. Her heart was so wounded and raw, she did not sense the danger to herself or to him. She snuggled into his arms, allowing his comforting presence to wash over her. He kissed the top of her head and held her tightly.

"What do we do now?" he asked her quietly.

Several wicked thoughts ran through her head. But just before she was about to suggest one of them, she remembered what Odin had said about Athena comforting him in his grief. She suddenly understood why he had given in to her advances, and it frightened her, especially when she realized how precarious her own position had grown. Odin had not loved Athena but merely used her for satisfaction and comfort. She found herself in a similar situation, but she had much more than physical attraction drawing her to Vidar. He had connected with her soul in a way Odin had quite neglected. And she wanted to experience everything Vidar could offer her. The impulse was stronger than it had ever been before, and her usual methods of resisting failed her. But the fear that she was only using the general pricked at the back of her mind. And she worried that Vidar, who had become as dear to her as her sons, might understand her better than she understood herself. But perhaps not. He had been wrong about Odin.

"Frigga?" he whispered, interrupting her thoughts.

"Yes?" she murmured as she pressed closer to him, afraid he would tell her to return to the room she shared with the king.

"Why don't you stay with me tonight?" he suggested. "In my room. You can take the bed, and I'll sleep on the settee. I tend to fall asleep there most of the time anyway. Then I'll be certain to wake up on time, and I'll know you're safe and comfortable."

"But how will I get out in the morning?" she asked, looking up at him through still-wet lashes.

"You can go invisible and follow me out in the morning," he offered. "We just need to allow enough time so I'm not late for my post."

"You're more worried about that than being caught with the queen in your bedroom?" she teased.

When he chuckled shyly and a blush stole across his chiseled cheekbones, emotion overwhelmed her. Feeling as though she must express her heart somehow, she placed two of her fingers against her lips and simultaneously pressed them against his in a mock kiss. She felt his body tense and sensed the action had almost proved his undoing. He reined himself in with extraordinary effort and hugged her instead of kissing her.

"Don't do that again if you expect me to behave myself," he groaned.

"Oh, fine," she pouted playfully. "I'm just so grateful for your offer … but how will I get inside your room? I would have to knock to let you know I'm there. I could send the sound inside the room so only you hear it, but I would have to time an illusion perfectly with your coming to the door to hide its opening and closing. I don't know if I have the mental strength left to do it."

"There's no need for you to strain yourself, my queen. I'll use the device now to go back to my room. Then I'll go out to the banquet hall balcony for a while to give you time to catch up," Vidar offered. "Meet me there, invisible, and touch me somehow so I know you're there. Then you can follow me to my room. No one will suspect a thing."

"I like this plan," she cooed. "Perhaps we'll have a new meeting place."

His eyes widened. "This is a one-time thing, Frigga," he protested. "We cannot risk something like this regularly, especially when the king returns to the palace."

"You don't tire of meeting here?"

"I never tire of spending time with the queen," he whispered.

He kissed her forehead, then drew out the device and disappeared. For a moment, Frigga scolded herself for what she was doing. Was it really any better than what Odin had done twice now? She and the general had not allowed themselves to go past a certain boundary, but would Odin see it that way? When she remembered how he had tried to manipulate her, regardless of whether or not he had succeeded, her anger grew hot, and she made her decision.

I don't care what Odin thinks, she told herself haughtily.

She turned herself invisible and silently made her way to the banquet hall balcony. She stood at a distance for a moment to admire Vidar from behind, then crept closer and placed her hand on his arm. He stretched nonchalantly, then walked briskly to his own door and opened it, which activated the lights. He bent down briefly to scrape something that was not there off of his boot. She slipped into the room, touching him as she passed so he would know. He followed and shut the door, then pushed a few controls to turn off his motion sensors as she surveyed her surroundings. The general's room seemed much like him—handsome but stark in its masculinity. The few pieces of sturdy furniture lacked the opulence of most of the palace furnishings, but they bespoke comfort, just like Vidar did.

She dropped her invisibility and turned to him. He stood there in the center of his room, staring at her as if he could not quite handle her presence among his treasured things. She stepped close to him and wrapped her arms around his waist, toying with thoughts she knew she should not have.

"Maybe this wasn't a good idea," he murmured as he stepped back slightly.

She saw that golden light in his eyes and guessed what he was thinking. "Are you asking me to leave?"

"No," he whispered.

She smirked at him but decided not to torture him any further. She ran her finger along the dark wood of his bed frame instead of down his chest like she wanted. "Tell me about your bedroom set, Vidar. These aren't palace furnishings."

"My father was a woodworker. He made that headboard and footboard for my mother as a wedding gift," he explained. "When I moved into the palace, Odin allowed me to replace the furniture he provided with these."

"How lovely," she gasped, taking a second look at the bed. She gestured to the armoire and the desk. "Did your father make those too?"

He nodded, then led her over to a corner of the room she had not yet noticed. "And you'll recognize this."

She smiled when she saw the two-headed wolf statue standing in the corner, then shyly asked. "Do you still have my note and the key to Laufey's room?"

"I do," he said softly. "I haven't ever needed the key, but I keep it in a box with your note and all of the letters I've written to you over the years."

"You wrote me letters?" she gasped. "May I see?"

He blanched. "I never thought I would ever say no to you, my queen. But I'm not ready to show you."

"Why not?" she prodded.

He blushed deeply. "If you love me at all, please don't push me. Having you here is hard enough for me. If I let you read those letters, in my room, with me standing here …" He closed his eyes and took a deep breath. "It's so much easier to justify this … whatever we have … if we keep to what we've already discussed."

"Very well," she sighed, knowing he was right. "You are such an honorable man, Vidar. I trust you completely."

He beamed with joy at those words. "You give me hope, Frigga."

"Hope for what?"

"I dare not say any more," he murmured. "Is there anything you require for the night, my queen?"

She desperately wanted to rush to him, but she restrained herself. "I think I'll be quite comfortable. Thank you, General."

She settled herself into his bed and lay there awake, listening to him shifting into place on the settee. "Vidar?" she finally spoke.

"Hmm?" he answered sleepily.

"Are you comfortable over there?"

"Yes, though I'd much rather be over there," he chuckled.

"I … I think I'd better go back to the royal chambers," she stammered.

She heard him sit up. "Have I offended you, my queen?"

"Oh no, of course not," she hurried to reassure him. "This just feels … wrong. I may have to accept not being able to sleep tonight."

He yawned. "How can I help?"

"I don't know," she sighed.

She heard the floor creak slightly as he approached and knelt by the side of the bed. She put out one hand, which he grasped tightly. She peered at him in the dark, fighting the urge to yank him into the bed with her. He changed into a sitting position, still holding her hand, and leaned his head against the wall. She felt her body relax and her eyelids grow heavy.

She woke with a start, subconsciously looking for Odin. Then she remembered where she was. Vidar had left his position by the wall sometime during the night and lay sleeping on the settee. When he heard her movements as she got out of the bed, he opened one eye, then sat straight up as if he too had forgotten she had spent the night in his room.

"Good morning, my queen," he said softly. "I'm glad you were able to sleep after all."

"Yes, thank you so much," she answered, rubbing her arms to warm herself. "I suppose I'd better get ready to have breakfast with the princes."

"Are you cold?" he asked curiously.

"Aren't you? It feels like winter is nipping at our heels," she replied with a little laugh.

"Strange," he commented. He walked over to the window and peeked out. "There's snow on the ground. But why? We're not even ten days into the harvest moon!"

Instantly, Frigga knew why. "Oh no!"

"What is it?" Vidar asked with alarm.

"It's Thor. It has to be," she cried. "Any type of unusual precipitation is almost always Thor. He's never made it snow before. What if something's wrong? I have to go to him!"

"Here!" Vidar quickly drew out his transport device and thrust it into her hands. "Go to your room, then walk—or run if you must—to Thor's door. Send a guard for me if you need me."

Too distressed to ponder his willingness to break his oath to his order for her son, she listened carefully as he showed her how to use the device, then followed his instructions to the letter. She felt a strong pull, then blinked twice when she found herself standing in her room. Not taking even another moment to relish the thrilling sensation of that type of travel, she rushed out of her room and down the hallway to Thor's room.

7

The towheaded young prince sat huddled in a frost-covered corner in his room, tears flowing down his face.

"Thor?" Frigga said softly as she approached. "Tell me what's wrong."

He turned his back to her, though not before she saw embarrassment all over his face. She knelt beside him and drew the boy into her motherly embrace, pressing his head against her chest. He sniffled as his body relaxed. He stayed there for a few minutes, then pulled away to wipe his nose on his sleeve. She did not chide him for his bad manners but simply waited patiently for him to speak.

"I had a terrible dream about Father," he finally said with a shudder. "At least, I hope it was a dream. Is he … has he …"

"Your father is recovering well, Thor," Frigga soothed him. "I had dinner with him last night."

"That was last night," he pointed out, trembling as he huddled closer to her. "He died early this morning. The guards told me … in my dream … I think."

"Most bad dreams are fears being released by the mind, Thor," Frigga reassured him. "They very rarely mean anything."

"What if it does mean something?" he asked fearfully.

"Would you like me to go check on him?" she asked.

"Would you?" he chirped hopefully. "May I go? I want to see him for myself."

"I'm sorry, Thor, but no visitors but the general and me," she replied.

"Why the general?" Thor whined.

"Don't you like the general?" Frigga asked in surprise. "He's your father's closest friend."

"I like him just fine, Mother," Thor grumped. "He's a great soldier and a good teacher. And I know there's no one more loyal to Father. Well … maybe one."

"And who is that?" Frigga asked with laughter in her voice.

"Me, of course," he spouted. "Don't laugh, Mother."

"You are very loyal to your father," she agreed, pulling him forward to kiss him tenderly on the forehead. "You're a wonderful son, Thor."

He grinned at her and wiped his eyes. "Don't tell Father I was crying."

She nodded, understanding how embarrassed he was. But remembering how Odin would not allow himself to truly grieve or show much emotion, she told Thor, "There's no shame in showing how much you love someone. I know you want to be tough, but you're allowed to feel too."

He looked at her with questions in his eyes as he cocked his head. "Then you can tell him I'm worried about him and want to see him."

"I think he'd like to know that," she responded. "I'll tell him."

"Thank you, Mother!" Thor exclaimed, throwing his arms around her in an uncharacteristic show of affection. "I'm sorry about the snow."

"You've never done that before," she chuckled.

"Then how did you know it was me?" he demanded.

"Who else could make it snow at the beginning of the harvest moon?" she teased. "And I'm sure there isn't snow anywhere else on Asgard. We'll need to work on your control a little more during our next lesson."

"Mother!" he complained.

She winked at him. "Please give Loki and Baldur my love at breakfast. I'll go straight to the House of the Healers, just for you."

"Will you have lunch with us?"

"I'll try," Frigga affirmed. "Now, give me another hug, and I will see you later."

He hugged her tightly, then abruptly let her go. She smiled fondly at her son, who looked so much like her. But no one could deny he was Odin through and through. The boy rose to his feet and gallantly offered his hand to help her rise as well. She dusted off her rather wrinkled dress, which Thor suddenly noticed.

"Mother, did you sleep in your clothes?" he asked, his eyes widening.

"Yes, and I rushed straight here when I realized you needed me," she admitted. She chuckled as she looked down at herself. "I suppose I'd better clean up before I see your father."

"I think you're pretty no matter what," Thor said shyly.

"Thank you, dear one," she said fondly as she tweaked his nose and tousled his reddish-blond hair, laughing when he swatted at her hand.

"I'm too old for that," he protested.

"No, never. You'll always be my dear one," she informed him.

"Would you like me to walk you to your room?" Thor offered, puffing out his chest to appear more manly.

"I'd like that," she agreed softly.

She took his arm, enjoying the time with him as he proudly escorted her back to the royal chambers. Even though he was shorter than she was, she knew he would likely tower over her someday, even if he never got as tall as Baldur.

Back in her room, she cleaned herself up and changed clothes, then summoned her guard escort to take her back to the House of the Healers. She had given no credence to Thor's dream, but when she found Odin's room empty and the bed made as if no one had been there, irrational fear crashed through her spirit. She rushed into the hallway to find someone to tell her where the king had been taken.

Seeing none of the healers, she sent one of her guards to find Eir while she paced worriedly in the hallway. What if Thor's dream had been real? What if Odin had died while she slept in the general's room? But why wouldn't they have notified her? What if they had tried but discovered she had not been in her own room?

As she took another turn in her pacing, wringing her hands as she did so, she heard footsteps and glanced in the direction of the sound.

"Odin!" she cried with relief when she saw him approaching with the orderly. Then she grew slightly angry. "What are you doing out here?"

"I've been released," he explained. "They took me to the therapy room to do some tests to check for lingering damage, then decided they have no reason to keep me here."

"But you've still got your eye covered! Where's Eir?" she demanded.

"Here, Your Majesty," Eir answered as she joined them, followed by the guard Frigga had sent. "Apologies! General Vidar told us you planned to take breakfast with the princes. We were not expecting you."

"That was the plan … until Thor made it snow at the palace," Frigga said.

"Thor made it snow?" Odin repeated with amusement.

"Yes. He wanted me to tell you he's worried about you and wants to see you."

"I was hoping to surprise you and the boys by showing up at the palace for breakfast," Odin lamented. "I guess the final tests took too long."

"I'm glad you didn't do that!" Frigga exclaimed. "I might have fainted again. Now, who's going to explain about your eye?"

"It's worsened," Eir said grimly. "I recommend we do the surgery today while we still have a chance to save it, but the king is stubborn."

"Why don't you want to do the surgery, Odin?" Frigga asked.

When Odin glanced at Eir and the guards, Frigga surmised he did not want to discuss anything in front of them.

"Did you miss breakfast?" Odin asked Frigga instead of answering her.

When she nodded, Eir spoke up quickly. "So did the king. I'll have the orderly bring two breakfast trays here immediately. Why don't the two of you discuss things while you wait?"

Odin offered Frigga his arm and walked with her back into the room he had occupied. "How did you sleep?"

"I had a hard time at first," she said truthfully. "But I finally did get some rest."

"I'm glad," he said softly. "I was worried about you."

Immediately struck with guilt, Frigga had no idea what to say. She masked her face and changed the subject. "Now that we're alone, will you tell me why you don't want the surgery?"

Odin grimaced. "I want to give it more time to heal itself."

"You cannot fool me that easily, Odin," she contested. "After everything, you still cannot tell me the truth."

He sighed deeply. "Fine, Frigga. If you want me to say it, I'm afraid."

"There's no shame in that," she reassured him.

"A king isn't supposed to be afraid," Odin argued stubbornly.

"Says who?" Frigga demanded. "It takes courage to even admit fear. Once you figure out what you're afraid of, you can deal with it."

"I'm afraid of losing my eye completely," he admitted. "As long as my eye is still in my head, I can hold onto hope that my sight could return."

"But Eir said it's getting worse, not better," Frigga pointed out.

"I know," he sighed. "I haven't told her this, but it's been hurting."

Frigga gazed at him with sadness and concern. "You know what you need to do, don't you?"

He nodded as one tear slid down his cheek. She kept this observation to herself, knowing how Odin felt about anyone seeing him cry. She sat with him in silence, but no more tears followed. When the orderly brought their breakfast, Odin told him to fetch Eir. Then he ate quickly, not saying a word.

When the healer arrived, Odin solemnly told her, "I'm ready."

"Odin, aren't you going to tell her?" Frigga prompted. "Or do I have to?"

He glanced at Frigga, frowning slightly. Then he blurted out, "My right eye has been hurting since I woke up this morning."

Eir groaned. "Oh, Your Majesty! Why didn't you tell someone?"

"What does that mean?" Odin demanded.

Frigga placed one hand over his to calm him.

Eir carefully answered, "It means it may be too late. But I think we should try it anyway. I'm fairly certain it's your only chance to regain sight in that eye."

"Fine," Odin grumped. "Let's get it over with."

General Vidar appeared in the doorway. Frigga had not seen him since leaving his room.

Odin smiled at his friend, instantly cheerful. "Vidar, I'm glad you're here. There's been a change of plans."

"Oh? I've just informed Lord Bragi you've been released," Vidar told him. "But no one else."

"Good," Odin said. "They're going to try to fix my eye. I'll be here for a while yet."

"Shall I inform Lord Bragi?" Vidar asked.

Before he could answer, Frigga interjected, "Odin, I really should let the princes know you're doing better. Especially

Thor. I can let Bragi know if you want Vidar to stay with you."

"Whatever the king wishes," Vidar said graciously. "Bragi had just finished the official statement to Asgard when I spoke with him. I brought it with me."

Odin reached out to take the paper Vidar held out to him and perused it. "Very good."

"May I read it?" Frigga asked.

Odin hesitated, then handed it to her. "I suppose you'll see it eventually."

Frigga read it over quickly, then narrowed her eyes at Odin. "You're calling it a stroke?"

"I knew you'd be unhappy about that," Odin sighed. "Frigga, what else can I do? I've told you, Eir, and Vidar the truth. And we all agree it would do more harm than good to explain it any other way to our people."

"Did you tell Eir and Vidar the reason you used your gift that way?" she asked quietly.

He glanced over at the healer and the general. "Yes, briefly. And they've agreed it doesn't need to be discussed any further."

Frigga forced herself not to twist her mouth into a sneer. *Of course they did,* she thought bitterly. *What other choice do they have? What other choice do I have? I said I forgave him, as always. Maybe Vidar is right that I have forgiven too much ... but Odin actually admitted his own wrongdoing to them. That's a good sign, isn't it?*

"We really should get the king into surgery right away," Eir prompted, seemingly uncomfortable with the tension.

"Frigga, do you prefer to stay or return later?" Odin asked, which surprised her. "I'd like you both here when they're done with me. But it doesn't matter to me who's here for the actual surgery."

"No one's allowed in the surgical area, Your Majesty," Eir informed him.

"How long will it take?" Frigga asked her.

"It's hard to predict. It could be several hours," Eir answered. "Or it may not take that long at all."

"Both of you go," Odin said decisively. "Frigga, if Vidar takes care of Bragi, then you can see the princes and return quickly."

Frigga gave Odin a quick peck on the lips, then followed Vidar out of the House of the Healers. They did not speak at all until they had almost reached the palace, though Frigga sensed growing agitation in the general's body language.

She wished she could grab his hand, but since she could not risk it, she merely said, "Things are going to be just fine, General."

He shook his head. "I may have been wrong about how Odin viewed us, but I don't think I'm wrong about this. And if Odin loses that eye, I'm worried about how he'll treat you. I've seen several soldiers lose limbs or body parts, and there's a grieving process that goes along with it."

"Let's not borrow trouble," Frigga responded, trying to hide the trepidation she felt at his words.

But he knew. He glanced at her, then remarked, "I think we already have. But I want you to know I'll be here to help you through whatever's coming."

"Thank you," she whispered, hoping her eyes told him how much she appreciated his offer.

He smiled at her tenderly, though he dared not touch her. As they entered the palace, she straightened her shoulders and lifted her chin. Vidar went one way to locate Bragi, and she took a different corridor to find her sons. She found them in the library, hard at work on their lessons. Baldur had taken a break from his own studies to help his younger brothers since Frigga had not been available to teach them.

Loki looked up from his textbook as the door opened, spotting her first. "Mother! Have you come to take over our lessons?"

"I'm afraid not, Loki," Frigga answered. "I've come to tell you how Father is doing. Then I have to return to the House."

"Is he well?" Thor asked cautiously, fear sparking in his blue eyes so like her own.

"When is he coming back?" Loki demanded.

"Let Mother speak," Baldur chided.

Frigga laughed, which immediately eased the tension on everyone's faces. "He's just fine, boys. And he might come back today or tomorrow. We won't know until they finish trying to fix his eye."

"You mean it's not better?" Thor asked.

"No, it's not," Frigga admitted. "But everything else has healed beautifully and much faster than anyone expected. We should all be grateful he's doing so well."

Baldur peered at her with concern in his dark eyes. She was not entirely certain she believed her own words, and he knew it. She smiled at him, hoping he would understand not to press her.

He drew near her and placed one hand on her shoulder. "Are you alright?" he whispered.

She nodded. Then all three of her sons surrounded her in a hug.

"Now don't make me cry, boys," Frigga chuckled in an attempt to keep her emotions in check.

"It's alright, Mother," Thor said with a knowing smile. "You're allowed to feel."

"Thank you, Thor," she said, patting his arm. "Get back to your lessons. I'm not certain when I'll be able to return. Baldur, you'll look after your brothers?"

"Of course, Mother. I can handle everything here," Baldur stated proudly.

"Then I'll leave things in your capable hands. Thank you, all of you, for being so well-behaved and understanding," she praised them.

All three of them beamed at her. She memorized the mental picture they made together, noting how different they were in appearance and personality, yet equally precious to her. Tall, strong, but gentle Baldur stood with one hand on Loki's small, wiry shoulder and the other resting on Thor's stockier frame. The younger boys instinctively stepped closer to their oldest brother as he tightened his grip in a silent message of comfort.

Though loath to leave them, she forced herself to hurry out of the library. When she found the general still closeted with Bragi, she went down to the kitchen to instruct the cook to prepare special Asgardian cakes for Thor and Baldur as well as a berry tart for Loki since he hated cake. When she returned to Odin's main office, she enhanced the sound to hear Vidar and Bragi still deep in discussion. She leaned against the wall and, feeling strangely sleepy, sank farther and farther down until she folded herself into a comfortable position on the floor.

The door opened and Bragi stepped out, not noticing her right away because he was flipping through some papers he held. She tried to scramble to her feet, but in her haste, she bent her ankle underneath herself just as she put her full weight on it.

"Your Majesty!" Bragi exclaimed when she gasped in pain. "What are you doing on the floor?"

The nobleman offered his hand to help her, but Frigga simply could not rise to her feet, even with his strong arm for support.

"I've hurt my ankle just now, Lord Bragi," she explained, flushing scarlet with embarrassment. "I cannot get up."

"Forgive me, Your Majesty, but you cannot stay there," Bragi declared. Not waiting for an answer, he hollered behind him, "Vidar, the queen needs assistance."

Vidar strode out of the room and quickly assessed the situation.

"It's only my ankle," Frigga protested.

"I'll carry her to her room, Lord Bragi, and see that she's settled there until we finish here," he offered. "Then I'll take her back to the healers once we're done."

"Get on with it then," Bragi said hurriedly, turning his attention back to his papers.

Vidar lifted Frigga up and carried her to her room, keeping his face void of emotion. She sneaked one peek, then avoided looking at him, feeling incredibly embarrassed over the whole incident.

As he passed one of the guards in the hallway, Vidar

barked, "You there! Bring some ice to the royal chambers at once. The queen is injured."

"Right away, sir," the guard answered automatically, then hurried in the opposite direction to obey.

When they reached the royal chambers, Vidar left the doors open and gently set her down onto her lush settee. She settled into the rich crimson pillows with a sigh of relief, though a sudden throb from the movement made her inhale sharply.

"Swing your leg up here so I can look at that ankle," Vidar instructed, his eyes brimming with concern.

"I don't think you should, Vidar," she murmured, blushing as she spoke. "I only tweaked it a bit."

The guard hurried into the room and wordlessly handed a pack of ice to the general.

"Thank you," Vidar acknowledged him. "Inform Lord Bragi I will be with him shortly. After that, you may return to your post."

The guard clapped his fist to his chest twice and bowed, then left, slamming the door behind him in his haste. Vidar jumped slightly.

"I didn't expect him to do that," he laughed at himself.

"You aren't usually so jumpy, Vidar," Frigga pointed out with concern.

He sighed. "I know it. I'm worried about the king. And now you."

"I'm fine, really," she reassured him. She lifted her leg onto the settee, wincing slightly as she accidentally jostled her sore ankle again.

"Stretch out your leg if you can," Vidar instructed. "I'll help you elevate it."

He grabbed two more pillows from the bed and handed her one to wedge under her knee. He helped her place the other one by gently holding her calf so as not to put undue pressure on her foot or ankle. She shivered slightly at his touch, for though he was completely respectful, there was something rather intimate about the process.

He lifted his eyes to meet hers and smiled shyly. "Apologies, my queen. I know my hands are rough."

"I think being around me is making you lose your gift," she snickered as she brought her other leg up onto the settee to lean back into a more comfortable position. "I wasn't thinking that at all."

He wrapped the flexible pack of ice around her ankle, then knelt in front of her. "I know, Frigga. I don't always let on what I understand, though I freely admit I can be wrong. But I'm usually not."

"And here I thought I had an effect on you," she pouted playfully.

"You have a powerful effect on me, my queen," he murmured. "But I dare not stay long lest someone starts any gossip. That guard knows I'm in here."

"Then I'll make this fast," Frigga said softly. She reached out to place one hand on his face and softly kissed his cheek. "Thank you for taking care of me."

"You're welcome," he said huskily, closing his eyes at her touch.

He rose to his feet, then grabbed one more pillow and a soft, golden brown blanket from the bed. He helped her lean forward and placed the pillow behind her, then draped the blanket over her.

"I'll be back as soon as I can," he told her. "Try to rest."

She nodded and closed her eyes, her mind briefly touching on the newly formed memory of Bragi's comment to Vidar that some of the staff seemed uneasy despite the explanation for the king's condition. Sharing Vidar's opinion that it was of little concern, she fell asleep quickly, not even hearing the door open and close. Only moments seemed to have passed when she felt a hand gently cup her face. She opened her eyes to see the general kneeling in front of her again.

"I thought you said you were going?" she teased, placing her hand over his.

"I've already gone and come back," he chuckled. "You've been asleep. You must have needed it. All these late nights with me, no doubt."

"What time is it?" she asked.

He stood and checked the timepiece on the fireplace mantle in the sitting area of the royal suite. "It's almost noon. That took quite a bit longer than I intended. Can you walk?"

Frigga stretched and swung her legs back down, then tentatively tested the ankle she had tweaked. "I think so."

She stood and took a few steps. She limped slightly, though most of the throbbing in her ankle had stopped.

"I'm glad it's feeling better," Vidar said. He grinned mischievously. "Although, I was looking forward to carrying you all the way to the House of the Healers."

She walked over to him, gaining strength as she moved. She draped her arms on his shoulders. "I'll let you carry me some other time. I enjoyed the last time, even though I couldn't show it."

He slid his arms around her waist as his lips parted slightly. She could not tear her eyes away from his mouth except to glance at his eyes, which smoldered with golden light. Lacking the willpower to deny herself or him, she felt her eyes close involuntarily as he tightened his embrace. When he did not kiss her, she opened them again.

"Not here," he whispered. "Not now."

"Why not?" she asked softly, feeling a wicked urge to overcome his inhibitions by tempting him further.

"You share this room with the king," he stated flatly.

She suddenly came to her senses, feeling embarrassed and ashamed. "You're right. My emotions are all over the place. Please forgive me."

"No, it's not your fault," he insisted. "We'd better check on Odin. He must be in recovery by now."

But when they arrived at the House of the Healers, Eir met them at the door to inform them the king was still in surgery.

"What's taking so long?" Frigga queried impatiently.

"Your Majesty, I don't know how to tell you this," Eir sighed. "There's simply no way to soften the blow."

"Then just tell me," she demanded, noting how the general stiffened beside her.

"We had to remove his eye," she said quietly.

Vidar bowed his head as Frigga gasped, "But why? I thought you were just going to determine if you could fix it or not!"

"When he had his stroke, as we've decided to call it, he burst several vessels that carry blood to the retina. Blood had been slowly pooling behind the eye, which was likely causing the pain and pressure he'd been experiencing," Eir explained. "In order to stop the bleeding, we had to cauterize the burst vessels. New blood vessels can grow behind the eye, which can be problematic because they don't always grow back correctly. We could have tried to seal those off if that had happened, which wouldn't have restored his vision, but he would have kept the eye itself. Unfortunately, there was just too much damage."

Frigga felt like her own eyes would cross from all of the information. Without thinking, she felt for General Vidar with one hand. He understood immediately and supported her just as she felt the room sway.

"Your Majesty!" Eir exclaimed. "Are you alright?"

Frigga took a deep breath. "Yes, I'm just a little overwhelmed. I'm not certain I understand it all."

"She needs to sit down," Vidar interjected. "Oh, and would you examine her ankle? I almost forgot."

Eir looked questioningly at the queen, who chuckled sheepishly and said, "I tweaked it a bit. I think it will be fine."

"Let me take a look," Eir insisted.

She led Frigga to a chair and examined the ankle while she nodded in approval at Vidar's description of how he had treated it.

"You're right, Your Majesty. Your ankle is only slightly strained," Eir confirmed. "But that walk over here wasn't the best thing for it. Stay off it for the rest of the day if you can. Alternating heat and ice will likely help. And perhaps some Asgardian ointment if you'd like it. We can provide all of that for you, but I'll leave it to your discretion. The king will want you here with him anyway. If you care for it properly today, it will likely be as good as new after a good night's sleep."

"Thank you, Eir," Frigga replied somewhat abruptly. Far more concerned with Odin's condition than her ankle, which she could tell would heal itself eventually, she prompted the healer, "What other damage was there to the king's eye?"

"Most of it was due to the amount of blood and fluid pressure," Eir replied. "If we had operated even twelve hours earlier, we would have been able to save the eye, though not his vision."

"For some reason, knowing his vision loss was irreparable anyway makes me feel better," Frigga admitted. "Will he wear a prosthetic eye now?"

"Eventually, yes. We had just finished inserting a temporary implant when you arrived," Eir said. "I had my apprentice take over so I could explain the situation to you." Seeing Frigga's worried look, she hastened to add, "She's very capable. She only needed to baste the eyelid shut so everything can heal properly."

"When can we see him?" Frigga asked quietly, trying to absorb everything she had been told.

"My apprentice should be finished by now," Eir mused. "We put him to sleep for the surgery. It should only be about another hour before we take him back to his room. Would either of you like a lunch tray while you wait?"

"None for me," Vidar replied.

"Did you eat this morning?" Frigga asked.

Vidar shook his head sheepishly.

"Then I insist you eat now," she half scolded. "I need you to keep up your strength."

"As you wish, my queen," he conceded with a respectful bow.

Eir hurried off. Vidar followed Frigga back to the room where Odin had stayed before the eye surgery. Vidar closed the door and enveloped Frigga in a hug before a word could be spoken. Shocked, she started to push him away, thankful the window curtains were still closed.

"Please don't," he murmured. "Just let me hold you for a few seconds. For my own comfort, as selfish as that may sound."

She melted into his embrace, remembering how Odin had shut her out even in their shared grief. Vidar's need for comfort in that moment brought comfort to her own spirit. True to his word, he released her after mere seconds, then sat abruptly in the chair by the door with his head in his hands.

Frigga walked over to him and placed her hand on his shoulder. "You must not blame yourself, Vidar," she whispered.

He looked up at her. She was stunned to see tears shimmering in his eyes. "Frigga, I'm worried about you," he admitted. "Yes, I'm grieved for the king, but if he hurts you again in this new grief—"

"I cannot think that way," she stopped him, shuddering at the thought. "I may have to lean on you through this. If you can continue to be a friend and a comfort to me, perhaps I can stay strong for the king. Can I rely on you?"

"Yes, my queen," Vidar murmured. When a knock sounded at the door, he stood quickly and quietly urged her, "Sit here. You're supposed to be staying off that ankle."

She sat obediently, watching as Vidar opened the door and helped the orderly bring in two lunch trays. She did not care about the food and only ate because she had insisted the general do so. Neither of them seemed inclined to speak again. Frigga's nervousness grew as time passed until she realized she was working herself into a frenzy. She took several deep breaths to calm herself just as the orderly returned to collect the trays.

"The king will be back in about fifteen minutes," he informed them. "I hope you don't mind if I take care of a few things in here?"

"Do you need us to step out?" Vidar asked.

"No, but perhaps you can move the queen's chair next to yours, General? Just so I have more room to move around," said the orderly.

Vidar nodded. "Eir told her to stay off her ankle. Should I—"

"You are not picking up this chair with me still in it," Frigga protested, afraid that was what he had been about to suggest. "I'd just as soon hop over there."

"I thought I could act as a crutch with the chair in my other hand," Vidar said. "If the queen would permit me, that is."

"General, why don't you carry the queen, and I'll move the chair," the orderly offered. "We are pressed for time, if you'll forgive my boldness."

Frigga stood so the orderly could move the chair as Vidar scooped her up to take her to the new spot across the room. The orderly busied himself with setting up equipment and making the bed. He paid them no more attention and soon left, leaving the door open.

Frigga flashed Vidar a shy smile. "I could get used to that."

"What?"

"I really like it when you carry me," she whispered.

He blushed. "Enough of that, my queen. We're getting careless."

She fell silent as they waited for Odin to be brought back to the room. She wondered what the general was thinking, slightly irked over how he had rebuked her, though he had been gentle … and correct.

He wordlessly reached out and squeezed her hand just once, then dropped it to continue to stare at the wall across from them. The minutes ticked by as if there were a phantom timepiece in the room. She felt the urge to pace. Forgetting Eir's admonition to stay off her ankle, she stood abruptly.

Vidar immediately grabbed her hand. "Where do you think you're going?"

She remembered her injury and sank back into her chair with irritation. Feeling like a bratty child, she seethed, "You're getting a little too bold, General Vidar."

"Apologies, my queen," he muttered.

But she saw the hurt flit across his face and chided herself for allowing her frustration and impatience to spill out on him. Before she could apologize, she heard the hum of an electric stretcher just outside the door. She leaped to her feet but sat down again when Vidar shot her a warning look.

He helped the orderly move a rather pale Odin into the bed. Stark white bandages covered the king's right eye. His left eye remained shut.

"Is he asleep?" Frigga asked the orderly.

When he shook his head sadly, Vidar and Frigga exchanged worried glances.

Without opening his good eye, Odin spoke in a gravelly voice. "Leave me, all of you."

"But Odin, you said—" Frigga began to argue.

"I know what I said," he snapped. "Just go!"

Frigga opened her mouth to insist she would not leave him, but Vidar quietly urged, "Let's go, my queen. We'll come back later."

"On second thought, Vidar, you stay," Odin barked.

"As you wish, my king." Vidar had responded exactly as expected of him, but Frigga saw anger in his eyes as he addressed the orderly. "Please assist the queen to the room next door while I hear what the king would say."

"Why does the queen need assistance?" Odin demanded, turning his face in the direction of the general's voice.

"She injured her ankle earlier today," Vidar answered. "Eir does not want her walking."

"Fine, do as he says," Odin commanded the orderly, waving one hand without opening his eye.

Frigga's heart sank even further when she detected the king's lack of concern for her. She felt tears prick at her eyes and a lump form in her throat. She accepted the orderly's arm and slowly moved with him out of the room. Vidar closed the door firmly behind them. Frigga could not hear the words he spoke with the king, only slightly raised voices. Her spirit was too wounded to enhance the sound waves.

The orderly helped her lie down on the bed in the adjacent room, then left to perform his duties elsewhere. She curled up her body in an attempt to wield off her sadness, but the tears came anyway. She did not hear the door open or sense anyone near her until Vidar knelt beside her bed. He placed his hand on her forehead, then moved it across her temple and down her cheek in a tender caress. She felt her lip and chin quiver again but could not speak.

"I've closed the door," he whispered. "Odin is sleeping now. No one will disturb us for a while. We can talk if we keep our voices down."

She sat up and made room for him to sit beside her on the bed. As he held her tightly, comfort washed over her from his warmth and caring.

"What did the king say?" she finally asked when she could trust her voice.

"Not much," Vidar admitted. "Especially when I rebuked him and warned him not to take his circumstances out on you."

"You did?" she gasped.

"Perhaps you're right. Perhaps I have grown too bold," Vidar mused.

"I should not have said that," Frigga sighed. "Odin isn't the only one taking his grief and pain out on other people."

"Think nothing of it, my queen," Vidar responded. "I am not entirely certain he considered my words. But I know he grieves. And he doesn't trust himself. He gave the order that any healer or orderly who attends him must be male. He will not even see Eir."

Frigga gasped, utterly speechless at this news. Vidar gazed at her with concern, which loosened her tongue.

"And does he still insist he will not see me?" she asked.

"He doesn't want you to see his grief or pain," Vidar explained.

"But I want him to turn to me in his grief," she said quietly, with frustration. "Why won't he just turn to me? Instead, he turns against me." The tears she had stemmed threatened to break through again. "I cannot do this alone."

"You're not alone," he soothed her, rubbing her arm and shoulder as he spoke. "I'm here."

"Oh, why can't I have you both?" she muttered in frustration, too overwrought to care how she sounded.

But he let her comment pass. "Eir says you can stay here in case the king becomes more reasonable after he sleeps. But she warned me that it may take days for him to come out of this dark depression that hangs over him."

"Did she say how we can help him?" Frigga asked.

"She thinks it's a good sign for him to be willing to see me. But she's keeping him sedated for now," he informed her. "She doesn't have the staff to subdue him if he flies into a rage."

"Does she think he would?"

"Some men do while recovering here. He's lost a significant part of his body," Vidar answered. "It's a risk. And Odin is too strong even now."

"What do you think I should do?" she asked.

"I think we could give it one more try to see if he'll let you visit him," Vidar said. "If he is of the same mindset by dinner time, perhaps you should return to the palace."

All of her independence seemed to have abandoned her, and the lonely nights in Odin's chambers stretched before her in an unbearable length.

"Alone?" she asked fearfully.

"Of course not," he reassured her. "I'll go with you."

She breathed a sigh of relief. "When is dinner time?"

"In a little over an hour," he answered.

"I've lost all sense of time," she admitted. "I thought it was earlier than it is."

"Will you be alright if I leave you here for a little while?" Vidar asked. "I should be with the king when he wakes."

She nodded, then asked, "Would you grab me a book from the waiting area before you return to him? And could you bring me some Asgardian ointment as well?"

"Of course, my queen."

Vidar kissed her forehead and hugged her once more, then left the room. He returned shortly with a book about horticulture and a small jar of ointment. She applied the concoction to the soreness just above her foot, then tried to read. Unable to focus, she stared at the ceiling for a while, counting the small cracks in the alabaster. The pain had ebbed considerably; she was just about to disregard Eir's instructions and walk over to the window when Vidar entered the room.

"The king is asking for you," he told her as he shut the door.

She rushed over to him without realizing what she was doing. At the look on Vidar's face, she laughed and assured him, "My ankle doesn't hurt anymore."

"Good," Vidar said. "I don't know how Odin would respond if I had to carry you in there."

"The orderly didn't carry me," she informed him. "I simply leaned on him."

"Good," he repeated. "I didn't want him touching you."

She laughed. "Don't get jealous now."

"You've felt jealous," Vidar stated a little defensively.

"How did you know that?" she gasped. Then she laughed. "Never mind. That was a stupid question. I'm so happy I could kiss you."

He grinned and winked at her. "Later."

"I might hold you to that," she flirted shamelessly.

His eyes burned slightly, but he simply stated, "The king awaits you."

8

Odin sat propped up, studying his long, slender fingers with his good gray eye as if preparing himself for something. He glanced up when he heard Frigga draw near his bed.

"Frigga, I apologize for my rudeness earlier," he said stiffly.

"You're forgiven," she said softly as Vidar set up a chair for her by the bed. "You weren't yourself, and you've sustained a great loss."

"I'm still not myself," Odin responded, looking at his fingers again. "I … I cannot predict how I'm going to act right now. I've already caused so much damage to you. I think it's best for you to return to the palace."

"I want to be here with you," Frigga contested.

"I know," he said, glancing at her again. This time, he held her gaze long enough for her to read the grief in his good eye. "Please let me have some dignity."

"What dignity?" she asked indignantly.

"That my queen not see me like this," he answered quietly, dropping his eye again. Before she could retort, he changed the subject. "I see you are walking on your own. Are you well again?"

"Yes, I simply strained my ankle," she answered. "The general had me ice it as quickly as possible. I've rested most of the day."

"I'm glad to hear it," Odin responded. "And how are the princes?"

"They're worried about their father," Frigga told him honestly. "They want to be with you as much as I do."

"Doesn't anyone understand my need for privacy?" Odin erupted.

Frigga jumped away from him at the volume. She looked at Vidar in consternation.

"Forgive me," Odin murmured, squeezing his eye shut. "But I warned you, Frigga. I seem to be unable to control myself. I *am* trying, but it wears me out. Please ..."

As Odin trailed off, his eye still shut, Vidar gestured for her to honor the king's wishes.

"Very well, my king," Frigga agreed, her heart squeezing with anguish. "I'll dine with the princes tonight and stay at the palace until you send for me. And I will come just as soon as you want me."

He opened his intact eye and reached out his hand for her. She took his hand and almost fell as he pulled her into an awkward hug. She kissed his forehead, then hurried out of the room. Vidar spoke briefly with the king before joining her in the hallway.

"He does not wish to eat," Vidar told her. "If he keeps that up, Eir will prescribe a nutrient feed for him again."

"Can you not reason with him?" Frigga pleaded.

"I've tried," Vidar admitted. "He wants me to return in the morning. Maybe I can get him to eat then."

The two of them walked back to the palace somewhat slowly since Frigga's ankle had begun to throb again.

"When do you want your device back?" Frigga asked, mincing her steps to minimize the soreness.

"I'd forgotten all about it," Vidar muttered. He glanced at her as they walked. "Would it help or hurt to meet tonight?"

"I honestly don't know," Frigga murmured. "I don't know how to handle what's happening to my husband, and I don't want to be alone tonight, but—"

"Say no more," Vidar interrupted. "If you give me back the device, I'll come to you. If you keep it a little while longer, would you come to me?"

"Yes," she said softly. "I like your room. It's comforting, like you are."

"Just one more time in my room then," he suggested. "We really cannot make this a habit. And I will need that device back sooner rather than later."

"After tonight, we'll go back to Laufey's old room," she agreed.

When they reached the palace, they found they were too late for dinner. The princes had already eaten and gone horseback riding. With the king holed up at the House of the Healers, gloom had settled over the entire estate. The cook fixed plates of food for the queen and the general, which they ate together in silence. Vidar excused himself fairly quickly. Frigga gave instructions to the guards that she was not to be disturbed except for word from the king. Then she waited in the library for her sons to return, watching from the window. When she finally spotted them, she hurried out to greet them, ignoring the protests of her ankle.

"How is Father?" Thor asked eagerly.

"How are you, Mother?" Loki interjected before she could answer.

Baldur merely gazed at her, no doubt sensing the tumult of her emotions.

"We've been waiting for you all day," Thor informed her. "You missed lunch and dinner."

"Let her speak, Thor," Baldur chided.

Frigga fought the tears welling up in her eyes. "I need to talk to you, my sons," she began. "Would you rather go to the library or Baldur's room?"

"Baldur's room!" the younger two boys cried with delight.

They loved any opportunity to invade their brother's space. Baldur chuckled, but he cast a worried glance at his mother. He offered her his arm as the four of them walked down the long corridor and up the flight of stairs that led to his room. Frigga leaned on him gratefully, wincing every so often as her ankle throbbed again, but she kept her physical pain to herself.

She sat down on the chaise lounge in Baldur's room as her sons gathered around her. She quietly updated them on their father's condition, skimming over how volatile he had been.

"Then Father will be just fine!" Thor cried gladly.

"He's missing an eye, stupid," Loki said fiercely. "How does that sound fine to you?"

"Don't call me stupid," Thor growled.

"Not now, boys!" Frigga said sharply. "And Loki, mind your tongue."

"Mother, would Father permit me to see him?" Baldur asked. "Perhaps I could ease his emotional turmoil."

"Father doesn't need that," Loki scoffed. "He's too tough."

"Loki, what's gotten into you tonight?" Frigga scolded, concerned by his uncharacteristic harshness. "Your father has feelings. And this is very hard for him. When he does return, we'll have to be very supportive and brave." She allowed a note of warning into her voice. "And we must not stare."

"Why? Does it look awful?" Thor asked quietly.

"I haven't seen it, Thor," Frigga told him. "And he'll probably keep it covered until they make him a prosthetic eye to look like his old one."

Thor sighed with relief. "Then he'll be back to normal eventually."

"Mother, what about my offer?" Baldur prompted her.

"It's a fine idea, Baldur," Frigga answered. "Why don't we see what General Vidar thinks in the morning?"

"Are you going back with him?" Baldur asked.

"No, your father wants me to stay with you," she told him.

Loki's face brightened immediately. Frigga decided to spend some alone time with her youngest son at bedtime to probe into what the boy might be feeling. She spent an hour reading stories to them, which even Baldur enjoyed, then walked Loki to his room while Baldur took Thor to his.

When they reached Loki's room, he hugged his mother impulsively. "I'm so glad you're back, Mother. I've missed you."

"Oh, my sweet boy," she murmured as she pulled him closer into her warmth. "I've missed you too."

"May I show you what I've been working on?" he asked excitedly.

"Of course!" She followed him into his room and watched as he formed a glowing green ball of light. "That's beautiful, Loki!"

"I love this color," he murmured, staring at the glowing orb.

"I like it too." Frigga smiled softly, reminded of Laufey yet again. The petite giantess had always gravitated toward green as well, especially when choosing fabric for the dresses Frigga made for her as her pregnancy progressed. "I would wear it more often, but your father prefers red."

"So does Thor," Loki muttered, making the ball disintegrate. He looked at his mother. "Why does Father love Thor the most?"

"Oh, Loki, why do you think that?" Frigga cried.

Tears welled up in his eyes. "He always notices everything Thor does but nothing I do. I think he likes Thor even more than Baldur!"

She knelt in front of him and wrapped her arms around the boy. "Thor is the most like him, you know, even though he looks like me."

"I wish I looked like you," Loki said softly.

She shook her head. "You are exactly the way you're supposed to be, Loki." She leaned close and whispered, "And I'll tell you a secret. *You* are the most like me."

"Does that mean you love me the best?" Loki asked impishly.

She laughed. "I love you very much, Loki, but I love Baldur and Thor too."

"You love a lot," Loki remarked. "Maybe Father doesn't know how to love everyone like you do."

Frigga suddenly felt unbelievably sad. "Your father does love you, Loki. You'll see it someday."

"Then why won't he let me go see him?"

"He won't let Thor go either," Frigga reminded him.

"He might let Baldur," Loki pointed out. "And then he might let Thor too. What if he doesn't let me?"

"Oh, my son," Frigga sighed. "You must not think that way. You're only hurting yourself. I know your father has not always paid as much attention to you, but he must grow and learn just like everyone else. I know he loves you. In fact, just before this happened, he told me he couldn't see how anyone wouldn't be fond of you."

Loki's eyes flared the bright green that meant he was happy. "Maybe he'll see better without his eye," he suggested with a shy smile. "I'll try to think good thoughts."

His words struck Frigga as containing wisdom beyond his years. She hugged him, then kissed him goodnight.

She took her time making her way to the royal chambers since her ankle had endured far more activity than it should have. She sent one of her guards for more ice and a heat pack, then sat on the settee to follow Eir's instructions from earlier, pondering her time with her sons. The cold permeated her skin and banished the pain effectively, but the warmth was even better. She started to doze off but suddenly remembered the general might be waiting for her. She cast off the heat pack, then dressed in her prettiest blue gown, not quite knowing why. She fished the device out of the hidden pocket in her other dress and transported herself to the general's room, which was empty.

She settled herself on his settee, wondering where he had gone and when he would return. After just a few minutes, another door inside the room opened, one she had not noticed before, and the general stepped through.

She stood, brimming with curiosity. "Where have you been? Where does that door go?"

He stopped in his tracks and stared at her, then smiled with admiration shining in his eyes. "Frigga, you look absolutely beautiful."

"Thank you." She dipped her head, smiling sweetly. "It's been a while since anyone has told me that … well, besides Thor."

"Odin loves red, but I love blue," Vidar murmured, drawing near her as if in a trance.

"And Loki loves green," Frigga chuckled nervously, filing that bit of information away. "You didn't answer my question."

Vidar shook his head as if to free his mind of certain thoughts, still staring at her. "What question?"

"Where have you been?" she repeated impatiently. "And where does that door go?"

"Apologies, my queen," he said softly. "I knew you were coming at some point tonight, but you took me completely by surprise. Did you dress up like that just for me?"

Frigga crossed her arms and glowered at him. "You're stalling."

He laughed. "I really am stunned by how beautiful you look. But since you won't let the matter drop, I'll answer your question as long as you never tell another soul."

She nodded. "I've kept this secret, haven't I?" she reminded him, showing him the device. Then she gestured to him and to herself. "And this one."

"I went to another realm," he told her, seeming to enjoy her visible surprise. "Behind that hidden door is a passageway King Borr built, which leads to a secret portal. That's why Odin gave me this room."

Frigga felt shocked and intrigued all at once, daring to ask, "Which realm?"

"Midgard." Vidar had hesitated at first, but eagerness spilled into his tone as if wanting to impress her. "I had business there on Odin's behalf. I apologize for keeping you waiting."

"I've only been here a few minutes. I had to ice my ankle again and almost fell asleep," she admitted, processing this new information as she wondered how much he would reveal to her. "Can you tell me about your trip?"

"No, I cannot, my queen," he said softly, his eyes glowing as he looked at her. He took a few steps toward her. "There are things I cannot tell even you when it comes to matters of state."

"I understand," she murmured as she closed the remaining distance between them.

Although still curious about his short trip to Midgard, she found herself ceasing to care as he took her into his arms as he so often did when they met in secret. But tonight, something felt different. Their mutual grief over Odin had bonded their spirits together even more strongly. She had not thought much about how close they had come to crossing boundaries earlier that day, but alone with him in his room, the memory flashed through her in a rush, along with all of the emotions tied to it. And not only did she find herself unable to navigate the complexity of her feelings for both men, she could not separate them in her mind. Just as Vidar's face had morphed into Odin's features in her dream so many nights ago, she imagined he had become her husband somehow. She slid her arms around his neck and pulled his mouth down to hers. He offered no resistance. And just as quickly, he was no longer Odin but Vidar again.

But it was too late. She had kissed a man who was not her husband.

She could not lie to herself; this was no innocent mistake. She had imagined too many times what it would feel like to kiss Vidar and had, in fact, craved physical intimacy with him. She pulled away to gauge his reaction and saw her own desire mirrored in his eyes. This proved her undoing in the moment as she let her guard down even further. Before the guilt had a chance to set in, she kissed him again.

He moaned softly against her mouth and tightened his arms around her. Then he broke away and rested his forehead against hers as he smiled at her with more love and longing than she could bear.

"You were right," he said shakily.

"About what?" she asked breathlessly.

"That we wouldn't stop at just one kiss," he groaned, pulling her to himself again. "And now I fear I cannot stop at all. Even though you imagined him at first—"

"What?" she cried in dismay, stepping away from him. "How did you—"

"I've seen you kiss Odin," he reminded her. "That first kiss was exactly how you used to do it, reaching up for him like that. But the second—"

"This gift of yours is getting out of hand," she teased. "How can I ever fool you?"

"Why would you want to?" he asked, his eyes suddenly guarded.

"I wouldn't," she reassured him, stepping close to him again. "Yes, I saw him at first, but now it's only you."

He kissed her this time, hard and hungrily. As his lips crushed hers and stole her oxygen, she feared she would pass out.

"Air!" she gasped.

He released her at once and sat down heavily on the settee. "Forgive me," he whimpered, his eyes wide with shock and realization. "I got carried away." His voice fell to a mortified whisper. "I … what have I done?"

Frigga's lips burned where his had been, both with desire for more and horror at what she had started. She locked away the guilt clamoring for her attention, then sat down beside him and reached for his hand.

"It wasn't just you," she comforted him, aching over the agony etched on his handsome face.

"Then what have we done?" he whispered, squeezing her hand as he looked at her lips.

"What we've wanted to do for a while now," she answered flippantly, longing for him to kiss her again. "Nothing has to change."

As if he could not resist, he allowed his eyes to rove over her, then forced them back to her face with a look of sheer panic.

"Everything has changed!" he exclaimed, rising to his feet and pacing the floor as he grabbed his hair with his hands.

"I … I thought this was what you wanted," she stammered in confusion.

"It was … *is*," he answered distractedly.

"Do you still love me?" she asked, terrified she would lose him now.

He sat back down beside her and hugged her fiercely. "Yes, I still love you."

"Then kiss me again," she commanded him when he released her.

He smirked at her. "No."

"Yes," she insisted as she grabbed his tunic with both hands and pulled him to her until their lips almost touched.

"Does the queen enjoy tormenting her general?" he sassed as he pulled back slightly.

"*My* general?" she asked in mock surprise.

"Yes," he murmured as he cupped her face with his hands. "Yours, only yours."

"Then obey me," she demanded playfully. "Or I will be forced to take punitive action."

He chuckled. "Such a clever queen." As he sought her mouth again, he murmured, "Command me at will."

Then he kissed her with such passion, Frigga longed to throw away every caution and inhibition to give herself fully to Vidar. And from the way he clenched his hands against her back as if to keep them from wandering, she guessed he wished for full satisfaction as well.

Suddenly, her mounting guilt escaped from where she had contained it. Dismay and shame flooded her, for she knew she had purposely tempted him after he had tried to exert discipline and treat her with honor.

What am I doing? she silently screamed at herself.

He broke away and dropped his head. "I ... I cannot do this," he panted. "I want to, Frigga, so badly. But ... I can sense your guilt … and …" He took a deep breath. "You are the wife of the king—my closest friend and my brother in bond. As much as I want you to be, you are not mine."

His words produced a surprising effect in Frigga. Though she had been thinking along the same lines, she suddenly felt rejected and even more ashamed. She dropped her eyes and turned her body away from his, staring at her hands in her lap.

"Do you think me wicked, Vidar?" she asked quietly. "Do you no longer respect me?"

"No," he breathed, drawing the word out softly and soothingly as he gripped her shoulders. "It's because I respect you. And if you are wicked, then so am I."

"You are not wicked," she objected forcefully. "You are … everything my heart desires."

"Do you wish to torment me again, my queen?" he asked huskily.

"Yes," she groaned. She traced his mouth with one finger and grinned when he shivered. "But I will not. We've crossed a line. I fear we cannot go back."

"We can try," Vidar murmured. "Please don't dismiss me now."

"I have no intention of dismissing you," she informed him indignantly.

"Then permit me one more," he begged, reaching for her again. But he stopped himself and sighed. "Frigga, if we both stay here tonight, we're going to end up in my bed together."

"Are you asking me to leave?"

"No, I will."

"Now how would that look?" she teased. "The general sleeping outside his room?"

"I could go back to the ..." His voice trailed off as his face turned ashen and he spoke again, as if to himself, "How will I face Odin tomorrow? I've kissed his wife multiple times. And I've dared to want more." He stared at Frigga with a glazed look in his eyes. "So much more."

Without another word, he strode to the door and left her sitting there on his settee. The door did not close behind him but swung wide open. She made herself vanish, then carefully placed the transport device onto his pillow where he would be sure to see it. She looked around just once, then hurried to the royal chambers as quickly as she could despite her aching ankle.

As soon as she entered the room she had shared with Odin for centuries, sorrow washed over her. She threw herself onto the bed, sobbing as she reflected on her behavior. She had promised to forsake all others when she married Odin. But she had justified meeting another man in secret because Odin had neglected her and she needed a friend. Vidar had been a welcome escape at first, but she had allowed herself to fall in love with him. Not only that, she had kissed him passionately and almost ... But no. She had not. They had crossed a line, yes, but not *the* line. She calmed herself and dressed for bed, then fell asleep with that comfort lingering in her mind.

Suddenly, she sat straight up, sensing someone in the room.

"Odin?" she asked groggily.

"No, it's me."

Frigga knew his voice instantly but had no idea what to expect since he had abandoned her in his room. She grabbed the blankets to cover herself as he knelt beside the bed. She could not see his face clearly.

"You left," Vidar stated softly.

"You left first," she shot back defensively.

"I had to clear my head," he explained. "I went out to the banquet hall balcony. It's a good place to think."

"Did you expect me to wait?" she asked with slight irritation. "I had no idea what you were doing."

The moon broke free from a cloud outside and shone a beam of light through the window, illuminating both of their faces.

"You've been crying," Vidar observed.

"And sleeping," she pointed out. "How long were you out there?"

"I don't know," he admitted. "I found the device when I returned and came straight here."

"I think I've been asleep for an hour or two," Frigga guessed.

"Could we talk?" Vidar asked quietly. "We cannot let things stay the way they are right now."

"I agree, but I don't know what to do," she responded. "Did you think of anything while you were out on the balcony?"

"Several scenarios went through my mind," he replied.

"Tell me," she prompted.

"The most severe is to never see each other again, but because of who we are, we'll have to see each other … unless I request a transfer somewhere other than here," he stated.

She shuddered. "I hate that idea."

"I don't like it either," he muttered. "Another option is to free yourself from Odin legally. He has betrayed you twice. It doesn't seem right to me that you should never have happiness when other Asgardian women would not have tolerated the king's behavior. He would have been booted out on his ear if he were anyone else."

She snickered at the mental picture, then cocked her head as she considered his suggestion. "What about my sons? And how would I support myself?"

"I would support you. I may not match the king in wealth, but I've done well for myself over the years," Vidar stated proudly. "And I haven't figured out what to do about the children. Baldur will be a legal adult soon, and Thor would probably want to stay with his father. Loki would side with you."

She shook her head. "You're talking about splitting up my family, Vidar. It isn't like you to even suggest this. The king just lost an eye. You would wound him further?"

He sighed heavily. "If he found out what we've done, it would wound him even more."

"More than my leaving him? Surely not! Don't you think he would guess the reason?" she argued.

"Not if we waited to come together," Vidar explained. "He would still have my friendship as a comfort. Then, in the proper time, I would make my intentions known … after he's moved on."

"When he finds another wife?" she asked incredulously. "He might not. Borr never did."

"Borr's wife died tragically," Vidar argued. "It's not the same at all. Odin has found comfort with other women in the past. I'm confident he would remarry. And until then, I would keep you somewhere safe and visit you whenever I can. At least this way, we can protect Odin somewhat."

"I think you underestimate him. His pride would not allow him to accept my departure," Frigga said quietly, wondering where the sting was that usually accompanied any thought of Odin with another woman.

Had she numbed herself to him that effectively? Or was this strange ambivalence a side effect of her unfaithfulness?

"You could be wrong, you know," Vidar argued, desperation creeping into his voice. "Maybe he would free you willingly because of what he's done to you."

"He would never free me willingly. He views me as his possession, and in his mind, his queen is a symbol of his honor," she declared as a deep heaviness settled in her heart. "Don't you realize the king could twist things to his advantage? He might have me branded as a traitor if I try to pursue legal action against him for adultery, especially since it was so long ago. There wouldn't be a safe place for me on Asgard."

"What if you took temporary refuge in another realm? Vanaheim, perhaps?" he suggested.

"And what would I tell my brother? He would be so ashamed of me," Frigga sighed.

"Wouldn't he be more likely to take issue with how Odin treated you?" Vidar asked, his tone gentle and persuasive.

"If he did, he might declare war on Asgard to defend my honor," Frigga pointed out.

"King Gylfi would not start a war he could never win," Vidar scoffed. "He needs Asgard!"

"And you're willing to risk lives if you're wrong?" Frigga gasped indignantly. "The lives of your people and mine?

And leave Vanaheim vulnerable to attack when Asgard ends the alliance?"

Vidar sighed deeply as he dropped his head in shame and defeat. "You're right," he muttered bitterly. "I only have one other suggestion. It's a bit of a middle ground."

"What is it?" she prompted, tears distorting her voice as she recognized the hopelessness of their situation.

"We continue as we have but maintain appropriate boundaries," he said firmly. "And that will be no easy task."

"Most of the time, the best course is not the easiest," she murmured sadly. "I think that's what we must do. Maybe if we stop spending so much time together, we can go back to being friends."

His face twisted at her words. "Friends?"

"You said once you were content with friendship," she reminded him.

"Are you content with friendship?" he shot back.

"No," she sighed. "But what choice do we have? Isn't it better than nothing?"

"I don't know," he muttered. "Didn't *you* say we couldn't go back?"

"And *you* said we could try," she retorted. "What we need is something to focus on besides each other."

"Maybe you're right," he sighed. "I'll think about that and let you go back to sleep now."

"Vidar?"

"Hmm?"

"When will I see you again?" she asked, unable to hide the longing in her voice.

He tenderly kissed her forehead. "That doesn't sound much like going back to being friends, my queen."

"I know. What if we just go back a little instead of back to the beginning?" she suggested. "We could love each other in heart and spirit but not in body."

He looked hopeful. "Loving you in heart and spirit has been my reality for hundreds of years. I respect you enough to restrain myself."

Frigga held her hand out to him, smiling when he folded it into his own. "What should our boundaries be?"

"Let's discuss that when we're both rested," he suggested.

"Good idea. I feel so much better now that we have a plan," she murmured, feeling sleepy again.

"And now I can face Odin in the morning," he said more cheerfully. He kissed her forehead again, then stood. "I'll see you at breakfast, my queen."

"Oh! That reminds me," Frigga said. "Baldur wants to try to ease Odin's emotional anguish."

Vidar cupped his chin with one finger resting on his nose as he pondered this. "That's a good idea. I'll discuss it with Baldur, then bring it up to the king."

"Thank you," she whispered.

He nodded, then vanished. She fell asleep greatly comforted and assured that as long as they were careful, they would not have to part from each other.

9

"**Y**ou look especially pretty today, Mother," Thor remarked as he worked under her guidance to keep his weather gift under control.

The general thought so too, Frigga reminisced with satisfaction.

She had taken extra care in her appearance just for him, donning a blue dress and a simple sapphire necklace since she would not be seeing Odin that day. Her ankle felt as good as new, just as Eir had predicted. And since she had slept well, her reflection that morning had radiated with renewed energy. Vidar had shown just enough admiration for her to see when she had arrived for breakfast in the family dining room. Otherwise, he treated her as cordially and respectfully as always, giving no indication of what had happened between them. He did not stay long but took Baldur with him to the House of the Healers, leaving Frigga to turn her attention to resuming lessons with the younger boys.

"Are you smiling because of what I said?" Thor asked innocently, bringing her back to the present.

"Of course. And thank you, Thor," she answered quickly, telling herself her response was mostly true. "Now, think of something that makes you really happy, but don't let yourself use your gift."

"Are you happy about Father getting better?" the boy pressed his mother. "You seem different this morning."

"Stop trying to get out of your lessons, Thor," Loki taunted him.

Thor stuck his tongue out at Loki as Frigga laughed, "Come now, boys! I haven't worked with you in days. Let's focus, shall we?"

"Can we go outside later?" Loki asked slyly.

"Now who's trying to get out of lessons!" Thor retorted indignantly.

"I said *later*," Loki remarked haughtily.

He formed a ball of red light and threw it at Thor, who shielded his eyes and ducked, making the light missile splash into his hair.

Loki burst out laughing. "Thor has bright red hair!" he chortled, grabbing his sides as Thor's face turned almost as red as his hair.

The light faded quickly, but Thor's anger did not. Before Frigga could stop him, Thor summoned a rain cloud right above Loki's head and drenched him. Loki sputtered indignantly and sent a piercing shriek right into Thor's ears. Thor clapped his hands over his ears but kept his wits enough to form a swirling wind that picked Loki up and dumped him onto his hindquarters. Normally, Frigga would have stopped them immediately, but she was impressed by their wit and their display of power. And seeing the humor in the situation, she broke into peals of laughter, which stopped the princes more effectively than if she had lectured them or grabbed them by their ears again. They looked at each other, grinning foolishly, then joined their mother in her laughter.

"What's going on in here?" Baldur's good-natured voice interrupted their merriment. "I can't leave for a few hours and expect lessons to be done?"

"Well, who made you Mother?" Frigga demanded playfully.

"Someone has to be," he joked.

Frigga snickered, then directed Thor and Loki to work on their handwriting, ignoring their groans as she stepped out into the hallway with her oldest son.

"By your excellent mood, I'm guessing things went well with your father?" she prodded.

"Yes, his body heals itself quickly," Baldur remarked casually. "He is much better today. He's eating and allowing Eir to attend him now."

"How did he seem in spirit?"

"General Vidar is right. He's grieving. But he allowed me to see him," Baldur answered.

"Were you able to help?" she asked.

"Only a little," he admitted. "Eir warned me his brain is still somewhat at risk. So I eased into his emotions just briefly, long enough to give him some hope and comfort. The rest, he'll have to do on his own."

"Thank you for doing that, my son." She caught a glimpse of Mimir, the math tutor, coming down the hallway. She hugged Baldur and said, "We'll speak more later. I must return to your brothers."

"And I'll return to my own studies," Baldur responded.

Frigga watched him go, then led the kind-hearted teacher into the library, grateful to have a short break from instructing her sons. She settled down with a book she had not yet read and soon lost herself in its pages.

"My queen!" Mimir interrupted loudly.

Right in the middle of a battle scene, she sighed inwardly, looking up from the book in annoyance.

"Forgive me, my queen," Mimir continued, stifling a chuckle as his intelligent blue eyes glistened with amusement. "I've called three times now. That must be an excellent book."

The princes snickered behind their hands but quieted immediately at one look from their mother.

"Oh yes," she replied to the math tutor. "It's full of danger and intrigue."

"May I see?" He held out his hand for the book. "*The Thunder's Foe.* Oh yes, I know this book. One of my graduates, Odrerir, wrote this many years ago. His son Kvasir is turning out to be quite the writer himself. He's one of my students now."

Frigga nodded politely. "Please give the queen's compliments to Odrerir. Perhaps he would consider doing a reading at the palace?"

"I think that could be arranged," Mimir said with delight. "We can talk about that some other time. I must give you today's report on the princes, then be on my way to my next appointment."

Frigga listened as he recited their marks and pointed out where they needed to improve. Loki and Thor beamed with pride at Mimir's praise of their progress.

After a quick lunch, Baldur returned to the House of the Healers while Frigga took Thor and Loki to play in the gardens. Since Vidar had been with Odin all day, a lower-ranking guard stood watch. Frigga brought her book, which she finished as the sun caressed her with lazy afternoon warmth. With a sigh of contentment over the conclusion, mixed with sadness that the story had ended, she reluctantly closed the book and called to her sons. Just as they joined her with disgruntled groans at having to end their play, another guard approached with Lady Annette and Sigyn.

"Annette!" Frigga exclaimed with delight. "What brings you here?"

"Run and play with the boys, Sigyn," Annette instructed her daughter.

Thor and Loki whooped at the extension of their time outside and dragged Sigyn to wherever they had been playing as one of the guards hastened to keep up with them.

Annette turned to the queen. "Berg had a meeting with Bragi, so we tagged along to visit with you. How fares the queen?"

"Quite well. And you?" Frigga said, blushing slightly as she thought of how well she fared when Vidar was around.

"Well enough," Annette replied. "Berg has almost fully recovered. He's eager to get back to normal activity."

"Understandable," Frigga remarked. "I'm certain the king will feel the same once he returns to the palace."

"And how does he fare? So tragic to have a stroke so young!" Annette said sympathetically.

"Baldur brought a good report this morning," Frigga answered.

"Berg is hoping to see the king before we return home," Annette informed her. "What chance do you think he'll have?"

"I wouldn't risk it, honestly," Frigga said somewhat stiffly. "He has permitted hardly anyone to visit him."

Annette peered at her curiously. "You said Baldur brought a good report. Haven't you been to see the king today?"

Frigga pasted a fake smile on her face. "I'll go when he sends for me," she answered. "Until then, I have sons to school."

"Don't you ever grow tired of that?" Annette asked.

"Of what?" Frigga queried.

"Schooling. You've practically raised Baldur, but you still have many years ahead of you with Thor and Loki," Annette clarified. "I only have Sigyn, and I am weary of the monotony of teaching her."

"Why not hire tutors?" Frigga suggested.

"Berg wants me to teach her until she reaches her transition years," Annette said, making a face. "I'm so glad girls mature faster than boys."

Frigga laughed. "Oh, Annette, whatever would you do with yourself otherwise?"

"I'd travel and throw glorious parties when I'm home," she said without hesitation. "I married Berg for his money, you know." Annette giggled when Frigga let loose a scandalized gasp, then continued, "I'm not ashamed to admit it. I like fine things. Wealthy men have always been attractive to me. Isn't that why you married the king?"

"No, I didn't want to be a queen," Frigga said softly. "I married him in spite of his position."

Though not something she would ever share with Annette, Frigga briefly pondered what had drawn her to Odin, disturbed to find her understanding of the past clouded by her feelings for Vidar. Had Odin ever cherished her and validated her as much as the general did? Had she naively fallen for Odin's good looks and charm due to the immaturity of her youth?

Surely there was more to it than that, she thought with dismay as she struggled to grasp the memories she had recounted to Odin just days ago.

But Annette interrupted her churning thoughts, her tone laced with intent. "If you hadn't married him, I think you would have started the Idisi. Becoming a healer would have been too quiet a life for you."

For just a moment, Frigga imagined a life without Odin. Was Annette correct? Would she have started the group of Vanir warrior women instead of Lady Freya? Could she have met Vidar somehow and been free to love him?

To hide the sudden regret that filled her, Frigga laughed and teased, "You seem to think I'm wasting my abilities, Annette."

"You know I don't mean to criticize, Frigga," Annette assured her, dropping the formalities since no other nobles were present. "I simply wish more people knew how skilled you are. I've been wanting to see you fight someone since you showed Baldur how to use his sword all those years ago. You must have learned for a reason."

"I've probably forgotten how by now," she said lightly.

"Oh no," protested Annette. "I'm certain it's like sharing a man's bed. You never forget how."

"Annette!" Frigga scolded, blushing furiously. She smoothed her dress to maintain her dignity, then said, "There's no place for women who wield swords on Asgard."

"Maybe there should be," Annette retorted.

Frigga cocked her head, wondering what motivated the noblewoman to say such things. But before she could continue, the boys came rushing back with Sigyn close on their heels, hollering at them to wait for her. The guard lagged so far behind them, Frigga could barely see him.

"Mother, we found a yellow salamander in the pond!" Thor announced when he had caught his breath.

Loki panted beside him with his hands on his knees. Sigyn caught up with them and fell on the ground, gasping for air.

"Thor tried to frighten me with the poor thing, but I like salamanders," Sigyn boasted. "He was so cute! He even let me hold him for a little while."

Thor rolled his eyes just as Loki said, "She's not so bad for a girl, is she, Thor?"

"Yeah, you should take her rabbit chasing with you the next time you get lost in the wilderness," Thor teased.

"Leave Loki alone, Thor!" Sigyn said fiercely when Loki glared at his brother. "Or I'll … I'll … punch your teeth in!"

Loki glanced at her in surprise, looking decidedly embarrassed. Startled by this rare show of temper from the little girl, Frigga hid a smile as she realized the clear implications of the child's reaction.

Apparently, so did Thor, for he howled with laughter. "Loki's got a girlfriend!" he cried in a sing-song voice.

"I can take care of myself, Sigyn," Loki said arrogantly, crossing his arms across his chest. "I don't need a girl to fight my battles."

Sigyn's little face fell, and her sweet blue eyes filled with tears.

"Loki, be kind," Frigga scolded gently. "And Thor, don't mock your brother."

Loki hung his head and mumbled an apology. Sigyn nodded but moved to stand close to her mother, glaring at Thor, who merely smirked at her.

"This is exactly why we need something like the Idisi on Asgard," Annette whispered to Frigga as she hugged her daughter close to her side. "So that we can fight if we must."

Frigga stared at her friend as an idea sparked in her mind. Wanting some privacy to discuss it, she chirped, "No harm done, right, children? Why don't you all run to the kitchen for a snack?"

The three children exchanged surprised glances, then ran off before she could change her mind. Frigga grabbed Annette's arm excitedly as they followed, the two guards trailing behind them.

"What is it?" Annette asked in alarm.

"You've given me an idea, Annette. A wonderful idea, although I daresay you thought of it first!" Frigga exclaimed.

"I did?" Annette wrinkled her nose in confusion.

"You said we need something like the Idisi on Asgard," Frigga reminded her. "But all women of Vanaheim are trained to defend themselves, though they don't normally go to battle with the men. If war ever comes to the home front, they are always ready to hold their own."

"Really?" Annette gasped. "That's what we should be doing!"

"Yes, exactly! We need a training program for Asgardian women who want to learn how to fight," Frigga said excitedly.

Annette stared at her. Then a wide grin spread across her face. "Like fencing?"

"Fencing, other types of sword fighting, Vanari—"

"What's that?" Annette interrupted.

"Vanari? It's a fighting art my people created," Frigga explained. "It's beautiful … like a lethal dance."

"And you know how to do it?" Annette queried eagerly.

Frigga nodded.

"Well enough to teach others?" the noblewoman pressed.

"All I can do is try," Frigga murmured. "If I could train a class of thirty to forty women, perhaps they could each train their own classes."

"Then you'd have your own Idisi," Annette pointed out gleefully.

"Not quite," Frigga chuckled. "The Idisi are special forces—spies and assassins. After Freya failed to capture Odin's heart, she poured her fury into the girls she trained. And they were fierce indeed."

"So are you, Frigga. You have to do this," Annette practically gushed. "Even if we never have to defend ourselves, what a gift this could be! For one thing, it's dreadfully boring to have an armed guard with me everywhere I go. The common women move about freely. Why can't I?"

"It's unlikely anyone would kidnap a common woman," Frigga pointed out.

"No one has ever tried to kidnap me," Annette harrumphed. "If I could defend myself, wouldn't that be a sufficient deterrent to anyone who might consider harming me? My guards simply take up space. I think the one assigned to me today was as bored as I am, though he never complained."

"What would he do if he were released from guard detail, I wonder?" Frigga mused.

"Perhaps we should ask him," Annette giggled.

"Perhaps, but not yet. There is much to think about. I'll have to convince King Odin and his war council," Frigga pointed out.

"You won't be doing it alone," Annette promised her. "Ithunna, Gladys, and I will be right there beside you." She winked at Frigga. "And we're all married to war council members who enjoy nightly companionship."

Frigga burst out laughing. "Annette, you are truly awful. And I love you for it."

Annette laughed with her. "Why mince words?"

Frigga frowned slightly. "We cannot approach the war council without a plan. How will we pay for it? Where will we train? Who will be eligible for enrollment?"

"Details," Annette scoffed.

"But those are questions they'll ask," Frigga insisted. "If we have those answers first and can show them the benefits, we'll have a greater chance at approval."

"I have complete confidence in you, my queen," Annette said lightly, patting Frigga on the arm as they reached the kitchen.

"Let's keep this to ourselves for now," Frigga whispered.

"What took you so long, Mother?" Thor demanded happily.

"And why did you let us have a snack right before dinner?" Loki asked.

"So many questions!" Frigga laughed. "I noticed you didn't ask that before you ate your snack, Loki."

"Why would I?" Loki snorted indignantly. "Then you might have seen my point and changed your mind."

"Perhaps I hoped you wouldn't eat so much at dinner if you had a snack first," Frigga suggested with a wink.

"Does that mean you'll do this more often?" Loki asked hopefully.

"That depends on whether or not I see what I'm looking for," Frigga said breezily as she ushered the three children out of the kitchen and down the hall toward the family dining room, where they sometimes entertained special guests when the king was not present.

"That child is deviously smart," Annette whispered to Frigga. "The makings of a king."

"Yes, but Loki will never be king," Frigga chuckled softly. "Still, he's an asset to Asgard, there's no doubt of that."

"Under your guidance, he'll become a fine man," Annette said thoughtfully. "Berg wants to approach Odin about Sigyn as a potential bride for Prince Baldur someday, but if that isn't acceptable to the prince, then perhaps—"

"Annette, it's too soon to even be thinking about that," Frigga cut her off. Then she smiled at her rather forward friend. "But I will say I'd be in favor of your sweet daughter marrying any of my sons."

They reached the family dining room where Lord Berg and Lord Bragi waited for them. Berg kissed his wife and scooped his daughter up into his arms. Even though Annette had joked about marrying her husband for his money, Frigga recognized her eagerness in his presence as well as the affection in her voice when she spoke of him. They were well-suited for each other.

Vidar seems to be a better fit for me, she told herself as her thoughts returned to trying to remember why she had fallen for Odin.

During the meal, she let the conversation flow around her as she mused on Odin's kingly strength and wisdom. More often than not, he seemed to know exactly how to handle every political situation as it arose. A skilled diplomat, he always sought to protect the weak and desired the happiness of his people.

But he neglects the happiness of his wife, she thought bitterly.

After dinner, she said goodbye to Berg and his family, promising Annette to send for her soon to discuss and plan their idea.

"What idea?" Berg asked.

"We'll keep that to ourselves until we flesh it out more," Frigga said, casting a warning glance at Annette.

She felt a slight pang of guilt because she wanted to discuss it with Vidar that night but did not want Annette revealing anything to her husband. The nobleman held a lot of swaying power, and Frigga needed him on her side. But if Lord Berg did not approve of the queen's plans, he might shut them down immediately.

Annette winked and nodded at the queen to indicate she would not speak of it yet, then left with her family.

After they had gone, Lord Bragi turned to the queen. "Your Majesty, would you permit the young princes to go fishing with me? There are a few hours left before nightfall."

The boys immediately begged Frigga to let them go. Since the nobleman had no children yet and seemed to enjoy spending time with the princes, she laughingly gave her approval.

"Where is Lady Ithunna tonight?" she asked, wishing she had been present to share in the excitement of her idea.

"She is at home, my queen," Bragi answered. "Her mother has been staying with us or she would be here. She'll be disappointed she missed visiting with you and Lady Annette."

Frigga dipped her head in a nod, smiling to herself as she decided to surprise Ithunna with a visit. After Bragi left with Thor and Loki, Frigga changed into her riding outfit— a form-fitting gray dress that only came to her knees and a pair of soft riding breeches. After she slipped on her riding boots, Frigga hurried to the palace stables. As she saddled her lovely gray mare, Sigurna, Odin's black stallion pawed and snorted in his stall to protest his mate's imminent departure. Descended from a long line of rare eight-legged horses, Svadilfari had always been high-spirited, one of the reasons Odin preferred that breed. Sigurna nickered softly and shook her black mane at the truly unique animal, stamping one of her four hooves as if to tell him to settle down. Frigga patted her neck and crooned to her as she swung herself into place with just the slightest creak of leather.

Once they left the stables, Frigga spurred Sigurna across the palace bridge and took the left fork that led to the edge of the wilderness where just a few isolated houses were scattered, including the home of Bragi and Ithunna. The pounding of Sigurna's hooves against packed dirt settled Frigga's body into a natural rhythm as the scenery flew by them. She had not ridden her horse in months, let alone with no armed escort. Rejoicing as the wind whipped her hair away from her face, she felt as if she had returned to the days of her youth when she rode freely across the plains of Vanaheim.

She arrived at Bragi's manor faster than she wished but enjoyed the surprise on the face of the young manservant who rushed to stable her horse. A maidservant answered when Frigga knocked on the beautifully carved oak door. With wide eyes, the doe-eyed girl curtsied several times as she led the queen to the sitting parlor of the grand home. At the maid's insistence, Frigga sat down on a comfortable settee by the window. The sheer white curtains afforded her a beautiful view of the manicured front lawn and the weeping willow tree she had passed at the beginning of the winding path that led to the door.

Lady Ithunna came flying into the parlor in a matter of minutes, once again wearing a stunning purple that made her dark hair shimmer.

"Why, Queen Frigga, what a lovely surprise!" she gushed as she smoothed her dress. "What brings you here?"

"I don't mean to interrupt your visit with your mother, but Annette and I have been hatching an idea I'd like to discuss with you," Frigga answered.

"My mother retired to her room after dinner, my queen. It's just us," Ithunna stated. "May I offer you something to drink?"

"Thank you, Ithunna, but I cannot stay long. Bragi has taken the boys fishing, so I should return before dusk," Frigga replied.

"And how does King Odin fare?" Ithunna prompted.

"Better, I'm told," Frigga answered. "But really, we can dispense with the pleasantries. I am so eager to tell you about this."

"Of course. Go ahead, Your Majesty," Ithunna said graciously as she sat down in a luxurious armchair across from the queen.

Frigga recounted her conversation with Annette, enjoying the excited flush that stole over Ithunna's cheeks as she spoke. When the queen had finished speaking, Ithunna held up one finger, then hurried out of the room. She returned quickly with one of Bragi's fencing swords.

"Show me something," Ithunna urged as she handed the weapon to Frigga.

Frigga smiled, delighted by the chance to demonstrate what she knew. She took her stance, gripping the sword firmly. Then she lunged forward, minding her footwork, and quickly snapped back to her original position.

"Now teach me to do that," Ithunna begged with shining eyes.

Frigga helped Ithunna plant her right foot forward and parallel to the sword she held, with her left foot perpendicular to and a shoulder's width apart from her other foot. She showed her how to turn her body to the side with her knees bent slightly over her toes for the proper stance.

"Always place your heel first when moving toward your opponent," she instructed Ithunna. "Now lunge forward toward me like I just did."

"Oh, this is impossible to do in a dress," Ithunna complained when she stepped on her hem and almost fell over.

"Mind the hem, Ithunna, and keep a grip on your sword," Frigga chided her. "You may *have* to do this in a dress someday, so you must learn."

"Can you do it?" Ithunna challenged.

"Yes, of course," Frigga answered in surprise. Then she laughed. "But it is easier dressed like this. The problems with dresses are usually in the sleeves, bodice, or length. If you must, kick out right before you lunge to keep the fabric away from where you land with your foot. You'll learn to be aware of where your feet are and where they need to go. Now, try again."

Frigga worked with Ithunna until she could move correctly in a dress. The noblewoman grew tired and frustrated a few times, but Frigga was patient with her. They did not notice how late the hour had grown until they heard horses approaching. Frigga looked out the window to see the sun vanishing below the horizon as General Vidar and Lord Bragi stopped their horses in front of the house. Frigga watched as the men dismounted, silently admiring the general's movements as he swung one long leg over his glistening, chestnut brown stallion and hopped down to land perfectly on both feet.

He does everything well, she thought to herself with pride.

The same stableboy appeared to take their horses as Ithunna joined Frigga at the window.

"Why is the general here?" Ithunna gasped.

"I came out here alone," Frigga answered sheepishly. "Bragi must have brought the boys back sooner than I expected and guessed where I went. I really should have been back before now."

"Look at me," Ithunna wailed. "I'm drenched in sweat. I cannot be seen like this!"

"Go wash up," Frigga told the distressed noblewoman. "I'll meet them outside."

"You're sweaty too!" Ithunna protested.

"Not quite as much. And I don't care anyway," Frigga insisted. "Hurry now!"

When Ithunna obeyed with a frantic look in her eyes, Frigga rushed out to meet the men, still holding Bragi's sword. As soon as Vidar saw her, relief transformed his face, followed by anger.

"Queen Frigga, what will the king say when he hears you left the palace without an escort?" he thundered. "And what are you doing with that sword?"

"Have care, General," Bragi admonished him. "You are addressing the queen."

"Apologies, Your Majesty," Vidar said in a calmer voice. "The king has entrusted your safety to me, and I do not think he would approve."

Frigga hid her consternation as she realized how upset he must be, for he rarely addressed her that way. "No harm done, General. The king would most assuredly approve of your fervor in your duty."

Bragi chuckled, seemingly oblivious to the tension between the queen and the general. "General Vidar might have overreacted, Your Majesty, but he is not wrong. I would also like to know what you plan to do with my fencing sword."

Frigga smiled as disarmingly as possible and held out the sword as she walked toward them.

"Welcome to the future, gentlemen," she said soothingly. "Imagine if a noblewoman could defend herself so well, she did not need an armed guard except in rare circumstances. Do you realize the manpower such a thing could free up for other tasks?"

Vidar and Bragi exchanged bemused looks, making Frigga bristle slightly.

"And who will teach you such defense?" Bragi said rather condescendingly.

"I have had the proper instruction since I was a girl," Frigga responded hotly, irked by his tone. "And I will teach other women the same."

"Now, Your Majesty, let's be realistic," Bragi began.

"Draw your sword, General," Frigga commanded.

"What? No!" Vidar protested.

Bragi looked at him nervously and whispered, "I think that was an order, General. You'd better humor her."

Vidar sighed wearily and drew his sword as Frigga took her stance. She lunged toward him so quickly, all he could do was blink as she knocked the sword out of his hand.

Bragi burst out laughing. "How have you survived battle for so long, Vidar?"

Vidar flushed and grabbed his sword. "She took me by surprise!" he defended himself. He took his own stance. "Try that again, my queen."

Frigga dipped her head with another disarming smile to acknowledge his request. Instead of lunging this time, she advanced quickly and, with several quick flicks of the wrist, nicked the hand that held his sword before he could take one step forward. When he did not drop his sword as she expected, she retreated quickly. He advanced on her with frightening speed, but she maintained her wits as he forced her to parry his blows, which she knew were not at his full strength. However, she also knew she could never defeat him by strength alone. She leaped to the side to make him turn, then seized that moment to kick him in the hip. As he stumbled, she gathered the strength in her legs and launched herself into the air for another kick, which knocked him to the ground. She used the impact to propel her body backward perfectly so she landed on her feet in a Vanari crouch, still holding the sword. The general tried to get up but stopped when he felt her sword at his throat. He held both his hands up near his face in surrender, grinning at her with open admiration.

"And I'm even better with a short sword," she declared before she allowed him to scramble to his feet.

Bragi stood there with his mouth hanging open in shock. Frigga brushed her tousled hair away from her face and smoothed her riding costume.

"The queen's abilities know no bounds," Vidar praised her.

"I cannot do all of that in a dress," Frigga admitted. "But even if I were armed with a dagger or a slightly longer sword, I could hold my own against someone who threatened me."

"Can you teach Ithunna to do any of that, my queen?" Bragi breathed.

"I've already taught her a little, my lord," Frigga informed him. "I would like to approach the king and the council with a plan to train Asgardian women to defend themselves when they have need."

"They will not be easily persuaded," Bragi said quietly. "But after what I just saw, you have my support."

"Thank you, my lord," Frigga chirped happily. "I really should return to the palace now. I didn't intend to stay away so long. And I do apologize for worrying both of you."

"I still don't think it's wise for you to travel alone," Vidar admonished her gently.

"Well, I won't be alone now," she replied saucily. "Lord Bragi, would you please have your man bring General Vidar's horse and mine?"

"Of course, my queen."

As Bragi hurried off to obey, Vidar turned to Frigga. "Do you have to return to the palace immediately? Or can we take a detour?"

"That sounds rather scandalous, Vidar," she whispered.

"Trust me," he whispered back.

Bragi returned quickly and took the sword Frigga held out to him. The stable hand approached soon after with both horses. Vidar and Frigga mounted their animals, then rode off toward the palace.

Once they were well out of sight from Bragi's manor, Vidar took the lead and guided Frigga across the countryside toward a secluded spot by a gurgling stream. The deepening shadows of dusk crept over the land. Tiny insects flashed specks of white light from their bodies as they flitted around three weeping willows with leaf-laden boughs that seemed to lament the passing of late summer into autumn.

"Fireflies!" Frigga exclaimed, pointing them out as she looked around her. "In all my time on Asgard, I've never been to this place."

"My parents used to bring me here when I was a boy," Vidar told her. "I'm certain other Asgardians know about it, but I've never brought anyone else here."

"The general honors me," she said softly.

Vidar dismounted and allowed his horse to drink from the stream. Even though Frigga did not need help getting off her horse, she accepted his assistance just for the excuse to be in his arms again. As he lowered her to the ground, the expression on his face made her wonder if he was thinking about how romantic the setting was. As she remembered kissing him, the heat built in her face and she found it hard to catch her breath. A soft nicker distracted her.

"Your horse seems to be making moves on Svadilfari's mate," Frigga chuckled, pointing to the two horses nuzzling each other and talking to each other in their language. "Sigurna doesn't seem to mind much either."

"Horses are not monogamous," Vidar said lightly. "If Svadilfari were here instead of Vasili, she would likely act the same with him."

"You make my horse sound so fickle," Frigga teased as she placed her hands on his shoulders and peered up at him.

"Isn't she?" Vidar murmured.

"Horses may not be monogamous, but there are mares who choose just one stallion," Frigga replied. "I believe it is the stallion who is fickle, for he will chase down any mare who strikes his fancy. And if she rejects him, he immediately moves on to the next one."

Vidar narrowed his eyes. "Are we still talking about horses? Surely you don't think I am like a stallion."

"No, of course not," Frigga reassured him. "And I am no mare."

"No, the queen is even more than I realized," Vidar said huskily as he lowered his head to kiss her.

But Frigga moved away. "Don't, Vidar. I'm still sweaty and wind-blown from fighting and riding."

"I don't care," he asserted. "So am I."

"What about what we said last night?" she asked.

"To not get carried away again?" he answered with an overly innocent air.

"To discuss appropriate boundaries after we rested," she laughed.

"I was hoping to at least kiss you again," Vidar admitted sheepishly. "You don't have to let me. I really missed you today."

"I missed you too," she replied. "And I *am* sorry I scared you. If you had reacted any more strongly, Bragi might have suspected something."

"I was incredibly relieved to find you there unharmed, though angry that you put yourself at risk like that," he told her. "But as you said, no harm done. Bragi is none the wiser, and this even works to my favor. If you had not gone to see Lady Ithunna, I could not have spent time with you tonight. I'm afraid I have to leave for a few days."

"You're leaving?" she asked flatly. "On another errand for Odin?"

"A continuation of my work on Midgard," he clarified.

"And you still cannot tell me about it?"

"I'm afraid not," he admitted. "Baldur will stay with the king as he continues to recover. He's doing much better today, which I noticed you haven't asked."

She hung her head. "I hadn't yet."

"His spirits are lifted with Baldur around. And he's making progress."

"I'm glad to hear it. But I'm sure Baldur will tell me more. Let's not spend our time together talking about Odin. Will you return to me in one piece?" she asked tentatively.

"I'll do my best," he chuckled. "It isn't an expressly dangerous errand. And you have plenty to do to prepare your plan for the war council. You might not even notice I'm gone."

"No, I'll miss you terribly," she contradicted him with a well-placed pout. Then she smiled brightly as she imagined presenting her plan before the council. "Does that mean you support my idea as Bragi does?"

"Yes, my queen," he answered as he slipped his hands around her waist to pull her closer. "I'll even fight you again if you need to demonstrate your skills for the council."

Deliriously happy over his approval, she threw her arms around his neck without thinking. In seconds, they were kissing even more passionately than they had the previous night. Being outside in a secluded area as the darkness deepened made her feel reckless. Carried away by the moment and the intensity of her emotions, she entered an emboldened state of mind as he thrust one hand into her hair and pulled her body against his with his other hand spread wide against her back.

Suddenly, Vidar's stallion whinnied and stamped his foot. Vidar jumped away from her, breathing heavily.

"Frigga, I'm out of control," he gasped, frantically looking around as if he expected to be arrested any moment.

"So am I," she sighed as she took several deep breaths. "I simply cannot resist you."

He drew near her again and gently cupped her face with one hand. "Then I won't put you in a position like this again."

"I suppose we cannot handle it," she agreed with a tremendous sense of regret.

"The memories of these last two nights will stay with me when I'm away from you," Vidar told her. "Thank you at least for that."

She cocked her head at him. "I've caused you pain, haven't I?"

"More pain than I ever thought possible, my queen," Vidar said honestly as he caressed her cheek with his thumb to take the sting out of his words. "But the same dagger that wounded my heart keeps me alive as well. Remove it and I'll bleed to death."

"I know a thing or two about healing, you know," Frigga said seriously. "There is no recovery from a wound like that unless the dagger is removed as quickly and safely as possible and surgery is performed to repair the heart. And even if you heal, you're never the same again."

Vidar chuckled at her miniature lecture. "No, Frigga, there is no surgery possible to repair my heart if you walked out of my life. But you are right about one thing—I'll never be the same again."

Though his words pierced her, the thoughts they triggered distracted her. Remembering what Annette had said about having her own Idisi, she grabbed his arms excitedly. "You've just given me an incredible idea!"

"Tell me," he prodded, seeming to enjoy the excitement on her face despite the change in subject.

"On Vanaheim, all women are taught basic defense principles from childhood, in case we are ever overrun again. But after Odin rejected her, Freya started a small company of women warriors called the Idisi," Frigga began.

"Yes, I know of the Idisi, though I didn't know Freya was the mastermind behind the organization," Vidar interjected. "Is that how she got over her heartache? I thought she married someone else."

"No, never, though many tried."

"I've read some of the stories," Vidar chuckled. "So what about the Idisi?"

"Freya has always kept her methods secret. But I believe they are trained much like your Valiants," Frigga answered. "What I was thinking about just now was starting my own Idisi with the healers."

"With the healers?" he repeated incredulously.

"Yes! In a way, you've given me the power to hurt you or heal you. My Idisi could have the same power if they were trained in warfare as well as the healing arts," she explained. "And if they traveled with the troops, it could significantly cut down on our losses."

"But most of the healers chose that profession because they don't want to bring harm, only healing," Vidar pointed out. "Especially the men."

"Not all the soldiers in the Seventh Corps wanted to be Valiants, did they?" Frigga argued. "All I need is a small group willing to attend to the wounded on the battlefield … who are not afraid to fight."

"Would you teach them?" Vidar asked.

"I can teach them some things," Frigga said. "But I would need someone very skilled in warfare to help me."

"Who did you have in mind?" Vidar asked with an ironic glint in his eyes.

"The finest, handsomest, kindest, bravest general I've ever met," she said flirtatiously, walking her fingers up his chest as she spoke.

"It's not me you have to persuade, my queen," Vidar answered, though he smiled at her words. "If you get this past Odin and the war council, I'll do it."

She smiled gratefully at him, then murmured, "If only—"

Vidar stopped her with one finger over her mouth. "There's no use in entertaining the if-onlys and what-ifs anymore. This is where we are. This is what we have."

"What are you saying, Vidar?" she asked quietly.

He shrugged. "I'm coming to terms with the fact that I'm hopelessly in love with my best friend's wife."

"Hopelessly?"

"My cause is hopeless, isn't it?" he asked her, looking at her strangely. "Unless Odin dies or casts you away, I'll never have you."

She shook her head. "Even if he died or cast me away, I wouldn't be free. We've discussed this before. I chose to be a queen because I loved a king even though I never wanted it. But I am beginning to see how I can use my position for the good of the people. And though we cannot love each other fully, together we could build something incredible. Something for Asgard."

"Together," Vidar murmured in agreement, caressing her face again as his eyes softened with tenderness. Then he sighed. "We should return to the palace."

"Vidar?"

"Yes?"

"I haven't given you a proper goodbye," she said softly. "And I won't be able to once we get back."

"What exactly do you mean?" Vidar asked. "I don't think we should kiss each other again."

"Ever?" she asked in disappointment.

"I don't know, Frigga," Vidar answered. He bit his lip and looked away. "What about Odin?"

She sighed. "I've not thought of Odin much today."

"He'll likely return to the palace before I do," he informed her. "And while I'm away, you'll—"

"Do you think I'll forget you?"

"No, of course not. But I think you'll do what you should and reunite with your husband," he responded.

She regarded him seriously, unsure of what to think of his words. Instead of speaking, she kissed him softly on the cheek, then mounted Sigurna. He followed suit and mounted Vasili. When they reached the royal stable, Vidar remained behind while she walked into the palace alone.

Baldur strode up to her as soon as she entered the large doors of the palace entrance. "Mother, where have you been?" he demanded angrily.

Frigga stared at him in surprise. It was unlike Baldur to show anger. "Watch your tone with me, young man. I am your mother!"

He took a deep breath and started over. "We've been incredibly worried about you. Why did you leave without telling anyone where you were going? Even the stable guards didn't know where you were."

"I went to see Lady Ithunna," she answered breezily. "Lord Bragi and General Vidar found me there. And here I am, home safe."

He frowned. "You've got all the palace staff talking, Mother. Some of them think you sneaked away to carry on some dalliance." He smiled as if at a memory, then said, "General Vidar was quite angry. He told them to hold their tongues or lose their positions."

"He didn't say a word of that to me!" Frigga gasped in consternation.

"Perhaps he felt it inappropriate to even bring up to the queen," Baldur pointed out.

Frigga nodded, though her thoughts raced and hurdled over each other. Had Vidar thought there might be someone else? Was jealousy the real reason for his anger? If she could be so careless with her marriage vows, what would prevent Vidar from fearing she would be careless with his heart as well? No, she would not entertain such thoughts. Surely, he had just wanted to protect her from gossip.

Aloud, she said, "I had hoped to take more time to work things out, but it seems I must act quickly for my own reputation."

"It's salacious gossip, Mother," Baldur said with a shrug. "Anyone who knows you would never believe it. They say such things because they are not free of impurity themselves." He paused. "Work what out?"

Frigga breathed a sigh of relief, feeling assured Baldur must not suspect anything between his mother and the general. She smiled at her son. "Come, Baldur, I have something to tell you."

He walked with her and listened intently as she recounted her conversations with Annette and Ithunna as well as her sword fight with General Vidar.

"That must have bruised his ego a bit," Baldur chuckled, delighted by the whole thing. "I do have some concerns about these ideas of yours, to be honest. But if you can iron all that out ahead of time, you should definitely do this."

"Will you help me?" Frigga asked eagerly. "I'd like to present it to the war council at their next meeting."

"That's in four days," Baldur remarked dryly. "Why not wait until the next one?"

"I do not wish to wait that long. And if I move quickly, it will silence anyone who would dare accuse the queen," she said indignantly.

"Oh, Mother, now I wish I hadn't told you," Baldur sighed. "People will talk. And once Father returns, they won't dare say another word about it."

"Do you know when your father is returning?" she asked.

"No, but the surgery site is healing quickly," Baldur answered cheerfully. "Eir says he can attend the council meeting for certain."

"What of his moods?" Frigga asked cautiously.

"I think he should see you," Baldur stated. "I've eased his depression as best as I can, but I think a visit from you would do tremendous good."

"He doesn't wish for me to see him," Frigga reminded him.

"That's what he says," Baldur mused. "But I sense loneliness in him."

Guilt and compassion washed over Frigga in an instant. "I would go, but what if he succumbs to wrath at my appearance? What if it does him harm or sets him back?"

"I'll go with you, Mother," Baldur offered. "I think he'll be happy, but if he flies into a rage, we'll leave."

"Do you think there's a chance of that?" Frigga asked. "I'm not concerned for my own safety. I'm concerned for his."

"He's been gaining control of himself," Baldur answered. "Eir only sedates him at night now. I really think you're what he needs most, Mother."

"Very well," Frigga sighed, though her heart filled with dread at the prospect of facing Odin so soon after her behavior with Vidar.

She barely slept that night, but the following morning, she gathered her dignity and followed her oldest son to brave a visit to the king.

10

"Good morning, Father," Baldur said cheerfully. "I've brought you a surprise."

"Good morning, Baldur," the king answered. "Is it the news I'm being released from this prison of forced relaxation and rest?"

Frigga waited in the hallway as her son had advised. She noticed how strong Odin's voice sounded, and though he spoke sarcastically, she picked up on his desperation to move on with his life.

Baldur beckoned for Frigga to enter. She tugged on her red anniversary dress nervously, hoping the care she had taken with her appearance would overcome any misgivings he might have toward her for coming without his permission.

She need not have worried. His good eye lit up as soon as he saw her.

"Frigga!" he exclaimed, sitting up as straight as he could. A warm smile spread across his face. "Now, this I did not expect. You said you would only come if I called for you."

"I decided to risk it," she told him.

"Risk what?" he asked.

"Your anger," she admitted. "I didn't know how you would receive me. But I wanted to see you."

He grimaced slightly. "Baldur and Eir have managed to keep me under control."

"And how do you fare?" she asked, drawing near to take his outstretched hand.

"Stronger by the day. I'm eager to leave this place and return to the palace." He smiled again and breathed deeply as if to capture her essence and keep it with him. "It is so good to see you, Frigga. Tell me what you've been up to."

She exchanged a look with Baldur, silently asking if she should tell the king of her plans. Baldur shrugged, which Frigga interpreted as meaning it could go either way. But the king's mood seemed fine and, realizing she would have to tell him eventually, she filled him in on the last few days, leaving out her secret time with Vidar, something she desperately tried to banish from her mind in the presence of her husband and son.

Odin chuckled when she recounted once again how she had defeated the general. "I would have loved to see that. I had forgotten you were trained to fight." He wrinkled his brow and quietly asked, "So, Bragi supports your idea, does he?"

"Yes, and so does Vidar," she answered. "He said he would fight me again in front of the council."

"At least I know he would never hurt you," Odin murmured.

"Father, I also support Mother's ideas," Baldur interjected. "But I have some concerns."

"As do I," Odin admitted.

Eir bustled in before he could elaborate. "You are looking well this morning, my king! The presence of the queen is good for your health."

"Well enough to leave, caretaker?" Odin asked rather darkly. "Or should I call you my jailer?"

Eir firmly set her jaw. "Let me look at that eye. We need to change the dressing."

"What eye?" Odin grumped, his voice rising. "There is no eye!"

"Odin—" Frigga started to admonish him.

"What, Frigga?" Odin snapped. "Don't tell me how to behave. You have no idea what it's like for me now. You haven't been here!"

Frigga clenched her mouth shut as her eyes smarted with tears. The recent memories she had been ignoring swarmed her, forming a relentless, overwhelming guilt. When she wordlessly turned and left the room, Baldur followed.

He silently wrapped his arms around his mother. "Don't blame, Father," he whispered. "He can be cruel, but it comes from a place of deep anguish. He is trying."

"He blames me for not being there when he asked me to stay away," she huffed as her anger dried up her tears.

"I know," Baldur comforted her. "Give him time."

She turned away and set her fist under her chin, fighting to control her emotions. She must not let her son guess the true reasons for her anguish.

Eir joined them in the hallway. "The king's eye socket looks exactly as it should, but these mood swings are not good for him or anyone else. I want to keep him a little longer—for observation."

"Eir, I think the king might cause more trouble if you keep him any longer," Frigga sighed, relieved to have a possible task on which to focus. "What if you released him to my care? You know I can do what needs to be done."

"My queen, I worry for your safety," she said hesitantly.

"If things were to escalate beyond either of your control, he could become physically violent."

"Odin has never once raised a hand to me," Frigga informed Eir briskly. "But if it comes to that, I can defend myself if I must. And he has just been reminded of it."

"What do you mean?" Eir asked warily.

Frigga quickly summed up her idea and described her fight with Vidar. Eir's light brown eyes sparkled, making her lovelier than Frigga had ever considered her to be.

"I'm in," the healer announced.

"What?" Frigga's surprise was so great, she automatically reacted as if she had not heard or understood.

"This is one healer who would love to be able to hold my own in a fight," Eir clarified. "I think it could be beneficial, maybe even save Asgardian lives."

Impulsively, Frigga hugged Eir. "You'll be the first of my Idisi."

"You need to come up with your own name, Mother," Baldur chuckled.

"I should, shouldn't I?" Frigga murmured thoughtfully. "This is something new, something different."

"Let's discuss this later, Your Majesty. We need to decide the right course for the king. He needs something to focus on, but it must be something that does not overtax or stress him," Eir informed Frigga. "That's another reason for him not to return to the palace. You and I both know he will resume his normal activities without hesitation."

"What should we do?" Frigga asked.

"This project of yours might be the solution," she suggested. "If you seek his advice, it could be enough."

"You might be right," Frigga agreed. "Baldur, I have an idea."

"Another one?" he laughed.

"I have plenty of ideas, thank you!" she said with playful indignation. "If I get all of your concerns down on paper in front of your father, he might jump into the discussion and give his own opinions. He was quite reasonable and even pleasant until Eir mentioned his eye."

"I'll bring you a notebook and a writing instrument," Eir offered. "I think this will work."

The healer dashed off, then returned quickly with a leather-bound book filled with clean white paper and a beautiful black calligraphy pen. Frigga took them with respectful care, guessing Eir had retrieved them from her own belongings.

When the queen reentered Odin's recovery room, he was staring listlessly out the window. Without addressing him, she sat down in a nearby chair and opened the notebook with the pen poised to begin writing. He raised an eyebrow when he saw her but said nothing. Baldur took another seat.

"I'll write down the questions I expect the council to ask," Frigga began. "We can add any additional concerns you might have, Baldur."

"What are you doing?" Odin asked flatly.

"If you don't mind, Odin, we have plans to make," Frigga said smartly.

"Why don't you do that somewhere else?" Odin demanded. "I'm supposed to be resting."

"Honestly, Odin, I think you've rested quite enough," Frigga said. "If you don't want to help, that's up to you, but I would like to hear your opinions on the matter."

He blinked his remaining eye twice, then returned his attention to the window.

Frigga quickly penned some questions, then read aloud, "Who will be eligible for enrollment? Where will we train? What costs will be involved?"

"Good questions, Mother," Baldur praised her. "I also want to know what you will be teaching all the women as opposed to this elite group you want to start. Will the regular program be required of women like the rite of passage is required of men? How long will the training be?"

Frigga made those notes, then looked up. "What other questions and concerns?"

"How will you determine if the healers can stomach the battlefield? How will you prepare them for the horrors of war?" Baldur queried.

Frigga blanched, but Odin peered at his son.

"The same way you were prepared," he informed the crown prince.

Frigga wrote all of this down, smiling to herself. "What else?"

"Will they be cavalry or only trained on foot?" Baldur added.

"I had not thought of that," Frigga admitted. "Freya's warriors used to ride winged horses from Olympus, but I'm not certain if they still do."

"Dragons," Odin said, looking out the window again.

"No, they never rode dragons," Frigga chuckled.

"You shall ride dragons," Odin clarified, a smile crossing his face. "Frigga the Fierce."

"Is he still on a sedative?" Frigga asked Baldur.

"No, I most certainly am not," Odin said indignantly.

Baldur shook his head, grinning to himself.

"You want me to ride a dragon?" Frigga repeated, aghast. "Don't you think horses are a little more practical?"

"Train them on regular horses as well, if you like," Odin said with a wave of his hand. "But you know we won't be able to get winged ones. Dragons are the only other creatures who can fly that are large enough to bear a rider."

"They are too large," she protested.

"There are smaller dragons on Muspelheim," Odin mused. "Beautiful sleek creatures, not too much larger than a winged horse."

"Can they be ridden?" Frigga asked curiously.

"The fire giants ride the bigger ones, so why not?" Odin remarked, turning his gaze on her. "If anyone could manage it, you could."

Frigga dropped her eyes, pleased but confused by his compliment.

"He's right, Mother," Baldur agreed heartily. "The dragons are fierce, but the ones we saw seemed loyal to their riders."

"A healer could stabilize a wounded man while guarded by a dragon," Odin added. "And even the smallest ones I've seen look strong enough to bear someone out of a fight."

Frigga scribbled furiously, excitement welling up inside her. "How would we acquire such creatures?"

"We already have one," Odin announced proudly.

"What?" Frigga gasped. "How did I not know this?"

"I didn't have the chance to tell you before this happened, and I had quite forgotten until now," Odin admitted. "The dragon was a gift from the new king of Muspelheim. Gjallar has been taking care of her at the Bifröst stables."

"A female?" Frigga asked with delight. When Odin nodded, she continued, "And these creatures can be stabled like horses?"

"Not quite. We made accommodations for one dragon," Odin said. "But if we had a fleet of them, they'd need their own housing."

"And how would we acquire that many?" Frigga asked, noting the cunning gleam in Odin's eye.

"Write that question down," Odin instructed. "Let's start with one to see if it's feasible before I discuss that part any further."

"You already know, don't you?" she teased, grinning at him as he did his best to look innocent. "Very well, Odin. Keep your secret … for now."

When the king actually laughed, Frigga felt warmth steal through her body. She stood and sat on the edge of his bed, then tenderly placed one hand on his whiskered cheek.

"You're going to be just fine, aren't you?" she whispered.

Baldur grinned, then stepped out to give them privacy.

Odin regarded her with his good gray eye. "Are we going to be?"

"You know my loyalty," Frigga responded uncomfortably. "To you and to Asgard."

"Yes, I do," Odin murmured, dropping his head to look at his hands.

Frigga sensed her answer was not what he had hoped to hear, and the emotional wall fell back into place between them. She went back to her own seat, stuffing down the surge of guilt attempting to resurface.

"What other problems do you foresee, my king?" she asked abruptly.

But as she began to write down his suggestions, her focus shifted to her plans as her excitement and anticipation grew from the dawning realization that they could actually happen. And including Odin was proving to be precisely what he needed. Though she wondered if he only approved of her plans out of desperation for a distraction, she was wise enough not to question it.

As the days flew by, she involved him more and more, keeping him abreast of her meetings with the healers and noblewomen supporters. She stayed too busy to think of Vidar during the day, but alone in her bed at night, thoughts of the general engulfed her. Each time, a deep ache would settle in her heart as she wondered how he fared on Midgard. But sleep always brought her sweet relief. And so, the time passed quickly as Odin improved in health and mood.

11

The palace brimmed with a hullabaloo of excitement and anticipation, for the king was finally returning.

Frigga had sent word earlier for preparations to be made for his homecoming, then hurried to the palace with Baldur to ensure her instructions were carried out to the letter.

To her satisfaction, the savory aroma of spit-roasted boar and buttered cabbage, Odin's favorite dish, danced on the warm air from the kitchen. And the maids scurried about in the process of thoroughly cleaning from the servant quarters to the royal chambers.

By the time King Odin stepped through the palace doors with his royal escort, the atmosphere felt as though it might pop if anyone had to wait any longer. The staff had lined up to welcome him without prompting and without exception.

My, how our people love their king, Frigga thought as she watched their eager faces.

Odin smiled and waved at everyone and thanked them for honoring him. Frigga stole a few glances at him. Since he would not be fitted for his prosthetic eye for a number of weeks, Eir had given him a black eye patch to wear, which Frigga found rather dashing. His happiness and relief over his release made him look even handsomer than his kingly garments—a crimson and gold embroidered tunic accented by sharp black trousers.

He is quite a man, she thought, surprised at her renewed attraction to him.

Had it sprouted anew from working on a project together without arguing? Or perhaps it was merely his confidence and regal bearing as he dismissed the servants.

She suddenly felt the repressed energy of her youngest sons and pushed aside her musings to place one calming hand on each of their shoulders. They had almost exhausted their effort to heed her earlier warning not to rush their father when he arrived. Just before she feared they could contain themselves no longer, Odin reached out his arms for the two boys. They quietly and carefully went to him, murmuring how glad they were for his return.

Crouching lower to keep one arm around his younger sons, neither of whom quite reached his chest, Odin gestured with the other for Baldur and Frigga to join them. Completely surrounded by her husband and her sons, Frigga reveled in their togetherness in that moment, marveling at how much she had missed it. Then Odin straightened to his full height and allowed Thor and Loki to pull him by the hand to the family dining room. He did not even seem to mind their chatter and engaged them both as if he had every spare minute on Asgard to listen to them, which warmed Frigga toward Odin even further.

After a delightful, relaxed dinner, Frigga led Odin to their chambers, determined to follow Eir's instructions to get him to rest.

"I can still see, Frigga," Odin chuckled. "I'm not quite at the point where I need to be led by the hand. I only let the boys do it because they need to feel needed."

"Well, so do I. Stop complaining, and let me do what I can," Frigga scolded him as she opened the door for him and ushered him inside.

"It is so *good* to be back!" Odin exclaimed, looking all around him. Then he turned to his wife, who hurried over to close the curtains. "You've done so much already, Frigga. I doubt I would have survived had it not been for you. And I haven't treated you well at all, have I?"

She bustled around the room in a flurry of activity, feeling wary and uncertain of the changes in him. Would they last or was he just happy to be home?

"I understood, Odin. You've been through a lot," she threw over her shoulder.

"Frigga, stop fussing and come here!" he laughed.

When she meekly obeyed, he enveloped her in his arms. She relaxed against him slightly, enjoying his warmth though she prepared to keep him at bay. The king's earthy musk filled her nostrils, enhancing the refreshingly clean smell of their suite. The memory of Vidar's pleasant traces of cedar and spice tickled at the back of her mind. Both scents had a powerful effect on her, just as both men did, which she hesitated to admit to herself. But as Odin held her with confidence and expectation, his embrace seemed diametrically opposed to the gentle comfort and suppressed longing of Vidar's arms. She suddenly felt ashamed for comparing them as she sensed a fragile vulnerability in her husband. But then he moved in such a familiar way, she knew he was about to kiss her. She eased herself away from him, wincing slightly at the wounded expression he tried to hide.

"Do I repulse you now?" he asked quietly as he tried to turn his covered eye away from her.

"Of course not," she crooned as she moved a stray lock of his jet black hair away from his face. "It's not your eye that makes me hesitate."

"What is it then?"

She sighed, knowing she could not tell him the whole truth. "Do you remember when I asked you for time?"

"Yes," he affirmed. When she paused to try to find the right words, he cocked his head and gazed at her solemnly. Then he kissed her forehead. "I understand. I won't pressure you. I'll leave it to you to let me know when you're ready."

This act of understanding and selflessness, coupled with the respect he had shown her since preparing for the council meeting, unlocked a part of her heart. Her attraction to the king increased tenfold. In fact, all of her pent-up and denied desire for Vidar began to bubble into this new yet familiar awakening toward Odin.

What is happening to me? she asked herself as she reached out her hand to stop Odin as he moved away from her.

He turned to her in confusion, then looked from her hand on his arm to her face. She smiled shyly at him, feeling a thrill of response when hope dawned on his face. For some reason unknown to her, she suddenly wanted to see what would happen if she loved him in body again. Was it more than just a desire for satisfaction that drew Odin, or even Vidar, to her? Was the act of physical intimacy some sort of key to a deeper part of men? If so, could she unlock the heart of her husband as he had just unlocked part of hers?

She kissed the king as she had kissed him before she knew about Laufey, urged on by his overwhelmingly positive response. But just as things were beginning to progress, she suddenly remembered what Vidar had said—that she would and should reunite with her husband. The memory shriveled up the desire she had begun to feel again for Odin.

"Slow down … please … Odin, stop!" she gasped as he started to undress her.

He stepped away from her as if she had physically pushed him. "Why? What's wrong?"

"I thought I was ready, but I'm not," she said apologetically.

She could tell by Odin's breathing how hard he was fighting to control himself. He stared at the floor and shrugged her off when she tried to touch him.

"You shouldn't have done that, Frigga," he said somewhat angrily. "You just made it a lot harder for me to resist my desire for you. Why torture me with a taste when you had no intention of following through?"

Frigga stared at him as her own anger started to get the best of her. "Just when I think you could love me for me …" She trailed off, knowing she was not being fair or accurate. "Odin, please forgive me. I know I'm not making sense. I simply cannot seem to get control of my thoughts."

"I know what that's like," he said sympathetically, his anger fading. "I wandered in darkness for days after I lost my eye."

"I know," she whispered, dropping her eyes. "I would have been there for you, but you—"

"I was a fool who didn't know what was best for him,"

Odin interrupted her. "Frigga, I don't just need you in body. I need your presence. I need your support. I need your fire."

"There were a lot of your needs in there, Odin," Frigga pointed out. "Perhaps you should consider what I need." Seeing the confusion on his face and fearing what he would say next, she muttered, "Right now, I need some air."

She hurried out of the room, ignoring him as he called after her, "Where are you going?"

She fled from the palace, both relieved and disappointed when he did not follow. Thinking only of getting to her horse to ride out her confusion and anguish, the tears hit her before she reached the stables. Sigurna stamped her feet as Frigga sobbed through saddling and mounting her. Both Svadilfari and Vasili watched her, nickering softly as if they understood her pain.

As she rode out of the stable toward the bridge, she thought she heard a man shout. She continued on, quite certain none of the stable guards on duty had seen her. It was not until Sigurna had almost reached the wilderness that Frigga suddenly heard galloping hooves behind her. She looked over her shoulder to see if a guard had followed her after all, but the rider wore black rather than the red stable livery.

A wave of fear washed over the exposed and vulnerable queen. She had not even bothered to grab a weapon in her distress. She kicked Sigurna's sides frantically, trying to coax more speed from the horse, who was already breathing heavily. The sound of flying hooves grew louder. Knowing she would be overtaken shortly sent a rush of adrenaline through Frigga. She used the reins and her feet to signal for

Sigurna to turn and charge past the other horse, hoping the move would take the other rider by surprise. He would have too much momentum to follow immediately. If she succeeded, she could dash off to the side in the darkness and hide in the outskirts of the wilderness.

"Frigga, stop!" the other rider shouted as he tried to grab her reins.

She knew his voice just before she saw Vidar's face in a sliver of moonlight released from the shifting clouds. She immediately reined in her horse and dismounted.

"Why would you scare me like that?" she demanded angrily, keeping a firm hold on Sigurna's reins as Vidar also dismounted.

"*I* scared *you*? You nearly gave me a stroke to match Odin's!" he retorted with just as much heat in his tone. "I returned from my trip just in time to see you taking off looking like your life was over. Every worst-case scenario flew through my mind. Didn't you hear me yell when you left the stable?"

"I didn't know it was you," Frigga retorted defensively. "I couldn't see who was pursuing me or even where you came from."

"And you don't have a weapon, do you?" he demanded. When she shook her head, he sighed heavily. "If I had overtaken you, what was your plan?"

"I would have fought you hand to hand," she answered hotly.

"You would have fought bravely and been defeated quickly," Vidar insisted. "The reality is that you are not strong enough to physically fight most men. What if I had ill intentions?" He shuddered. "What if we had found your body in the morning?"

She had no idea what to say.

He continued, "This is not how a commander acts. How can we trust you to lead a group of women when you cannot manage your own emotions?"

She tried to interrupt him, but he had not finished.

"Why would you run off this late at night? And where were you going?" he demanded, not bothering to let her speak as he added, "Does Odin even know you're out here?"

As quickly as the snap of a whip, she grabbed his sword and held it to his throat. "Are you quite finished, Vidar? Who is it who cannot manage his own emotions? You were so worried about me, you didn't even see that coming, did you?"

He frowned and took his sword from her. "Well done," he conceded.

"Now, let me address your concerns," she said calmly, for she recognized he had a valid point and wanted to put his mind at ease, lest she lose his support as well. "I am not a man. And I will not command like a man. My fighters will not fight like men. We have no interest in trying to be men. But with your help, we can protect ourselves from those who would abuse us. And while we may never attain the level of warrior that you have, we can be of some help in saving lives."

"I don't disagree with you on any of those points, Frigga," Vidar informed her. Then he paused. "Those who would abuse you? What has Odin done to you?"

All of the fight drained out of her. "Nothing," she sighed. "He returned to the palace today and to our chambers tonight."

"How does he fare?" Vidar asked, stiffening slightly.

"He's doing well physically, but I've upset him," she said. "I almost … but I couldn't—"

"Don't say any more," Vidar interrupted her.

"But I didn't—"

"I understand, Frigga," Vidar cut her off. "You needn't explain yourself to me. I don't care to imagine how you kissed him or how far things went before you stopped him."

She blinked rapidly as more tears threatened to spill. "I left the palace to clear my head, Vidar. I told Odin I needed air. I couldn't love him that way while thinking of you."

The ghost of a smile crossed his face, but he shook his head. "This has to stop."

Her heart froze mid-beat. "What do you mean?"

"You know what I mean," he whispered hoarsely, avoiding her gaze.

"You're ending our relationship," she stated flatly. "And forcing me back to Odin."

"Frigga, I asked you to consider legally freeing yourself from him, but you wouldn't," he said somewhat bitterly as he met the intensity of her gaze, then dropped his eyes again.

"How could I? With everything that's at stake?" Frigga demanded, waving one arm wildly to emphasize her words. "And now, on the eve of possibly the most significant day of my life, you would dismiss me so callously? I didn't think you had such cruelty in you."

Vidar's eyes flashed. "You call me callous, toy with my heart, and question my honor. Perhaps you should reconsider who is cruel."

Frigga gasped, emotional wounds gaping open within her. She turned away from him and buried her face in her hands.

The tears did not come, only a dry anger like the desert winds that plagued the westernmost part of her homeland. And he did not comfort her like he usually did but maintained his distance. Wordlessly, she grabbed Sigurna's reins and hoisted herself onto her horse.

Frigga fixed Vidar with her gaze again and spat, "I don't know what happened to you while you were away. But tonight, you have shown me you are no different than Odin."

He lifted his chin, his eyes hardening with an icy determination as he coldly stated, "Then back to Odin you shall go."

She took off as if fleeing for her life, urging the poor horse faster and faster until tears finally flew from her face into the wind she and Sigurna made. She felt as though her heart bled within her. How could he betray her like this? He had never spoken so frigidly to her in all the years she had known him. He had promised to love her, to be her friend, to stay by her side, and to help her with her presentation to the war council. And she had trusted him implicitly. But this new behavior of his was far too close to how Odin had treated her in the past. Had she seen a glimpse of the real Vidar? She angrily brushed aside her own wrongdoing and refused to consider how she had hurt him.

But deep inside, she knew she was being unfair to him by only listening to herself without considering his perspective. As her anger ebbed into grief, she listened carefully, hoping to hear the pounding of his horse's hooves behind her, but he did not come after her, just as Odin had not.

She reached the stables in record time, then tended to her horse as she composed herself. She slipped into one of the palace guest rooms to clean herself up, feeling an acute sense of loss. When she finally returned to the royal chambers, Odin seemed to be asleep. She changed into her nightgown in the darkness and crawled into the bed.

"Frigga?" the king murmured softly.

"Yes, my king?" she answered warily.

"Where have you been?"

"I went for a ride," she told him.

"Alone?"

"Yes, alone."

"That was unwise," he scolded, propping himself up on his elbow to peer at her in the dark.

She forced a laugh. "You'll have to get used to that with this new program."

"Hmmm," he grunted, sounding less than convinced.

"Odin, you still support this, don't you?" she pressed.

"Of course. But I don't care for the idea of my queen running around outside by herself after dark," Odin contested. "It isn't safe."

"Then why didn't you follow me?" she asked quietly.

"You said you needed air, so I was respecting that." Odin paused, then sheepishly admitted, "And honestly, I didn't know you wanted me to."

"It would have been nice," she retorted softly.

"Then I've let you down yet again," he murmured. "I never seem to be able to figure out what you want."

"Don't talk that way, Odin," Frigga chided. "It makes me feel awful."

He sighed, then murmured, "You sure do smell nice. Like jasmine. After all that time with the healers, I hope I never smell lavender again."

In spite of herself, she laughed. "I washed up in one of

the guest rooms so I wouldn't wake you. It's a good thing I didn't use the lavender soap."

He groaned playfully at her teasing, then tentatively asked, "Would you permit me to simply hold you tonight?"

"Of course, husband," she responded quietly.

He slipped his arms around her. With his warmth at her back, she lay awake for quite a while, wondering where Vidar was and if she could even face him on the morrow. Finally, she allowed herself to sleep, knowing she needed her strength for her presentation.

When she awoke, Odin still slept beside her. She flipped over on her side and watched his chest rise and fall. Though just shy of Vidar in height, the king's chest was deeper and his muscle structure denser. She idly wondered which of the two was stronger. Or were they evenly matched? After a few minutes, Odin opened his good eye and smiled when he saw her watching him.

"Finally! A chance to be the first to wish the loveliest woman on Asgard a good morning," he murmured in a low, contented voice.

She leaned over and kissed him lightly on the mouth. "And a fine morning it is."

"Are you ready for this afternoon?" he asked, furrowing his brows slightly.

"I will be," she said confidently. "But there is much to do. I'm meeting with the women after breakfast to go over the final details."

"I'm so proud of you, Frigga," Odin stated. "Have I told you that?"

"No, but it's nice to hear it," she said silkily. The ache in her heart eased slightly at his words. She smiled mischievously and combed her fingers through his full black beard. "This could use a little trimming."

He sighed at the sensation. She grinned and began to massage his scalp. She had forgotten how much she used to love the soft thickness of his hair. She breathed in his familiar scent as he leaned into her touch.

"You do know how to torment a man," he groaned.

The similarity between his words and Vidar's from several nights before was too much.

She withdrew her hand and muttered, "I'll stop."

"No, don't stop," Odin pleaded.

She stared at him, unsure of what to do. He propped himself up on his elbow like he had the night before and peered at her. With just one eye, he seemed even more intense than he had been with two, especially in the morning sunlight. Despite her confusion and previous pull toward him, she felt like squirming away but feared he would start asking uncomfortable questions. As much as Vidar had hurt her, she did not want to be the cause of his downfall. With that thought hovering in her mind, she surrendered herself to Odin, merely going through the mechanics until he was satisfied.

When it was all over, he kissed her on the nose and murmured, "This is the best morning I've had in years. Thank you, Frigga."

She nodded to acknowledge him and turned her face into his chest so he would not see her conflict. When he climbed out of the bed to get ready for the day, she lay there feeling dirty and weak.

"Frigga, you'd better hurry," he prompted her.

She sighed and started her own morning preparations. When she had finished, they went down to breakfast together. She smiled at the antics of her younger sons as they competed with each other to impress their father, trying her best to keep her emotions hidden from Baldur. But to her relief, he seemed more in tune with the king. While Odin listened to his sons update him with more of their childish news, Baldur nudged Frigga with his elbow.

"I haven't felt Father's happiness like this in years, Mother," Baldur remarked quietly. "How ever did you do it?"

She blushed deeply. "Never you mind, Baldur."

He glanced at her quickly, then blushed himself. "Oh," he chuckled. "Of course."

To her relief, one of the palace guards entered to announce that Frigga's guests awaited her in the grand ballroom.

Thankful for the interruption, the queen hurried off after the guard to the elegant room, which always felt vast and empty when not filled with people. Even the gathered women seemed small as they clustered around the artwork Frigga had commissioned to give the councilmen a visual of armor and weapons for her elite group of healer warriors.

"Her Majesty, Queen Frigga of Asgard," announced the guard, moving aside to allow her to enter.

Frigga's co-conspirators clamored over each other to greet her in their fervor of excitement, then quickly drew her into their discussions. Since there had not been time for Frigga to see the dragon, they had decided to propose the use of horses until the dragon initiative could be finalized. The drawings depicted an equestrian majesty that the queen hoped would engage the imaginations of the council members.

"Could I really look like this?" breathed Eir, holding up a picture of herself dressed in battle gear.

"Why not?" Frigga laughed. "I could make you look like that now."

She used her light gift to change Eir's appearance into the fierce but feminine warrior drawn on the sheet of paper the head healer held. The other women begged for her to transform them too.

"Why don't we go to the council looking like these drawings?" gushed Lady Gladys, who had entered their number late but with just as much zeal.

"No, that would only make them think we are playing at war if we go masked in illusions," Frigga cautioned. "And I'm not strong enough to do all of you at once. I wish we'd had time to make what we've designed. But even without them, we shall emerge triumphant today!"

The other women cheered, then poured themselves into the final touches as Frigga continued to boost morale and encourage everyone with more optimism than she actually felt. But surrounded by her supporters, her inner confidence grew to match her brave words until she knew she was ready to boldly stand before the war council.

12

Frigga stood by the king at her usual place in the banquet hall as the herald announced each of the guests for the pre-meeting luncheon she had arranged. Odin winked at her once as laughter and conversation filled the hall. No one had been told the reason for the gathering except the husbands of the women presenting the proposal.

As they sat down to eat, Odin remarked, "General Vidar should have arrived by now. Have you seen him?"

"Didn't you send him on an errand, my king?" Frigga queried casually, though her heart smarted at the mention of his name.

"Yes, but he was supposed to return yesterday," Odin answered, searching the small crowd as if the general had slipped in unnoticed. "How will you fight him to show your skills if he's not here?"

"Perhaps the keeper of the gates can locate him?" she suggested.

"I don't allow Gjallar to seek out the general because of the secrecy of some of his missions," Odin whispered. "That mental block has stood for so long, he couldn't find Vidar if he tried."

Frigga pondered that information, marveling at the implicit trust Odin placed in his boyhood friend, then asked, "Do you have a substitute you would suggest?"

"There's no one else I trust to be careful with you," Odin said distractedly, still looking for the general.

Frigga sipped her goblet of sparkling water silently. After what had happened last night, she was not at all certain how the general would interact with her. She did not have to wonder long, for just a few minutes later the herald announced Vidar's arrival. The circles under his eyes suggested he had not slept, but his uniform was pressed and clean. His sword swayed with his movements as he approached the king and queen. Frigga carefully masked her face with light illusion to hide the anguish she felt in his presence, not trusting her own acting skills. Vidar had no such power, and the deadness in his eyes haunted her.

"My king, forgive my tardiness," Vidar apologized, his tone flat and void of emotion. "I was delayed."

"No matter," Odin answered graciously. "The important thing is you're finally here. I will hear your report after the council meeting."

Vidar nodded wearily.

"Vidar, you look exhausted," Odin observed. "Are you fit to compete against the queen?"

"If the queen still wishes it," Vidar replied. He glanced at Frigga and nodded politely. "Your Majesty. You look well today."

"Thank you, General," she answered, bowing her head slightly. "I hope you will not go easy on me."

He bowed, but Frigga saw just the hint of a wry smile.

"Eat while you can," Odin instructed him.

Vidar nodded, then hurried off to get himself some food. Frigga watched him go, keeping an illusion of disinterest pasted on her face. She saw him look back only once but knew he would not be able to see past her facade.

"He looks awful," Odin murmured.

"Well, perhaps you've been working him too hard, my king," Frigga suggested glibly. "He was quite worried about you when you were at the House. Couldn't that errand have waited?"

"The timing was exactly what it needed to be," Odin stated sternly, making Frigga feel he had just firmly planted her in her place. Then he unexpectedly wrinkled his brow as he glanced at her. "But I could have been kinder to him."

"I'm sure he understood, as I did," Frigga reassured him, wondering at his humble acknowledgment. "Perhaps you can make it right with him when he gives you his report."

Odin nodded thoughtfully. But rather than approach his friend, the king soon called for everyone's attention, then announced the council meeting would start in thirty minutes, beginning with a special proposal by the queen. The noblemen all exchanged looks, except for the three husbands of her closest supporters. Frigga watched Berg carefully, knowing several of the councilmen would vote as he did. He had allowed Annette to be part of the planning but had not voiced his true opinion, despite Annette's sly but unsuccessful prodding. Frigga wished she knew how he would respond, but she comforted herself with the knowledge that Bragi and Trebent were in favor of the proposal.

The minutes flew by as she tried not to wring her hands. She imagined she felt Vidar's eyes on her several times, but she ignored him. Finally, King Odin offered her his arm to escort her to the ballroom, where the council meetings were usually held to foster a sense of equality between the king and his lords. She sailed regally through the carved oaken doors, light as a feather on her husband's arm, then took her place by his side at the head chair of thirteen cushioned but sturdy seats set firmly in a wide circle on the glossy wooden floor. The twelve councilmen filed in and stood by their chairs, but Vidar stayed with his guards near the doors as the rest of the women entered.

Odin gestured for the councilmen to take their seats and for everyone else to gather around the inner circle. "Gentlemen and trusted council members, before we conduct our normal business, I present to you Queen Frigga and her guests with a proposal to better the kingdom of Asgard."

Frigga stepped into the circle to address the councilmen. "Gentlemen, have you considered the resources we waste on armed guards for the noblewomen of this kingdom, protecting them during mundane everyday tasks that present no real danger?"

The councilmen exchanged glances.

"What if all Asgardian women, even commoners, could defend themselves?" she continued. "Crimes against women would decrease, and more guards could turn their attention to jobs more fitting to their skills and interests."

The guards exchanged glances and murmured to each other excitedly at that comment. Vidar kept his eyes forward, his expression blank, almost listless.

Emboldened by the reactions of the guards, she proposed, "And that is why I would like to initiate a program to teach the women of Asgard self-defense."

The councilmen began to murmur to each other in quite different tones than Frigga had heard from the guards. Odin silenced them with one hand, then gestured for her to continue.

"I will give a series of classes for thirty to forty women at the arena. We will only charge a small fee for materials and weapons," Frigga declared. "If more express interest, I will choose from those who show the most promise. Once I begin classes for the women chosen, I will train them for one year. Any expenses exceeding fees collected will be taken from the royal treasury. After I have trained this group to match me in skill, those who desire to do so will teach classes in other regions of Asgard until every woman who wishes to learn has been taught. We will also integrate training for primary aged girls as part of their regular curriculum. It will take time to implement, but I believe staggering the changes like this will make it easier for everyone to adjust. This program will not be required but strongly encouraged. After things are moving smoothly, we would only employ guard details in circumstances of high danger or when a family feels the need, as well as for ceremonial escort here at the palace."

"Forgive my impertinence, Your Majesty, but what makes you qualified to give such training?" Lord Shronner asked. "What did you mean by matching you in skill?"

"Never mind that. I want to know why we should even spend time and resources on such a venture," interjected Lord Delling, a white-haired council member with a stern and craggy face. "Our guards have no other tasks better suited to them than protecting the noblewomen. Something like this simply is not needed."

"Perhaps it seems so now. But what of times of war? What of the fact that the common women already have no escorts to defend them?" Frigga responded calmly. "If all women learned defense, we could hold Asgard even during a time of invasion. The Vanir have prepared their women to defend their homes for centuries now."

"This is not Vanaheim," was his only reply.

Frigga resisted the urge to smirk at his rather weak response and decided to address what he had left unsaid. "I acknowledge that Vanaheim has dealt with more conflict than Asgard, but we have repelled invasion exactly because we have been prepared."

"Asgard is prepared," Lord Delling stated emphatically.

"Why only prepare the men, Lord Delling?" Frigga shot back. "Those without swords can still be slain by them. Should we do things as we have always done simply because the risk has not yet presented itself?"

Lord Delling furrowed his brows, but Lord Shronner spoke up again. "These are valid points, my queen. But I would like answers to my questions. And I echo Lord Delling's statement that guards are best suited to protect the noblewomen. What else would they do?"

"I will address that in a moment," she assured him. "But returning to your questions, Lord Shronner, I was trained to fight with a fencing sword, a dagger, and a short sword as well as with a hand-to-hand fighting style called Vanari," Frigga informed him. "I will demonstrate. General Vidar, would you join me, please?"

As Vidar obeyed, a look of excitement transformed Lord Bragi's handsome face, making him look boyish as he nudged the councilman next to him.

"The general will simulate an attack on a noblewoman, and I will show some possibilities for self-defense. General, make your move," Frigga commanded as she turned her back on him and pretended to be distracted.

When he grabbed her from behind as if to hoist her up into the air and carry her off, she bent forward from the waist, then drove her elbow into the side of his head. He released her immediately and stumbled backward, grasping where she had struck him. She pressed a hidden trigger at her waistline, releasing tiny clasps that locked her layered skirts in place. In one swift movement, she ripped them off to reveal simple riding breeches underneath a long, slightly fitted tunic that had appeared to be the bodice of her dress. Everyone in the room gasped but the king, who had known about the modifications to her dress, and the general, who advanced on her again, seemingly ready for anything now. Unaffected by how scandalized her audience sounded, she hurriedly bunched up the skirts, then flung the bulky wad of fabric at him.

She waited for Vidar to free himself, then held up her hand. "Hold your position, General." She turned to the councilmen, who either stared at her with open shock or averted their eyes completely. "Gentlemen, there is no need to avert your eyes. I understand you are not used to seeing me like this, but as you can see, I am fully dressed and the king has no qualms over my appearance."

Almost as one, the men looked to their king as the women stifled giggles behind their hands. One side of Odin's mouth twitched up slightly, but he merely nodded and gestured for her to continue.

"I appreciate your show of respect and your concern for modesty," Frigga affirmed them. "And I'm not suggesting turning our culture upside down by changing our standards of dress. These particular modifications were designed centuries ago by Vanir women so we could flee uninhibited when necessary. In a public place, I would have already fled to safety or been defended by people around me. If not, a well-placed knee to the groin would have incapacitated my attacker, but I chose not to subject the general to such agony."

"Thank you for that," Vidar muttered as he rubbed his head with a wry face.

The councilmen stifled their laughter.

"In a more remote location, I might not have anywhere to flee, which would require different strategies. And since I am now better dressed for it, I will demonstrate how I would handle being threatened by the sword," she announced.

Several councilmen watched with mouths agape as Frigga grabbed her fencing sword, a saber she had chosen from the armory for its lightweight and flexible blade as well as the bell guard curved around the handle to protect her hand. She took her stance as Vidar drew his own weapon, a beautiful foil with an ornate guard surrounding the handle and pommel, one she had secretly admired over the years.

There was no taking him by surprise this time. Underneath his smooth exterior, Frigga detected a focused determination. As she advanced on him, he parried and thrust as if he were fighting a man. Frigga was hard-pressed to hold her own against his strength, which she imagined was driven by the emotions he could not quite keep from showing in his eyes. She concentrated only on defeating him, utilizing Vanari breathing methods to maintain her composure. As he brought his sword through the air to slash at her yet again, she raised her own and drove him back slightly. With flawless Vanari technique, she whirled around to distract him, minding her footwork, then leaped into the air with a solid kick to his chest. He stumbled backward but did not fall. He ran toward her, sword raised, but she twisted her body perfectly to place herself behind him before he could adjust. Her smaller size and swiftness of foot proved to her advantage. In a flash, she knocked the foil out of his hand. Keeping her saber at the ready, she quickly drew a small dagger out of her bodice, which she held against his throat with one hand. With a swift movement of his own, he threw her off, knocking her weapons to the floor. Then he whirled around to face her, fists and jaw clenched.

"Enough!" King Odin cried, rising abruptly from his seat. "We've seen enough."

"I've certainly seen enough," Lord Delling remarked wryly. "The queen has surprising skills, but she is no match for the strength of a man. If the king had allowed this completely inappropriate match to continue, the general would have injured the queen."

Fury mixed with dismay crossed Vidar's face for a moment, but he quickly smoothed his features and waited for further instruction.

"I don't know about that," Lord Bragi piped up. "I think she could have done serious damage of her own if she were truly in danger. This is the second time I've seen the queen fight the general. She beat him the first time because he was not expecting her to do so well. And that, I believe, would be an advantage in employing a program like this for self-defense. Any foreigner who might invade would expect our women to be defenseless. And if they were to wear dresses like the queen's, our enemies would not regain their wits as quickly as Vidar did, even if they could come close to the skills and strength of our esteemed general."

Several of the other noblemen nodded in agreement as Vidar dipped his head in acknowledgment of Bragi's compliments. When Frigga thanked the general, he bowed respectfully and retrieved her discarded skirts, which he handed to her before returning to his men.

She reattached the garment, then informed Lord Bragi, "Dresses such as this would be beneficial but not imperative. And there could be times when tearing off a layer of skirts would not be conducive to a fight, as we Vanir have also found. I can teach the women how to discern the best methods for different situations, as well as how to effectively sword fight in regular dresses with these weapons, which we can more easily conceal."

As she spoke, she passed out the artwork showing several of the weapons she wanted to have made for the women. The shorter, lighter blades of deceptively strong metal combined with delicate but practical guards would enable the fairer sex to carry the swords without growing tired but still effectively wield them in a fight. The noblemen looked over each drawing as Frigga watched carefully to gauge their reactions. Several of the guards strained to see the papers. Their interest reminded Frigga to address the question of what the guards would do without the mundane task of accompanying noblewomen everywhere.

"Now, gentlemen, as you look over the swords, do remember that Lord Delling and Lord Shronner stated there are no tasks better suited to a guard than protecting a noblewoman," Frigga began. "And while there are guards who believe the same, there are those who would welcome other opportunities. I have interviewed several of them. They listed such aspirations as joining General Vidar's Valiants, serving on the war council, training foot soldiers, and even serving as spies or ambassadors to other realms."

Vidar looked at his men in surprise as several of them straightened their shoulders and stood taller at the queen's words.

A new council member Frigga did not know spoke up. "Is this really something for the war council to vote on when it will not be required? Shouldn't the king decide, as he usually does for social programs?"

"This is no mere social program, Lord Asger. We are discussing defense and distribution of weapons. The support of the war council is absolutely necessary," Odin replied. "Does anyone else have anything to ask the queen?"

"Wouldn't arming our women allow for said weapons to be used against them?" Lord Gunnar asked, his brow wrinkling with genuine concern.

"The men are already armed, Lord Gunnar," Frigga reminded him. "And a man who intends harm will use his weapons. If he knows a woman is armed, he will think twice about bothering her. And if he does not know, as Lord Bragi pointed out, then she has the element of surprise."

Lord Gunnar nodded thoughtfully, avoiding the intense gaze of his father, none other than Lord Delling.

Clearly irritated by this, the older nobleman spouted, "I would advise the council against this. I fear it will cause more harm than good. Women will lose respect for their husbands and forget their rightful place."

"To what place do you refer, Lord Delling?" Frigga asked quietly.

"Motherhood and keeping the home, of course," responded the councilman.

Frigga chuckled, though her eyes flashed dangerously at this assertion. "My lord, I believe you know quite well that not all Asgardian women are mothers. And many of them have owned property and practiced trades for centuries whether they have families or not. I'd also like to point out that Vanir women have not ceased to keep their homes nor do they disrespect their husbands. It has taken nothing from their womanhood to know how to defend themselves, nor has it threatened the manhood of any man but those who would harm said women. Respect should be shown toward men and women alike. And continuing to put women in the position of being unable to defend themselves will certainly not foster respect but resentment."

Lord Delling snorted in complete disregard for her words. Frigga glanced over at the other women, who all bore looks of restrained contempt and anger on their faces.

The white-haired nobleman followed her gaze and addressed the women. "Next, you'll be wanting seats on the war council!"

"As a matter of fact, we just might," Lady Ithunna huffed indignantly. "War affects us just as much as you. When the men go off to battle, who runs things here? You act as if we haven't got any sense, Lord Delling!"

Frigga wanted to hug her but settled for her inward glee over the noblewoman's feisty response. Lord Bragi winked at his wife and nodded his approval, making her blush.

Lord Delling blinked at her words, then sputtered, "This is what happens when the king takes a foreign wife with strange customs."

Odin fixed the man with the intensity of his single eye and said menacingly, "I would caution you not to dishonor my queen, Lord Delling."

"Would you allow a woman to sit on your council, my king?" the older man demanded.

"Perhaps. I might appoint one of them to replace you," Odin responded, his one eye twinkling with amusement at his own words. When Delling began to sputter again, Odin reassured him, "Relax, Delling. We are not discussing new council members at the moment. But do manage your words with more care."

"Of course, Your Majesty," Delling sighed, staring at the gnarled knuckles on his right hand before lifting his eyes to meet Odin's expectant gaze. "I mean no disrespect to any woman, including the queen."

The king nodded with satisfaction, then announced, "The queen has another proposal to present to the council, after which we will vote."

Frigga smiled warmly at Odin for his defense of her, then passed out the artwork depicting her group of healer warriors. She saw several eyebrows go up at the sight of the images.

"What is this?" Lord Berg demanded, waving the paper she had handed him. "Teaching our women self-defense is one thing, but these look like women going to war as a man does."

"Only for the express purpose of saving Asgardian lives," Frigga answered. "Which one of you has the picture of the healer Eir?"

"Is this it?" Lord Trebent asked as he held it up.

She peered at it from where she stood, then nodded. "Please pass that around, Lord Trebent, so the other councilmen can look. Our second program is developing an elite group of warrior healers. I'd like Eir to join me so she can explain why this initiative is necessary."

Frigga gestured for Eir to come forward to speak her part. The healer did so with quiet confidence. Every man in that room held her in high respect, for she had helped many people in her role as the head healer. And no one doubted her grit.

"My good councilmen, if my support of the queen surprises you, I would ask you to consider my story," Eir began. "I am the daughter of a common foot soldier who served Asgard with his life. After he died in battle, my mother opened her own business supplying fine jewelry to the noblewomen. She was robbed and murdered near the end of King Borr's reign. Though her killer was captured and brought to justice, if the queen's first program had been available to her, she would likely be here with me today. And this second program we are now discussing might have saved my father as well. If you vote in favor today, there could be an Asgardian child living right now, maybe a little girl just like me, who will not lose her parents as I did."

Lord Delling squirmed in his seat slightly as heavy silence blanketed the room.

"I understand it is difficult to be reminded of how Asgardians fared under King Borr. We must remember that though he inherited quite a mess from his father, he did his best to rule in fairness," Eir continued. "And King Odin has done even more to improve Asgard. Contrary to Lord Delling's words, the king's marriage to the princess of Vanaheim, now our beloved queen, has been of great benefit to Asgard, especially to the healers."

Frigga blushed as she felt all eyes upon her. She met Vidar's gaze for a moment, then turned her attention to the growing discomfort of several council members, including Lord Delling.

"Queen Frigga brought her knowledge of herbs and Vanir healing techniques with her and willingly shared them with me and my predecessor," Eir informed them. "This knowledge has enhanced our treatments for soldiers injured in battle and saved other Asgardian lives. And this initiative to teach healers to fight will save even more. We have lost soldiers for no other reason than because we could not get to them in time. We healers have discussed the importance of getting the wounded to us as quickly as possible, but not one of us has ever considered being present on the battlefield itself."

"Because it's ludicrous and unnecessary!" one of the councilmen burst out, a fair-haired man slightly younger than the king. Frigga tried to remember his name as he continued, "We already move the wounded to the House of the Healers through the Bifröst. If we need a faster solution, why not build temporary portals from the area of conflict directly to the House of the Healers?"

"Bifröst travel is not always safe for injured soldiers, Lord Harald. I am sure you've felt the sensation of the energy draw," Eir responded firmly. When he nodded thoughtfully, she continued, "If too much energy is drawn, the result is quite painful, which any formerly wounded soldier can confirm. And since quite a bit of energy is needed to keep a severely injured soldier alive, expending it could kill him. Portals take too long to build anyway, especially at the size that would be needed. It's an impractical security risk at best."

Frigga suddenly noticed how intently Vidar was listening. She made a mental note to ask him why, wondering if his portal building experience had sparked an idea. Then she remembered he no longer wanted to continue their relationship. She felt a squeezing sensation in her chest but stuffed it down and returned her attention to the discussion.

"If we were present on the battlefield, we could stabilize seriously wounded soldiers to give them the energy needed for Bifröst travel," Eir continued. "We cannot possibly eliminate all casualties, but imagine the good we could do!"

"There's wisdom in your words, Eir," Lord Berg declared. "Most of you know my father's brother died on Svartalfheim from battle wounds that could have been healed here. Not only do I support this initiative, I think the healers should train some of our soldiers in more than just basic wound care. It goes both ways."

"An excellent suggestion, Lord Berg," Eir responded. "I cannot understand why no one has suggested any of this before. Perhaps Asgard's nobility has a tendency to get stuck in their ways."

She looked at Lord Delling and the two oldest councilmen near him when she said this. Frigga stifled a laugh, then looked over at the other men as she imagined the vote.

Odin in favor, Bragi in favor, Trebent in favor. Berg in favor, which should sway both Asger and Harald. Delling against, Gunnar possibly against, if only to please his father, she thought to herself. She glanced at the men Eir had included in her subtle barb toward Delling. *Nimski and Magnus will vote against. Chet, Shronner, and Einar could go either way.*

"How do you propose to train the healers, Your Majesty?" Lord Gunnar spoke up.

"Alongside the other women, at first," Frigga answered. "The healers in the initiative will also receive specialized battle training, including horseback maneuvers and psychological preparation."

"From whom?" Lord Einar interjected, leaning forward with great interest.

"From me," Vidar said firmly when Frigga hesitated. When she smiled gratefully at him, he nodded and continued, "I'll prepare a series of the same exercises used to train my Valiants, but I'll work with the women separately since modifications will be required."

"Well, we all know the healers have strong stomachs," quipped Lord Chet. "I'd be against any other group of women doing this, but I do believe the healers could pull it off."

"Male healers will not be prohibited from joining, Lord Chet," Frigga corrected him.

"I don't expect any will care to join," Eir interjected. "Most of them have no desire to face battle. And we will still need healers here to receive the wounded as they are brought to the House."

"Shall we take the vote?" Odin suggested. "Does anyone feel the need to discuss either proposal further?"

"I've been ready to vote," announced Lord Asger impatiently. "Let's move on with it."

Most of the other councilmen nodded their agreement. Frigga took a deep breath. Judging by the last few questions, she felt success within her grasp. But the excitement within her came with a deep sense of responsibility.

"As in everything we decide here, I expect you to vote according to your conscience," Odin reminded them. "I am in favor of both, but that does not mean punitive action will be taken against anyone who votes against. I started this war council under my father, with his permission, to bring an end to monarchs who made unilateral decisions regarding war. Please keep this in mind as you consider your stance on the matter."

"My king, may I add a final word?" Frigga spoke up. When Odin nodded, she looked each councilman in the eye as she said, "The past is the past, gentlemen. Let us learn from it and think to the future as your king has always done."

Odin suppressed a smile at her praise. "Lord Berg?"

"In favor," Berg responded firmly.

"As am I," Bragi affirmed.

"Against," Nimski voted, just as Frigga had expected.

"In favor," Delling stated. When she stared at him in shock, the older man added, "Although with a condition. I would like to request a trial period of five years, after which we will evaluate each program to see if it has met expectations."

"Even I could agree to that," Magnus spoke up. "I had

planned to vote against, but this suggestion seems wise. King Odin, shall we amend the proposals in this way?"

Odin looked at Frigga, who nodded eagerly, confident she could easily prove herself within five years. "Consider the proposal amended," the king declared.

"Then I vote in favor," Magnus agreed.

To Frigga's delight, all the other councilmen followed suit.

"Nimski, do you wish to say something?" Odin prompted when the old man opened his mouth, then clamped it shut.

"Your Majesty, I foresee many problems with these ventures," Nimski said slowly. "However, my vote was cast before the proposals were amended. If this is indeed the will of the council, I will not impede it. I must admit I am curious to see where we stand in five years."

"Thank you, Nimski," Odin said congenially. "The proposals pass for a period of five years, after which we will discuss any progress made."

Frigga restrained herself from jumping in triumph and calmly thanked the councilmen for their support. As Odin directed the meeting to the next thing on his agenda, she gathered her drawings and lead the women to the banquet hall, where they all erupted with the squeals and rounds of congratulations they had kept carefully controlled until that moment.

"I take it things went well?" asked an amused, deep voice from a corner of the hall, causing all the women to jump in surprise.

"Baldur!" Frigga exclaimed.

He pushed himself off the wall, where he had been leaning

unnoticed, and approached the group. "Does Asgard have an elite band of warrior healers?"

"Not quite," Frigga said with a laugh. "We have a lot of work to do. But both proposals passed, almost unanimously."

She filled Baldur in, delighted when everyone laughed at her reenactment and imitations of the councilmen.

"You still need a name for your Idisi, Mother," Baldur reminded her. "And I think I have the perfect one."

"Let's hear it!" Eir prompted.

"Valkyries," Baldur said triumphantly. "It means *chooser of the slain* in one of the Midgardian languages."

"How do you know that?" Frigga queried, intrigued and impressed.

"I read about it," Baldur said with a shrug. "And since they'll be training a lot like Valiants, it fits quite well."

"Valiants and Valkyries," Frigga murmured. "I like it!"

"So do I," Eir agreed.

The other women nodded eagerly in approval of the name.

"Will you be a Valkyrie?" Annette asked the queen.

"Of course," Frigga answered in surprise.

"Surely not!" objected Lady Gladys. "You are the queen! Odin will not allow you to go traipsing about on the battle-field."

Frigga looked sharply at the younger noblewoman. "Why, Lady Gladys, how could I not lead by example?"

"Lady Gladys is right," Ithunna said softly. "We cannot risk the queen. Even Odin does not go to battle except in dire circumstances."

Eir placed a gentle hand on the queen's arm. "My queen,

there is no battle in sight yet. You train as you see fit. Then you will be prepared when the time comes. We have much to do and plenty of time to work out the details."

Frigga examined the faces of each of the women as dismay tickled at the back of her mind. What if she had to stay home while the other Valkyries went to war? Would she have a chance to prove herself? Or would her life continue as it had before the general befriended her?

As if her thoughts had made him materialize, Vidar appeared at the banquet hall doors. "Your Majesty, the king has summoned you."

Baldur shooed her in that direction, then turned to the women. "Well, ladies, why don't I show you what my mother taught me years ago while you wait for your husbands to collect you?"

"I have no husband," Eir reminded Baldur with a laugh.

Frigga joined the general at the doors. "Is the king finished with the council, General?" she asked, keeping her tone formal.

"Please come with me," he responded in an equally stiff tone.

She followed slightly behind him, not beside him as she usually did. They did not speak to each other, but she felt the squeezing sensation in her chest again. Vidar led her to Odin's least used office, a small room near the banquet hall.

"Wait here," he instructed her. "The king will join you soon."

Frigga wanted to call after him as he turned on his heel and strode out of the office. But she hesitated a fraction of a second too long. He had shut the door firmly behind him without so much as a glance in her direction.

13

Frigga fought back tears as she sat down at the carved oak desk and ran her fingers along the smooth wood. Something about its workmanship reminded her of the furniture in Vidar's room. Would everything whisper to her of the forbidden love she had lost?

She wandered around the little used office for a while, inspecting the bookshelf and the maps on the wall as she wondered why Odin kept her waiting there. She went to the window and peered out at the palace grounds. Suddenly, she spotted a small wooden figurine carved in the shape of a howling wolf, tucked discreetly in the corner of the window.

Did Vidar leave this here? she thought as she picked it up.

When she ran her fingers over it, she felt a tiny indentation around its nose, which she guessed might be a button. Intrigued, she grabbed a glass dip pen from the well on the desk and used the tip to press the nose. A hidden compartment popped into her hand from the base of the figurine, revealing a piece of paper curled within the glass walls of the cylinder. She used the pen to slide it out and unrolled it, her heart pounding. In a bold, sweeping hand were written the words

Forgive me, my queen.

Frigga mustered all of her strength to stem the tears stinging the corners of her eyes. Hearing voices outside the door, she hurriedly reassembled the figurine and thrust it into the hidden pocket of her dress just as King Odin and General Vidar entered the room together, deep in conversation.

"Most suitors don't wait so long to make their interest known," the king said with a sympathetic chuckle.

Frigga's ears perked up immediately. She arranged her face in a pleased smile, though inwardly her heart ached as she cheerily asked, "Have you finally found someone to share your life with, General?"

Vidar glanced at the window. His eyes widened slightly as he looked to the queen again. She nodded imperceptibly to communicate she had found the wolf and received his message.

"Sadly, no," Odin answered for the general. "Vidar spoke with Lord Gunnar about courting his daughter just now, but apparently Lord Nimski's grandson beat him to it. They plan to wed in the spring. I was encouraging him to act quickly the next time a woman catches his eye."

Frigga shoved down the jealousy and hurt threatening to overwhelm her. "How awful," she said soothingly. "That would have been a smart match too. But there are plenty of young and beautiful noblewomen around, General. I'm certain you'll find the right one soon."

"The queen's compassion suits her well," Vidar responded. "But I do not recover from such things as quickly as some."

The ache in Frigga's heart smote her again at his hidden barb, but she merely nodded graciously, refusing to give him the satisfaction of a reaction. "Of course. Any loss takes time to grieve."

Odin patted the general's shoulder. "You really should get some sleep, Vidar. Exhaustion makes everything worse."

"I'll take my leave then, if it pleases the king and queen," Vidar said quietly.

"Very well. I expect to see you at the banquet this evening, General," the king stated. "We have much to celebrate."

"As you wish, my king," Vidar replied.

He bowed to the queen, then clapped his fist against his chest twice in a salute to the king.

"Why did you keep me waiting in here, Odin?" Frigga asked after the general left, forcing her heartache to the back of her mind. "I have a lot to do before this evening."

"Didn't Vidar tell you?" Odin asked in surprise.

"He just told me to wait here," she answered. "Was he supposed to say something else? He isn't acting like himself."

"Poor Vidar," Odin sighed. "He seems quite devastated. I didn't even know he'd taken a fancy to the girl. You know, I've quite forgotten her name. There are too many of the nobility to remember."

"I don't remember her name either, only her face and her family," Frigga commented casually. "The general did seem quite taken with her at the last banquet."

"Oh, is *that* why you were watching the general?" Odin remarked with sudden realization. "I should have known. Well, Frigga the Matchmaker, it would seem you failed the poor fellow."

"It isn't my fault he waited too long," Frigga remarked indignantly, though she knew it was. *So much for his declarations that he would have no other woman but me,* she told herself silently. Aloud, she asked, "She must be a fickle thing to accept another suitor and agree to marry him in a matter of weeks. I wonder if she'll be there this evening."

"Probably, and no doubt with her new betrothed," Odin replied with a shrug. "Vidar has requested a transfer to the northern borders over this mess, but I simply cannot spare him. He'll have to move past it."

Frigga suddenly remembered when Vidar had suggested a transfer so they would not have to see each other anymore. "After he agreed to help with my Valkyries?" she spouted indignantly, hiding her dismay that he would take such action.

"Your what?" Odin said in confusion.

"Valkyries," she repeated. "That's what I'm calling my warrior healers." She explained the meaning, finishing with, "Baldur suggested it."

"It fits," Odin agreed. "But you needn't worry. I'm not sending Vidar anywhere."

Frigga smiled weakly as she desperately fought her emotions. "I'm not worried. I just don't understand. Why in the nine did he think a transfer was the right course? It isn't like him to break his word."

"He's not thinking clearly," Odin mused. "I hope some rest snaps him out of it. But enough about him. How do you like your new headquarters?"

"My new ..." her voice trailed off as his words registered. "Odin, you're giving me my own office?"

He grinned widely. "I thought you might be able to use the space. Now I'm glad Vidar didn't tell you. It's better seeing your reaction."

Overwhelmed with delight, Frigga rushed to Odin and hugged him impulsively. "Thank you, my king," she said happily. "And I can rearrange everything however I wish?"

"Just don't paint the walls pink," he responded, smiling down at her as the barely noticeable wrinkles around his good eye deepened.

She laughed, then noticed how weary he looked. "Odin, I think you need some sleep too."

"I'm fine," he began to protest. But when she crossed her arms and raised an eyebrow, he sighed. "I suppose I should rest for a few hours. Will you join me?"

"I wish I could, husband, but I need to check in with the cook and give some last-minute instructions to the maids and ..." Frigga trailed off as she saw disappointment flash across his face. "On second thought, I can spare a little time."

Odin grinned boyishly, then offered her his arm to return to their chambers. When they arrived, he eased into their bed. She lay down beside him and stroked his hair until he fell asleep. Then she kissed his forehead and left the room to complete the rest of her tasks for the banquet. Her energy levels were surprisingly high, considering all of the emotional trauma and sleep loss she had sustained. After she was certain the palace staff needed her no longer, she went back to the royal suite, but the king was still fast asleep. Her thoughts turned to the general as she fingered the wooden wolf statue in her dress pocket.

She went back to her new office and sat down at the desk. She released the hidden compartment and reread the note. Why did he seek her forgiveness? For how their relationship had passed appropriate boundaries? For his harsh words outside the palace the previous night? For pursuing Lord Gunnar's daughter? Her face twisted with pain and jealousy when she thought of how Vidar had spoken so animatedly with the girl at the last banquet. How was it she could reconcile with Odin, even show him love, but still feel such depth of anguish over losing Vidar? She had not enjoyed her forced time with Odin that morning, but his kindness to her recently made her think she could give him another chance. Should she pretend her feelings for the general had died until they finally vanished? The thought caused her chest to tighten again. How could she go through day after day, motion after motion, without his friendship or his love? What must she do to be free of this pain? When she feared her treacherous heart might drive her thoughts into insanity, she stood abruptly. The movement caused the small paper to float to the floor face down. She grabbed it in surprise, for Vidar had written something on the back.

She formed the words with her mouth, just below a whisper. "Come when you can."

Her heart leaped into her throat. He wanted to see her!

She reassembled the wolf figurine again and thrust it back into her dress pocket. How long had he been waiting for her? She cast an invisibility illusion over herself and hastened to Laufey's old room as fast as she could go. The door was locked, but she always kept the key with her. She eased the door open and slipped inside, muffling the sound of her movements. The general lay fast asleep on the bed. So changed were her thoughts that she followed her first impulse, disregarding any thought of the king, and climbed into the bed, daring to cuddle up next to Vidar.

He sighed in his sleep at her nearness, then opened his eyes. "Just a dream," he muttered as his eyes drifted shut again.

"Then let's never wake up," she murmured back as she slipped her arms around him.

He returned her embrace. Suddenly, he sat up and shifted away from her, frantically rubbing his sleep-laden eyes as he gasped, "This is real!"

"Yes, it's real," she answered in sudden confusion as she also sat up. Had she misunderstood his intentions and set herself up for more rejection? "You asked me to come, so I came."

"I was planning to say goodbye," he told her ruefully. "But Odin refused to grant me a transfer."

"I know. He told me," she replied. "Why are you here then?"

"I knew you got my message, so I wanted to be here when you came," he answered. "Plus, I owe you an explanation."

"Perhaps you'd care to start with Lord Gunnar's daughter?" she huffed, crossing her arms across her chest.

"Solveya?" He gazed at her with a cunning glint in his eyes. "Were you jealous, my queen?"

"Yes," she stated flatly, though she was thrilled to hear him address her in his usual way. "Was that your plan? To torment me? To show me how you've suffered?"

He shook his head. "My plan was to remove myself. Pretending to be heartbroken over Solveya was my alibi—my reason to leave this place."

"And what if she had accepted your suit?" Frigga asked dryly.

"I knew she wouldn't." He grinned at his own cleverness. "She's been secretly seeing Nimski's grandson for almost three years now."

"How did you know that?" Frigga gasped.

"Lord Flit is a colonel in the Seventh Corps. I overheard him talking to one of my Valiants about her while we were on Muspelheim," Vidar informed her. "Despite how well he's done for himself, he couldn't quite muster the gumption to speak with her father. When Solveya flirted with me at the last banquet, I understood her true intentions."

Frigga smirked with realization. "To spur her secret suitor toward some action?"

"Yes," he affirmed with a quiet laugh. "I have no doubt she'd be quite embarrassed if she knew I saw right through her. I played along, thinking it would be good for the young man to think he had some competition. I guess it worked. When I spoke with Lord Gunnar today, he told me Lord Flit approached him the very next day. They were going to announce it around the time of the king's illness, but they decided to wait. It fit into my plans better than I'd hoped, until Odin ruined everything."

"How long have you been planning this?" she asked quietly.

He dropped his eyes. "Only since our argument last night. I went back to Midgard and wandered around until I came up with it."

"Argument?" Frigga repeated indignantly, her anger returning as she remembered his words. "That was no mere argument. You ended our relationship. Harshly!" She shook her head suddenly. "Why am I even here?"

"Why are you here?" he asked softly, refusing to look at her.

"You asked me to come. You asked me to forgive you," Frigga reminded him. When he looked up at her, she dropped her eyes this time. "I've been utterly heartbroken. And I hoped—"

When he stopped her with one hand on her knee, she thought she saw the trace of a relieved smile, but he merely said, "I do hope you'll forgive me for hurting you, my queen. I honestly didn't anticipate Odin refusing my request."

"Well, of course he refused! Odin is right. You're not thinking clearly," Frigga fumed. "I cannot believe you decided the best course was to leave. You promised in front of the entire council to help train my Valkyries—"

"Choosers of the slain?" Vidar interrupted with a delighted grin. "What a clever name."

"It was Baldur's idea," she informed him. "You must read the same books. But don't change the subject, Vidar! What were you thinking?"

"Vale would have taken over the Valiants and trained your Valkyries," Vidar muttered.

"Vale is nowhere near your skill level," Frigga pointed out. "Did you even ask him?"

"Not yet, and it doesn't matter anyway," Vidar blurted out, rising to his feet. "Odin told me to face my heartache like a man." He snorted derisively. "If he knew it's you that I … and the *hypocrisy* of that statement coming from him …"

He trailed off, then turned to face her where she still sat on the bed. "What am I supposed to do, Frigga?" He sat beside her and grabbed her upper arms so quickly, she flinched. He relaxed his hold slightly as he pleaded, "Tell me what to do. What do you want me to do?"

"What happened to you on Midgard?" she asked quietly. "You have not been yourself since you returned."

"It has nothing to do with Midgard. I thought … I thought I could handle it," he sighed.

"Handle what?" she prodded.

He groaned and dropped his head into his hands. "I've made everything worse, haven't I?"

Frigga reached over and grabbed one of his hands. "Vidar, please … tell me what's bothering you."

"Am I really like Odin?" he asked her pitifully, looking at her with such agony, she felt his pain scorch her soul.

"Yes, you are very much like Odin," she answered honestly. "In all the best ways."

"Then why did you say it like an insult last night?"

"Why did you say what you said?" She looked down at their hands and intertwined her fingers with his.

"I've tortured myself over what I said," he murmured as he reached up one hand to caress her face. She closed her eyes and leaned into his touch as he continued, "I was angry and hurt. I thought if I ended things that way—harshly, as you put it—you would move on with your life. With Odin. And I would go off quietly somewhere and drown my pain somehow."

"So you tried to remove the dagger," she said, remembering their conversation the night they rode to the stream by the weeping willows.

"Yes, and I'm bleeding to death," he said sorrowfully. "It's one thing to leave this place and never see you again. It's quite another to face you every day, to see you with him, to imagine …"

When he trailed off again and looked away, she asked softly, "Do you understand why I cannot leave him?"

"Yes," he whispered as his gaze flitted to her mouth. He cupped her chin tenderly with his free hand, stroking her cheek with one thumb. "I don't like it, but I do understand. I see all the good you're doing for our people." He took a deep breath and continued, "When I first befriended you, I had loved you in silence from a distance for a long time already, but I kept no hope for myself nor did I dare to have the thoughts I have now."

"When did you first love me?" Frigga interjected. "You've never told me."

He smiled sheepishly. "I went with Odin to Vanaheim for the nobles' meeting to initiate the alliance."

"The day I met Odin?" Frigga gasped.

"Yes," he affirmed. "I wasn't nobility, so I stayed at the back of the room and watched. I spotted you long before he did. But I thought Lady Freya was the princess and you were her handmaiden."

"You saw Lady Freya?" Frigga asked with surprise, frowning slightly. "But you gave me the impression you had never met her when we talked about all the men who pined after her."

"I merely said I'd read some of the stories. I haven't met her. But yes, I have seen her more than once. And I never did see what all the fuss was about," he clarified.

"And you thought I was a handmaiden?" Frigga could not help but snicker at the thought.

"Her dress and jewels were far more elaborate than yours," he defended himself. "But you needed no ornamentation. I couldn't take my eyes off you."

"I never saw you," Frigga said with wonder. "Even in my memories, you simply are not there. Perhaps things would have been different if I had noticed you then."

"I doubt it. At the time, I would not have been permitted to marry above my rank," he reminded her. "By the time I had figured out my mistake, it was clear to me Odin was smitten with you. I excused myself and spent the rest of the trip in the stables with the other guards. Of course, I never told anyone out of embarrassment."

"So that's when you fell in love with me?" she asked, feeling slightly confused.

"It isn't quite that simple," Vidar admitted. "I was definitely attracted to you. But when Odin confided in me that the two of you had started courting in secret, I found brief happiness with another. After Borr's death, Odin told me what happened between him and Athena. The girl I was seeing had just ended our relationship, which made me far more harsh with him than I needed to be."

"Why did she end it?" Frigga asked, not wanting to hear another word about Athena.

"I wasn't ready for marriage, so she found someone who was," Vidar explained with a shrug.

"Do you miss her?"

He smiled wryly. "I haven't thought about her for years."

"What did you say to Odin?" Frigga asked.

"It's not really suitable for a lady's ears," Vidar sighed. "He asked me if he should marry you despite what he had done. And I told him he'd be a fool to let you get away from him … among other things."

"You said that?" she asked softly, squeezing his hand.

"To my great regret," he admitted.

"But why?" she asked. "You said it wouldn't have mattered."

"If Odin hadn't married you, you would have been spared all of the pain he caused you," he replied.

"But you might never have seen me again," she reminded him.

"True," Vidar acknowledged. He tightened his grip on her hand. "When you arrived on Asgard, I was not prepared for the effect you had on me the first time to increase tenfold."

Frigga closed her eyes and searched for the moment she had officially met Vidar.

"And this is Major Vidar," a younger, more carefree Odin stated as he gestured toward the slightly taller, decorated officer who stood at attention with his men.

Frigga stared curiously at the handsome young man, who briefly met her gaze before nodding and bowing as expected.

"We are honored to serve our new queen," Vidar said kindly, keeping his eyes straight ahead.

"I am honored to be served by such fine soldiers," she answered gladly, then turned her attention back to her betrothed.

"Don't let that perfect protocol fool you," Odin informed her as they walked away. "He's my best friend in all the nine realms. No one knows me better." He paused, his fierce gray eyes brimming over with love for his bride-to-be. "Except maybe you."

She sighed happily, then clutched his bicep as she looked back at the soldier, surprised to catch him staring right at her. He turned his head away so quickly, she was certain she had imagined it.

"Were you in love with me then?" Frigga asked shyly as she eased away from the memory, not wanting to remember any more of her wedding day.

"If I was, I didn't know it," Vidar sighed, as if he had just examined his own memory. "I've always thought you beautiful, but I knew you belonged to my best friend. Still, you did stir something within me. That wedding was not easy for me, but swearing fealty to you as my queen was as natural as breathing. After that, I stayed in the background and did my duty. I tried to ignore my physical attraction to you, but the more I learned about you, the harder it was to fight falling for you. No other woman compared to your grace, your kindness, and your character."

"And I was completely oblivious," Frigga breathed.

Since Odin rarely complimented anything but her looks, her heart lapped up his words like a thirsty animal. When Vidar spoke to her like that, she wanted nothing more than to fling herself into his arms.

Vidar shrugged again. "I learned to hide my feelings over the years. When I saw your unhappiness that day in the library, I could no longer stand by and do nothing. But over time, I sensed you felt something for me too."

"Of course you did," Frigga teased. "But when did you figure out that I was falling for you?"

"I was afraid to believe it at first, so I'm not entirely certain. But the day I left for Muspelheim, you gave me hope … boldness … I should not have come to you that first night we met in secret, but I just could not stay away. I wanted to love you in every way I'd imagined while I was away, so I pushed out every warning in my mind." He glanced at her as he said this, then looked down again. "I was both disappointed and relieved when we didn't even kiss that night."

"I was too," she whispered. "I had planned to give you everything, but I couldn't go through with it."

"I know," Vidar admitted. "For so long, I've made myself believe your happiness was all that mattered. But I seem to have afflicted you with the same deep misery that has overtaken me. That's why I decided to leave."

"The dagger in your heart also lies in mine," she told him. "We are both pierced through and bound to each other. When you tried to remove the dagger, I bled as well."

"Is Odin your surgeon?" Vidar asked as he stared at the floor.

"If he is, he's a clumsy one," she scoffed, remembering their time together that morning.

Vidar stiffened. "You went through with it, didn't you?"

"I made myself," she whispered, wondering why she suddenly felt so ashamed.

Vidar dropped her hand as if she were a bee that had stung him. "When?"

"This morning. I had to keep him from asking questions. I ran out of reasons to keep him at bay," she defended herself. "You yourself said I should reunite with him."

He stood and paced the room. "What else did you expect, you fool?" he berated himself aloud. "You practically forced her into it!"

Frigga sat there on the bed as tears threatened to submerge her once again. "You must hate me now. I would hate me if I were you."

"You would hate me if I told you I had lain with another woman?" he asked, whirling around to meet her eyes.

"No," she sighed. "But I would be hurt, angry, and jealous even though I have no right to be."

"That's exactly how I feel right now," he told her. "Despite all my words to the contrary, I was foolish enough to think you wouldn't do it because you love me. But you love him too. I see now how truly asinine I've been. What good is my gift if I couldn't see this for what it is?"

"Vidar, it's not like I enjoyed it," she choked out. "I would rather it be with you."

He suddenly knelt before her and took her hands. "Then let it be with me," he begged, his voice desperate with longing. His eyes widened at his own words, and he shook his head. "What am I saying? Frigga, we've lingered here far too long. I have no idea what time it is."

"Neither do I," she said in dismay.

"Stay here," he instructed her. "I'll be right back."

He vanished, then reappeared. "It's almost six. The banquet starts at seven, doesn't it?"

"Yes, and the last time anyone saw me was when I went to my new office," Frigga said. "I'm going to have to pretend I fell asleep in there."

"We'd better go," Vidar urged her.

"Wait." She placed one hand on his arm before he could vanish again. "Where do things stand between us?"

"I don't have any real answers, but I love you as much as I ever did," he responded, kissing her on the cheek. "Do you think you could get away later tonight so we can talk again?"

"I'll try," she promised. "But Odin will not be tired if he's been asleep all this time."

"Has Bragi briefed him on everything since he's been back?"

"No, he hasn't," Frigga answered. She reached out one hand to feel his trim beard, briefly comparing it to Odin's full one. Filled with relief to have Vidar back, she murmured, "I'll see what I can do, my love."

"You've never called me that before," Vidar said softly as he placed his hand over hers and pulled it to his mouth to kiss her palm. "Somehow, someday, I'm going to find a way for us."

She took one last look at him, then cloaked herself with invisibility and hurried back to her new office. She carefully avoided bumping into any palace staff bustling around in the hallway. She slipped inside the small room she could now call her own, then pulled herself together and walked into the banquet hall. She praised the staff for their work, then rushed to the royal chambers.

Odin stepped out of the bathroom, freshly washed and dressed in his royal robes. "Oh, there you are, Frigga!"

"Why, Odin, you look splendid!" she exclaimed, taking in the rich red, embroidered fabric and cream-colored fur of his mantle, which complemented his red tunic and brown trousers.

"Thank you," he said distractedly as he adjusted the gold circlet perched on his black hair. "Why aren't you ready yet? I thought you had already gone down."

"I must have dozed off in my new office," she lied, finding it strange how easily it slipped out. "I just checked on things in the banquet hall. Everything is ready."

"Except you," he pointed out. "Hurry now!"

"Of course, my king," she mumbled. "I'll meet you in the hallway outside the banquet hall so we can go in together."

"Very well," he said. "I have business to discuss with Bragi before the banquet."

She nodded, then sighed when he left. She was quite familiar with this distracted mannerism of his. He had turned his focus back to being the king of Asgard. She marveled at her hurt feelings for as much as she did not want to be caught in her affair with Vidar, she did not like how oblivious Odin seemed to be to what was happening to his wife. How was it he had fallen back to taking her for granted within twenty-four hours of returning to the palace?

She had just selected a dress when the door swung open. She whirled around to see Odin step back into the room.

"I decided to come back for you," he informed her.

"What about Bragi?" she asked, pleased by this new development.

"I'll talk with him later," he said, his good eye gleaming with a look she recognized.

"Are you going to watch me get dressed?" she asked, pretending to be scandalized.

"Am I not allowed?" he teased back. "It's nothing I haven't seen. And I never tire of it."

"We have guests, my king," she replied flirtatiously as she undressed, noting the appreciation and admiration on his face.

"There's always something getting in the way, isn't there, my queen?" Odin shot back playfully.

She laughed, then grew serious. "We cannot change who we are, Odin. We'll just have to figure out how to invest time in our relationship around the responsibilities we have."

"Do early mornings work for you?" he quipped. "I could get used to waking up like we did this morning."

"No, that's not what I meant," she sighed in frustration as she changed into a soft, periwinkle blue banquet gown with off-the-shoulder cap sleeves. "This is what I was trying to say last night. I need more than the physical."

"So do I," Odin agreed in a surprised tone. He sighed. "I just don't always know what to do anymore."

"You did when we were courting," she reminded him, glancing at him in the mirror as she arranged her hair.

"That's because I was trying to woo you," he said with confusion. "It's different now."

"Why should it be? Did it ever occur to you, dear husband, that perhaps wives still want to be wooed? I am not some prize catch to be displayed and bragged about," Frigga said indignantly as she clasped a silver choker around her neck.

"Who do you think bought you that jewelry?" he huffed as she put on the matching earrings. "Doesn't that mean anything to you?"

"I've never cared about such things. You know that. I wear them for you and because of my position." She turned around and posed. "How do I look?"

"Just fine," Odin said without much thought.

"Just fine?" Frigga repeated with irritation. "You see, Odin? You think I want to be showered with jewels and gifts, but what I really want is for you to talk with me, open up to me, speak to me the way you did once."

"Frigga, that's not fair," Odin responded. "What's left to talk about after 1,400 years?"

"We're one year shy of that," Frigga corrected him.

"I was counting our year of courtship," Odin said wryly.

"Are you the same man you were back then?" she asked accusingly.

"You have made it quite clear that I am not," he retorted.

"Let's not argue," Frigga sighed. "I didn't mean to accuse. I'm certainly not the same woman I was 1,400 years ago. We don't even know each other anymore!"

"I thought we did," Odin responded candidly.

"So, you haven't tired of my body, but you tire of conversation with me," Frigga stated, ignoring his comment. "Why won't you connect with my soul?"

Odin blinked his good eye twice. "I thought we weren't going to argue. We have guests, remember?"

"Yes, of course," Frigga said disarmingly, forcing a smile, though her heart withered inside. "I'm ready." She held her hand out to Odin. "Shall we?"

He stood and took her hand. "You look lovely, Frigga. Is that better?"

She snorted in exasperation. "Is it really that difficult to pay me a genuine compliment, Odin?"

"What about what I said this morning?"

"That doesn't count," she said bitingly as she dropped his hand.

"Why not?" Odin asked in indignation.

"You had ulterior motives."

"I did not!" he burst out. "I had no expectations this morning." He jabbed his finger at her suddenly. "You started that! Why did you do it if you were only going to throw it in my face later and make me feel like some kind of …"

He stopped and took a deep breath to calm himself.

She folded her arms across her chest. "Why don't you finish what you were about to say?"

"No, I'm not going to finish it," Odin retorted, shaking his head. "I'm not tired of talking with you, Frigga. I'm tired of *fighting* with you." He threw his hands up in exasperation. "I don't want to do it anymore."

"Do you think I enjoy it?"

"I wonder sometimes," Odin muttered.

She gasped in disbelief and drew in a breath to blast him with her words, no longer caring they had a banquet to attend.

But before she could speak, he blurted out, "You're so much smarter than I am."

"Wha—" Shock drained her anger in one deflating blow.

"I cannot ever win in a battle of wits against you," he rushed on as she stood there blinking in confusion. His broad shoulders slumped slightly as he furrowed his brow and looked at the floor. "My competitive nature rears up when you push me beyond my capacity. And I don't want to admit it … but you run circles around me."

She felt a smile tugging on one corner of her lips. "The king of Asgard believes his queen to be smarter than *he* is?"

Odin groaned. "Don't ridicule. Do you know how hard that was to say?"

"Odin, I had no idea you felt that way!" Frigga exclaimed as compassion overflowed where her anger had been. "You seem so confident all the time, I never dreamed you had any insecurities."

"Well, I do," Odin muttered, avoiding her eyes.

"See? We still have things to learn about each other," Frigga declared. "The way you opened up to me just now … this is what I've wanted."

"It's not easy for me, Frigga," he told her.

"I'll try to be patient with you," she said softly, reaching for his hand again. With her other hand, she moved a stray tendril of hair away from his face and tucked it up behind his crown. "You're not only brilliant but a marvelous king. Let's go greet our guests before we're unfashionably late and people start to talk."

"Would you join me for an evening stroll after the banquet?" he asked impulsively.

"What about Bragi?" she reminded him. When his face twisted with frustration, she chuckled. "Take as long as you need with him tonight. Then we'll go on an early morning stroll before breakfast."

He nodded in agreement and kissed her lightly on the cheek, then escorted her to the banquet hall.

When the herald announced the arrival of the king and queen, Frigga saw General Vidar hurry from the balcony to join the throng of guests. Unlike Odin's indifferent response to her attire, Vidar's eyes lit up when he saw her. But he quickly masked his expression, replacing it with the mournful one anyone would expect who knew about his conversation with Lord Gunnar. And the way palace gossip traveled, it was easy to assume just about everyone in the banquet hall knew. Thankfully, Baldur had been correct that no one had dared to besmirch the queen's reputation once Odin returned. Her triumph at the war council seemed to be the main topic of discussion, though several people cast furtive looks at General Vidar.

Frigga spotted Solveya and Flit speaking with each other in hushed tones as they watched the general mingle with the other guests. She was too far away to enhance the sound when they approached him. After a few words, Flit clasped his fist to his chest twice and bowed respectfully to Vidar as Solveya curtsied. Frigga saw her flush deeply even from where she stood. Then the betrothed couple wandered off with their arms wrapped around each other. Vidar watched with furrowed brows, then went back out to the balcony.

Odin nudged her with a worried expression on his face. "Did you see that?" he asked her.

"Yes, my king," Frigga responded. "That was kind of Nimski's grandson to approach Vidar, though it looked painful for him. Perhaps the gesture will bring him closure."

"I've only seen him like this one other time, many years ago," Odin said quietly. "Perhaps I was wrong to keep him here."

"You should go talk to him," Frigga suggested.

"Ah, Frigga, I never know what to say," Odin said doubtfully.

"You're his friend," Frigga encouraged him. When Odin shook his head, she sighed, "Then I will talk to him first."

She moved with easy grace out to the balcony and stood beside the general as he looked out over Asgard.

"How am I doing?" Vidar asked her quietly.

"The king is watching," she responded. "No, don't look. Look straight ahead so he cannot read our lips. I asked him to speak with you, but he says he doesn't know what to say. He's reconsidering your transfer."

"Oh no, not now," Vidar groaned, burying his face in his hands.

Frigga used the opportunity to awkwardly pat him on the back so the king would see. She turned to catch Odin's eye and shrugged as if uncertain of what to do. She discreetly beckoned for him to join them, but Odin shook his head again. She turned her attention back to the general.

"He'll meet with Bragi tonight, but I don't know for how long. I can cloak you with invisibility as soon as we hear the king at the door if you can use your device quickly enough to get out of there."

He looked at her with wide eyes, then faced forward again. "I dare not come to your room."

"And I dare not leave my room without telling him where I'll be," she told him. "What if he comes back early?"

"Then we shouldn't meet tonight," he answered.

"My new office," she said quietly. "Wait for me there, and we'll figure out a better plan moving forward."

He nodded. Frigga returned to the king, who had been joined by Lord Gunnar.

"He's really taking this hard, isn't he?" Gunnar asked the queen as she took her husband's arm.

"I'm afraid so," Frigga replied. "Apparently, your daughter's interest in him was not what it seemed. He feels humiliated."

Gunnar grimaced. "Solveya was shocked to hear he took her flirtations so seriously. She didn't mean him any harm."

"Oh, of course not, Lord Gunnar," Frigga said soothingly. "She seems quite happy with Lord Flit."

"It's a good match. As honored as the good general is, he is too old for Solveya anyway, though I'm sure he desires offspring. As his years advance, he may grow desperate," Gunnar suggested. "Most women his age are married. And the younger women prefer men their own age."

"Not all of them," Frigga laughed. "I've seen some of the younger women flirt with him besides your daughter. He'll find someone eventually."

"He'll be far more cautious next time," Odin sighed. "It took him years to get over the last girl who broke his heart, though it was his own fault. He should have just married the girl, ready or not. He's always been unlucky in love. And you're right, Gunnar. He's running out of time."

"Well, if you're reconsidering his request for a transfer, that won't help him at all," Frigga giggled. "There aren't many eligible women where he wishes to go."

Odin laughed. "My dear Frigga, don't let your new project cloud your judgment. I know you're thinking of your precious Valkyries."

She kissed him on the cheek, casting aside any guilt over her manipulation. "I cannot fool you, can I, husband?"

Lord Gunnar grinned and averted his eyes at her display of affection.

"Besides, I'm thinking just a short trip might do him some good," Odin informed her.

"You could be right," Frigga agreed, relieved by this news. "Now, go talk to him. Please?"

"Very well," Odin sighed.

He clapped Gunnar on the shoulder, then strode to the balcony to speak with the general.

Gunnar shook his head. "Who knew my little Solveya could cause so much trouble?"

"Beautiful women always do, Lord Gunnar," Frigga laughed.

"Don't I know it," he sighed. "And you are no exception, Queen Frigga."

"I appreciate the compliment, but I'm not certain what you mean," Frigga replied somewhat stiffly, concerned the nobleman might suspect her ties to the general. Or worse, could Gunnar be flirting with her?

"I mean no disrespect, my queen," he hastened to explain. "I was simply referring to how you took the council by storm today, even when my father showed you no mercy."

She relaxed and laughed at the memory. "He was merciless, wasn't he? I was shocked when he voted in favor." She glanced around the room. "I don't see him this evening. Or your wife, come to think of it."

"He fell ill this afternoon," Gunnar informed her. "Silva stayed with him. I'm afraid I'll be leaving soon myself."

"I'm sorry to hear that," Frigga replied sympathetically. "Please tell Lord Delling the king and I hope for his speedy recovery."

Gunnar bowed. "I shall, Your Majesty."

He took his leave just as the herald announced the serving of the meal. Frigga had no opportunity to ask Odin about his conversation with the general until the lull before dessert.

"The general seems in better spirits," Frigga observed. "You must have helped him after all, my king."

Odin grimaced slightly. "I hope you don't mind, Frigga, but I told him a little of the trouble we've been having."

"Why did you do that?" she gasped, looking at her hands as heat stole across her cheeks.

"I just wanted to show him I identify with his pain in a way," Odin said softly. "I didn't say much, and I kept it discreet. Don't be embarrassed, Firefly."

"I'd forgotten you used to call me that," Frigga gasped.

"I'm trying to remember our courting days," Odin chuckled.

"I loved it when you called me that," Frigga whispered, slipping into the memory without effort.

Prince Odin of Asgard laced his long, strong fingers with Frigga's as they sauntered through the green meadow near their secret portal on Vanaheim. She breathed deeply of the warm summer evening air as the dusk settled into a deepening stillness. The shadows lengthened, and crickets began to hum with infectious energy while tiny twinkles of light flashed off and on around them.

"I wonder why there are so many fireflies tonight," Frigga sighed contentedly, squeezing Odin's hand as she reveled in his nearness.

"They're drawn to your light like I am," he rumbled as he abruptly stopped and pulled her into his arms.

She eagerly welcomed his kiss, easing into his chest as a feeling of warm acceptance washed over her.

He broke away to say, "Perhaps they think you're their queen."

She laughed, then quipped, "I'm no one's queen."

His handsome face grew serious as his gray eyes burned with an intensity that took her breath away. "Would you be my queen, Firefly?"

Her eyes widened with realization, but she could not help snorting slightly over the nickname. "Firefly? Do you find me flighty, Odin?"

"Never," he protested. He lifted her chin and softly and slowly proclaimed, "I find you beautiful ... fascinating ... pure ... and perfect." He paused and cocked his head. "The nickname suits you. Do you mind if I call you that?"

"I like it," she whispered as his words watered her soul. She linked her arms around his neck. "You can call me Firefly anytime you like."

"And what of my other question?" he urged eagerly.

"Yes, I will be your queen, Odin of Asgard," she answered shyly, closing her eyes in anticipation of the deep kiss she assumed would follow.

Frigga yanked herself out of the memory when it suddenly changed into Vidar kissing her in a similar fashion as fireflies lit up the willow trees around them. She frowned, squelching the urge to squirm under King Odin's single-eyed and intent observation of her during her silent reverie.

"Were you remembering?" he asked quietly.

"Yes, but we should not talk this way in public, my king," she murmured, dropping her eyes as demurely as she could muster.

"I suppose you're right," Odin agreed with a heavy sigh. "There's always someone watching, isn't there?" When Frigga nodded, he said, "I spoke with Bragi briefly, but we have much to discuss. What will you do while I meet with him?"

"I'll spend a little time with the princes, I suppose," she replied nonchalantly.

"Baldur and Hod are going night fishing," Odin informed her. "They're taking Thor and Loki with them."

"What?" Frigga involuntarily narrowed her eyes in consternation.

"Now, Frigga, I told them they could go," Odin reassured her. "You're not going to fuss about it, are you?"

She sighed, reluctant to relinquish her concerns over the wisdom of allowing the younger boys to go. "I suppose not. They're growing up too fast."

Odin chuckled knowingly. "We still have centuries with Thor and Loki."

"But only a hundred years left with Baldur," she reminded him.

Odin looked over to where the crown prince goofed off with his friend Hod and several other soldiers. "He'll start training as a Valiant tomorrow. My recovery has delayed it long enough."

"What about the short trip you mentioned for Vidar?" Frigga asked.

"It's only for a few weeks," Odin stated. "Vale will start Baldur's training. Then Vidar will take over when he returns with a clear mind."

"I'll work with the Valkyries until then," Frigga said as if she fully approved of her husband's plan.

"I'll try to be quick tonight," Odin offered. "But I cannot guarantee anything. At least we have our morning plans."

"I think I'll start setting up my office," Frigga said with sudden excitement as if she had just thought of it. "Why don't you come see what I've done when you're finished?"

"Don't overtax yourself," Odin warned.

She laughed. "I could say the same to you."

She could hardly wait to get to her new headquarters after Odin left the banquet with Bragi, surprised at how quickly she could switch to longing for Vidar's company again. But she remembered to speak with the noblewomen before they all left and scheduled a meeting at the arena in three days. Then she urged her sons to be careful as they prepared to leave for their night fishing trip. Finally, she rushed to the office with all of her drawings and plans. Since Vidar had not yet arrived, she spent a good hour arranging her desk and hanging her drawings next to the map. Just as she sat at her desk to take some notes, Vidar appeared in front of her, which caused her to nearly jump out of her skin.

"You scared me!" she chided him playfully. "What if I'd screamed?"

"I'm sorry," Vidar chuckled. Then he looked around the room in approval. "How long have you been here? You've done quite a bit."

"About an hour," she answered. "I told Odin I was coming here, so I had to have something to show for it."

"Do you need any help?" Vidar offered.

"That wouldn't do," she said with a smirk. "Odin might wonder how I did it myself if I had you move things around."

"True," he murmured, eyeing her with appreciation. "Have I told you how exquisite you look tonight?"

She blushed with pleasure at his praise. "Odin wasn't impressed."

"Yes, he was. I saw him watching you several times at the banquet," Vidar contested. "He's just forgotten how to tell you. I've heard the noblewomen talking. It seems to be an issue for married men."

Frigga rolled her eyes. "I simply do not understand why."

"Neither do I. If you were my wife, you'd probably get tired of hearing me say how much I love you," Vidar stated as he walked over to the window.

"Not likely," she giggled.

"Where is my little wolf?" he asked suddenly.

"In my other dress!" she gasped as her hands flew to her mouth.

"Don't leave him there. The hidden compartment won't work anymore if he goes through the laundry," Vidar warned. "Then we won't be able to write each other notes and hide them inside him, which was my reason for giving him to you in the first place."

"Where did you get him anyway?" Frigga asked.

"My father made him," Vidar said. He gestured to the desk. "This too."

"Your father was very talented," Frigga said, detecting sadness in the general. "I wish I had known him."

The general dropped his eyes, and Frigga sensed not to press him or continue speaking on that subject.

She joined him at the window. "We need a better hiding place. Someone might see the wolf here."

"The middle drawer of the desk is fairly deep. Keep him near the back," Vidar suggested.

"What if Odin decided to rummage through it? Does it lock?" she asked.

"It does, actually," Vidar responded, his face brightening. Then he frowned. "But there's only one key."

"Can you have another made?" she prodded.

"I suppose, but not anytime soon. Did Odin tell you he decided to send me away for a few weeks?" When Frigga nodded, he continued, "It serves me right for acting rashly."

"Where are you going?" Frigga asked with a slight pout.

"To the South Sea," Vidar answered. "Lord Berg owns property there. He wants to build a summer home."

Frigga blinked twice. "But what does that have to do with you?"

"He wants to surprise Lady Annette for her next birthday," Vidar chuckled. "And since she grew up there, she knows all the builders in that area. Plus, she keeps a close eye on their household expenses. He hasn't been able to figure out how to pull it off, so he asked Odin for ideas a while ago."

"I'm still not sure I follow," she stated with some confusion. "Are you going to build it?"

"Yes. It's been a long time since I've used the knowledge, but my father taught me everything he knew about construction and carpentry," he admitted with pride. "Odin is covering all of the expenses, including a generous stipend for me. Lord Berg will reimburse the king after he presents the finished home to Lady Annette."

"As exciting as that sounds, I wish you weren't going," Frigga admitted. "But I suppose this is what we have to do."

Vidar stepped close to her and folded her fingers over something cold and smooth. "Take this. I won't need it for a while."

She opened her hand to see Vidar's traveling device. She looked up with wide eyes at his grinning face. "Do you mean—"

"I want you to come to me there," he affirmed. "If you can. When you can."

"How are you going to get back to your room tonight?" she asked. "And what about your order?"

"Never mind them! But I guess I do need it to get back," he laughed as he walked over to the desk, then opened the middle drawer. "Leave the wolf in here. It should be safe for tonight. I'll sneak in here first thing in the morning and leave the device and a note with the location. I'll come early enough so no one sees me leave your office. Then I'll lock it behind me."

Frigga felt a surge of excitement well up within her. "What if I can't get away?"

He took her into his arms and kissed the top of her head, then let her go. "I'm not supposed to tell you this, but Odin told me he's leaving for Muspelheim again soon. If you plan it right, we'll have several nights together."

"Can you imagine?" she breathed, feeling her eyes sparkling with anticipation.

"Yes, my queen, I can," he murmured, reaching out to cup her face as golden light flooded his own eyes. He shook his head subtly and reluctantly dropped his hand. "But for now, I want you to keep your promise."

"What promise?"

"Teach me how to lock my mind," he urged her as he walked around the room investigating her work.

"That will take more time than we should risk tonight," Frigga informed him. "Odin has already been closeted for over two hours."

"What about suppressing a memory like you did with Laufey's?"

"Doing that yourself is a discipline of the mind that isn't really taught," Frigga said thoughtfully. "And it's not a healthy thing to do in my experience because it can lock unprocessed emotions into your psyche. Honestly, you've probably already done it without realizing it."

"Can anyone do it?" he asked curiously.

"Of course," Frigga answered. "Locking your mind makes it easier, but no memory is ever fully inaccessible unless it's changed or erased. A suppressed or hidden memory can release with all of the emotion attached but not usually on its own."

"But changed and erased memories are permanent?" Vidar asked.

She cocked her head at him. "As far as I know. I suppose something could bring them back, but I have never heard of it happening. Why do you ask?"

"Merely curious," he replied nonchalantly. "Honestly, locking my mind is more important. I don't want to leave it open to mind readers, especially Odin."

"I doubt he's read your mind in all the years you've known him," Frigga pointed out. "Why would that change?"

"What if he begins to suspect us again?" he muttered.

She sighed. "Very well. Come here." When he obeyed, she placed her hand on his forehead. "I'm going to enter your mind. I'll stay near the edges at first. When you feel me probe deeper, imagine parrying a thrust to push me out."

He nodded and closed his eyes to narrow his focus.

What will she see? she felt him think. *Will she look at my memories or all of the times I've imagined … she's pushing through, I can feel it.*

Frigga withdrew her hand since she could no longer hear his thoughts in her own mind. "All of the times you've imagined what?" she teased, though she knew the answer.

"Someday I'll show you … when you're ready to read my mind," Vidar suggested in a low voice.

"That might not be the best idea," she said seriously.

"Maybe not," he agreed, but his eyes betrayed the direction of his thoughts. "Was that the last thought you saw?"

"More or less. You blocked me quite well. Practice that mental block whenever you can, and you'll be able to block an intrusion into your mind when you feel it."

"Is that it? I thought it would take more time for you to teach me," Vidar said.

"I've only shown you how to sense and block an intrusion," she chuckled. "There's more to locking your mind than that. For instance, I'll need to show you how to prevent mental invasion even while you sleep. And knowledge isn't enough, just like when you train your troops. Practice is imperative."

"When is my next lesson, my queen?" he asked with boyish eagerness.

"We'll work on it when you return," she said playfully.

"I'm glad I have a job to do there," Vidar mused. "I need something to do besides walk the sand and dream of you for weeks."

"Will you dream of me?" she asked softly.

"Every night," he murmured, reaching out to hold her tightly against him. "Until you're right here again." But when she lifted her face to his, he released her and stepped back. "Odin could arrive any moment. I'd better go."

She nodded, feeling slightly strange about the whole encounter after he left. As she absentmindedly moved the same stack of papers to different parts of her new desk, she reflected on how they had both thought their relationship was over. How easily they had come together again! And yet, she did wonder why Vidar had not allowed himself to kiss her. Somewhat embarrassed by her lack of focus on what she was doing, though no one was there to see, she forced her attention back to the task at hand.

When another hour of sorting and organizing had passed and Odin still had not appeared, Frigga decided to risk going back to the royal chambers to retrieve the wolf. While she was there, she grabbed one of her smaller flower vases as her alibi in case anyone was watching. When she returned to her office, she placed the vase onto the window-sill, then stepped back to admire its simple beauty.

She was in the middle of examining her weapon plans when Odin stepped into the room and looked around.

"You've been busy, haven't you?" he commented. "It looks nice."

"Thank you," she said automatically, but inwardly she scoffed, *Nice? Vidar called me exquisite. Odin never uses such words.*

And because she had silenced the pricks in her conscience over planning to visit Vidar while Odin was off-world, she did not feel the guilt she usually experienced when comparing the two men.

"The vase is a nice touch," Odin said offhandedly.

"The room needed something pretty," she responded with a shrug.

"It already has something pretty," Odin said softly.

She squelched any pleasure at his words. Too many years of hurt and neglect had made her cynical. Deep down in her heart, she knew he was trying. But in some ways, she wished he would just go back to ignoring her. Lingering thoughts of Vidar made Odin's former apathy seem better to her than his clumsy efforts to make things right, especially since his compliments in the past had so often been linked to trying to initiate physical intimacy with her.

Surely he wouldn't try for twice in one day! she thought. *Was that why he called me Firefly?*

"Ulterior motives again, Odin?" she asked aloud.

He flinched. "Is that how you're going to view every compliment I try to give you?"

"I'm just drawing from past experience," she answered smartly. "We went for so long without physical intimacy, I'm worried you'll be more demanding now that I've given in to you."

"Have you no respect for me at all?" he huffed. "I'm not an animal. If you're just giving in to me and going through the motions, I'd just as soon go back to the way things were."

He cast one long, sad look at Frigga as she stood there with mouth agape. His words challenged her deep-seated belief about his motives. She again brought to mind the possibility that loving her husband in body could be the key to his heart. Did Odin want her for more than just his own satisfaction? Is that what he had been trying to say earlier? And what about Vidar? He wanted her too. What were his motives? The last time she had toyed with those questions, she had fled the palace and brought quite a bit of pain upon herself and Vidar. And now, it certainly appeared she had hurt Odin as well.

Was it only yesterday? she thought. *So much has happened.*

The silence grew unbearable. Odin finally looked at the ground and blinked rapidly. She had secretly wanted to see him cry, to show some vulnerability. But when he bit his lip, she realized she would not handle it well if he did.

She changed the subject and asked, "How did your meeting go with Bragi?"

He swallowed hard and held up his hand to request a moment. Then he said, "Frigga, you don't know how much I love you, do you?"

She stiffened. Then her shoulders slumped. "Please stop playing with my emotions, Odin."

"That's Baldur's power," Odin protested. "Not mine."

"Everyone has the power to yank another person around or manipulate them," Frigga retorted. "Baldur's abilities are just an enhanced version, a weakened gift because of his Olympian bloodline."

"You should not say such things, Frigga," Odin warned sternly. "Do you want the boy to believe he is weak?"

"Who taught him how strong he is?" she cried, striking her breast bone indignantly. "I did!"

"And I've done nothing?" Odin asked in a dangerously quiet tone.

"I didn't say that," she murmured, averting her eyes and clasping her hands in front of her. She sighed. "Why is it all we seem to do is fight?"

The anger that had flared in his good eye fizzled out. "I suppose we have centuries of resentment to work through. Somehow, I must show you I am not your enemy."

He approached Frigga cautiously and hugged her. She fought the confusion in her own mind, then extracted herself as gently as she could.

"I know you're not my enemy. I'm just not certain you're my friend," she muttered.

He flinched again but nodded as if in resignation. "I suppose I'll have to do something about that. Meanwhile, my queen, we have a busy day tomorrow. Perhaps we should retire."

"We do?" she asked in surprise.

"Yes, I have a surprise for you."

"What is it?" she asked warily.

"We'll take our morning walk as we planned, but after that, we'll ride out to the Bifröst," Odin informed her with a slow grin of anticipation growing on his face.

"What for?"

"To meet your dragon," he answered matter-of-factly.

"Really?" she squealed, unable to squelch her excitement.

"Yes, I need you to determine if the dragon initiative will work," he said, clearly enjoying her excitement. "I have to go back to Muspelheim soon. And I'd like to bring more dragons back to Asgard with me."

Frigga squealed again and almost knocked Odin over with an embrace of pure glee. He grinned widely, a surge of delight transforming his face into the man who took her breath away during their courtship days. His active participation in something that mattered so much to her brought a warmth that melted the angst she had felt only moments ago. She gladly accepted his proffered arm to return to their chambers, where they prepared for bed without any more discussion.

But that night, her anticipation and nervousness mixed together into a jolt of energy that made it difficult for her to sleep. She lay awake thinking of all her equestrian training as she made plans for how to tame and ride that dragon.

14

Frigga fought the urge to rush Odin through their morning walk, barely noticing the grounds she usually admired quite readily. Even breakfast with her family seemed interminable.

"Why are you so jumpy, Mother?" Loki asked with slight irritation during breakfast.

"Mind your business, Loki," Thor taunted.

"Thor, are you Loki's father?" Odin asked sternly.

"No," the boy answered sheepishly.

"Then let *me* be," Odin reprimanded him.

Loki's eyes brightened at Odin's defense of him.

But then Odin added, "Loki, you need to address your mother with more respect."

Loki dropped his head. "I'm sorry, Mother. I didn't mean to be disrespectful."

Frigga bristled, believing Odin's rebuke to be unnecessary.

But the king continued, "I know you didn't mean any harm, but your mother is the first woman you will ever love. The way you treat her will impact the way you treat your future wife someday."

Frigga's eyebrows nearly disappeared into her hairline as she stared at her husband with shock and admiration. He flashed his good eye at her somewhat sheepishly, as if to acknowledge he had not always done so well himself. But both Loki and Thor drank in their father's words with wide eyes. Baldur merely hid a smile as Odin returned his attention to his breakfast.

"To answer your question, Loki, your father is taking me somewhere exciting today," Frigga explained. "I'm just eager to get started."

"Why don't we get to go to exciting places with Father?" Loki asked bravely.

"Because you're not old enough yet," Odin stated firmly. "Someday you will go."

"To battle?" Thor prompted enthusiastically.

"More than likely," Odin answered as he lifted another forkful of baked eggs to his mouth.

"I want to see the places Father has been," Loki interjected. "And some of the places we've read about."

"Yes!" Thor burst out excitedly. "Think of the adventures we could have, Loki! We could see for ourselves if giants are as scary as they sound … especially those ice-hearted savages on Jotunheim."

Frigga and Odin exchanged a look. Her heart had warmed toward him again, but a chill stole through her when he did not correct Thor's careless words.

"Mind what you say, please, Thor," she sighed, wishing the king would show more support for her parenting, though she did notice how he silenced his son with one look when the blond boy opened his mouth to argue.

Frigga had approached Odin many times about the prejudices Asgardians held toward most other races. But he always brushed her concerns aside, which made it quite difficult for her to address how the prevalent attitudes of Asgardian culture influenced the children and even herself. When she was honest, she struggled with her own negative views toward Jotuns. But she had loved Laufey. And if Loki ever found out about his Jotun heritage, she did not want him to despise himself.

Her position was indeed precarious, for she could not in good conscience teach her sons an equality she did not fully embrace. Uncertain what she had expected Odin to say, she decided to let the matter drop yet again.

After everyone had finished breakfast without further discussion, the king and queen saddled their horses and rode to the Bifröst stables. Odin took a slower pace than usual to adjust to his single-eye vision. Sigurna seemed quite content to trot next to Svadilfari. And just as Vidar had predicted days ago, the mare showed her mate the same affection she had shown Vidar's horse.

When they arrived, the watcher and keeper of Asgard's gates led the king and queen to the dragon's section of the stables while his oldest son Heimdall kept watch.

"She looks like molten gold," Frigga gasped when she saw the sleeping creature.

Her scales rippled together in a glittering golden yellow that flowed onto her leathery folded wings. At Frigga's exclamation, the dragon opened a pair of bright orange eyes and raised her sleek head to peer at the newcomers. In that position, her full size was hard to judge, but Frigga estimated her to be slightly larger than a winged horse, though small enough to ride comfortably.

"No horns," Frigga observed with wonder.

"Only the males have horns," Odin told her.

"Does she have a name, Gjallar?" Frigga asked the keeper of the gates.

"I've tried to call her a few different things, but she didn't like any of them," Gjallar responded. He smiled fondly at the dragon, deepening the creases in his rich brown skin. "She's learned to trust me, but it took a little work."

"How did you do it?" Frigga asked curiously, noting how calm the dragon seemed despite the presence of the strangers.

"She seems to be able to understand me," Gjallar answered. "I told her I would not harm her each time I brought her food or treats. After a few days, she let me touch her. There's a spot behind her ears she likes me to rub."

"Where are her ears?" Frigga asked curiously.

The dragon lifted her head, then flared out triple flange ears, her brilliant and intelligent eyes gleaming as she stared at Frigga.

"Oh, there they are!" Frigga laughed gleefully. "What else can you do, sleek one?"

The dragon retracted her ears and stared at the door confining her. She raised her magnificent golden wings slightly, then brought them back to her sides.

She wants to be released, Frigga thought.

"I'll tell you one thing she can do," Gjallar interjected, his unusual coral eyes turning almost pink in his amusement. "We muck out her stall the same way we do for the horses. I've been using her dung as fertilizer for my garden. I don't even have to let it rest or dry out. I've never seen such yield. Or prettier, more delicious fruit for that matter."

"What does she eat?" Frigga asked.

"Mostly fish, but she likes brightly colored vegetables and fruit, especially yellow or red ones. I usually keep a stash of golden apples here. Those are her favorite so far," Gjallar stated.

The dragon perked up considerably at this turn in conversation. She lifted her scaly tail and swayed it back and forth, flaring the golden flanges at the tip.

"Would you get me one?" Frigga asked. "I'd like to try something."

Gjallar nodded and slipped away, then returned with one of the golden apples that grew in the grove in the palace gardens. The dragon sniffed the air and pranced a bit as Gjallar handed the apple to the queen.

"Let me in the stall," Frigga instructed.

"My queen, I don't think—"

"Do as she says, Gjallar," Odin commanded. "We're both armed and skilled enough to act quickly if anything goes wrong."

Gjallar hesitated but obeyed. Carrying the apple in front of her, Frigga approached the golden dragon, who watched her somewhat warily.

"Hello, my beauty," Frigga murmured soothingly. "You and I are going to be fast friends, aren't we?"

The dragon flicked out a slender black tongue and wrapped it around the apple, never taking her glowing eyes off the queen. But as she crunched it, she stayed perfectly still as Frigga reached out to caress the spot behind her retractable ears.

"Great Odin's Raven," Gjallar breathed.

"Gjallar!" Odin reprimanded him. "You know how I

hate that expression! And in front of a lady … the queen, no less!"

The keeper of the gates cleared his throat nervously and bowed. "Apologies, my king. And to you, my queen, for the strong language."

Frigga hid her laugh in her hand as she dipped her head in acknowledgment of his apology. The expression had been coined after Odin brought a pair of raven mates back from Midgard when he wandered that realm with Zeus. The sleek black birds had lived much longer than ravens usually did on Midgard. Even their offspring had fared better in the wild of Asgard. Now, Odin always kept a mated pair at the palace, where they irritated some of the fussier nobility. Despite the king's best efforts to squelch the epithet, his well-meaning subjects had somehow spread it to every corner of the realm. And every time someone used it in front of Odin, Frigga had to hide how amusing she found the whole thing.

"Just watch your language, Gjallar," Odin sighed. "Would you care to share what inspired your outburst?"

"It took me days to get that far with her," the esteemed gatekeeper admitted. "The queen astounds me."

"I think she trusts me because you do, Gjallar," Frigga guessed.

"Perhaps," Gjallar said with a thoughtful nod. "But I don't think so."

"Don't underestimate yourself, Frigga," Odin added. "You have an incredibly wholesome aura about you."

"Aye, she does," Gjallar agreed.

Frigga blushed. And when she looked at the king, she felt her heart softening toward him again. The dragon nudged her arm with her sleek and scaly head. Then the creature looked at the door again. Frigga cocked her own head. She tentatively placed her hand on the dragon's shoulder and felt a warm sensation pulsing through the creature's scales.

"May I enter your mind so I can understand you?" Frigga whispered.

When the dragon lowered her head slightly and pushed it under the queen's hand, Frigga entered her mind and found she could communicate with her in Asgardian.

I am Idunn, the dragon told the queen silently.

That is a lovely name, Frigga responded in kind. *Very similar to one of our noblewomen, the Lady Ithunna.*

That is well, the dragon thought back. *Then you are not likely to forget.*

Of course not. How could I forget one such as you? Frigga replied. *I am Queen Frigga of Asgard, and you are most welcome here.*

Greetings, O Queen, the dragon returned. *If you free me, I will serve you.*

Are you unhappy here, Idunn? Frigga asked her.

You are one of the most important people in this powerful realm. Much is expected of you, is it not? Idunn asked.

Yes, of course, Frigga answered, confused by her question.

Then you know what it is like to be cared for but still feel imprisoned, the dragon thought. *I long to feel the wind under my wings and soar on greater heights.*

I cannot even imagine what that feels like, Frigga mused.

Would you like me to show you? I have missed bearing a rider who shares my joy in flight, Idunn thought as her body quivered. *Your kind should fit nicely between the base of my neck and my wings.*

How do you know? Frigga asked.

I have carried Muspel children of many ages. Only two were bigger than you, Idunn said. *We Salir are too small for the adults.*

Salir? Frigga repeated inquisitively.

There is no word for it in your language, O Queen, Idunn stated. *It is what I am.*

Are you not a dragon then? Frigga asked. *And how do you know our language?*

I am a Salir dragon, she responded. *And I do not know how I know. I simply do. We are a race of stealth, finesse, and advanced intelligence. Because the Muspels train on us before they are fully grown, we never have the chance to bond with a rider for life like the Nagir do. They are the larger dragons. I have trained quite a few riders, but I was banished from my world because I lacked fighting spirit.*

Who told you that? Frigga thought indignantly as she felt the creature's sadness.

The Muspel who prepared me told another in my hearing, the dragon responded.

You were chosen as a gift for my husband, the king of Asgard, Frigga informed her silently. *To foster peace. You have great purpose.*

That is a better story, the dragon responded.

"What is she doing?" Gjallar asked the king as Frigga stood quite still with her hand between the dragon's eyes during this mental exchange.

But Odin silenced him with a quick shush and a wave of his hand.

He is your mate? the dragon asked as she stared at Odin. Then she closed her eyes and thought, *But you have another mate, another who holds your heart. I see him in your mind. I do not understand. Your kind is monogamous.*

It's complicated, Frigga answered quickly with growing alarm.

It had not occurred to her that the dragon might be able to see her hidden thoughts. And she had been so focused on communicating with the creature, she had been unaware of Idunn's mental probe.

Do not be afraid, the dragon stated as she opened her eyes to look into Frigga's. *I will keep your secrets, and I will help you if I can. You are wholesome, as your first mate has said.*

King Odin can also access your thoughts if he chooses. And he may not ask first, Frigga thought.

He can only access my thoughts if I allow him to do so, O Queen, Idunn declared silently. *You should have thought to protect your own. The division of your heart is compromising the power of your mind. I will not probe you further. I have seen enough to know you can be trusted, for you are one who loves much. If you need to speak to me again, you need not ask my permission. But next time, see to your own mind.*

I will heed your warning, Idunn, Frigga thought with relief, sensing she might be able to trust the dragon as she had not trusted anyone but Vidar. But this was not the time to reveal her heart any further. Instead, she asked, *How do I ride you? Like I would a horse?*

Only when I am walking or running. I will not accept a bit or bridle as the horses do here, but I can show you what the Muspels use to ride us if you know someone who can fashion one, the dragon thought. *When we are airborne, you must become one with me and keep your center of gravity low. You must strive for balance in your posture and squeeze with your legs but not too hard. My scales may be slippery to you, so you will need to use my fighting spikes to mount me and keep your position.*

As Idunn sent her thoughts to the queen, three gleaming ivory spikes emerged from either side of her neck.

Just like a cat unsheathing its claws, Frigga thought with delight.

I do not know what a cat is, the dragon thought back. *Are they tasty?*

We keep them as pets, not as food, Frigga returned with amusement.

Then I will not eat your cats, Idunn thought. *Am I to be a pet in this place?*

Perhaps the king planned to make you a pet, Frigga answered. *But he has given you to me. And I would like to be your rider for life.*

The dragon reared suddenly and expanded her wings, breaking their connection. At first, Frigga was frightened, especially when the creature threw back her head and roared. Gjallar thundered for the Bifröst guards as both he and Odin drew their swords and rushed to the stall door. Frigga shouted at them to hold as Idunn fell back onto all fours and lowered her head.

The queen looked the dragon in the eyes; no animosity or ill intent clouded their luminescent beauty. She gently placed her hand back on the animal's head and eased into her mind, keeping everything locked in her own but the communication link.

Forgive me, O Queen, Idunn thought. *I was overcome with joy. I would have liked to shoot a column of fire to the sky as is our manner of celebration, but I contained myself.*

I'm glad you did, or you would have burned down your living quarters, Frigga laughed silently. *I will explain to the men. Then we will ride together.*

Frigga released her connection with the dragon and turned to the gatekeeper, the king, and the guards who had answered Gjallar's call. "There is no danger here. She was rejoicing, not threatening."

The men all sheathed their swords in swift movements as the tension ebbed from their bodies. The subtle sound of metal sliding against leather hovered slightly in the air, lending a seriousness to the moment as Frigga realized how quickly Odin's soldiers had rushed to defend her. Grateful but sobered by their loyalty, she smiled brightly at the guards as Gjallar bid them to return to their posts.

"You can communicate telepathically with her?" Gjallar asked when only the three of them stood in the stable area.

"I can," Frigga confirmed. "Speak nothing of what you have seen."

Gjallar bowed respectfully. "The queen has a powerful gift. I understand the need to keep it secret. What will you do now?"

Frigga patted the dragon on the shoulder. "She has offered to let me ride her."

As Idunn lowered her head, Frigga used one of the spikes to swing herself up onto the dragon's back, then gripped the two lowest spikes on either side of her neck. She found she needed every muscle in her arms and legs to keep from sliding.

Gjallar opened the stall door. The dragon reared again and accidentally knocked Frigga harmlessly into the straw on the stable floor. Gjallar reached for his sword again, but the dragon immediately lowered herself into a submissive crouch and waited for Frigga to approach her again.

As soon as she touched the creature's shoulder, Frigga heard Idunn apologize to her in her mind. She quickly snatched her hand away as if she had been burned. Then she put her hand back on the same spot.

Idunn, how did you do that? she asked the dragon.

What do you mean? the dragon responded in confusion.

I can only read minds if I touch someone's forehead with my hand, Frigga thought.

It does not matter where you touch me, O Queen, Idunn returned. *And it is not your ability that allowed us to communicate. I can speak to the mind and read the thoughts of anyone who touches me if I choose. Until you had asked for permission to enter my mind, I had not chosen to read your thoughts. This form of telepathy is how the Muspels ride us. They even see into our hearts if we allow it. That is how our bond is formed. But when the children grow up, they switch to riding the larger Nagir. Then the bond is broken, as are we.*

Is that why they said you lost your fighting spirit? Frigga asked.

It might be true, the dragon mused. *Time will tell. Take your position again, O Queen. I will still hear your thoughts if you speak to me.*

Please call me Frigga, she thought as she mounted the dragon.

Very well, Frigga, Idunn responded.

Frigga clenched her legs and abdominal muscles to keep her balance as the dragon walked out of the stable into the open air. She was barely conscious of Odin shouting at her to be careful as he and Gjallar followed them outside to watch.

Hold tight. I'm taking off now, Idunn warned her.

As the dragon stretched out her wings to their full width and eased into the air, Frigga briefly felt as if her stomach had stayed on the ground. But as they gained height, she regained her strong constitution, using every bit of her strength to keep her hold on the dragon. Suddenly, she accidentally swallowed a massive gulp of air. Her chest burned with the pressure. As her focus shifted to the pain, she began to subconsciously loosen her grip on the dragon.

Hold on! Release the air! Idunn urged in her mind.

I cannot do both, Frigga thought with rising panic.

Then she proved herself wrong as she involuntarily unleashed an unladylike belch. She felt, rather than heard, the amusement of the dragon. And since no one else was around to scold her for bad manners, the slightly embarrassed queen laughed out loud, enjoying the freedom of their shared mirth.

Only a novice would make such a mistake, the dragon teased. *Try not to swallow any more air.*

As Idunn's powerful wings beat the air in majestic, mesmerizing movements, the wind whipped through Frigga's curls and tore at her riding dress. But Idunn's steady rhythm made it easier for the queen to stay seated. Still, since she could only experience a taste of the thrill of flying because of her precarious position, she wished she could relax enough to enjoy the view.

You will eventually, Idunn responded to her thought, which Frigga had forgotten to block. *It is easier to do this with an irscet.*

An irscet? Is that what you mentioned earlier? Frigga asked curiously.

Yes, it means something like dragon seat. It is both like and unlike a saddle, Idunn answered.

I can see a horse's saddle would never fit you, Frigga observed. *Your back is broader than my mare's. And your wings are much wider than I expected.*

Four stallions nose to tail cannot match the width of my wings, Idunn boasted. *And the feel of the wind beneath them again is like no other sensation. Your planet really is quite lovely. I think I will like it here, although it could be warmer.*

Frigga laughed. *It will get even colder in a few months. How do you fare in the winter?*

Muspelheim has no winter, though it grows cold at night sometimes, Idunn replied. *I can endure lower temperatures in most instances. I would only be in danger if my internal furnace went out. Yes, I think I will be quite happy here. Even in the winter.*

I hope so, Frigga answered silently. *How long are you able to fly?*

I do not know. I have never exceeded my limits, the dragon thought. *But I dare not go any further with you riding bareback. I will turn around, then start a practice descent to see how you handle it.*

What do I do? Frigga asked.

Keep your head down so the wind does not push you off my back, Idunn answered. *Be one with me. Remember balance and your center of gravity.*

Frigga felt herself slipping sideways as Idunn circled in the air. She tightened her hold, leaned in the opposite direction, and managed to keep her seat. But as Idunn changed her angle, Frigga lost her grip and flew over the dragon's head with a shriek.

This is it, she thought as her body flipped through the air at such terrifying speed, she could not even suck in enough air to scream again.

She spread out her arms and legs in a desperate attempt to slow herself down. She braced herself for the crushing impact of hitting the ground, hoping it would be over quickly. Suddenly, talons closed around her and arrested her fall. She let loose the terror she had not been able to release in one long wail of relief as she dangled from Idunn's grip. It had only been a few seconds.

I have you, Frigga, Idunn informed her silently. *I would never let you fall to your death. Clearly, we need to work on descension.*

Well, now I know you can lift someone my size, Frigga thought as she tried to calm her pounding heart.

Of course I can. Why does that matter? the dragon thought.

Someday, we may go to battle together and help move the wounded, Frigga replied.

I would like that very much, Idunn thought. *Perhaps I lack fighting spirit because I have always been more interested in protecting and helping than harming and destroying.*

You are extraordinary, Idunn, Frigga returned. *Are there others like you?*

Yes, there are others who feel the same, Idunn thought as she glided into an outcropping of rock that appeared to lead into a high mountain cave.

She gently set Frigga down and allowed her to clamber back onto her back. When the dragon took to the air again, Frigga found it easier to ride, for she had always been a fast learner.

As they flew back to the Bifröst stables, Frigga sent, *My husband is going to Muspelheim soon to bring back more dragons. How would he find ones like you?*

I can give him a list of names and qualities to look for in other Salir, Idunn replied.

And you can do that without letting him read your mind? Frigga asked with concern.

Yes. As I said, I will keep your secrets. It is not my place or my nature to inform your husband of your second mate, Idunn promised.

Do you have a mate? Frigga asked.

I have had three, the dragon answered, *And I have birthed seven offspring. Some of us are monogamous by choice. I would be with the right male, but I do not care to speak of that right now.*

Where are your offspring? Frigga asked curiously. *Should my husband bring them back with him?*

No, they are fully grown and have mates and established lives on Muspelheim, Idunn answered. *Our bonds with our offspring are strong, but we let them live their own lives and make their own choices even at a young age to foster the fierce independence needed on our world. Very unlike your reluctance to release your sons.*

Frigga laughed inwardly at her blunt boldness. *How much did you see of my life, Idunn?*

Much, was her only response. *I am ready to descend. Mind your balance.*

Frigga focused on keeping her center of gravity low this time and did not lose her seating, though she did slip forward slightly once or twice. Idunn seemed to be keeping a tight hold on her movements, allowing her wings to slice through the air with aerodynamic elegance as she surrendered her former altitude to the clouds above her. The specks below them took shape, becoming more recognizable. Then everything came into sharper focus as they rapidly approached the stretch of grass where they had launched into the air. Delighted to see Odin, Gjallar, and several guards watching with open mouths and awed expressions, Frigga gripped Idunn's girth tighter as the magnificent creature alighted on the ground without so much as a jolt.

As she slid off the dragon's back, Frigga sent one last message to her. *Thank you, Idunn, for sharing that experience with me. I will come to see you again soon. Please do not tell Odin I fell. He might not let me ride you again.*

I will tell your first mate only what he needs to know, the dragon agreed. *And I will continue to stay in the place they made for me until better accommodations can be arranged.*

The king hurriedly approached with Gjallar as the guards clapped their chests and bowed in deference to Frigga. Though weary from the ride, a bit windblown, and somewhat wobbly on her feet, she nodded graciously to acknowledge them. The open admiration on their faces made her feel like the heroine of some daring adventure, especially when they gave the dragon beside her a wide berth.

"Are you hurt?" Odin asked when he reached her, anxiously looking her over.

The dragon bounded over to Gjallar and nudged him with her head. He chuckled, but then his eyes widened with alarm.

"I'm fine, Odin," Frigga laughed as she watched the keeper and the dragon, assuming she was communicating with him.

After just a few moments, Gjallar led Idunn back into the Bifröst stables to settle her back into her stall. Frigga motioned for Odin to walk with her as they followed.

"What was riding a dragon like?" Odin asked.

She burst out laughing at the expectant, childish look on his face. "Would you like a turn?"

"I might," he admitted with a sheepish grin.

"You can ask her if she'll let you ride her when you speak with her," Frigga suggested.

"I don't think it's a good idea for me to speak with her," Odin said, his face sobering instantly. "What if I do more damage to my brain?"

"She says she can communicate with anyone who touches her if she chooses," Frigga informed him. "You wouldn't have to expend any of your own power. But she can probe your mind, so you would need to keep it locked."

"Honestly, I'm nervous about doing even that," Odin admitted. "Why do I need to talk with her?"

Frigga summarized their discussion around the plan to procure more dragons like her.

"Maybe you should come with me to Muspelheim," Odin remarked thoughtfully.

Frigga felt an immediate flare of excitement, followed by frustration as she realized that if she went with him, she would not be able to visit Vidar at the South Sea. But she had not left Asgard since her brother's coronation. Indecision settled in as she silently grappled with whether or not this opportunity was worth giving up her plans with Vidar.

"Is my suggestion that shocking?" Odin prompted. "I thought you would be eager to go."

"You've never taken me with you to another realm," she answered cautiously. "But Muspelheim? Are you certain that's wise?"

"You're probably right," Odin sighed, which made Frigga wonder if he had wanted her to go with him for more than just practical purposes. Straightening his shoulders, he continued, "Muspelheim is still dangerous. Perhaps it is not a good place to take my queen."

Disappointment welled up inside of her. The withdrawal of his offer made her want to insist on going even though she had been wondering if she should. Once again, she found herself in the situation of trying to figure out how she could have both options.

"I just rode a dragon bareback," she pointed out. "Perhaps I'm capable of more than you think."

Odin cocked his head at her. "Do you want to go or not?"

She sighed, resting one hand on the wooden frame of the main stable doors. "Yes and no."

Gjallar tentatively approached but stood at a respectful distance. Odin gestured for him to join the conversation.

"I have other business with the new king of Muspelheim," Odin informed Frigga. "I'm taking three council members and General Tyr with me. That should be plenty of protection. Bragi will take over here for Lord Berg with Vale assuming Vidar's duties. And the younger boys have Baldur and their tutors. You wouldn't necessarily be needed here like you have been on my other trips."

Frigga nodded thoughtfully, not wanting to reveal that none of this had even occurred to her.

"I was originally thinking you could work with the noblemen's wives while I'm gone," Odin went on, "but I do think you should choose the dragons you want. What if I bring home the wrong ones?"

"How are you getting these dragons anyway?" Frigga interjected, though she did not miss the uncharacteristic uncertainty in his voice. "Do you have some sort of agreement with the Muspel king?"

"He is indebted to me for helping him acquire the throne," Odin explained. "The first dragon was a gift to seal the treaty between us, but he's already told me we can trade for more if she pleases us. After all of the ill will, I believe King Baer is eager to stay in our good graces."

Gjallar suddenly spoke up, "Why not send the queen home through the Bifröst when she has finished her task? Then she can turn her attention to her duties while you focus on your meetings, my king."

"I'm not comfortable sending her alone, Gjallar, though I know your abilities," Odin contested.

"The king is right that no one is better suited to choose the right dragons for the Valkyries," Gjallar stated. When Frigga stared at him in surprise at his use of the new name, he grinned and explained, "Good news travels fast, Your Majesty. Idunn told me the rest. But my suggestion, my king, is to bring Prince Baldur and Hod with you. They've been to Muspelheim before and can return with the queen. She'll need help bringing the dragons back anyway."

"Gjallar, you are a man of great wisdom," Frigga exclaimed with pleasure.

"Indeed," Odin agreed. "Clearly this plan pleases the queen. We need only decide when to go."

"I have a meeting at the arena in two days," Frigga informed Odin.

"I can wait until after your meeting," Odin offered.

"I would prefer to get the dragons before I meet with them. The sooner, the better!" Frigga exclaimed. "I can reschedule through Gjallar if I cannot get back in time."

"Yes, I can do that. I would be glad to lend my assistance however it is needed," Gjallar offered.

"How quickly can you prepare temporary housing for five more dragons?" Frigga asked eagerly.

"Why five?" Odin challenged. "Surely you'll need more than that."

"Yes, but I don't think we should risk acquiring more until we have a permanent place for them," Frigga answered. "Six dragons will give me something to start training with, at least. Idunn still has to show me how to make riding seats. And what type of permanent housing we should build. Seeing it for myself on Muspelheim will help."

"Five more it is," Odin agreed.

Frigga felt as though she might burst from her skin with excitement, but she turned to Gjallar expectantly since he had not yet answered her question.

"What do you think, Gjallar? How quickly?" she prompted.

"If my men work around the clock, we could feasibly convert twenty empty stalls into five dragon quarters in a day or two," he replied. "Idunn's didn't take more than a few hours."

"What if you need them for horses?" she asked.

"We'll keep the easternmost stalls available, but I doubt we'll need them. We're at peace and most Asgardians are too preoccupied with the harvest season to travel," Gjallar responded.

"Well, King Odin, how soon shall we leave?" Frigga asked with a twinkle in her eyes.

He laughed. "I think you'd go now if I said the word, but we need a little time to prepare. Spend the rest of the morning with your dragon, Frigga. I'll take care of everything at the palace and return for you in time for lunch." When she nodded, he turned to the keeper of the gates. "Gjallar, send word to Baer to prepare for our arrival this afternoon. He was expecting me sometime soon, so it should not surprise him too much."

As Gjallar hurried off to obey, Odin escorted Frigga through the stable doors to Idunn's temporary living space. He distractedly kissed her goodbye then mounted Svadilfari, who had been contentedly munching hay from his place at the tethering post. Odin kicked his flanks and urged him out of the stable in a flurry of flying hooves. Sigurna watched them go, seeming as irritated by her mate's disinterest as Frigga felt herself. But reminding herself that they all had quite a bit to do, she decided not to allow Odin's rushed gesture to bother her any further. Instead, she carefully entered Idunn's stall and approached the resting creature.

The two of them spent the rest of the morning conversing and working on plans, including the design for a modified irscet dragon saddle. Frigga was so intent on their endeavor, she was quite surprised when Odin returned. When she registered how quickly she had forgotten him, understanding suddenly flooded her. Perhaps his focus made him forget her temporarily but had nothing to do with her value to him.

"Look!" she exclaimed, rushing over to him with the drawings she had made. "Idunn helped me design a dragon saddle for the Valkyries." She flipped over the page before he could get a good look. "And here are some ideas for housing." She flipped through those even faster. "And I wrote down all the names and characteristics for our new dragons."

"Frigga, slow down!" Odin laughed. "I didn't catch more than a glimpse. Show them to me at lunch. We have much to discuss and do."

15

Frigga felt as if she were in a dream as she stood with all the men on the dais of the great Bifröst portal. She had been grieving the sudden death of her father the last time she had traveled this way. Nostalgia and sorrow settled over her briefly as the huge shimmering portal sucked them all through and deposited them safely on Muspelheim as if nothing had happened. Excitement and anticipation quickly replaced her former emotions.

She looked around her at the rocky landscape littered with far-off volcanoes. The air felt thick and heavy like an unbearable summer afternoon that drives everyone inside for relief. Vidar's description echoed in her mind. She had imagined Muspelheim as frightening and dark, but the planet was not what she had expected. Vivid orange and coral colors streaked the hazy yellow sky with a strange beauty that took Frigga's breath away. She had not picked up a paintbrush in years, but the sight made her wish she could pluck one out of the air and paint the scene before it faded from her memory.

As Odin gestured for everyone to follow him to nearby towering gates of black iron, he leaned in to whisper to

Frigga, "Be glad we're far from the battlegrounds. The stench of the tar pits would knock you over."

She shuddered, noticing a faint but strong odor creeping over the land from somewhere in the distance. "Is this their capital city?"

"I suppose this is as close to a capital city that I've seen," Odin answered with a shrug. "Their way of life really isn't comparable to ours. But they could be powerful allies if we can overlook our differences."

Frigga saw movement at the gates, which swung wide open to admit the group. They crossed over a bridge carved of black glass that bore strange serpentine symbols. Below its shining surface, which almost perfectly reflected their images as they walked, a river swiftly flowed. The water was so clear, Frigga could see straight to the bottom of the gray stone river bed. She peered ahead of her, wondering why they had not yet seen a single fire giant.

At the end of the bridge stood a tall structure made of the same shiny black substance with similar carvings that reminded her of Idunn in a strange way, though they took no recognizable form. Two columns flanked the base wall, looking as though they had grown into twisted spires resembling a pair of horns. The wall between the columns had appeared seamless at first, but as they approached, two large doors soundlessly opened inward with a whoosh of sweetly-scented air, admitting them into a silent hall over-flowing with foliage and brightly colored flowers growing out of black rock.

Frigga stared at the indoor botanical garden in amazement and breathed deeply of the wholesome stillness. Despite the riot of color and fragrance, the surprisingly solemn aura made her feel she must keep her admiration to herself.

The others seemed to be under the same spell as King Odin led them toward a grouping of rocks in the center of the hall where a huge horned dragon lay curled up. The winged creature, which Frigga assumed was a Nagir, lifted his head and growled at the visitors as he flashed his fierce red eyes at them. As they approached the pile of deep gray, lightly speckled boulders that somewhat resembled a throne, Frigga registered the presence of a well-camouflaged figure perched cross-legged on the stone seat just as he placed a six-fingered hand on the burnt orange scales of the dragon to calm him.

"You've come earlier than expected, King Odin," the king of Muspelheim said in Asgardian as he unfolded his long limbs and stood.

His voice rumbled from deep within his chest even as his words flowed smoothly out of his mouth. Frigga almost expected lava to pour out with them. He looked exactly like the mental image Vidar had painted for her when he had described fire giants, his skin almost perfectly blending with the rudimentary throne behind him.

"They speak Asgardian?" Frigga whispered to Lord Shronner, who stood closest to her.

"They say they can speak any language," Shronner whispered back. "They don't usually bother much with the common tongue."

Odin silenced the two of them with a warning glare, then addressed the fire giant. "I have delayed returning long enough, King Baer."

King Baer flashed his fiery eyes at each person, his glance lingering longest on Frigga as he replied, "That is true, but your message gave us little time to prepare."

"If you had sent word asking for more time, I would have honored that request," Odin returned.

"There was no need," Baer replied solemnly. "We have readied ourselves to welcome you."

"I hope the effort was not too taxing," Odin responded grimly. "I will take your preference for more notice into consideration for my next visit."

King Baer nodded. "I was sorry to hear the reason for the delay in your return. How ironic to have lasted so long in battle only to lose an eye in your own land."

Odin grimaced slightly as the men around him bristled. Frigga fancied she saw a cunning smirk on the giant's face. She stifled her own indignation, then remembered Idunn's blunt mannerisms and wondered if this was the Muspel way and not an intended cruelty or threat. But before anyone could respond to Baer's comment, he turned his intense gaze on her again.

"Is this delicate bloom your queen, King Odin?" Baer asked. "I have never seen one of your females before." He cocked his head as he stared at Frigga, then remarked, "Or eyes of such blue. They are like my flowers that open their faces only to the morning."

"The king of Muspelheim speaks most beautifully," Frigga said humbly, curtsying before him and feeling pleased that his forward ways also extended to positive affirmation. "His speeches are as lovely as his receiving hall. I am Queen Frigga, and I have come with a proposal for

Your Majesty. I'm afraid I must confess my eagerness to visit your realm and present my request to you was a determining factor in the timing of our arrival."

Baer's deep gray lips formed a delighted smile, revealing a row of brilliant white teeth. The contrast was so startling, she could not help staring.

"It seems the queen has not seen one such as I either," he laughed, the sound bubbling from him like rolling thunder. "And if one such as you had need of haste, perhaps it was necessary. I will hear your request, Queen Frigga, and show you more of my gardens since they please your eyes. Such eyes!"

"I would love to see them, King Baer," Frigga replied demurely with another little curtsy.

She winked at Odin, who was not quite successful at hiding his irritation at the Muspel king's boldness.

"All of you are invited, of course," King Baer informed the others. "But first, we have prepared refreshment for the delegates."

After King Odin introduced each of the men, King Baer waved for them all to follow him. The dragon lifted himself off the shining black floor and ambled after his master, nearly knocking Lord Berg over with his tail. Frigga had expected the dragon to make more noise, but he moved almost soundlessly. She peered at the animal's feet and guessed he kept his talons sheathed when he walked.

Just like a cat again! she thought with glee.

Baer led them all through another seamless door to reveal a black table laden with fruits and vegetables of every color. White flowering trees and delicate ferns filled the edges of the room. When Frigga clapped her hands to her mouth in obvious delight, she heard a pleased rumbling like a cat's purr. To her surprise, she realized the king was making the sound deep in his chest. The dragon nudged him with his great head, and the king placed his hand on the creature briefly.

Then Baer informed the men, "Asgardian females are better company than you males. They do not hide so much."

Frigga laughed as the Asgardian men tried to disguise their agitation, which only proved his words.

"I am Vanir, King Baer, and only Asgardian by marriage," she corrected him.

"Truly? Tell me about your people," he requested politely as everyone sat down and began to eat.

"We are like Asgardians in almost every way, though we are not as wealthy or polished. And we have seen too much war," she began. She looked up at the clear ceiling of his home and wiped a little sweat from her brow from the humidity. "But we are a proud and skilled people, especially in the ways of science. We honor our healers and our warriors equally with dances, celebrations, and stories."

"Do you miss your homeland?" Baer asked curiously. "You speak quite wistfully."

"At times," she admitted. "I especially miss Vanaheim's wide open plains and the long, feathery grass I walked through when I had a chance to get away by myself."

She happened to catch Odin squinting his good eye slightly as she spoke and wondered what he might be thinking. She could not recall if she had ever shared that with him in the past.

"Alas, we no longer grow grass here," the king of Muspelheim declared. "We have found it to be a waste of the space we need to grow our food, though we are fond of flowers."

"Do you only eat fruits and vegetables?" Frigga asked curiously, thankful for the change in subject.

"No, we eat several types of serpents and lizards," he answered. "We also fish in the lakes past the volcanoes and tar pits. Some Muspels grow plants out in the open there. That's where we get our obsidian, which we use quite frequently, as you can see." He waved at the black glass of the table, floors, and walls, then placed one large gray hand over hers. "Your kind does not usually express such interest in ours. I am thankful for your husband's help in ending the war here, but not even he has asked much about our culture."

She resisted the urge to snatch her hand away from the heat in his touch. "I will see what I can do to remedy that."

She breathed a small sigh of relief when he removed his hand.

But he had noticed and hurriedly said, "My apologies! Did I burn you?"

"Only a little," she hastened to reassure him, showing him that not even a red mark remained. "Will we be meeting your queen, King Baer?"

"I have no queen. My dragon will choose one for me," Baer responded with a shrug. "He knows me as I know myself. I'm in no hurry."

"I only understand a little of such things, but I have spoken at length with the Salir dragon you gave us," Frigga replied. "The one named—"

"We do not speak aloud the names of our dragons here, Queen Frigga," he interrupted her. "I am surprised the Salir did not tell you that. Does she please you?"

"Very much so," Frigga replied, hiding her confusion over this news. "And I am sorry if I have caused any offense."

"You did not know." He winked at her. "We are even now."

She laughed, which delighted the king so much that he started to purr again. Then Frigga realized her mistake—the dragon was making the sound this time. When the king placed one hand on him again with closed eyes, Frigga guessed it was part of their communication. The Asgardian noblemen had watched all of this with fascination, but Odin looked slightly angry. Frigga made a note to speak with him as soon as they had a private moment together. But for now, she had a mission to fulfill. As King Baer eagerly listened, she described her dragon initiative and her first experience riding a dragon.

"Queen Frigga, you amaze me!" Baer exclaimed. "Daring and genius have made their homes in your heart." He turned to Odin. "King Odin, I will be a lucky Muspel indeed if my dragon chooses a queen for me like yours."

The dragon lifted his head at those words and gazed at Frigga as if memorizing her.

"You honor me and my queen," Odin said with a respectful nod.

Despite his gracious words, Frigga knew an emotional storm brewed under his polished exterior. She turned back to the Muspel king. "I am intrigued by your marriage customs, King Baer. What if your dragon selects a mate who is already married or does not wish to marry you?"

"It's a complicated process that isn't easy to explain," Baer laughed. "If a female caught my eye or my dragon's eye, he would communicate with her dragon to assess her availability and interest. Sometimes the female's dragon will approach the male's dragon. Now that I am the king, my dragon has had to turn several females away who had undesirable motives. I suppose that is only natural."

"Why not cut out the middle man?" Berg whispered to Shronner, who chuckled softly.

"Finally!" Baer exclaimed. "One of you almost dares to speak his mind. So, Lord Berg, what would you say?"

"I merely wondered why you need the dragons at all," Berg said nervously. "Why not just talk to the females yourself?"

The huge red dragon snorted.

Baer chuckled, then explained, "We do speak with our females, but when we are pursuing a commitment, what you call marriage, the dragons help us avoid the common pitfalls of most relationships. They have incredible insight into the psyche and can detect clearly what we only see dimly. Motives, kindness, even darkness. I have no doubt your queen already knows this, having ridden one herself."

Frigga nodded. "My new dragon says her kind is only sometimes monogamous. Are the Muspels the same?"

Baer grinned at her. "Yes. But I care not for casual relationships. I have had my fill of balancing multiple females. Now I want something real—just one person I can fully trust. And I am content to wait until my dragon and I find her. In a way, I envy you Asgardian men. You seem to find loyal mates much faster than we do."

"I have yet to find a wife," Shronner announced.

"Same with me," General Tyr chimed in. "It is no easy task."

Baldur and Hod exchanged glances with each other as if uncomfortable with the conversation.

Trebent had not said a word since they arrived and focused on the remaining food on his obsidian plate. But Frigga did not concern herself with that, as he had always been a quieter man.

"Perhaps we are not so different after all," Frigga observed.

"Perhaps not, O Queen," King Baer agreed. "Our methods are different, but we experience some of the same things. I have had my doubts as to whether or not we can understand one another enough for our new alliance to work, but what I have seen and heard today gives me hope. And now that you have helped me dethrone a tyrant, King Odin, I hope to change things."

"And *that* is why we are here, King Baer," Odin prompted. He pushed his plate back and stood. "And if you truly wish us to speak our minds and disregard political protocol, perhaps we can conduct our business expeditiously this time."

"Perhaps," replied King Baer, his eyes flaring slightly. "But I think you remember we do not rush things here. Still, you have shown an interest in my culture. And a desire to graft a part of it into your own. For that reason, I will compromise and speed things along this time, though it is contrary to my nature." He stood as well and gestured for Frigga to follow him. "Those of you who wish to see my gardens and my fleet of Salir dragons may join us. The rest of you, feel free to wait here and continue to refresh yourselves."

Odin strode to Frigga's side and offered her his arm. Baldur and Hod followed behind them, as did General Tyr. Lord Berg, Lord Trebent, and Lord Shronner whispered to each other, then joined the group. This immensely pleased King Baer, who eagerly led them through an overwhelming labyrinth of rooms filled with flowers, trees, and exotic-looking plants. One large room reminded her of the apple grove on Asgard, though the apples were a brilliant blood red. Another overflowed with prickly plants she had never seen before, which Baer warned them not to touch. These instructions were strangely hard to resist, but Frigga managed to curb her desire to stroke the fuzzier-looking ones. She found it odd how the king proudly told them the names of each plant but did not permit the names of the dragons to be spoken. And since she could not quite retain all of the information anyway, she decided to simply enjoy the experience of the tour.

As they stood in the last room, Frigga asked the king, "Do you live alone in this great house?"

"No, several members of my cabinet live here with me, as well as my servants, but they are all occupied with other tasks at the moment," he answered. "You will meet my cabinet this evening. We have led my people from here for all the years we have fought to improve our world. Horticulture has been my hobby, but it has also preserved my sanity. But come, to the dragons!"

He waved his hand before a wall. A small charm on his wrist flared slightly, and two huge doors opened inwardly as his main doors had.

Thirty enormous obsidian paddocks, each holding three to four dragons, lined both sides of a wide aisle. Roars filled the air as the multitude of Salir dragons reared into the air as Idunn had done when celebrating. Flames erupted from their mouths toward a black ceiling inset with clear glass windows that seemed so high up, three Muspels would have to stand on each other's shoulders to clean them. The Asgardians gaped with open mouths at the spectacle and stood stock still as if they could not take another step forward.

So many! Frigga marveled silently. *Are they happy to see us or the king?*

Baer's dragon let loose a high-pitched whistle, which silenced the Salir and brought them back to all fours.

"These are all yours?" Frigga exclaimed.

"In a way," Baer chuckled. "My people pay tribute to me with the Salir since no one really keeps them as companions. But they are really for our warriors, who begin their training here as children. We have another housing for the Nagir."

He motioned for them to follow him down the long aisle. The obsidian of each paddock framed thick clear gates that came to Baer's shoulder, designed to allow visitors to see in and the dragons to see out. Individual pools of crystal water rippled slightly as the group walked by and the dragons pranced about, showing off for their visitors. Their living quarters had no straw or other type of bedding, only the soft gray dirt that also covered the aisle floor. Frigga reveled in the sensation of her feet sinking into it as they walked.

One hornless vermillion dragon stayed curled up in a corner of a paddock on the left side when her companions rushed to their front gate to inspect the visitors as they passed. The others kept going, but Frigga stopped at the gate. The dragon lifted her head to gaze at Frigga with curious claret eyes, but she did not move. Since the fire giant king and the Asgardian delegates had moved far beyond the paddock, Frigga imitated the purring sound Baer had used and stretched her hand toward the top of the gate. She might have been able to make a poor imitation of the sound with her vocal chords, but her ability to manipulate sound waves enabled her to execute it perfectly. The other three dragons, two males and one female, cocked their heads at her. They all looked at each other, then back at Frigga. One male stepped forward to thrust his horned head over the gate to meet her hand. She locked her mind as she had done with Idunn, only keeping a mental communication link open.

What do you seek, Asgardian? he sent to her.

I wish to speak with the red female. Is she your mate? Frigga replied, not bothering to correct him as she had King Baer since the task at hand was far more pressing.

She has no mate, he informed her. *He was killed in a skirmish during the war, and she will take no other.*

I thought the Salir did not go to battle, Frigga thought in surprise.

Many of us roam free, he answered. *Sometimes battle comes to us.*

He broke the connection and let loose a series of pleasant-sounding trills and deep-throated growls. The vermillion female cocked her head and stared at Frigga, then tucked her head under her tail. The male Salir shook his head sadly at Frigga. But before she could do anything else, King Baer and King Odin appeared at her side.

"I want that one," she told them, pointing at the curled-up dragon.

"We rescued her from the plains," King Baer said. "She's healed from her injuries, but she hasn't done much more than lie there in days."

"She's lost her mate," Frigga informed him, watching the dragon, who had shifted in a way that made her think she was listening. "I know a little of how she feels."

"What do you mean?" Odin asked quietly, in a strange tone she did not know how to interpret.

Frigga turned to him but projected her voice so the dragon would hear. "I almost lost you, Odin. And the fear I experienced on that day was tangible. It drove reason from my mind. I can imagine her pain quite well, having had a taste of it."

When Odin smiled softly at her, Frigga wondered if he had feared she spoke of losing another. And perhaps she had been subconsciously thinking of Vidar and their brief yet painful separation.

King Baer interrupted her thoughts to ask, "What others please you? How many do you want?"

"I'd like to start with five," she replied confidently. "We can discuss more after we've established housing and everything else they'll need on Asgard. But I will not take any against their wills."

The vermillion female raised her head and peered at Frigga again.

"King Baer, may I enter the paddock?" she asked as she met the dragon's eyes.

"Frigga, no," Odin whispered urgently.

"I cannot allow that," Baer answered firmly.

"The dragon will not come to the gate to speak with me," Frigga protested. "I need to communicate my intent to her, to let her know my heart. The other dragons will not harm me. You trust them with your children, do you not?"

"Our children are taught from a young age how to defend themselves should a dragon become unmanageable. They are also born with thick skin and muscle strength that your kind simply does not have," King Baer stated sternly. "There are two males in there, and they can be unpredictable. Their teeth and talons could tear you to shreds."

"I've spoken with one of the males already," Frigga argued. "Ask them yourself if they will harm me."

"I do not speak with the Salir," the Muspel king snorted. "That is for children."

"Then why did they celebrate when we entered this area? They must be loyal to you for some reason," Frigga challenged.

"Their celebration was not just for me. Regardless, I care for them and provide them with riders," King Baer replied. "And if they wish to roam free, I allow it. They know kindness when they see it. But we have no reason to speak with each other."

"Perhaps you should anyway," Frigga dared to say. "You might find areas in which you can grow as a king. I, on the other hand, *need* to speak with them."

King Baer stared at Frigga, his mouth twitching slightly. Then he chuckled and shook his head. "You have a wholesome fire in you, O Queen. But if you were injured while visiting as a delegate, it could potentially harm future relations with your realm. If I consider speaking with the Salir that will not speak with you, would that pacify you?"

"For now," she conceded. "I have a list of names my Salir gave me, as well as characteristics we're looking for. But if you cannot know a dragon's name—"

"I said we do not speak them aloud," the king corrected. "Dragons only reveal their names to those they wish to know. If we spoke them aloud, it would be a betrayal of their confidence in us."

"I wonder why she didn't tell me that," Frigga murmured.

"You should ask her," King Baer returned. "The dragons may help you find the ones you seek." Then he turned to Odin. "We have yet to discuss the price of these dragons."

Frigga tuned them out to inspect the other paddocks. The rest of the Asgardians stood at the end of the long aisle, talking to each other and watching the dragons nearest them. She made her way toward her group, looking for other dragons that stood out like the melancholy vermillion female. Most of them seemed happy and full of life. Near the very end, one bright yellow male sat quite still as though he waited for her. When she reached him, he purred, which Frigga now understood meant he wished to communicate. She reached out her hand and allowed him to close the distance.

You have ridden one I know well, he thought when they connected. *I detect the faintest whiff of her scent on you.*

Yes, I am now her rider for life, she responded. *I am Queen Frigga of Asgard. How do you know my dragon?*

I am Brinn, brother to her last mate, the dragon responded. *Is she well?*

She is, Frigga answered distractedly. She pulled out her list of names to confirm why his name sounded familiar. *Brinn? Your friend asked me to bring you back to Asgard with me.*

She asked for me by name? he thought. His voice in Frigga's head seemed wistful and full of wonder. *But why did she tell you my name? Do you know hers?*

I do. Idunn told me several names, Frigga answered honestly. *I do not know why. I can only think she trusts me. And so can you.*

I know. I can sense your kind spirit. For that reason, I will tell you this—long have I sought her heart, Brinn sighed inside Frigga's mind. *But she chose two others and then my own brother. I cannot imagine why she would seek my company now.*

If you go with me, you'll soon know, Frigga told him. She explained why she was taking dragons to Asgard, then asked, *Will you go?*

I will go, he responded. *Tell me the names of the others you seek.*

She read the names silently into his mind.

Gronn and Plinn are dead, he informed her after listening carefully. *Farenn and Evonn have joined the dragon clans that run wild on the plains. The others are here. Of those, try Dwinn across the aisle first. He is the crimson dragon with the largest horns. And also Yolann, his second mate. She is the rust-colored one in the same paddock.*

What about his first mate? Frigga asked, glancing across the aisle. *Is she the golden dragon with them?*

Yes, and she is a feisty one. I doubt she would go. She is not on your list, so I will not speak her name, Brinn thought with amusement. *Idunn never did care much for her.*

And what about the other red male with them? Frigga asked.

Do not approach him, Brinn warned. *He hates your kind. He will harm you if he can.*

Thank you for the warning, Brinn. Do you know the vermillion dragon on the other end? She lost her mate in the war, Frigga thought.

I should not tell you her name either, Brinn answered. *I will say she is not on the list, but she will die if nothing changes.*

She seems perfect. It's strange Idunn did not mention her, Frigga mused. *But I would like to take her nonetheless.*

She did not list her former mates or her own offspring either. I do not always understand her, Brinn informed her. *The king is coming. You may seek me out again if you need further assistance.*

Thank you, Brinn, she thought.

She removed her hand from his head just as Odin and Baer joined her. She suddenly realized the other Asgardians had been watching her curiously.

"This one too," she told the two kings. She pointed toward the three dragons watching her from the paddock directly across from Brinn. "I will speak with those next."

"How are you speaking to the dragons, my queen?" Berg asked.

Baldur shifted his eyes from his mother to the other men nervously. He knew his parents both had some sort of secret mind power because Frigga had taught him how to lock his mind when he was much younger. But he did not know quite what they could do, just not to discuss it with anyone.

"You could too if they allowed you," Frigga answered lightly. "They speak telepathically through touch."

Lord Berg raised his eyebrows and peered at the yellow dragon as if he might be considering speaking with him. Brinn cocked his head at Berg, then purred.

"He's asking to speak with you," Frigga told Berg. "Put your hand on his head."

Berg looked at her with wide eyes, then did as she suggested. His eyes grew even wider as he communicated with Brinn.

The nobleman held the connection for several seconds, then turned excitedly to everyone else. "I could hear him in my head! He said—"

"That's for you to know," Frigga interrupted. "I'm certain you wouldn't reveal a private conversation with an Asgardian, Lord Berg. Nor should you when it's with a dragon."

"Oh, of course," he murmured, nodding at the bright yellow dragon, who turned his attention back to the other dragons in his paddock.

Frigga walked over to the enclosure across the aisle as the men made their way back to the entrance. She approached the golden dragon first, who had been watching with eager orange eyes. Her scales were only a slightly different shade than Idunn's, but she had a fierce look that was quite different from Frigga's dragon. Before Frigga could say anything, the dragon purred to signal she desired to speak with her. Frigga placed her hand on her head.

Greetings, noble one, the dragon said. *What is your purpose here?*

I am taking dragons with me to Asgard, she answered.

Did that fool across from us tell you I would go? she demanded.

He told me you would not, Frigga corrected.

That makes me want to prove him wrong, responded the dragon as her orange eyes blazed slightly. *But I do not wish to leave my home. Do you plan to ask my mate?*

I do, Frigga thought. *Is that acceptable or do you wish to discuss it with him?*

He is weak, the dragon huffed. *I never should have mated with him. And now I cannot get rid of him. Even when he took another mate, he still favors me. He is like tar stuck to my talons.*

Frigga hid her shock at the dragon's callousness and cinched up her locked mind even tighter. *Would you mind if I speak with him and ask him to come to Asgard with me?*

Not at all, she scoffed. *Take that ridiculous second mate of his too. Perhaps then I will have some peace.*

Frigga nodded and broke their connection. If the male was so taken with the rude golden dragon, how would she persuade him? She decided to approach the other female first, noticing how the male kept a wary eye on her and the hostile male, who looked as if he might be considering springing at her. Frigga kept a calm exterior, then purred at the rust-colored female.

How can I serve you, Queen of Asgard? the dragon asked quietly after they had connected.

How do you know who I am? Frigga asked.

Our king spoke your title, and the other dragons are discussing you, the rust-colored creature responded. *Do you not hear them?*

Frigga cocked her head and realized she had not registered the soft trills of the other dragons. *Then do you know why I am here?*

I do, and I will hear you, the dragon declared.

You are kinder than your rival, Yolann, Frigga observed. *She seemed not to know my purpose.*

She likely wanted you to tell her yourself. She acts gruffly to impress, Your Majesty, Yolann answered. *She is not as tough as she seems. But how do you know my name?*

Idunn has asked for you and Dwinn to join her on Asgard, Frigga told her. She explained why, then thought, *But if he is more loyal to your rival, as she says, I don't know how we will persuade him to leave her. She does not wish to go.*

Yolann snorted in Frigga's mind. *She is quite full of herself. Why would Dwinn take a second mate if he is as pleased with her as she thinks?*

She told me she is eager to be rid of him, Frigga mused.

At this, Yolann laughed silently, the feel of her laughter filling the open space in Frigga's mind. *She was furious when Dwinn chose me,* the dragon declared. *She thought they were mates for life and used him as her servant, expecting him to cater to her every whim. Now she pretends she cannot stand him. How rich!*

Frigga lifted her hand and pondered this. Two very different perspectives. What would the male say?

She replaced her hand and thought, *Will you go?*

If Dwinn does, Yolann replied. *He is my only mate, and I am loyal to him. I go where he goes.*

Frigga noticed Odin beckoning to her. *Will you speak to him for me?* she asked Yolann. *I must go for now, but I will return as soon as I can.*

When the dragon nodded, Frigga hurried back down the aisle to join the men waiting at the door they had all entered. The vermillion dragon raised her head as Frigga passed and cocked her head. The queen slowed her pace to meet her gaze. She smiled at the grieving creature, who closed her eyes slowly and dipped her head in acknowledgment.

"Did you see that?" Frigga whispered excitedly to Odin when she reached him.

"You are gifted, my queen," Odin said kindly. "I have no doubt she will return to Asgard with you. Perhaps she will be happier there."

"Where are we going now?" she asked.

"King Baer has prepared rooms for us all. The men will stay two to a room, and we will have our own," Odin explained.

"They're showing us to our rooms now?" she asked in surprise as they followed the others back the way they had come.

"Yes, we'll take a short respite, as they always do this time of day. After that, we men have business to discuss. Baer has provided an escort for you if you wish to return to the dragons to finalize your choices. Tonight, we dine together with his cabinet. And in the morning, you may take the dragons back to Asgard."

"And what are we providing in exchange for these dragons? Gold? Jewels?" she whispered.

"They have no use for such things," Odin answered with a chuckle. "Baer asked about our native plants. He has his heart set on Asgardian apple saplings, which Baldur and Hod will bring back from the palace nursery. Five per dragon."

Frigga laughed quietly so the Muspel king would not overhear. "Of course! From what I have seen of Baer's gardens, they lack nothing. It is an honor for him to choose Asgardian apple trees as his price."

After Frigga and Odin had closeted themselves in their guest room and cooled the air to their liking by adjusting the humming machine in the ceiling as Baer had showed them, Frigga turned with great seriousness to her husband.

"Odin, what's been troubling you?" she asked tentatively. "You've been acting strangely since we arrived. If I didn't know better, I'd say you are jealous of the Muspel king."

"He has not been subtle about how taken he is with you," Odin pointed out. "I do not wish to jeopardize our fragile alliance with this realm, but he had better remember you are my queen."

Frigga sighed. "Oh, you males, always asserting dominance. King Baer is no threat. He is a fire giant and—"

"And I have lain with a Jotun," Odin interrupted.

Frigga stared aghast at him. "Why would you bring that up?"

"Because race is inconsequential when it comes to attraction and temptation," he explained curtly. "There is beauty in all the realms."

"If you believe that, why do you permit the intolerance of your people toward other races?" Frigga asked in surprise.

"Oh, not this again, Frigga," Odin said with exasperation. "Don't you hear your own hypocrisy? You yourself just said Baer is not a threat because he is a fire giant."

"Just because I am not attracted to a fire giant does not mean I think myself better than he is," she huffed. "There are Asgardians and Vanir I am not attracted to either."

"Ah, but you didn't say you aren't attracted to him. You brought up his race, not I," Odin pointed out. "Deep down inside, you know they are different from us."

"Of course they are! And yes, I do think it would be dangerous and irresponsible for one of us to mingle with one of them. I already worry about what Loki will have to face when he begins to discover his Jotun powers," Frigga retorted.

"I do too, Frigga," Odin admitted. "I would delay that day as long as possible. He must not believe he is anything less than our son."

"And being half Jotun makes him less?" Frigga asked, her body bristling at the insinuation.

"Not at all! Don't twist my words, Frigga," Odin clarified tersely. "The hard truth is that others might make him feel so. That is the battle we must face with him."

"And that is exactly why I would not risk intermingling," Frigga explained. "Surely the Muspel king also understands how important it is to take a queen more suited to his genetics."

"Perhaps you are right," Odin yielded. "I still plan to keep an eye on him. Their culture is so strange. Who knows what morals they adhere to."

"Yes, they are quite different. Fascinatingly so, in my opinion," Frigga mused. "But I certainly do not hate them for being different like Asgardians do."

"The last thing I want is to fan the flames of the old hatreds," Odin defended himself.

"I wasn't suggesting you personally, Odin," she clarified. "But the people look to you. Perhaps it's time we educate them on how to celebrate differences rather than fear them."

"This alliance is one attempt to bridge our worlds," Odin replied. "But you have seen how stubborn Asgardians are."

"I certainly have," she muttered.

He shot her an annoyed look, then continued, "We cannot implement too many changes at once. Be patient and content with the strides we have made."

"Are you suggesting we settle?"

"Of course not," Odin sighed heavily. "Things will change over time, Frigga. I cannot make a decree to stop feelings of hate and prejudice. They have to figure it out on their own through education and exposure. That's why we got involved in the Muspelheim conflict—to foster peace. And someday, understanding."

"I thought you got involved because the former king made threats against Asgard," she contested dryly.

To her surprise, he laughed. "Well, there was that. This is why I say you're smarter than I am. You always see right through me."

She laughed with him, then sobered. "Not always. You've fooled me a few times."

He grew serious as well. "I don't ever want to lie to you again."

"Then don't," she said breezily. She almost added, *Is it really that hard?*

But she stopped herself in time, hiding the pang of guilt that struck her because she had been lying to *him* by hiding the true nature of her relationship with Vidar. And yes, it was hard. She had no desire to give up the general's love, even though she knew it was completely incompatible with her morality and the standards of her world. And deep within her, as much as he had wounded her, she did not want to give up Odin either or deal with the consequences if she revealed her true heart.

The dragons and the Muspels have more than one mate at a time. Why can't I? she thought rebelliously.

And she wondered if Odin had hidden his infidelity for similar reasons. But he had insisted he had not loved the women with whom he had lain. And her impression that men could pursue physical satisfaction with little to no heart connection had led her to accept that. Perhaps he had not wanted the fallout or to risk losing her. And so it had been safer to hide his wrongdoing. But it also begged the question of whether or not he truly loved her if he could be so calloused toward his former lovers. As her frustration and confusion mounted, her thoughts began to crash into each other. She realized Odin was staring at her. When she met his good eye, he took a deep breath.

"Frigga, we agree on more than you think we do. I wish we had more time to really deal with the issues that lie between us," he said morosely. The sadness in his tone tugged at her heart. "I can see how much I've wounded you in the past. I'm not the same man, just as you said. And I am trying."

"I know," she whispered. She drew near him and hugged him. "We are who we are."

He held her tightly, clinging to her as if he could not bear to let her go. She tried to gently extract herself, but he held on for a few more moments.

When he finally released her, she asked, "When does this short respite end?"

Odin checked his timepiece, a one-of-a-kind device that clocked the time on all nine realms. "In twenty minutes."

He snapped the lid shut to reveal the engraving on the front, which read *King Odin Allfather* above three interlocked triangles, the symbol every Asgardian king had borne to honor and remember the fallen. But only Odin had ever been called Allfather. His concerns for and sense of responsibility toward all the realms, even the dreaded and frozen Niflheim, had earned him that title some time ago. But Frigga never used it, for she secretly resented it. Over the years, it had just come to mean more of him she had been forced to relinquish to his kingship. And the irony of the title conflicting with his reluctance to address prejudice had struck her with derisive hilarity more than once. She suddenly realized her thoughts also contradicted themselves. She wanted him to make Asgard better but resented the time it had taken away from her as well as the distractedness into which he so often slipped.

As Odin walked over to the window and looked out on the unusual landscape, she tentatively sat on the large, square bed in the room. She felt the highly polished obsidian of the frame, enjoying the smoothness against her hand as she sank into the surprisingly soft and warm mattress.

She sighed with contentment and delight. "Odin, come try this bed! I think the mattress is filled with hot water!"

"We had beds of sand last time," Odin remarked. "The others probably have those again. I think you've warranted the special treatment, Firefly."

He sat down on the other side too quickly and accidentally flopped almost to the middle, knocking into Frigga. She laughed, which encouraged him to tickle her to make her laugh harder. When she begged him to stop, he did but stared down at her with a look she knew all too well.

She yawned to signal for him to not get any ideas. "How do I summon this escort Baer provided for me? I think I'd like to take a nap before I go back to the dragons."

"Just go to the enclosure when you're ready," Odin answered. "The escort will be waiting for you there."

He kissed her forehead as she lay there looking up at him with her curls fanned out around her. She saw the desire in his good eye and felt a shiver of response. She could easily transform him into Vidar in her mind to ignite passion with Odin, but something about the idea repulsed her. She touched his cheek with a soft smile, then turned on her side, hoping he would not feel rejected. He lay down beside her, but when she woke up from her nap, he was gone.

She made her way back to the dragon enclosure where a fire giant with coal black skin and flaming eyes stood guard. She smiled at him, feeling slightly fearful. He was very unlike Baer, and she was alone.

"Have you been waiting long?" she asked sweetly.

He stared at her with eyes ablaze, then grunted as he pointed to a long, pale scar down his throat. She realized with a start that he could not speak. She almost suggested she could read his mind but thought better of it. The Muspels did not need to know she possessed that gift.

Instead, she nodded and said, "I understand. Did one of my kind do this to you?"

He shook his head and gestured to himself.

"One of your kind?"

He nodded.

She sighed sadly. "My deepest condolences for your loss and suffering. And I thank you for escorting me."

He bowed slightly, then opened the dragon enclosure. The Salir stayed quiet this time but focused on Frigga and the Muspel as they walked toward them. The first male she had spoken to trilled as she drew near him, then purred his request to speak with her.

As soon as her hand connected with his scaly orange head, he thrust into her mind, *I wish to go with you, Asgardian.*

Will you tell me why? she responded.

The male shifted his eyes to the vermillion dragon, who had moved closer to the gate and sat gazing at Frigga. *Because she has decided to go,* he said simply.

What is your name? Frigga asked boldly as she looked him over.

He puffed out his chest. *I am Frinn.*

And I am Frigga, she chuckled. *Not so different, are we?*

We are very different, Queen Frigga, he said seriously. *But I have heard your plan, and I crave something different in my life. And if it wins her heart ...*

Frinn trailed off as he looked again at the female, who had taken a few steps toward the gate.

Frigga reached out her hand and called, "Will you speak to me, beautiful one?"

The dragon slowly took several more steps until she stood next to the orange male. She lowered her head and allowed Frigga to touch her. Frigga waited patiently for her to open communication.

Finally, the female thought, *You are wise and kind.* She shifted her eyes toward the male. *So is he. He suggests my heart might heal on your planet. Do you think it so, O Queen?*

I have found healing in many places, Frigga answered. *On Asgard, you will be treated well. We have a great work to do, which may give you a purpose beyond your pain.*

I want to live again, the red dragon admitted.

And so you shall, Frigga thought. *Will you tell me your name?*

I am not ready, she responded. *When I tell you my name, you will know I trust you.*

Can you tell me why my dragon did not tell me to keep her name secret as they do here? Frigga requested.

She may have assumed you knew how sacred our names are to us, the vermillion dragon mused.

Then I have betrayed her unwittingly, Frigga thought with dismay. *But she told me many other things about your kind, even how to ride her, but nothing about this.*

Speak with her about it, the dragon suggested. *I cannot speak for her.*

Frigga nodded. *We will return to your new home in the morning. Please tell Frinn.*

The dragon trilled to the orange male, who acknowledged her with a dip of his head. Frigga made her way down to the other end, where the other three dragons waited. She approached Dwinn first.

Yolann and I have decided in your favor, Asgardian queen, the crimson dragon spoke. *My first mate now prefers the other male, which suits our situation better.*

Frigga glanced at the hostile dragon, slightly alarmed at how he paced and glared at her.

Do not be afraid, Dwinn said. *He knows I will kill him if he tries to harm you.*

Why does he hate my kind? she asked.

One of your males killed the last Muspel who trained with him, Dwinn explained. *He had just graduated and fell in his first battle—the son of the tyrant who used to rule Muspelheim. Their bond was strong.*

Frigga felt her eyes fill with tears. Rather than answer the bigger red dragon, she projected her voice to tell the other, "I am deeply sorry for the pain we have caused you. To cut down one so young and full of life is an atrocity to be grieved, regardless of whose side he fought on. May he be at peace."

The dragon stopped pacing abruptly as Frigga finished speaking. Yolann went to him and nuzzled his head with hers. The two of them curled up together and paid no more attention to Frigga or the other two dragons.

She will ease his grief, Dwinn thought confidently when Frigga touched him again. *She was a good mate to me for a time. Now we can all move away from the past.*

You are refreshingly positive, Dwinn, Frigga thought.

I have no reason to be otherwise, he responded.

Frigga rubbed behind his retractable ear, which surprised and delighted the dragon. Then she turned her attention to Brinn, who had been patiently waiting for her.

Is everything settled? Brinn asked her.

Yes, Frigga answered. *Thank you for your help. You, Dwinn, Yolann, Frinn, and the vermillion female will come with me to Asgard in the morning.*

I eagerly await it, Brinn responded. *Until then, my new queen.*

Frigga smiled at the dragon, then left the enclosure with her Muspel escort. She expected him to go back to his post, but he gestured for her to follow him. Then he led her to the room where they had taken refreshment earlier. To her surprise, the Asgardian delegates sat across from six fire giants of various appearances at the large obsidian table.

Their size and fierceness intimidated her, and she felt her spirit quake slightly. She gulped and nodded at the grinning King Baer. As strange as he had first seemed to her, she considered his familiar face a welcome relief. Odin held her chair out for her as she joined the two monarchs at the head of the table.

"Am I late?" she whispered to Odin.

"No, not at all," he whispered back. "We've met with the cabinet members already. I was going to fetch you, but Baer sent some sort of signal to your escort just a few minutes ago."

Frigga smiled at the fire giants as Baer introduced them all, then engaged in polite conversation throughout the simple meal. They had many questions about her dragon initiative, which she answered gladly. The more she conversed with the Muspel cabinet members, the more comfortable she felt. But once the dinner ended, the adrenaline and excitement fled her body, replaced with exhaustion. Much to her relief, returning to the comfort of the strange bed soothed her sore muscles and weary spirit. Odin seemed equally exhausted and fell asleep quickly. Despite her fatigue, she lay awake until the silence mixed maddeningly with the swirling cauldron of her thoughts. Frustrated over her inability to rest, she decided to visit one of the botanical garden rooms, where she stumbled on King Baer tending to a bush overflowing with bright pink, star-shaped flowers.

"Queen Frigga," he greeted her with surprise. "Are you well? Did you need something?"

"I didn't mean to disturb you. I have not been able to sleep," she admitted. "I thought I'd enjoy your indoor gardens for a while."

"Something troubles you," he observed.

"I hope I do not offend you, but I have been wondering why monogamy is optional in your culture," she admitted cautiously.

He chuckled. "It has always been that way. Since you've been honest with me, I'll be honest with you. For most of us, pursuing multiple partners has not made us happy. Monogamy is held with high respect, but many in my culture believe it to be too restrictive. Unrealistic. Even unnatural."

"Mating does seem to be complicated for the dragons," Frigga observed.

"Many here live their lives without ever knowing sacrificial love," he stated. "Our civil war has shown us we have been far too focused on greed and power. I hope to change that. And perhaps by choosing monogamy myself, more of my people will take that path as well. You cannot change hearts by legal decree … only force them to your will, which eventually leads to rebellion … depending on the decree." He paused and flashed his brilliant white smile. "I'm not suggesting a removal of all laws, of course."

"Odin said something very similar a few hours ago," Frigga said thoughtfully. She straightened her shoulders. "King Baer, you are wise. I truly hope you find a queen worthy of you."

He dipped his head in acknowledgment of her words. "I will have your dragons ready for you in the morning, Queen Frigga of Asgard."

She curtsied, then returned to her room, where sleep finally welcomed her.

16

Frigga hurried behind her husband to the area where Gjallar would transport her, her two helpers, and the five dragons back to Asgard. The serpentine winged creatures remained calm, but energy rippled under their scaly skin.

King Baer stood waiting with several of his own attendants. He flashed one of his brilliant white smiles as he handed her a complicated-looking contraption. "A parting gift, O Queen."

"Is this an irscet?" she asked excitedly. Expecting it to be far heavier, she accidentally jolted it upward, then giggled with slight embarrassment over her overcompensation. "It's lighter than I thought it would be."

"It is a training irscet for a Muspel child. It belonged to the late son of our former king. His followers burned everything else he owned. But his childhood Salir somehow managed to hide this away until we captured him. My people believe it is cursed," Baer informed her. He winked when Frigga raised one eyebrow at him, then continued, "As I anticipated, you are wiser than that. It should be a suitable size for your female warriors. And if any modifications are required, I have no doubt the queen of Asgard will find a way."

Frigga smiled at him gratefully, though a pang smote her heart when she remembered the pain and anger of the

Muspel's childhood dragon. She tucked her feelings away as she carefully turned the irscet over in her hands to inspect it.

"So many straps and buckles," she observed, fingering the two long straps that likely buckled under the dragon's belly in front of and behind the wings. "Will you show me how to strap it on?"

"Of course," Baer answered as he beckoned for Dwinn to draw near.

Odin peered over her shoulder with fascination. "It's a beautiful red! It does look heavy though."

"It weighs less than Sigurna's saddle even though it's broader and longer," Frigga told him as she handed it to him to see for himself. She laughed when he made the exact same mistake she had, despite being warned. "What did I tell you, my king?"

He grinned sheepishly, then announced, "I like the tapered section at the back. And the higher horn."

"It's very sleek looking," Frigga added, reaching out to run one hand over the contraption.

"Does this long harness at the front attach to the dragon's neck?" Odin asked as he pulled up a cylinder set with three clasps on each side.

"Yes, and the rider can clasp or unclasp the spike attachments with these controls here," Baer responded casually, showing them both the tiny buttons that hooked into the harness. He quickly saddled Dwinn as the two reigning monarchs of Asgard watched carefully. "The rest is self-explanatory. It's built for riding a Salir, but we based much of the design on a horse's saddle."

"But how? You have no horses here," Frigga pointed out. She cocked her head as Baer removed the saddle from Dwinn's back. "Although, come to think of it, my Salir knew about horses, but not about cats."

"I know of cats," Baer chuckled as he handed the irscet back to her. "Tasty but not worth the effort, in my opinion."

Frigga grimaced as Odin, Baldur, and Hod all tried to stifle their amusement. She glared at them, then prompted, "The horses, King Baer?"

Baer grinned at the restrained mirth of the Asgardian men, then began to explain, "Many centuries ago, a group of horsemasters stumbled on our realm after escaping Aaru—"

"Dreadful place," Odin muttered darkly with an uncharacteristic shudder.

Frigga glanced at him curiously but with some suspicion. She had heard the tales of the dreaded realm of emptiness and despair, which was not even considered one of the nine. Ofttimes referred to as Helheim, it was a barren wasteland at the very base of Yggdrasil, a dumping ground of sorts that was nigh impossible to access or leave through regular travel, which had always made her wonder where the stories had originated. And now, the tone in Odin's voice held a strange familiarity. Could he have experienced Aaru in his travels? But if so, why would he have never mentioned that to her?

Before she could interject, Baer continued, "Yes, the tales alone nearly froze the blood of my elders. I was a mere child at the time. They begged for refuge, almost mad from what they had endured to escape."

"How *did* they escape?" Frigga asked. "And with horses, no less!"

"They would not speak of it," Baer replied. "Others of their kind had escaped before them, but they had no way of knowing if they had survived or where they had gone."

"What happened to the ones who came here?" Baldur asked, but he cut his dark eyes over to his father in that way he had when sensing a shift in emotion.

"They lived among us for a time until they had regained strength of mind and limb, then went searching for the rest of their number," Baer answered. "None ever returned. But they taught us a great deal about irrigation and, of course, riding. Before they came, only the boldest of us dared to fly because our only option was bareback. This is why you each must hold your queen in high esteem, for she has done what few have."

Odin bristled again at Baer's obvious admiration, but Baldur and Hod gazed at Frigga with new respect.

"Have you ridden bareback, King Baer?" Hod asked, addressing the Muspel king for the first time.

"I have, young one," Baer responded proudly, "though it was many years ago. When you return with my apple trees, I will tell you the tale."

Hod nodded, his unusual golden eyes gleaming with excitement over the whole exchange as a devilish grin lit up his face, so much like Gjallar's (whereas his older brother Heimdall's looks favored their late mother). Though his skin was not as dark as Baer's, and deep brown rather than gray, Frigga suddenly noticed that Hod's smile was just as startling a contrast, perhaps more so because he rarely showed it.

Frigga chuckled to herself; the boy was so quiet until he had something bold to say. He had spirit, of that there was no doubt. It was no wonder her oldest son had bonded with him.

Baer returned his attention to her. "Does my gift please you, Queen Frigga?"

"Oh yes! I can hardly wait to try it!" she gushed as she stroked the beautifully curved seat. "I meant to ask earlier what this is made of. It looks like dyed leather, but it feels much softer."

"It is jörmungandr skin," Baer informed her.

"What in the nine is that?" Frigga giggled, mulling the sound over in her mind and wondering if she would ever be able to say it correctly.

"They are large, smooth-skinned serpents that mainly reside in our sulfur lakes, although they are one of the few creatures that can live in almost any type of water. But they are pests that plague our lands," Baer replied, his face twisting with disgust. "Playful at times, even friendly, but they get too big and eat many of our fish. And some of the bigger ones are quite dangerous. Still, they serve their purpose ... like most wildlife."

"I want one," Odin whispered petulantly.

Frigga shook her head slightly but otherwise ignored his boyish plea to ask, "Are they naturally red?"

"No, they are a pale gray," Baer answered. "We dye our irscets to match our dragons. And when we fly in battle or formation, we paint our skin so that our riders blend with our dragons as much as possible. But you must make your own traditions and your own dragon saddles. Your Asgardian leather will work nicely."

Frigga clasped the dragon saddle as closely as she could to her body and breathlessly thanked the king of Muspelheim, who grinned at her with matching delight but stepped back to allow Odin to bid his queen goodbye.

"I really do want one of those jörmungandr things," he whispered as he attempted to hug her around the irscet.

"Oh, Odin," Frigga sighed softly, feeling a sense of frustration well up inside of her as she realized there was little she could do about it. The creatures would likely become part of Asgard as the ravens had. "Please choose a small one, if you must."

"And just one," Odin promised quietly. "We don't need a pest problem on Asgard."

Gratified to hear this consideration, Frigga planted a modest kiss on his cheek. Odin gave her a pleased look, then clapped Baldur and Hod on the shoulders to bid them farewell.

"Look after your mother, Baldur," Odin commanded sternly.

"When have I ever *not*, Father?" Baldur teased with mock indignation.

Odin smirked at his son, then out of the side of his mouth, quipped, "Keep him out of trouble, Hod."

"Easier said than done, Your Majesty," Hod answered in his easy manner. "But you know he's always safe with me. We'll return as quickly as we can."

As soon as Odin stepped back, Frigga felt the magnetic pull of the Bifröst and, within seconds, the three of them were standing on the main Bifröst portal dais, safely on Asgard with the five dragons, who shook slightly from the experience. Gjallar and Heimdall planted themselves in front of the creatures and looked them over for any adverse effects from portal travel. Satisfied, Gjallar led the way to the newly finished stalls he and his men had prepared, leaving Heimdall to watch the Bifröst gates.

Idunn awaited them inside the stables. The other five dragons surrounded her immediately, trilling and growling in their dragon language as they looked over their new surroundings with pleased airs. As soon as Frigga felt certain they were settled comfortably, she and Baldur saddled their horses and rode together to the palace, allowing Hod a little time with his family.

On arrival, Baldur went to retrieve the twenty-five apple saplings for his return to Muspelheim with Hod. Frigga hurried to her office, worried she would not have enough time to get ready for her meeting at the arena, which she had not had to postpone after all. She busied herself with her preparations, then took a break for a quick lunch with Thor and Loki, who were bubbling over with curiosity about the dragons. She indulged their questions as best she could, describing their glittering scales, fierce demeanors, and proud gaits.

"They sound pretty," Loki remarked wistfully.

"Do they breathe fire, Mother?" Thor asked around a rather large turkey leg, one of his favorite foods.

"Yes, and what a sight it is," Frigga exclaimed, not bothering to tell him to mind his manners as she usually would. Instead, she described what she had seen in the dragon hall on Muspelheim as her sons listened with wide eyes and gaping mouths, finishing with, "They have a culture and language of their own and must be treated with the utmost respect."

"They talk?" Thor asked in surprise. "I thought they were just big animals."

"All animals talk in their own way, Thor," Loki retorted.

"They do not," Thor scoffed. "I've never heard them say anything."

"You just don't pay attention," Loki murmured as he moved his empty plate to the side. "Cats purr, dogs bark, snakes hiss—"

"I like snakes," Thor interrupted brightly.

"Yes, we know," Loki sighed with a dramatic roll of his bright green eyes. "My point is they're all communicating something. You just have to listen."

Frigga smiled proudly at the boy, who beamed back at her when she said, "Loki is right, Thor."

"Well, I don't understand any of them," Thor muttered.

"You would understand the dragons," Frigga encouraged him. "Perhaps someday, you'll get the chance. But I'm afraid I must leave you for my next meeting, my sons. Mind your guards this afternoon."

Both boys groaned but nodded obediently. Frigga spread wide her arms and drew them in for a warm embrace, then hurried to the ballroom to meet the women.

They all had the same questions about the dragons, much to her amusement and annoyance, especially when repeating the same answers used up half of their allotted time. But undeterred, Frigga brought their attention back to determining eligibility for the first women to train in her two programs.

"But don't we want all the women to learn?" Lady Gladys asked, wrinkling her pert little nose in confusion. "Why would we disqualify anyone for the self-defense program?"

"Overexertion can be dangerous for a woman who has not exercised much," Frigga replied carefully. "And since we might have to limit class size at first, if we make the specifications clear, the women who don't currently meet those qualifications will have time to work up to a level of fitness to start with the next class."

"Queen Frigga is right," interjected Eir. "And if we use inspiring language and even provide coaching for achieving those levels, the women who are not ready will be motivated to strive for more."

"Who's going to do that?" Lady Annette demanded.

"Eir, I think you're the most qualified," Frigga suggested, employing her most encouraging smile.

"More than likely." Eir's answering smile held an appealing confidence sprinkled with a touch of delightful mischief. "And if I bring on some of the handsomer male healers as assistants, that might inspire more women to join our fitness program."

"I'd join for that," Lady Gladys bragged as the other women giggled their agreement.

"Ladies, ladies!" Eir laughed. "Leave the single men to me!"

"Oh, Eir, you're too good for any man," Gladys sighed. "And you're always so focused on your duties. How you work in the House with all those beautiful men without pining for any of them, I'll never know."

"Why, Gladys, what would Lord Trebent say?" Lady Ithunna crooned teasingly.

"The same as any of our husbands?" Lady Gladys chortled. "As long as they get theirs, I doubt they care much. We can look as long as we don't touch. Right, ladies?"

Frigga cocked her head, wondering if the pretty noble-woman's assertion was true. The thought of either of the men she loved pining after other women wounded her. Did men not feel the same? She had a feeling Gladys might be sorely mistaken and wondered if she and Trebent were as happy as they seemed publicly, calling to mind the nobleman's quieter-than-usual demeanor on Muspelheim. Perhaps they struggled as much as she and Odin had, bearing their pain in secret because of their position. Suddenly, Frigga noticed how sad Eir seemed. Had something about the conversation bothered her? But there was no time for further reflection. As Frigga gently steered the women back to their plans, she decided to invest a little more time into her relationships with the two women. Perhaps they could encourage one another.

After the meeting, Frigga walked with Eir to the palace doors, looking for the opportune moment to ask about her mood earlier. But the healer kept the conversation running about logistics for her fitness program, almost as if avoiding any other topic.

Finally, Frigga interjected, "Eir, all of that sounds fantastic. Starting with gentle exercises and building into a more robust program is an excellent idea. But you are more than capable, and I would like to discuss something else with you."

"Of course, Your Majesty," Eir responded dutifully, though her light brown eyes changed from animated to veiled.

"You seemed unhappy when the women were teasing about your male healers," Frigga began, keeping her tone warm and gentle. "I sense an emotional wound you keep hidden."

"And hidden it shall remain," Eir stated with gravity. "I have seen and borne much in my years, Queen Frigga. It is a burden I alone must carry."

Frigga sighed, sensing not to press her. "Eir, you are someone I trust implicitly. I hope someday you feel the same about me. If you ever need to unburden yourself, I am here."

"Thank you, Your Majesty," Eir responded. "I am well aware that some things can fester in the heart. Perhaps someday I will face it, but today is not that day."

"I understand," Frigga replied as she reached out one hand to grasp the healer's shoulder. "I carry my own burdens close to my heart."

"Does the queen need to unburden herself?" Eir asked kindly.

Frigga smiled wistfully but with irony. "Perhaps someday. But today is not that day."

Eir chuckled and placed her hand over Frigga's to squeeze gently before letting go. "Well played, my queen. Until that day."

Frigga nodded, feeling a strange regret over not opening up to Eir. But she knew she could risk no such thing. And it had occurred to her that the healer might also carry a forbidden love she dare not reveal. She pondered that possibility as she hurried to her office, hoping Eir's possible target of affection was someone other than Vidar or Odin, then spent the rest of the afternoon and early evening poring over the royal statements about the program, which would be issued to every household when ready. With tryouts to be held in one week and so much more work to do, her eyes began to cross from fretting over how to manage it all. Her thoughts turned to Vidar as they often did in moments of stress and discouragement. She wondered what he was doing that moment as she began to ache from missing him. Then she remembered she had not yet retrieved the wolf and the device from her desk. She opened the drawer and rustled things around in search of the hidden items. At first, she thought Vidar had not succeeded in stashing them, but then her hand brushed against the cold metal of the device just as she spotted the dark wood of the wolf. She eagerly opened the secret compartment, which held Vidar's location and a short note.

"The nights will be long and cold until we meet again," she read aloud, barely above a whisper.

She pressed the note to her chest and closed her eyes, wondering how soon she could go to him. With Baldur gone, she knew she must attend to Thor and Loki first. Somewhat reluctantly, she made her way to the family dining room where she dined with her youngest sons. She allowed Thor to persuade her to play a few games with them, then indulged Loki when he clamored for her to read to them.

When she could finally justify extracting herself, she beckoned for one of the guards. "Please see to it that the princes are settled for the evening. I am weary from my journey and my day."

"Yes, Your Majesty," he acquiesced respectfully. "I'll ensure you are not disturbed."

"Will we see you for breakfast, Mother?" Loki asked eagerly.

"No, my son," Frigga said wearily. "I am quite worn out. I think I'll sleep through breakfast." When his handsome little face fell, she laughed and added, "But I will see you at lunch, and we'll spend all afternoon in the gardens."

"What about lessons?" Thor asked.

"Oh, of course," Frigga sighed. "Baldur isn't here. I suppose you'll have the morning off until Mimir arrives."

Loki and Thor whooped loudly, congratulating each other as if they had gotten away with some trick.

She laughed, enjoying their exuberance. "See that you watch out for each other and stay out of trouble," she warned them. "If my rest is disturbed, no gardens."

They sobered instantly and nodded with wide eyes. Then they quietly hurried off to their rooms with the guard.

Frigga dragged herself to the royal chambers, tempted to sleep before whisking herself off to the South Sea. But as anticipation surged through her, she felt a sudden bolt of renewed energy. She locked the door and arranged her pillows to look like a sleeping form, though she was confident no one would dare enter. Then she changed into the same dress she had worn the first night she had kissed Vidar and arranged her hair carefully. Pleased with her appearance, she mentally targeted the location on Vidar's note and activated the device.

17

Frigga found herself standing in a humble two-story cottage. A cozy kitchen with pots and pans hanging from the ceiling opened into a sitting area with a desk exactly like the one in her office, as well as a worn-looking settee and a matching chaise lounge. The soft blue curtains were drawn, and a fire crackling on the stone hearth glowed with a charming warmth. Though she had never been there before, something about the place felt like home in a surprising way Odin's palace never had. And somehow, something she had always felt was missing settled over her in the utter tranquility of the moment.

A cheerful whistle sounded from the second story. Then she heard someone running down the stairs. She quickly made herself invisible, unsure of who or what to expect.

Vidar appeared from around the corner, wearing only a pair of loose breeches and a towel draped across his bare shoulders. She covered her mouth with her hand to stifle her gasp at the sight of him. But it was too late. He whirled around to locate the sound, his face fierce like the warrior she knew he was.

With a pounding heart and dry mouth, she revealed herself.

"Frigga!" he exclaimed. He tried to cover his exposed skin with the towel. "I wasn't expecting you so soon."

"How do you fare?" she asked quietly, trying not to stare at him.

Odin had always been well-built and powerful, but marriage always seemed to have a way of adding a little extra around a man's waist. Vidar had no such softness, and his muscles gleamed in the firelight as if begging to be touched.

"Fine, thank you," he answered with a little uncertainty. "Why don't you make yourself at home while I make myself more presentable?"

"Are you not presentable?" she asked with feigned innocence. "Your appearance meets with your queen's approval."

He blushed, chuckled slightly, and looked down all at once, which made him even more endearing and irresistible to her.

"That may be so," he said, "but your general would feel more comfortable wearing more clothing. I'll return quickly, I promise."

She nodded. When he ran back upstairs, she turned her attention to a painting veiled in shadow in the corner. She peered at it as the dancing flames from the fire revealed a beautiful woman and a handsome man with a strong resemblance to Vidar. A dark-haired boy in his transition years and an adorable little girl posed with the adults.

When Vidar returned minutes later, she still stood gazing at the painting.

"Is that you?" she asked softly, pointing to the boy.

"Yes," he answered, his tone wistful and sad. "This was my family."

"Then this little cottage is—"

"Where I grew up," Vidar finished for her. "I am originally from the South Sea, just like Lady Annette."

"But you said your parents showed you that lovely place near Lord Bragi's manor. With the willow trees and fireflies," Frigga pointed out in confusion. "And you speak more like you are from Valla, although not entirely like Odin or Berg. Certainly not like Annette."

"My parents grew up in Valla," he explained. "That place with the fireflies was their trysting place. When they tired of the city, they moved here, before I was born. But when we visited my grandparents, we would always stop there."

"So you learned your parents' manner of speaking?" Frigga guessed.

"Yes, and I never lost that accent like so many people do here," Vidar said proudly. "You haven't lost yours either. After all this time on Asgard, you still sound Vanir."

Frigga glanced at him anxiously. "Is it really that noticeable? I'm so used to the Valla accent, I had quite forgotten I don't sound the same."

"I love the way you speak," Vidar said softly. "It reminds me of this place. Always has."

Frigga smiled with relief. "How ever did you meet Odin? On one of your visits?"

"Yes. My father would bring furniture to sell in the marketplace. We were just commoners making a modest living when King Borr hired my father for several projects of his. Odin and I were instant friends and played together whenever we could, sometimes in the marketplace, other times in the village. Borr even let him come out here to stay with us every summer, which made the nobles talk. But Borr didn't care. He trusted us. And my father was very fond of Odin." He smiled at his memories, though the same lingering sadness he always had when speaking of his family hovered over him. "We had some grand adventures in this house."

"Odin never told me about this place," she admitted. "Why didn't you tell me?"

"I wanted to surprise you," he chuckled. "Father used his profits to improve the cottage whenever he could. It was his pride and joy, so my mother and I kept it up even after the …"

When he trailed off, she turned to him and laid her hand softly on his arm. "What happened, Vidar?"

He looked away, trying to hide the tears in his eyes.

She turned his face back to her and prompted, "I know there was some tragedy, but Odin never told me the details. In fact, he really hasn't told me much about his friendship with you at all."

"I haven't talked about it since it happened," he answered with a catch in his voice. "Mostly because my mother rehashed it enough for both of us."

"And I had never told anyone what happened with Laufey," she reminded him. She caressed his cheek and encouraged him, "It's time, my love. Let me be here for you."

"I cannot refuse you anything when you call me that," he whispered hoarsely. "I should warn you … I have never wept for them."

"Perhaps you should," she suggested. "It's not good to keep that bottled up inside you. If you need to weep, then weep. I don't mind."

He grabbed her hand and led her over to the settee. They sat down together, and she kept a tight grip on his hand as he began his story.

"I had just finished my transition years when it happened," he spoke softly. "My father had been training me to be a carpenter like him, but I wanted to train with Odin as a soldier. We argued about it a few times, including the night he left for several weeks to work on one of Borr's projects. I wanted to go to Valla with him. I told him I could help him at the palace so he could come home sooner, but he guessed my real reason."

"Visiting Odin?"

"Enlisting in the army," Vidar corrected.

"And did he guess using the same gift you have?" she asked curiously.

"Yes, I inherited his gifts," he affirmed. "My mother and my sister could manipulate light but not quite the same way you do. My parents used to make rainbows together. Lilari and I learned how to do it too."

He stopped talking, his face contorting with pain.

"So did your father let you go with him to Valla?" Frigga prompted, hoping the refocus would help him regain his composure enough to continue.

"No, he told me he needed me here with my mother and my sister. I grew resentful while he was away. I felt trapped. I wanted to see the world and visit other realms like Odin did." His voice shook and a few tears squeezed out. "I was supposed to be watching my sister that morning, but I sneaked off to practice sword fighting with my friends. I didn't know my father had returned. When my mother rushed out to greet him, they both spotted Lilari wading out to sea. She had done it countless times, but when she saw my father, she tried to hurry back and lost her footing. She was swept away by an undercurrent."

Frigga felt her own eyes fill with tears as a lump of empathic pain lodged in her throat. She knew the ending but waited patiently for him to finish.

"He swam out to save her ..." Vidar trailed off, then inhaled deeply and swallowed hard. "They both drowned."

Frigga leaned her head against his shoulder to comfort him, grieved by his story. "And you blame yourself," she stated softly.

"Yes," he choked out. "And so did my mother."

"What?" Frigga lifted her head and stared at him.

"She couldn't swim. She said if I had been there, I could have saved them." Restrained tears garbled his voice as he struggled to control himself. "She was right."

"No," Frigga contested in a soothing tone. "If your father, who was stronger than you, couldn't save her, there's no way you could have."

"Then I would have drowned in his place," Vidar said bitterly. "And they could have had more children."

"Did she say that to you?" Frigga gasped in indignation.

He nodded, then slumped forward with his head in his hands.

"Your father would have tried to save you both," Frigga told him. "And your mother would have been bereaved of all three of you."

"He could control water, remember?" Vidar informed her. "But he wasn't strong enough for the sea. She said he tried. Perhaps the two of us together—"

Frigga shook her head. "You cannot believe that. It would have taken far more than just the two of you to fight all that water with just your gifts. You would have drained all your energy and drowned anyway. That may be what happened to him."

"But if I had stayed with my sister, none of it would have happened," he argued, glancing at her with red, watery eyes filled with a deep-seated pain.

Frigga sighed. "You don't know that. A thousand scenarios could have taken place if one detail was slightly different. Yes, you should have stayed with your sister. But your mother was wrong to blame you. Perhaps she could not face her own sense of guilt and denied it by blaming you. How awful it must have been for her to stand helplessly on the shore knowing she could do nothing to save them. Whatever terrible things she said to you were likely out of grief."

He wiped at his face furiously, catching his tears before they could slide down. "She was unbearable. Fits of rage and uncontrollable weeping. She took to constantly drinking ale, drowning her sorrow until she was a shadow of the mother I knew. I did everything I could to please her, to help her. I kept up the house, took over Father's business, and put my life on hold. It was never enough. I was never enough. And in the end, I failed her too."

With that, his tears finally burst forth from him like a flood. She silently held him, stroking his hair as he unleashed years of pent-up anguish. She had never seen a man cry like this, and she wished with all of her being to comfort him somehow.

"I-I'm sorry to lose control like this," he finally stammered.

"You needed to weep for them," Frigga reminded him gently. "And you did warn me."

He chuckled slightly. "I wasn't prepared for it myself. I do feel better now, thank you."

"Why do you think you failed your mother?" Frigga prodded quietly.

"Because I could never help her heal. She died a few years later," he answered.

"Vidar, may I speak plainly?"

"Of course," he responded, grabbing both of her hands. "You can always speak your mind with me."

"You did not fail your mother," she assured him. "Speaking as a mother myself, I think she failed you. You needed her as much as she needed you. But she let her own pain blind her."

His eyes filled with tears again. "Frigga, you are the most compassionate person I know. And I have no doubt you would have known just the right thing to say to my mother too," he told her as he drew her close and rested his chin on her head. "You're like water and sunshine to a wilted plant. And I love you more than I've ever loved another living soul. More than my father, more than my sister, more than Odin. Definitely more than my mother."

Frigga snickered despite the seriousness of the moment, which relieved his tension as he chuckled with her.

"What happened after your mother died?" she asked.

"I joined the military and let this place fall into disrepair. I've been working on it as I can over the last century or so." He looked around with pride. "It's almost where it should be."

"It is a lovely home," she observed. "You've done well."

"I've done more than usual the last two nights, hoping you would come soon," he admitted. "If things had been different, I would have brought you here as my wife."

She drew in her breath sharply. "You would have married me?"

"Without hesitation," he said with a grin. He stood and lifted her to her feet. Then he asked tentatively, "Would you have married me?"

"If things had been different," she said quietly.

And in that tender moment, they both understood how strong their bond was. They somehow knew the love they felt for each other could have led them down a different path if Frigga had not committed herself to Odin centuries ago … if their circumstances had indeed been different. A bizarre sense of pain mingled with surprising delight smote her.

And almost as if her brief thought of the king had resounded in his own mind, the general stepped away slightly, the strange smile on his face seeming to echo what she felt.

He drew a deep breath, then offered, "Come on, let me show you around."

She followed him throughout the cottage, enjoying his boyish eagerness and pride as he showed her each room and the work he had done. The house was indeed charming, with three small bedrooms and a bathroom upstairs. A circular window in the upstairs hallway was the only one without closed drapes. She peered out to see the moon reflected on the crashing waves of the ocean and a seemingly endless stretch of white sand.

"What a gorgeous view!" she exclaimed. "If I lived here, I might never want to leave."

"I actually prefer the view from the palace balconies," he admitted sheepishly as he glanced shyly at her. "And the view across the banquet table."

She turned to him with a mischievous smile. "You prefer looking at me to the beauty outside?"

Instead of answering, he pulled her away from the window and into his arms. "I am so happy to have you here, where we can be free. I never could have planned anything better than this."

She nestled against him and listened to his heart beating. "I couldn't wait to get here."

"How long can you stay?" he murmured.

"I locked my door and told the palace staff not to disturb me. But I did promise Loki I'd have lunch with him and Thor tomorrow."

He pulled away and looked at her with concern. "No one thought that suspicious?"

"Not at all," she laughed. "They know how tired I am. I just returned from Muspelheim this morning, you know."

"Muspelheim!" he exclaimed. When she nodded with a smile she could not suppress, he prompted, "Tell me everything!"

"Here in the hallway?" she laughed.

"Let's go back downstairs," he suggested. "I should check on the fire anyway."

She followed him to the sitting area, then settled herself on the settee. She admired him in the soft glow, watching his muscles flex under his simple white tunic as he stoked the fire.

He turned suddenly. "Why are you smiling?" he asked with a knowing grin.

"I think you know," she teased.

"Yes, I do," he admitted as he came over to her. "But sometimes I like to hear it. It gives me an ego boost."

"Far be it from me to deny you an ego boost," she laughed as he sat down beside her. She linked her hands behind his neck and drew his head close to hers. "You are an extremely handsome man. I am quite attracted to you."

His cheeks reddened as his grin widened. "It really is different hearing you say that out loud than just knowing it."

"You're blushing," she teased.

"Of course I am," he chuckled as his gaze flitted to her mouth as it always did when he wanted to kiss her. "You have quite the effect on me when you talk like that."

"Maybe I should do it more often," she teased. She traced his lips with one finger as she crooned, "You are strong yet gentle, fierce yet kind, daring yet humble—"

"Would you like something to drink?" he interrupted suddenly, standing so quickly, she lost her balance.

At first, she felt offended, but seeing how red his face was, she burst out laughing. "Too much?" she asked.

"I'm not used to so much positive affirmation, especially here," he muttered, averting his eyes as he stepped back a few paces. "Let's just say it's a good thing you aren't reading my mind."

She stood and approached him slowly. His eyes began to glow as she did.

"I don't have to read your mind," she said softly. "Your eyes tell me."

"The way you move," he whispered as his eyes blazed. "When the firelight catches the red in your hair … and that dress makes your eyes even bluer. Frigga, if you knew …" He shook his head. "Did you want a drink or not?"

"What do you have?" she relented.

He breathed a sigh of relief. "I have a little milk from the local village. And water, of course. I've never been one for mead or ale, but I might have a bottle of wine."

"Water is fine," she answered.

When he went to get it, she folded her arms and enjoyed the warmth from the fire.

"Are you hungry?" he called from the kitchen. "I have some bread and fruit."

"No, thank you," Frigga called back.

He returned with a glass of water for her and milk for himself. Then he sat down beside her and listened to her tell him all about riding Idunn and traveling to Muspelheim. His face paled when she described her fall, but he relaxed when she reassured him she had never been in any real danger. She felt so at ease with him, she did not realize she had told him the dragon's name until it was too late. Her hands flew to her mouth.

"What's wrong?" he asked with concern.

"I shouldn't have told you her name!" she cried in dismay.

When he raised an eyebrow, she hastened to explain their strange culture.

"So you still don't know why the dragon didn't tell you not to reveal her name to anyone?" he asked.

"Today was such a rush, I never had a chance," she sighed. "I'll ask her the next time I see her."

"Well, you know I can keep a secret," he said as he took her empty water glass. "Has Vale started training Baldur and Hod?"

"I would imagine so," she answered with a shrug. "Odin said something about it."

"How is it you don't want Baldur to be a Valiant but you see no issue with becoming a Valkyrie yourself?" Vidar asked curiously.

She sighed. "Because I know myself and my abilities."

"Do you doubt Baldur's?"

"It's hard for a mother to let go," she defended herself.

"Just don't do what my mother did to me," Vidar stated with some bitterness. "She was so against my joining the military, she poisoned my father against the idea and never once considered how it was my life."

"And your father didn't understand?"

"Just like me, he had blind spots," Vidar responded. "And my mother was definitely one of them. But how he loved her!"

"I think you are like him then," Frigga declared. "You have a great capacity for love."

"So do you," he murmured, dropping his eyes to her mouth again.

He stood abruptly and took their empty glasses into the kitchen.

"How is Berg's project going?" she asked, following him this time.

"It's taking shape," he said proudly. "Berg gave me an excellent idea of what he wants." Then he turned to her excitedly. "Would you like to see?"

"Can we risk that?" she gasped. "What if someone sees me?"

"It's dark enough," he said with a shrug. "If you're still not comfortable with it, stay invisible."

"Then lead on, fearless warrior," she laughed.

"Can you make me invisible too?" he asked with a mischievous gleam in his eyes. "It might look odd if someone spotted me walking around the site this time of night."

"Of course I can," she teased. "A clandestine operation, just the two of us."

"You're not too tired?" he asked with sudden concern. "It's about a twenty minute walk from here."

"Why don't we ride?" she suggested.

"I only have one horse," Vidar replied.

"Vasili?" she asked. When he nodded, she offered, "He's dark enough that I might be able to hide us all if we ride him together."

"I like the sound of that," he murmured, then gestured for her to follow him out to the modest stable near the cottage.

She cloaked them both as they walked. Once inside the stable, Vidar mounted Vasili, then offered his hand to swing her up behind him. She wrapped her arms around his waist and exerted all of her effort to swathe them in darkness, refracting the light of the moon as it filtered through the spaces in the stalls.

"It's too much," she gasped as she slipped off the horse. "I'm not strong enough tonight."

Vidar also dismounted. "We'll walk. If you get tired, I'll carry you."

"Can we try again next time?" she said softly. "I'm afraid I've expended too much energy."

He nodded, though she could tell he was disappointed.

She walked over to him and kissed his cheek. "Would you carry me back to the cottage?"

"Yes, my queen," he murmured.

When he lifted her up into his arms, she rested her head on his shoulder and breathed deeply of his scent. Not having to walk gave her enough strength to make it appear as if he walked alone. He carried her back inside and set her gently on the settee, where she reappeared.

"That was strange," Vidar mused. "I've never carried someone I couldn't see."

She smiled at him wearily and rested her head on the back cushion of the settee, which she found to be a surprisingly comfortable position.

"Are you spending the night here?" he asked her with some reservation.

Frigga pouted slightly, her feelings hurt. "It doesn't sound like you want me to stay."

"I do want you to stay," he protested. He ran one hand through his rich brown hair. "I thought perhaps … I'm just not certain … That is, I don't think …" He sighed, then blurted out, "Oh, confound it all!"

He plopped down beside her and gathered her to himself, making her heart race. But rather than engage in the passion of their last two encounters, he began kissing her slowly … intimately … changing angles with each kiss but keeping his mouth unbelievably soft against hers. He cradled the back of her head with one hand while he caressed her shoulder with the other. Odin had never kissed her that way, and the general's tenderness affected her even more than his passion had. She shivered with delight as he started kissing her jawline. A sudden jolt of energy surged through her.

"Vidar?" she whispered breathlessly.

"Hmm?" he murmured.

When she hesitated, he gently bit the soft tissue of her earlobe. The sensation almost drove her wild, but she forced herself to maintain control.

"I'm dangerously close to letting it be with you," she admitted, using his words from days ago, when he had begged her to love him physically just once. "If you ask it of me again—"

"No," he interrupted, stopping her from continuing her declaration. "I will not ask it of you again."

"Why not?" she asked quietly. "I know that's what you want. We've already gone this far." She suddenly realized she had reached a new level of desensitization to their illicit relationship, but she shoved that aside. "Somehow, I think what we're doing now, what we've already done, would grieve Odin just as much as taking it all the way. At this point, I think we might as well. There's no going back."

"Perhaps," Vidar agreed as he leaned forward to kiss her softly again. "But in my own mind, it's easier to live with my choices if I refuse to fully indulge my desire until the day we can be together without Odin's invisible presence looming over us."

"What if that day never comes?"

He cocked his head and gazed at her seriously. "I cannot think that way. Not anymore."

"But we have to be realistic," she pleaded, ignoring her guilt for actively trying to seduce him. "This could feasibly be our last chance. Our last night."

"Frigga, I know what you're feeling," he said somberly. "I feel it too. But I want our first time to be everything it should be."

"Were you only teasing me?" she asked petulantly.

"I was testing my limits," he admitted. "And giving us a taste of what could be so we'll both look for a way to make it happen someday."

"That was dangerous," she warned him, somewhat playfully. "You might have unleashed more than you can handle."

"More than I can handle?" he scoffed arrogantly. "I'll prove to you what I can handle as well as how great my resolve is."

"How?" she prompted as an eager smile played about her lips.

"Come with me," he said gallantly.

He quickly put out the fire and gently led her by the hand to his manly looking bedroom. She found it hard to breathe and resisted the surprising, sudden urge to flee.

"Don't be afraid," he admonished her softly. "You trust me, don't you?"

"Yes, I trust you," she answered firmly.

He let go of her hand, then walked over to the small dresser he had shown her during his tour. He pulled out a long, pale blue nightgown and handed it to her with a shy smile.

"Was this your mother's?" she asked quietly, feeling both strangely nostalgic and disturbed all at once.

"No," he snorted, shuddering slightly. "I bought it yesterday on impulse."

"You planned this?" Frigga gasped.

"Maybe subconsciously," he admitted sheepishly. "I was more or less thinking you might need something to wear if you stayed here. And if nothing else, it reminded me of you."

"Whatever did you tell the vendor?" she teased, holding up the nightdress, which was fairly modest yet designed to enhance a woman's feminine figure.

"Only that it would be nice to have if I had any female companionship to forget my troubles," Vidar answered. "And we both laughed raucously as men do."

Frigga narrowed her eyes. "Do they now?"

"Yes, Frigga, they do," Vidar chuckled. "It might be frowned upon now, but casual encounters still happen."

"I'm not naive enough to think they don't," Frigga said somewhat testily. "But I had thought better of you. What of your reputation?"

"I was only playing a part. And I'm sure he thought no more of it, considering my reputation with the ladies was somewhat scandalous around here when Odin and I were young. That isn't who I am now, but if word should happen to spread around, it fits with the scene I set at the palace of a heartbroken man," Vidar said softly. He looked at her with an adorably pleading expression and tenderly put his hands on her shoulders. "Please, my queen, let's not ruin the rest of our evening with any more talk of the past."

"No, of course not," she answered meekly as she looked over the gown again, satisfied with how he had handled the situation. "I can see how the interaction might actually serve to keep our relationship hidden."

"That occurred to me as well. Now, go down to the bathroom and get ready for bed," he instructed.

She looked at him quizzically but obeyed. She could not see herself in it but sensed it suited her well. The fabric of the nightgown pressed against her skin as softly as Vidar's caresses had felt, making her eager to return to him.

She brought her dress back into the room with her and innocently asked, "Where should I put this?"

He did not answer, obviously focused on exploring her with his eyes.

"Vidar?" she prompted, holding out the dress.

He reached out to take it, then responded with a slight tremor in his voice, "I'll lay it over the chair here. Are you comfortable?"

"Very," she answered with a smirk. "But you don't seem to be."

"I'm sorry. I didn't expect that nightgown to be quite so flattering. But since I'm proving a point, I'll see it through." He removed his tunic and threw it over her dress on the chair, then turned around to let her get a good look. "It's only fair I torture you a little since I'm torturing myself to prove to you how much I can handle."

She bit her lip. Though she had already seen him shirtless once, the second time was far more difficult.

If he can deny himself, so can I, she lectured herself.

He turned down one side of the bed. "You sleep here," he instructed her.

After she tentatively lay down, he pulled the blankets over her. Then he shut off the overhead lights and climbed in next to her, enveloping her with his arms. She froze as memories of Odin holding her in their bed washed over her, but when Vidar did nothing further, she relaxed.

"Good night, my queen," he murmured against her hair.

"Good night, my love," she responded, already feeling sleep closing in on her.

18

W*here am I?* Frigga asked herself in a daze.

The sunlight felt different. Her bed felt different. When she opened her eyes to see Vidar sleeping beside her instead of Odin, she panicked.

"Oh no, oh no, oh no!" she muttered frantically as she scrambled out of the bed.

"What's wrong?" Vidar asked in alarm, sitting up and rubbing his eyes.

Her sense of reason and morality had risen with the sun, and she averted her eyes from his bare torso. Then she noticed how she was dressed and grabbed one of the blankets to cover herself.

"Did we … did we …" She could not bring herself to say it out loud.

"Don't you remember?" Vidar asked as he got out of bed and drew near her. "I didn't waste all my effort, did I?"

When the events of the previous night flooded her memory, she breathed a sigh of relief. "I remember now." She lifted her chin and winked at him. "You've proven yourself quite well, General."

He chuckled, then sobered quickly. "I'm glad we didn't go through with it after the way you reacted just now. We made the right choice."

"I feel quite good about that, actually," she admitted with another relieved sigh. "Thank you, Vidar, for not giving in to me. My inhibitions were unusually low last night. I'm embarrassed."

"Don't be," he said kindly. He grabbed her dress from the chair and handed it to her, then slipped on the tunic he had accidentally knocked to the floor. "I have a little time before I have to leave."

"Enough for us to have breakfast together?" she suggested hopefully.

"I can make us some eggs if you'd like," he offered.

"Yes, I'd like that," she agreed happily. "I'll go change, then meet you downstairs."

When she joined him in the kitchen, he gestured for her to seat herself at the wooden table, which bespoke Vidar's father's workmanship with its sturdy simplicity. The general had already set out a pitcher of milk and some fruit, which she nibbled at while Vidar cooked the eggs in the popular Asgardian poaching method.

"Did your father make your table and chairs?" she asked.

"No, I did," he said proudly as he finished spooning the eggs onto two plates already set with toasted bread.

"You're just as talented as he was!" she exclaimed. She eyed the plate Vidar set before her as her stomach growled slightly. "And this looks delicious. Thank you!"

He brought his own plate and more bread to the table, then sat down with her. After they finished eating, he refused to let her help clean the kitchen, insisting she stay seated.

A knock at the cottage door startled them both. She vanished as Vidar went to answer it. Seated at the wrong angle to see, she had to content herself with enhancing the sound.

"Father sent me to tell you he'll bring the stone to the construction site this afternoon," a young woman's voice said cheerily in response to the general's surprised greeting. "He apologizes for the delay. Mother and I baked you a berry tart to help make up for it."

"It's just as well. I've gotten off to a late start today anyway," Vidar responded. "Thank you, Patrice."

"Don't overwork yourself, Vidar," the woman lectured in a maddeningly familiar way. "I'll see you later."

Vidar closed the door and placed the tart on the counter, then turned to Frigga as if bracing himself for an unpleasant reaction.

Frigga regarded him coolly. "I think that's my cue to leave."

He sighed. "Frigga, I know what you're thinking, and it's not—"

"She sounded quite lovely, actually," Frigga interrupted nonchalantly. "Was the nightgown really for me or for her?"

He burst out laughing. "Patrice is my only cousin, the daughter of my father's younger brother. He took up stonemasonry after my parents died. He's providing the alabaster I need for Berg's summer cottage."

Frigga dropped her head in shame over her jealousy. "I'm sorry I jumped to conclusions."

He knelt before her and gently lifted her head to kiss her lightly on the lips. "When will you believe me when I say you alone hold my heart?" He did not seem to expect an answer but stood, then asked, "It appears I don't have to be back at the site for a few hours. What shall we do?"

She grinned at him mischievously. "I didn't get enough sleep."

"No?" he asked with an equally sly grin. "Neither did I." He held out his hand to her. "Shall we?"

She took it gladly, then allowed him to lead her back upstairs. They cuddled up with each other on his bed fully clothed, justifying a few soft kisses until they fell asleep again. Frigga awoke to the sound of someone pounding at the cottage door.

"Vidar," she whispered urgently. Then she gently shook him when he did not respond right away. "Someone's at the door."

He jumped up, then ran down the stairs, leaving her alone in his room. She closed her eyes and snuggled into the indent he had left on his pillow, wishing she could bring it back with her to the palace.

When he returned, she had almost dozed off again. He smiled down at her lying in his bed, then reached out to smooth her hair away from her face.

"We've been asleep for just under two hours, my queen," he informed her.

"Who was at the door?" she murmured lazily.

"A deliveryman with a load of wood," he answered. "He doesn't know where to go, so I told him he could follow me over there."

"He's still here?" she gasped, sitting straight up.

"He's waiting outside," Vidar reassured her. "I told him I had to come back inside for a moment. Will you be able to get away tonight?"

"I'll do my best," she promised. "I don't think Odin will return for several days at least."

He kissed her, then hurried out. She lay back down on his pillow for several minutes, wishing she did not have to leave. But reminding herself she would likely see him that night, she finally eased herself off the bed and transported herself back to her suite in the palace. She changed her clothing, then hurried to the family dining room for lunch, surprised to find she was the first one to arrive. She waited for her sons, wondering what delayed them. She heard Thor and Loki before they entered, arguing about whose fault it was for being late.

With an amused smirk, she met them at the door with her arms crossed and one eyebrow raised. "And where have you two been?"

They exchanged worried glances.

Then Thor spoke up, "Don't be angry, Mother! We're sorry we're late. Aren't we, Loki?"

"Yes, we're terribly sorry," Loki said morosely.

"You haven't answered the question, boys," Frigga pointed out sternly, hiding her amusement.

Both of them hung their heads.

"Boys!" Frigga prompted, drawing the word out with her tone full of warning. "One of you had better speak up. I'm not as concerned about your tardiness as I am about your sneaky behavior."

A sudden pang of guilt shot through her. Who was she to talk about sneaky behavior?

Thor spoke up. "Master Mimir canceled lessons today. We had nothing else to do … so we … we wanted to see the dragons, Mother."

"Well? Did you?" she asked.

Both boys nodded, trying to hide the smiles forming on their faces.

"You're not in trouble," she laughed. "Come and tell me about it."

They grinned at each other and ran into the dining room, clamoring over each other in their eagerness to tell her how big they were and how they shimmered in the sunlight.

"Slow down, boys," Frigga chided, her eyes sparkling with amusement. "All I can understand is you both like what you saw of the dragons."

"Like them?" Loki scoffed playfully. "I love them! But are we getting any green ones?"

"I don't think they come in green," Frigga remarked thoughtfully.

"What a travesty," the boy muttered, his eyes graying a bit as they did when he was unhappy or disappointed.

"Loki's new favorite word," Thor chimed in, his good-natured face still as cheerful as ever. "I don't think he even knows what it means. I keep telling him he means tragedy."

"He's using it correctly, Thor," Frigga informed him. "Travesty means a distortion, imitation, or debasement of something held in high esteem."

"Like dragons not being green," Loki added. "It's a travesty and a tragedy."

"Master Mimir muttered that word when he graded my fractions worksheet," Thor grumbled, his face falling.

"I told you it wasn't a good thing, Thor," Loki teased. "I'll help you if you'd like. Fractions are easy for me."

"Thanks, Loki," Thor replied brightly.

Though pleasantly surprised at her son's response,

Frigga was immensely pleased to see them getting along. "You two are being quite nice to each other today."

"I'm just glad we're not in trouble," Thor admitted. "I might pound Loki later if I feel like it."

"Just try it, Thor," Loki retorted. Then he grinned at his mother. "We thought you'd be upset that we left the palace. But we did forget to tell you that Colonel Vale went with us."

"Perhaps you should have led with that," Frigga chuckled. "I'm proud of you that you had the sense to ask an experienced adult to accompany you, but I still would have preferred it if you'd asked for permission first and not tried to hide it."

"We didn't want to disturb your rest," Loki told her sheepishly. "You asked us not to, remember?"

Guilt clawed at Frigga's heart, coupled with relief that no one had discovered her absence. But she merely smiled and stated, "And that was very thoughtful and obedient of you both. All in all, no harm done."

"The keeper of the gates wouldn't let us get very close at all," Thor complained.

"He did exactly what he should have done," Frigga informed the blond boy. "At least you got to see them."

After lunch, Frigga took the boys for a long walk in the garden as a guard trailed behind them. Thor ran ahead, then brought her back a lily from the pond. Not to be outdone, Loki plucked a white rose from a rosebush as they passed by.

"Because you're so lovely and pure," he told her innocently.

Frigga's eyes immediately welled up with tears. *I am not pure,* she thought, remembering her night with Vidar. *What would my sons think of me if they knew?*

"Mother, what's wrong?" Loki asked with concern. "Don't you like the rose?"

"Oh yes, very much," she reassured him. "Don't ever lose your sweetness, Loki."

He hugged her tightly, then ran off down the path with Thor. Since the guard maintained his distance, Frigga enjoyed the brief moment to herself, though she looked forward to a time without a guard escort at all. Her mind turned to her programs, then to her sons' excitement over the dragons. If she took them out there again, they could get a closer look. Perhaps the activity with them would distract her from the condemning thoughts threatening to assault her.

"Would you boys like to see the dragons again?" Frigga asked when she caught up to them. "Up close?"

They both jumped into the air, shouting their affirmation at her as she laughed with delight.

"Private, send word for the royal cariole," Frigga instructed the guard. "Tell the driver to leave the top down so we can soak in the sun."

Loki and Thor exchanged excited glances as the guard hurried off. Riding in such style was a rare treat for them, especially with the roof retracted.

"The cariole, Mother?" Thor asked in surprise. "Just for us?"

"Well, why not?" Frigga said impishly. "Just because it can fit six people doesn't mean it has to."

"Are we allowed without Father?" Loki asked with some trepidation.

"Why wouldn't we be?" Frigga asked in surprise.

"We've never ridden in it without Father," Thor spoke up. "Besides, I heard one of the servants say the door handles are solid gold."

"Why would that matter?" Loki asked. "There's a lot of things made of gold in the palace."

"Because they're made for the king," Thor responded quietly.

"And who am I?" Frigga teased.

"The queen," Loki answered firmly.

"And who are you?" she pressed, fixing both boys with a loving gaze.

"The princes," they answered together.

"That's right. And the cariole is for the royal family. The guard had no objection, did he?" she reminded them. When they shook their heads, she added, "But if you don't want to take the cariole, there's always horses. They're faster, after all."

"No, the cariole is perfect!" Loki hastened to say as Thor nodded his agreement vigorously.

Frigga laughed, then beckoned them to follow her to the palace doors to wait, where they chattered with excitement for their impromptu outing in the beautifully ornate, horse-drawn carriage.

When the elegantly dressed driver arrived, he hopped down from his perch and bowed, then opened the smooth white door to allow Frigga and the two boys to climb inside. Then he firmly shut the door, climbed back onto the driver's seat, and prodded the horses to set off for the Bifröst. The boys settled into the red plush seats with pride and joy on their faces and in their posture. Frigga relaxed against the soft cushions and watched them revel in the experience, gratified to see them behaving like little gentlemen. And just as she had anticipated, the gorgeous weather made the trip even more enjoyable.

As they neared the stables that temporarily housed the dragons, Gjallar hurried to meet them.

"My queen! My princes! What a pleasant surprise!" he exclaimed. "And quite convenient for me."

"Why? Have you heard from the king?" she asked as the driver helped her get out of the carriage.

"Yes, Your Majesty," Gjallar confirmed as he helped the boys down as well. "He contacted me this morning. Their business has gone better than expected, thanks in part to you."

"Excellent news, Gjallar!" Frigga said enthusiastically as Thor and Loki fidgeted beside her from boredom. "Did he say when he plans to return?"

"Tomorrow at midday. He is bringing King Baer and two members of his cabinet with him," he answered.

"Fire giants are coming here?" Thor gasped, his young voice spiking higher in fear.

"Oh!" Frigga gasped, ignoring her young son in her shock. "That is a bold move."

"He said it's time to educate," Gjallar replied. "And that you would know what he meant."

Frigga smiled to herself with pleasure that Odin had considered her words on Muspelheim. But she had not expected her husband to return so soon. She suddenly became aware that Thor and Loki were pressing into her as if trying to hide behind her skirts, much like they had as toddlers.

"Don't be afraid, boys," Frigga reassured them. "I've spent time with them, and it was quite pleasant. They are well-mannered and fond of plants, especially flowers. Does that sound so bad?"

Both of her sons shook their heads, but the apprehension in Thor's eyes remained.

"King Odin has also requested that you arrange a banquet in King Baer's honor," Gjallar added.

"Tomorrow?" she cried in dismay. "That's not much time."

"No, he will only host an informal luncheon with the war council tomorrow. He wants the banquet scheduled for the following day," Gjallar corrected.

Frigga breathed a sigh of relief. "That's a little better. Is King Baer bringing an entourage?"

"Just the two cabinet members," Gjallar answered.

"Very well," Frigga responded lightly. "I'll see to everything. But for now, we've come to visit the dragons. My sons would like a closer look."

Gjallar beckoned for them to follow him. All six creatures lifted their scaly heads as the four of them approached. Thor and Loki could barely contain their excitement. But as they gushed over the sturdy, twisted horns that gave the male dragons their fierce look, Frigga approached Idunn and purred to her.

You have learned about my culture, Frigga, Idunn thought with delight as they connected.

I have indeed, Idunn, Frigga answered. *King Baer told me they do not speak the names of their dragons aloud. I must confess I told several people your name.*

I did not wish to impose too many of our ways on you, O Queen, Idunn admitted. *I was afraid you would think them unseemly and offensive. When I probed your mind the day we met, I saw something there ... something you are only beginning to understand about yourself, but I do not wish to speak of that.*

I find a mind probe to be far more intrusive than speaking someone's name, Frigga said somewhat indignantly, wondering if the dragon spoke of her struggle to fully embrace such a strange culture even while desiring to change her own thinking to be more accepting.

The dragon laughed within Frigga's mind. *I agree with you. A mind probe is more intrusive. I have spoken with the other dragons, and we will not impose the name restriction upon you.*

No, please allow us to honor your culture as we can, Frigga declared. *But can you tell me why you do not wish your names to be known by everyone?*

Keeping our names hidden from others strengthens our bonds with our riders, Idunn answered carefully. *Even on Asgard, I am certain a level of familiarity and trust sparks from knowing someone by name.*

Yes, of course, Frigga answered.

By choosing when to share that information, Idunn continued, *we protect ourselves from those who might seek our harm. For there is power and purpose in every name. If you wish to honor our culture, that is well. And better for us.*

I might not fully understand, but there is wisdom in your words, Frigga told the dragon. *And yes, your custom is worth honoring. Only Odin, Gjallar, and Vidar know your name, and I will speak to them about it.*

Vidar, Idunn repeated. *You speak his name with tenderness and great affection. Have you told your husband of your second mate?*

I have not, Frigga answered testily. *He would not accept it. Our culture would not accept it.*

Idunn merely gazed at Frigga, then thought, *I should like to meet this Vidar.*

Frigga brightened considerably. *I would like that as well. I wish I could ride you today, but I left the irscet King Baer gave me at the palace. And I have much to do to prepare for his visit.*

King Baer is coming to Asgard? Idunn asked. When Frigga confirmed it, she thought, *How interesting, but I will not speak of my concerns. I see you have brought two of your sons. May I speak with them?*

Yes, but I would not tell them your name, Frigga warned. *They will not understand.*

Then I will wait until they are older, Idunn thought. *And I thank you, my queen, for respecting our ways, strange as they are to you.*

Are the other dragons adjusting? Frigga asked.

Yes, you chose well, Idunn praised her. *I am content, and they are content.*

Is Brinn content? Frigga teased good-naturedly.

Idunn merely responded, *Time will tell.*

But as Frigga gathered Thor and Loki to return to the palace, she smiled to herself when she saw Idunn and Brinn nuzzle each other. She sincerely hoped for their happiness, especially since she feared she and Vidar would never be free to love each other as they wanted.

Before she left, she pulled Gjallar aside to tell him not to reveal Idunn's name to anyone and why. Though puzzled by the whole thing, as a man of respect and honor, Gjallar agreed without further question. Thankfully, he had only introduced Idunn to his sons and could warn them as well.

After dinner and a brief consultation with the palace staff about the luncheon and the banquet, Frigga retired early again, eager to return to Vidar's cottage. She felt in a way as if she were leading two entirely separate lives. One version of her embraced her responsibilities as queen, bonded to Odin by a strong sense of duty, though not without love. The other longed for a simpler life, a taste of which she had enjoyed with the general. Though she would not enjoy the prestige or wealth of monarchy with Vidar, a life with him would be filled with deeper understanding and passion, which carried a great deal of weight and importance to her. Could she manage to cling to loving them both? What if she were forced to choose?

She decided not to allow such thoughts to dampen her mood as she prepared for meeting with Vidar again. After all, she did not have to make any decisions beyond how she would be spending the evening. The king was not at home, and her general awaited her.

19

The cottage was empty and dark when Frigga arrived. She kept herself invisible and quietly crept upstairs. Twilight was just beginning to deepen into dusk as the shadows lengthened. From the upstairs window, she saw Vidar walking the sand, though he kept his distance from the ocean. She hurried out to him, checking to make sure no eyes could possibly see her before she made herself visible.

"Vidar, what are you doing out here?" she asked when she reached him.

She saw fresh tears on his face and tenderly wiped them away.

"I was saying goodbye," he answered in a low, broken voice. "Finally letting them go." He turned to her and hugged her close. "You gave me the strength. Thank you."

"I'm glad I could help," she replied softly. When he released her, she looked around her, drinking in the stark and simple beauty of the beach. "It's lovely out here. I would think you'd never want to leave."

"I get restless," he said as he stared out at the crashing waves. Then he turned to her again. "But I would stay or go wherever you are."

Though she wanted to listen to Vidar woo her with his words, she also felt the pressure of their limited time.

"Odin is returning tomorrow," she told him abruptly.

"Let's go inside," he suggested.

"Didn't you want to show me Berg's beach house?" she reminded him.

"I don't want to waste any time with that tonight," he informed her. "You probably won't be able to come back again. Let's make the most of it."

"I do want to hear how the rest of your day was," Frigga told him.

"Then we'll talk first," he offered, swinging his hand with hers as they walked back to the cottage.

"First?" she repeated as her heart leaped into her throat. "And what are we doing after that?"

"You'll see," he said vaguely, grinning cheekily at her.

He opened the door and ushered her inside. She hid herself as soon as he turned the lights on, though she doubted anyone would be out there at this time of night. She revealed herself again only after he had drawn the curtains. Finally comfortable enough to relax, she filled him in on the events of her day while he built a fire.

"The king of Muspelheim, here on Asgard," Vidar breathed in wonder. "Half of me wishes I could go. The other half is relieved I cannot."

"It won't be the same without you there," she said softly.

"And now your dragon insists on calling me your second mate and wants to meet me?" Vidar chuckled. "I really don't know what to think of that."

"I trust her," Frigga reassured him. "Now, what about your day?"

He joined her where she sat on the settee. "There's not much to tell. I worked the rest of the day, came home, and ate dinner. Then I went out on the beach." He gathered her into his arms. "I missed you, as always. I've really looked forward to tonight. Last night was wonderful."

"Yes, it was," she agreed happily. In her mind, she was no longer Queen Frigga and imagined herself instead as a commoner free to love the man she wanted. "Were you hoping for more of the same?"

"Not quite," he murmured with a low laugh. He stood and retrieved an unimpressive wooden box from the desk. "I brought this with me from the palace in case anyone decided to snoop around in my room while I'm gone."

"Who would do that?" she objected.

"It's not worth the risk," he said simply as he removed the unadorned lid and handed her the box.

She looked inside to see the note she had written to him to start their secret meetings resting at the top of a stack of handwritten letters. "Are these your letters to me?"

He nodded, his smile shaky and uncertain as he sat back down beside her. "I thought about reading them to you, but I might not be able to stand it."

"Please try," she pleaded with him softly. "I love the sound of your voice."

"How about you read a few first? Then we can decide what we should do after that," he suggested with a shy grin.

"Odin wooed me through letters before he had our secret portal built," Frigga told him, winking at him playfully. "Are you certain you want to do this?"

He took her hand and squeezed just once, gulping slightly as he did so. Taking the gesture as a wordless affirmation, she scanned the first letter, which seemed to be the first he had ever written. Then she read it again, allowing the poetic words to quench her soul.

My beloved queen, I doubt I will ever have the courage to speak to you of how I rejoice whenever you are near. I dare not tell you how my first waking thought is how to bring back your smile and your laughter. You have been unhappy for so many years, I could not bear to stand aside and do nothing any longer. But where will I find the courage to even speak to Odin about treating you the way he should? I have faced death, battle, and many enemies. They have not made me tremble and falter as this does. But I promised you I would do what my heart rebels against doing. And so I shall. For you. Even though it means growing old without ever knowing your love, a fear I have long known I would have to face someday.

"Did you write this after that first conversation in the library years ago?" she asked, feeling as though her heart had turned to goo.

He nodded, his eyes brimming over with tenderness at the memory.

She reached for another letter, which spoke of his first attempt to speak with Odin and his frustration at his perceived failure. Letter after letter chronicled the progression of their relationship. The suppressed desire and desperation in his words built a heat within her that crept into her cheeks. She glanced up now and again to see Vidar watching her anxiously as she kept reading. When only three letters remained, she closed her eyes and released all of the air in her lungs in a shuddering sigh.

"Do you see why I didn't want you to read them when you first asked?" Vidar asked. "It was too dangerous."

"And it's not anymore?" she returned in confusion. "Do you have any idea what these letters do to me?"

"Of course I do," he murmured as he leaned forward and kissed her temple. "But I am just as resolved as I was last night. And now I've made a decision."

"What decision?" she asked.

"I'll tell you when you're finished reading," he assured her.

"I've read more than a few," she pointed out. "It's your turn to read to me. And then we'll see how resolved you are."

His eyes sparked with a determined, proud flare. But she saw the golden glow in them and shivered to imagine what he might do. He reached for the box and pulled out the last of the letters, clearing his throat nervously as he looked shyly at her. Then he began to read.

"My beloved queen, every night that passes without you nestled close to me, where I wish you belonged, has been utter emptiness to me." He glanced up and smiled as she shifted her body closer to his. Then he kept reading, his rich voice enveloping her like a warm embrace. "The taste of your lips is sweeter than the honey of the northern borders. The cascade of your curls mesmerizes me like shimmering firelight, and the devastating blue of your eyes shines clearer than the summer sky. Do I dare tell you how your soft curves speak to me as if calling out for my touch?" He groaned softly and reached out for her, then withdrew his hand before he made contact. He took a deep breath and finished, "My darling, if I cannot find a way to make you mine, I might perish from keeping myself from you."

Frigga had inched herself closer and closer to him as he read, deeply affected by his longing. He looked up at her and laid the letter aside.

"When did you write that?" she whispered.

"While I was on Midgard before our argument," he answered as he showed her the thicker paper. "This is Egyptian papyrus."

"Egyptian?" she repeated curiously. "Well, now I know where you've been going."

"Someday, I want to take you with me," he confessed. "But I shouldn't tell you any more."

"Not tonight, for certain," she agreed. Then she boldly murmured in his ear, "I am calling out for your touch."

He turned to her and kissed her as if he were starving for her affection. She surrendered herself to his need, completely disregarding anything but how his letters had made her feel. His muscles tensed as he tightened his grip on her. Then he released her and grinned as she clutched at him dizzily.

"There," he said smartly. "Now I know I can handle just one kiss."

"I cannot," she groaned, trying to pull him back to her. "Not after that."

But he resisted her. "No, my queen. I have two more letters to read, remember?"

She took a deep breath and nodded.

He kissed her cheek, then turned his attention to the second letter. "My beloved queen, I have wounded myself beyond recovery. And you as well, I fear. The pain on your face when I sent you back to Odin broke me into a thousand bitter shards, knowing I put it there. All I ever wanted was to bring you joy. Now I find myself in the terrible position of having to separate from you for your own good. But I fear I am deceiving myself. Perhaps it is because I cannot bear to think of you sharing Odin's bed instead of mine. I am dying inside, facing the rest of my life without you. I cannot eat. I cannot sleep. There is no other course but to soldier on. My only comfort is to imagine Odin might begin to love you the way I do once he has gained better perspective. You could teach him as you have taught me in our many years of friendship, which I will grieve losing for as long as I have breath. Farewell, Frigga."

His voice broke slightly, making Frigga's eyes sting with tears. Hearing his pain from that night brought to mind her own emotions. And she did not want to think about losing him again.

"I'm so glad that night wasn't the end of our story," she said with a tremor in her own voice.

He looked up just as a few tears slid down her cheeks. He set the letter aside and kissed where the tears glistened. "Don't cry, Frigga. In a strange twist, Odin provided us with another way by sending me here. If things had not happened the way they did, I would not have the resolve I have now."

"Not to consummate our love?" she asked. "Is that the decision you made?"

"Yes. And I would still be floundering, uncertain of what to do, stealing moments like these with no objective in sight," he answered. "Now that I've decided we will not travel that road, out of respect for you and your marriage to Odin, I feel free to express my love in other ways with the hope we will be together in every way someday."

"But how?" she asked.

"Let me read the last letter," he suggested. He picked up a stark white paper. "My beloved queen, I've accepted that I cannot live without you, so I cling to the hope of a future I have only dared to envision in my darkest moments. One that has been taking form the more time we spend together. I know it as certainly as I know the curve of your face, the scent of your skin, and the sound of your footsteps. Even if I have to wait a thousand years, you are worth every second. Laws change. Circumstances change, including political situations. But my love for you will never cease. I don't know when or how. But I feel something coming that will make everything right again. If we can ride the tide and weather the storms together, we will still be standing with our love stronger than ever when the way is clear. Will you stand with me until that day?"

"Did you write that today?" she breathed.

"Yes. Before I went out to the beach," he answered.

"And what are you asking from me exactly?" she pressed.

"I want us to hold fast to each other and figure out our future together," he explained. "We'll be who we are, doing our duty by the king, serving him as we should, knowing we love each other, and waiting for the day of fulfillment."

"Don't you realize what that means for me?"

He grimaced. "It cannot be helped. I'll have to live with it."

"And what am I supposed to do? Live with it too? Loving him in body when I'd rather be loving you?" she demanded indignantly.

"Frigga, you don't fool me, just as you didn't fool your dragon," Vidar responded. "You still love him. You really do have two mates somehow, though I don't understand it myself. I only have room in my heart for you."

"My feelings toward Odin are mixed and confusing," she admitted. "I don't want to—"

"Just be with him enough to allay suspicion," he encouraged her gently. "Imagine me if you must, like you imagined him the first time you kissed me."

"I would feel ashamed to do that!" she protested.

"I didn't say it was ideal," Vidar admitted. "This will be just as hard for me, maybe even harder. I have to go without satisfaction completely. But I'm willing to do it for you."

"I don't understand why!" she argued. "I'm willing to give myself to you. But you'd rather I give myself to Odin simply because—"

She stopped herself abruptly before accusing him of not wanting to share her, realizing how awful it sounded. Why should either of the men she loved be content to share her? They were not dragons, after all.

"I'd rather wait to have all of you when it's right, Frigga," Vidar corrected her. "I already have to live with coveting another man's wife. My best friend's wife. To take what you offer me would destroy what honor I have left. And then … you wouldn't love me anymore."

"That's not true," she whispered, even as she wondered if she only deceived herself to get what she wanted. "You're afraid, aren't you?"

"Perhaps. I don't know what giving in will do to either of us, especially without some stability. I need my resolve, Frigga. We both do," he explained patiently. "Everyone has a breaking point. And I'm trusting you not to push me beyond mine. I'm glad to know I'm stronger than I thought I was, but it took every ounce of discipline from my military training not to pounce on you last night. Feeling your body next to mine was almost my undoing."

"Then I'd better return to the palace," Frigga said with disappointment, feeling slighted and rejected though she understood his position.

"No!" he objected a little too forcefully. Then he softened his tone. "I don't want you to leave. Not like this." He pulled her to himself and kissed her forehead. "Frigga, I'm asking you for the only commitment I dare to ask right now. Odin aside, will you be true to me? Will you wait for me?"

"Yes," she murmured softly. "But I don't see how the way could ever be clear for us. And I don't want to live without you."

"You won't be living without me," Vidar contested as he caressed her cheek. "We'll see each other almost every day once I finish here. We have work to do … together … for Asgard. Remember?"

"But what about moments like this?" She pulled his head down and kissed him feverishly. Then she let him go, teasing, "Now I know I can handle just one kiss."

"And you have me wanting more," he whispered huskily. "I want everything that kiss promised."

"Are you still resolved, my love?" Frigga asked him quietly, not wanting to tempt him too much despite her own desire.

"Yes, I am," he said firmly. "And I'm not saying we cannot show each other any affection when we have a chance to safely be alone. But we need to be open and honest with each other when we feel like we're losing control. We need to protect each other and our relationship."

"You make it sound like we're courting," she chuckled.

"In a way, yes," he affirmed. Then he laughed. "In a very unconventional way."

"Then I agree," Frigga said, feeling a surge of emotion. "Since this will likely be our last full night together for a long time, will you permit me to see how strong I am?"

He smirked at her. "Against my better judgment, yes, my beloved queen. You may once again command me at will."

Her heart thrilled within her. She leaned forward and kissed along his jawline like he had done to her the previous night, enjoying the prickle of his beard against her lips. She heard his breath quicken, which encouraged her to push things a little further. When she kissed a spot below his ear, a soft moan he could not quite silence broke the stillness that hovered over them both.

"Are you alright?" she whispered.

"I wasn't expecting that," he groaned. "But I'm still in control."

"Good," she murmured wickedly as she kissed him a little lower and a little harder. "How's this?"

"Still … in control," he choked out. "Just don't go any lower."

She worked her way back up and sought his mouth again. "I like this game," she murmured.

When she ran her fingers through his hair, he moaned again and started kissing her with more heat than she could handle. He gripped her shoulders tightly to keep his hands in one place, then moved one to grasp the back of her head to bring her closer.

"When are we going to stop?" he panted when they took a break to breathe.

"I'm still in control of myself," she said saucily. "Aren't you?"

"Yes, but not for much longer," he admitted. "Promise me you won't push me too far."

"I promise," she repeated.

But he continued kissing her, pushing the line of where and how himself. She found herself trying to regain the upper hand but did not want to admit how dangerous the situation had become. Within minutes, they had crossed into unrestrained fervor.

"Forget everything I said about waiting," he paused long enough to say. Then, between several hard kisses that inflamed her further, he pleaded hoarsely, "Let's go upstairs … please … Frigga … let me love you fully."

"Stay strong," she murmured, retreating to a safe distance to allow him a chance to recover.

She was secretly pleased with herself for driving him to that point, though she had no intention of indulging his plea. She now had her own resolve whereas he had lost his, for she had kept her wits about her enough to know they would be filled with a deep regret if they gave in to their lust. And since she and Odin had resisted their desire for each other until their wedding night, she already had that inner discipline from which to draw. Vidar seemed to be reaching for his own reserves of self-control as he struggled to calm himself down, clenching and unclenching his fists until his body finally relaxed.

"That was close," he gasped. Then he grimaced. "So much for my discipline and self-control."

"It doesn't take much, does it?" she sighed with the beginning pangs of guilt. "If we're going to succeed at this plan of yours, we'd better not test our limits again. Last night, you held us fast. Tonight, I did."

"Thank you for that," he muttered.

"I understand now," she told him. "The pull is too strong. All it would take is one night where we both lose our grip, and it's over."

"Over?" he repeated indignantly. "Are you saying you would leave me as soon as I gave you everything?"

"No, of course not!" she exclaimed in dismay. "But I think slaking our lust could slay our love. You were right about waiting."

He smiled at her tenderly. "It isn't just lust to me, Frigga. I love you. More than you could know."

"I do know," she said as she smoothed back his hair, which she had left in disarray during their fit of passion. "It isn't just lust to me either, but I have to acknowledge how deeply I desire you. As much as I want to spend the night with you, I know I'll lose my resolve as soon as we're curled up in bed together. And you are weakened from what happened just now. I dare not stay here."

"I know," he sighed. "The nights will be long and cold without you, but we'll be together again soon. Some time apart will do us good. At least now we know where we stand."

"Together," she murmured, kissing him one more time before she activated the device to return to the palace.

She dressed for bed, trying not to think about seeing Odin the next day. Instead, she focused on her inflated pride in resisting temptation. She knew she could not say she had been faithful or pure. She knew she had fallen in love with another man, her husband's best friend. But at least she had not given in to him completely. She clung to that like a piece of driftwood in the churning sea of her choices.

I've done nothing wrong, she tried to tell herself.

But sleep did not come as easily as she expected. And when it did, she once again dreamed of Odin changing into Vidar and back again, then disappearing entirely. She tossed and turned most of the night, then finally fell into a deep sleep in the early morning. The sensation of a familiar, tender kiss on her forehead yanked her from an almost comatose state.

"Odin?" she gasped in confusion when she opened her eyes. "You're home early!"

"I didn't mean to wake you," he told her as he climbed into bed with her. "You look so peaceful and beautiful. Go back to sleep."

She snuggled up against his chest, half asleep but awake enough to be incredibly thankful she had not spent the night at Vidar's cottage. As Odin stroked her hair, she slipped into an even deeper sleep. When she awoke, she was alone in the bed. She sat up and looked around, wondering if it had all been a dream. She dressed hurriedly and checked the timepiece in their suite, then ran to the library where Thor and Loki sat with Mimir, hard at work on their lessons.

"Has anyone seen the king?" she asked casually.

"I don't believe he has returned yet, Your Majesty," Mimir answered with confusion. "If anyone would know, it would be you."

"Thank you, Mimir," she said. She turned her attention

to her sons. "Mind your tutor, boys. Father is coming today, if he is not here already. I'm going to find out."

"See you at the luncheon, Mother!" Thor called after her.

Frigga threw her hand up in a hasty wave as she rushed out the library doors. She hurried to Odin's main office. Empty. She checked his other two offices and then her own. Also empty. She stood in the hallway by the banquet hall, utterly confused. She had not been fully awake, but Odin's presence had seemed so real. Yet, now she could not find him. She was beginning to think she might be going mad when she heard voices in the banquet hall. She opened the doors and walked inside to see several of the palace staff and a handful of guards busily moving things around to prepare for the luncheon. No sign of Odin. She nodded at the servants as they looked quizzically at her.

One of the guards asked, "Are you looking for the king, Your Majesty?"

"Yes, have you seen him?" she answered.

"He showed those Muspel creatures to the guest rooms. Then they all went out to the Bifröst," the guard told her.

She breathed an inward sigh of relief, then registered what the guard had said. "Creatures? You're referring to the king of Muspelheim and his delegates, I presume?"

"Yes, Your Majesty," he returned.

"In that case, I would caution you to show a little more respect to our guests, Private!" she rebuked him.

"M-my queen?" the guard stammered. "I meant no disrespect."

"You spoke of them as if they are animals, but they are nothing of the sort," she chided him. "We can learn much from those different from ourselves."

He blinked and responded, "Of course, Your Majesty."

She judged by his veiled, polite expression that he had automatically reacted with what he thought he was expected to say. She shook her head sadly. Perhaps Odin was right that it would take more than she anticipated to overcome prejudice and old hatreds.

Feeling slightly discouraged by the exchange, she left the banquet hall to change into her riding outfit. Since she did not want to be bothered with a guard escort, she grabbed a dagger from Odin's collection, then rode out to the Bifröst by herself.

20

As Frigga approached the temporary housing of the dragons, King Baer looked up from his discussion with Odin and his two cabinet members to break into a wild and brilliant smile.

"Finally, a friendly face!" he rumbled. "Greetings, Queen Frigga!"

"Greetings, King Baer!" she returned. "Welcome to Asgard, all of you!"

The two Muspels with him smiled at her as well but did not speak. Odin merely nodded at the queen, but his smile and the light in his good eye told her he was happy to see her. She thought about Vidar's assertion that she still loved Odin. Remembering how frantic she had been to find the king, she knew the general had discerned the truth. But even she did not understand how she could love two men. Perhaps she should ask Idunn.

The fire giants huddled together, conversing in their own language. Frigga frowned slightly. Since well-mannered Asgardians and Vanir never spoke their native languages when even one person in their presence could not understand, she found their behavior suspicious and rude. Odin saw the furrow in her brow and stepped close to her.

"Remember they are not Asgardians nor Vanir and they do not observe our ways," he quietly urged.

"Indeed," Frigga muttered. She raised an eyebrow at him. "So, you have returned early. This morning wasn't a dream after all."

"Did you think it was?" he chuckled. "You were in quite a deep sleep. I was surprised to find you abed at that hour, but I'm told you were quite busy these last two days."

"Yes, I was. I went looking for you when I awoke and found you gone," she hissed, embarrassed and mildly confused by how her concern had turned to anger. "What kind of a cruel trick were you playing, making me think I had gone mad?"

"You went looking for me?" he asked with a pleased grin, ignoring her barb. "I'm glad to hear you missed me that much."

"It's only been a few days, Odin," she said, looking away with an overly casual shrug.

"I've missed you," he informed her lightly. "That's part of why I returned when I did. Well … that, and I needed to scope things out before I brought Baer and his delegates."

She snorted slightly. "Then don't pretend it was for me."

Odin blinked twice, then turned his attention to the Muspels, who had stopped talking and were clearly eavesdropping. Frigga quickly composed her face, realizing she had dishonored the king in front of his guests.

"We should return to the palace for the meal we've prepared for you," Odin told them. He then addressed his wife. "Are you riding in the cariole with us?"

"Thank you, my king, but I rode Sigurna out here," she answered.

"Alone?" Odin questioned, his tone holding a hint of warning.

"I'm fine, my king," she reassured him. "It's broad daylight, and I am armed. If you prefer that I ride with you, I could have a guard bring Sigurna back. But first, I need to have a word with my dragon."

Odin grimaced but did not argue, most likely due to the blatantly interested observation of their guests. "We will go ahead then. Would you like an escort to return with you?"

"I will decide whether I need one when I'm through," she answered bravely.

"Very well. Don't be late," Odin relented.

As soon as the king and the three fire giants left, Frigga rushed to Idunn and opened their line of mental communication.

Hello, Frigga, Idunn thought. *Things are not well.*

Are the Muspels unhappy? Frigga asked cautiously. *What did they say, if I may ask?*

My loyalty is to you now, O Queen, so I will tell you what I know, Idunn declared. *They are not comfortable here. Asgardians stare at them with fear or undisclosed hatred wherever they go. Had you not arrived when you did, they would have left. As it is, if this lack of welcome does not change, they will not stay for your banquet.*

They said all that? Frigga asked incredulously.

More or less, the dragon answered lightly. *You should know not all communication is with words.*

What can we do? Frigga asked worriedly.

Let it be, Idunn advised. *I believe this attempt to bridge your worlds was ill-timed. Your people are not ready. You and your first mate must make up the difference to help them be at ease, but you cannot force your people to accept the fire giants.*

My first mate, Frigga repeated. *Idunn, how many mates did you have at once? Of the three you had?*

I never had more than one at once, she answered. *But when a female has multiple mates, it is most often because they make up for a lack in each other. If one of my mates was lacking, I simply found another. I didn't care for balancing two or more. As I told you, I had never found one who was all that I desired. Until now.*

Brinn? Frigga asked.

Yes, Idunn replied, almost shyly. *I was blind to him for so long. I am thankful for another chance. He may be my mate for life, which is a rare thing for us. As I said, time will tell.*

I am happy for you, Frigga thought. *We will ride together soon.*

She broke the connection, then rode Sigurna back to the palace, pondering Idunn's words. She knew Vidar made up for a lack in Odin—tenderness, understanding, and his way with words that unlocked her heart. But what possible lack could Odin make up for in Vidar? Was there something else she did not understand about herself?

She surrendered her horse to the palace stable guards, then rushed to the royal chambers to dress for the luncheon. She had been wearing various hues of blue or purple lately, but she chose a red dress to please Odin. But when she entered the banquet hall, she felt quite uncomfortable when King Baer's flaming eyes lit up with pleasure at the sight of her. She dropped her own eyes and focused on the other guests.

Only Odin's war council and the royal family had been invited to this first entertaining of the Muspel king and councilmen. Frigga took her place between Odin and Baldur at the royal table and silently warned her younger sons to be polite with a single motherly look. Thor's pale skin and nervous shifting made Frigga fear he might bolt from his seat, but Loki stared at the Muspels with an obvious fascination that bordered on rude. The Asgardian council members who had not seen fire giants before behaved worse, eyeing their guests with wariness and trepidation. Even the delegates who had traveled to Muspelheim seemed uneasy.

"You have a fine family, King Odin," Baer remarked.

"Thank you, King Baer," Odin returned politely.

The servants brought in the food on dishes that clattered from their shaking hands. Frigga and Odin exchanged worried glances as the fire giants tried to ignore the almost palpable fear and tension in the room. Frigga began to ask them questions about their progress in rebuilding after the war, which helped everyone relax. Even Thor's face returned to a normal color as he enthusiastically began eating his portion of suckling pig, sliced golden apples, and candied turnips. He ignored the lightly steamed assortment of green vegetables, as was his habit. Frigga had given up fighting with him to eat his vegetables years ago.

At least he ate the turnips, she told herself.

Loki finished his food quickly, as usual, and seemed to be absorbing every word he could. He always had been a curious, observant child.

To Frigga's relief, the rest of the meal passed without incident. Odin led the men and the fire giants into the ballroom for some additional business, leaving Frigga and her three sons in the banquet hall. Loki and Thor started playing with the silk hanging from the ceiling, which Frigga would normally scold them for doing. Instead, she ignored them and walked out to the balcony.

Baldur followed her. "Mother, what's troubling you?"

"Many things, Baldur," Frigga responded honestly. "I encouraged your father to deal with the fear and prejudice Asgardians have toward those unlike them. He finally heeded my words. And now, it seems my actions have drawn the Muspels into this situation."

"You are not responsible for the choices of others," Baldur encouraged her. "Only your own."

"Thank you, my son," she replied, though his wisdom did not lift her spirits.

Because she kept her mind locked around Baldur, she knew he could only read her surface emotions. She hoped he could not sense how the absence of the general weighed on her. Could she bring herself to do what Vidar had requested of her? When would they be together again? She stopped herself from thinking such things when Baldur did not return to his brothers but watched her questioningly.

She turned to him and forced a smile. "Do not worry about me, Baldur. Why don't you take your brothers outside before they tear apart the banquet hall?"

He chuckled, though the apprehension in his eyes remained. "As you wish, Mother." Then he strode away, hollering, "Thor, put that down! Will you two ever stop acting like wild goats?"

But the laughter in his voice showed he was not cross. Frigga smiled to herself as her sons traipsed out of the hall, then turned her attention back to her view of Asgard as she remembered how Vidar liked to come out there at night to think. She soon lost herself in thought and memory until an intense heat suddenly closed over her hand. She gasped and pulled away from the burning sensation.

King Baer towered over her. "My apologies, Queen of Asgard. My anger has made my skin hotter than usual."

"Anger?" she repeated fearfully, stepping away from him.

"Not at you, O Queen," he hastened to assure her.

"At my people," she guessed.

"We may be allies on paper, but we have no true friends here," King Baer proclaimed. "Save perhaps you."

"What of the king? What of my oldest son?" Frigga countered.

"They fear us," Baer said in a dead tone.

"King Baer, please give it time," Frigga pleaded. "I've spoken with my husband at length about this. He invited you here to initiate change. But remember what you yourself said—legal decree cannot change hearts. How long will it take for you to enact change in your own world?"

Baer cocked his head at her. "Truly you are a wonder, O Queen. If you were a Muspel, I would seek your hand without hesitation."

Frigga gulped. "I-I'm flattered, O King, but—"

"Fear not," he laughed, cutting her off. "I have no plans to take a bride from outside my realm. And I respect your marriage. There should be more Muspels like you." He glanced behind him briefly. "There should be more Asgardians like you."

She straightened her shoulders. "If it's ever going to change, we must all deal with a little discomfort."

"Perhaps you are right," Baer said thoughtfully. "I had come to bid you goodbye and thank you for treating us as your equals. But a wise king heeds wise words. We will suffer a little longer."

"Then you will stay until the banquet tomorrow?" Frigga asked eagerly.

"We will stay," he responded, flashing his brilliant white smile.

"King Baer, forgive my boldness, but you are indeed a wise king," Frigga declared. "You will find your queen. And when you do, I hope you will let me know so I may rejoice with you."

"Gladly," he said, flashing his smile again.

Then he bowed and hurried off, no doubt to inform Odin and the two Muspel cabinet members of his change of plans.

Frigga turned back to look over Asgard. She felt a little lost. She had seen Vidar almost nightly since they had taken the step from friendship to an affair, though she told herself it was not really an affair as long as they did not give in to their desire for each other. She drew in a long breath and reminded herself she had lived without Odin countless times. She could endure a few weeks without Vidar. And maybe, just maybe, an opportunity would present itself for her to go to him. She sighed to herself as she imagined surprising him.

"What are you thinking about?" sounded a familiar voice to her right.

"Many things," she answered honestly as she turned to Odin with a disarming smile. "For one, I'm glad you're home." And she found it to be true. "Where are our guests?"

"Apparently, they take their afternoon rests whether it is hot or not," Odin chuckled, "which leaves my afternoon open for you."

"Does it indeed?" Frigga said warily, stepping away from him slightly.

"Don't be alarmed," he murmured as he drew her into a tender hug. "I resisted my desire for you when we were courting. I resisted for years on end more than once. I can wait for you again until I've repaired the damage I've done. It's the best way I can think of to show you I don't have ulterior motives, as you like to put it."

Frigga rested her head on his chest, pondering his words and the change in him. But the reminder of how coldly she had treated him in the past smote her. With his arm around her shoulders, they looked over Asgard together until Odin finally spoke again.

"What did you say to King Baer to change his mind?" Odin asked. "Nothing I said quelled his anger over how the luncheon went. I feared relations were damaged beyond repair, but he returned to say they would continue the course."

"I said something very similar to what you said about time and patience being needed ... when we were on Muspelheim," Frigga answered, looking up at him. "And I added this—if it's ever going to change, we must all deal with a little discomfort."

"Smarter than I am once again," Odin sighed. "Whatever would I do without you, Frigga?"

She smiled, pleased by his words. "You're not without me, so there's no need to discuss it."

"I have something else I wish to discuss with you anyway," Odin informed her. "An idea I had."

"Before you do, why did you permit the Muspel king to speak with me alone if you were concerned about his intentions?" Frigga asked curiously.

"Do you remember when you said I suspected you of unfaithfulness because I was not faithful myself?" he prompted as he turned her to face him.

"Something like that," she said seriously.

"I suppose you were right. It was my own failure that drove me to entertain such fears. But you've never given me reason to doubt you in all of the years we've been together," Odin declared. "So I've decided to put those thoughts out of my mind and choose to trust you."

Frigga felt the blood drain out of her face, but she used her illusion-casting ability to hide her reaction. Then she nodded and smiled sweetly, murmuring her thanks for his trust, all while her traitorous heart thumped in time to the guilt pulsing through her.

"What was your idea, Odin?" she reminded him, desperate to move away from the topic.

"Oh, yes … Would you be willing to give a speech in honor of the Muspels at the banquet tomorrow?"

"What would I say?" she gasped.

"Describe their planet and their way of living," Odin suggested. "Bridge the gap. Show our people they need to open their minds."

"And what about you, Odin?" Frigga prodded. "Have you opened your mind?"

"I'm working on it," he admitted. "Remember, Frigga, I've

seen things you never have. It is not easy to overcome the horrors of war."

"Can you share them with me?" Frigga asked. "I might see battle myself someday."

"No, you will not! I would never permit that," Odin protested vehemently.

Frigga checked her immediate surge of anger, recognizing how futile it would be to argue with him. No amount of logic would move him. She would have to be patient and change his mind subtly over time. Instead of lashing out, she turned her gaze back across Asgard.

"No arguments?" Odin asked in surprise.

She shook her head. "The king's word is law."

"Frigga, please try to understand," Odin pleaded. "I don't even go to battle myself except in the most dire of circumstances. I would be ashamed to let you go while I stayed behind."

She nodded. "I do understand."

Odin regarded her with doubt as if he expected further conflict. But since she did indeed see the wisdom in his words, though she refused to fully accept them, she remained silent and calm.

"I think I'd like to work on my speech in my office," she finally declared, smiling at him reassuringly.

"Very well. We'll dine in the banquet hall with the Muspels again at seven," Odin informed her. "Don't be late."

"What about the princes?" Frigga asked. "Baldur took Thor and Loki outside to play."

"I'll see to them," Odin offered. "You have a speech to write."

He winked at her and walked away with his easy, confident stride. She found herself admiring him from behind, noting his strong, broad shoulders and the muscular calves his breeches did not quite hide. He turned to look back at her at just that moment and grinned when he saw her watching him. He winked again, causing her to blush slightly. She did not hide the color moving across her face, for she knew it would send a positive message to her husband to allay suspicion as Vidar had asked. Grateful as she was for Odin's commitment to foster healing before approaching her again, Frigga wondered how long either man in her life would realistically wait for her. The fact that they were both willing to set aside their desire filled her with a validating comfort, coupled with no small amount of confusion.

She decided to put them both out of her mind for the time being, then hurried to her office and focused her mental energy on writing down all her memories from Muspelheim. She wrote of the landscape, the food, the plants, the dragons, and the kindness of the hosts. As she penned her thoughts, they turned to her desire to overcome prejudice, assumption, and misunderstanding. Remembering how the Asgardians had tolerated the presence of the Muspels at the banquet with little verbal resistance, she realized how subtle prejudice could be … even just a fleeting thought that the person in the room who is different from the rest must be a threat. And that sadly common spark, when left unchecked, could grow into a consuming fire of mistrust and fear leading to mistreatment, abuse, and even war.

And how many times has this happened in the past? she asked herself.

Most of Asgard had responded eagerly to the call to defend the Muspels in battle under King Odin's leadership, to free them from the tyranny they had endured and to end the civil war that had ravaged the fire planet. Had it not been compassion after all, but a sense of duty toward those deemed lesser? And now that the war had been won, did this deeply rooted negativity toward the fire giants reveal how hearts truly felt?

She could argue that the reception had been a tremendous success from the standpoint that it had even happened in the first place. Yet, the delegates had been acutely aware of every tremble or furtive look, more than likely due to their own fears in visiting Asgard. Perhaps they had expectations of being ill received and every response fueled that preconceived notion. The more she wrote, the more she recognized decades of fear and misunderstanding that must be undone at the most basic level. These two people groups might have vastly different cultures, but at that basic level—in the seat of their emotions—they were not so different as they seemed. Muspels and Asgardians both desired acceptance, respect, and the safety of knowing they were cared for and loved. They lived their lives and formed their societies based on the same foundations.

Hours passed by without her notice as a flurry of words poured out of her with an eloquence she had not even known she had. When she finished, she sat back and surveyed with mounting satisfaction what she had penned. An idea for a gift to the Muspelheim delegates began to tickle at the back of her mind. She excitedly shared this with Odin in whispers between courses at dinner that evening, then in more detail before they retired for the night.

"Frigga, you are not only smarter than I am, you are a genius!" Odin praised her when she showed him her work. "We are definitely doing this! And you've inspired me with another idea."

"Tell me!" she demanded playfully as she cuddled with him in their bed.

"If this goes over well, I want to offer a program to teach other cultures … beyond our existing training for ambassadors and spies," Odin began. "We could even build a school dedicated to such an endeavor, bringing in retired soldiers and spies to share their experiences."

Frigga's eyes shone with wonder. "You, my king, are the genius. What an incredibly marvelous idea!"

"I want to present it at the next war council meeting," he decided.

"But that's not until spring!" Frigga reminded him.

Odin chuckled, leaning over to kiss her gently. "Well, that gives us plenty of time to prepare, doesn't it?"

21

Frigga took a measured breath to calm the queasy feeling in her stomach. She had just given the bravest speech she had ever delivered, folding in a condensed version of her experience on Muspelheim and her key points on prejudice from the pages she had written the previous night.

A stillness had fallen over everyone, even the children. Every eye in the banquet hall seemed glued to her, unblinking and almost unrelenting. The Muspel trio did not move a single muscle, their frightening eyes flaming more intensely than usual. Frigga had no idea what to do as she surveyed a sea of unreadable faces.

Feeling as though she must fill the deafening silence with a stronger conclusion, she mustered her courage to speak up once more. "We must come together with understanding, embracing our differences and celebrating the strengths of our cultures. For there is beauty and dignity in all the realms, if we will but look for it."

She bowed her head to step down from the dais where she stood. Suddenly, a slow clap sounded from one corner of the room. Then a smattering of applause began to gather momentum until the room thundered with approval. The Muspels looked around them with pleased glances. Several Asgardians began clamoring for their attention with questions about their world. And just like that, a tentative window of communication opened.

Frigga looked around her with wonder as growing clusters of Asgardians formed around each of the three Muspels, who began to tell their own stories of their homeland. Their rumbling laughter and earthy voices mingled with lilting Asgardian tones as the formerly charged atmosphere became relaxed and lively.

Odin made his way over to her and slipped his arm around her waist. "Just look what you did, Firefly."

She leaned into him and remarked, "Not on my own, Odin. The speech was your idea. But when will we give them our gift?"

King Baer suddenly leaped onto the dais in one bound from where he stood. "Asgardians!" he bellowed, which immediately silenced everyone in the hall.

Frigga noticed a few people start at the sound as it fled to the ceiling. The guards instinctively placed their hands on their swords as if to ready themselves for what might happen next.

Baer merely glanced at them before continuing, "Today is indeed a day to celebrate! We are newly established allies by decree, but now, we Muspels pledge our loyalty to King Odin Allfather and to Asgard. Should you ever have need, we will fight to the death for you. I, King Baer of Muspelheim, swear it!"

The fire giant held his six-fingered hand out to Odin, who strode confidently to the dais to take it. Rather than clasp arms in agreement, as Frigga had expected, the Muspel king intertwined their arms and quickly bound their wrists together with some type of obsidian armband, which began to glow red in the center. The guards rushed the dais to defend their king as the people collectively gasped. The two Muspel delegates crouched slightly as if they too intended to protect their own king.

"Hold your ground!" Odin shouted, his face changing from surprised anger to wonder. "He has not harmed me."

"Have no fear, Asgardians!" Baer requested calmly. "You will see what I am doing in a moment."

The guards withdrew to a respectful distance, though they kept their hands on their weapons. The atmosphere reverted back to suspicion, and time itself seemed to stand still.

Entranced, Odin watched the pulsing light encircling his own wrist and then Baer's. Every Asgardian in the room watched with fearful awe, but the fire giants merely lifted their chins as Baer began to hum. The sound felt like a warm, lazy lullaby. The red light circled faster and faster until it seemed the entire black object glowed with it. The humming stopped, the fire giants stamped their feet twice, and the armband unclasped itself and fell into two separate pieces.

King Baer caught them before they hit the ground and handed the smaller one to Odin, who took it with eagerness.

"Let it be known that your king now wields Gungnir, a Muspel weapon electromagnetically forged from my own Draupnir," Baer informed everyone as he held up his own armband. "No one may touch it but Odin; it will respond favorably to him alone."

He showed Odin how to press something on the side, which immediately transformed the armband into a fearsome black spear. The people gasped and murmured their admiration as Odin examined the beautiful weapon with awe. Baer showed him another place to press, which turned it into a great staff. And one more manipulation brought it back to the form of an armband again, which Odin immediately clasped onto his left arm as the spectators began to whisper to each other excitedly.

"With it, you may summon me from wherever I may be, for my lifeblood and our alliance are bound within it," King Baer finished. "And mine will call to you, Allfather, for your lifeblood and our alliance are also bound in mine."

"And I will come if ever you should call me," Odin promised grandly. "Thank you, King Baer! We also have a gift of peace and goodwill for your people, though I fear it pales in comparison to yours."

The king of Asgard nodded to his queen, who retrieved a parcel wrapped in red silk. She joined them on the dais and knelt before the king of Muspelheim, holding the parcel up to him. Baer took the gift and allowed the silk to fall to the floor to reveal a beautifully hand-drawn, leather-bound book. He flipped through the pages with fascination.

"This is … this is …" The Muspel king could not seem to finish his sentence.

"It is my memoirs of Muspelheim, O King," Frigga interjected, "in detailed book form, for you to share with your people. The first of many other books about your homeland, I hope, that we may all read and learn. We had our artists and scribes work without rest to make it, as well as a matching copy for us to keep here."

The king pressed his fingers against his eyelids briefly, then said, "If you believe this pales in comparison, King

Odin, you do not yet understand Muspels. This is priceless. Queen Frigga, you honor us all!"

Then, in front of everyone, he lifted Frigga to her feet and planted a fiery kiss right on the top of her head, which sent a bolt of warmth through her instead of burning her. The people gasped and looked to Odin to see how he would react, but he merely nodded at Baer, then brought Frigga to his side to announce the close of the banquet. She felt a passing tension in his stance and wondered how he felt about it. But it appeared he had accepted that the Muspel king posed no threat. The rest of their guests seemed unable to even catch their breath from quite possibly the most memorable and unusual banquet they had ever attended. They quietly paid their respects to the Asgardian monarchs and the Muspel delegates, leaving in excited huddles until only the royal family and the three fire giants remained.

Odin transformed his new armband into the spear again and examined it carefully, exclaiming, "This weapon is extraordinary, King Baer!"

"May I try it, Father?" Thor begged excitedly.

"Did you not heed, little one?" King Baer asked sternly. "Only your father may touch it."

"Little one?" Loki snickered as he shoved Thor slightly.

Frigga shot them both a warning glance, sensing their simmering energy. "Baldur, please take Thor and Loki to bed," she requested, guessing the lateness of the hour was affecting them. "Say goodnight, boys."

When the three princes obeyed, Odin asked Baer, "What will happen if someone else touches Gungnir? Like my queen, for example?"

"It will burn her or anyone else who comes into contact with it," Baer explained. "And, of course, Gungnir will not transform for anyone else. Keep it safe and the weapon will serve you well."

"Will it make more like yours does?" Frigga asked innocently.

The other two fire giants looked at each other with shock, but Baer chuckled. "Only Draupnir has that power, and it is a fearful one. I could arm an incredible force if I so choose, but I choose not to do so. It is far too dangerous. Power like that should not be wielded by any one being."

"But you could have saved countless of your own people as well as mine," Odin protested.

"At what cost? To make myself every bit the despot we deposed?" Baer challenged fiercely. Then his face relaxed. "Besides, it would not have been a guarantee. Even armed with these, one can die. Battles are best won by wit, strength, and the sweat of one's brow."

"I cannot argue with you there, O King," Odin said with admiration. "Can we persuade you to stay until morning?"

"No, Allfather, though I thank you for your hospitality. This visit has far exceeded my expectations," Baer replied. He bowed slightly to Frigga, as did the other Muspels. "Fare thee well, fair queen. Until we meet again."

"I hope it will be soon, perhaps when you have found your own queen," Frigga answered, curtsying with a warm smile. "And I thank all three of you for visiting us."

When they nodded at her with their bright eyes flaming, Odin kissed her cheek. "I'll try not to be too late coming to bed tonight."

She watched the four of them go, then dragged herself wearily to the royal chambers. She settled onto the bed, thinking about Odin's idea for furthering education about other realms. She felt as though she had just dozed off when the doors opened and Odin burst into the room.

With childlike delight, he jumped into the bed with her. "You were magnificent tonight, Firefly!" he praised her. "I should have gotten you more involved in politics long ago. The way you smoothed over everyone and opened their eyes." He flopped backward and linked his hands behind his head to stare at their ceiling. "I'm so amazed, I'm almost speechless."

"Almost!" she chuckled, pleased by his praise.

He rolled onto his side and reached out to hug her without thinking. She cried out in pain when Gungnir touched her skin.

"Oh no! Frigga, I'm so sorry," Odin gasped. He immediately unclasped the black armband and threw it away from the bed.

"Odin, don't be so careless!" she scolded as she rubbed the red mark on her arm.

"I'm truly sorry. I didn't mean to hurt you," Odin murmured anxiously. "I forgot!"

"No, you big oaf!" Frigga laughed. "I meant don't throw away such a priceless gift on my account."

Odin looked at her strangely. "Frigga, you are more priceless to me than any weapon, even one as incredible as that. I don't want to burn you again."

"Just put it somewhere safe at night," she suggested, warmed by his words. "Or under your pillow where you can reach it quickly if you need it."

"Don't go anywhere," he told her playfully as he got out of bed and retrieved the armband. "Gungnir doesn't look harmed."

"That's a relief," she chuckled.

He thrust it under his pillow, then gently took her arm. "Let's see if you're harmed."

He tenderly kissed the fading redness, which had a surprising effect on Frigga. Her eyes widened as her breath caught in her throat suddenly.

"Did that hurt?" Odin asked worriedly.

"No, Odin, of course not," Frigga reassured him. "You're being so tender and respectful right now. And all of your praise just a few minutes ago. And what we accomplished together tonight …" Her words had been spilling out of her, but she stopped suddenly and stared at her husband. "We make a powerful pair when we work together instead of fighting each other."

"Yes, we do," Odin murmured in a low voice. He hugged her close to himself again.

"You're making me reconsider keeping you at bay, husband," Frigga remarked ruefully.

"I'm sorry," he sighed, releasing her immediately.

"And that made me feel worse," she admonished him playfully. "Just kiss me already."

He gulped slightly. "You're not going to tease me again, are you? Because I thought—"

"Odin?"

"What?"

"Stop talking."

And with those words, she opened herself to him as she had not in years, even connecting with him this time. Everything felt new and different. She did not need to slip into thoughts or imaginations of Vidar as she had feared, though a part of her remained bound to the absent general even as she loved her husband in body. But somehow, that did not bother her as it had. Instead, she experienced an incredible relief over keeping the two separate in her mind for the most part. And as Odin whispered words of endearment and pronounced his love to her, she felt happier with him than she had in centuries. During those moments, at least, it seemed perhaps her wounds might heal.

22

Frigga stood at the window of her palace bedroom and stared out over the picturesque view, not really seeing much. The past few weeks had been a flurry of activity, from the Muspel banquet to the tryouts at the arena for the first women joining her programs to the start of training for the regular self-defense program. All of it seemed a blur to her. She had kept such a frenzied pace that exhaustion was beginning to take a toll. She and Odin had spent many late nights planning their proposal for the war council to consider in the spring, which had deepened her love for the king in some ways. Their arguments lessened and their actual conversations increased. But her attachment to Vidar remained strong.

How I miss him, she sighed to herself, feeling unbelievably melancholy.

There had been days on end when she had not had time to think of him at all, especially while enjoying her time with Odin. But because her love for the general was as real as everything she had felt for the king and she feared fully trusting Odin again, the pain of her separation from Vidar drained her emotionally. And during moments like these, she wondered if Vidar experienced the same stretches of time without thinking of her. She wondered what he might be doing and how he fared. Would he meet someone in the marketplace or about the village? Did she alone truly hold his heart as he claimed? Or would it be better for them both if the general did move on with another woman?

"Frigga!" Odin exclaimed as he burst into the room as he often did when he was excited. The habit was terribly undignified but endearing all at once because he only acted that way with her. As if full of boyish energy, he practically bounded to where she stood. "Bragi says the fish have really been biting these past few days with the extra rain."

"Does he now?" she asked automatically, suddenly annoyed as she wondered why she should care about how the fishing was.

"Do you remember that little fishing hole we went to when I was just teaching Baldur to fish?" Odin prompted her.

"No. Have you forgotten how much I hate fishing?" she grumped.

Odin wrapped his arms around her. "What's wrong, Firefly?"

"Nothing," she snapped. Then she sighed. She could not tell him the real reason. "The rain has been so dreary. I miss the sun."

"At least the farmers have brought in most of the harvest," Odin reminded her.

"Yes, I am thankful for that," she said thoughtfully, her spirits brightening as she remembered the autumn harvest feast would take place in just shy of a week.

"So, that old fishing spot where I used to take Baldur?"

he prompted as if they had not spoken of anything else, which irked her further.

The last few days, it had seemed to her that he had reverted back to his old distracted ways. Perhaps all their relationship problems were resolved in his mind.

"What about it?" was all she said.

"Bragi went yesterday. He said there were more bass hiding near the surface than he's ever seen. I think we should go," Odin concluded.

"Who's we?" she asked warily, turning her attention back to the window just as another rainstorm darkened the horizon.

"The boys and I, for certain," he replied excitedly. His face dropped slightly. "I assume you don't care to go. Would you mind if I took them for a few days?"

Frigga immediately saw her advantage in the situation and flashed him a reassuring smile. "Odin, I think that's an excellent idea. The princes need time with their father."

"That is exactly what I was thinking!" Odin returned with a bright smile. "I'm glad you agree. We'll get everything ready and be off before lunch."

"If this rain stops, I might practice flying with my dragon," Frigga murmured.

"I don't want you doing that when I'm not there," Odin cautioned. "The last few attempts with that contraption of yours did not go well."

"It's called an irscet," Frigga corrected him. "It just isn't the right fit for me. And the one the leather workers tried to make for me was a dismal failure. I've tried to tell you before … the dragons do not have enough understanding of our anatomy to help rework it. I need General Vidar to target whatever we're doing wrong whenever he returns."

"He'll be back for the harvest feast," Odin informed her. "You can talk to him about it then."

"That doesn't help me today," Frigga protested. "I'm not sure what you're so concerned about. I've ridden bareback, remember?"

"I didn't know how dangerous that was when you did it," Odin countered gently. "I'm not doubting your abilities. I'd just feel better if you waited until you have a proper dragon saddle."

"Very well. I'll find something else to do," Frigga sighed.

"I know you, my lovely queen. You won't be bored," Odin said flippantly as he started changing his clothes and putting together a journey pack. "I think three days should be perfect, don't you?"

Frigga knew she could answer with anything and he would not hear it, so great was his focus on his task at hand. So she chose to let the question pass, becoming distracted by her own plans as she helped him and the princes prepare for their impromptu trip. After they were finally on their way, she warned the staff not to disturb her with any palace matters, informing them she had much to do.

She closeted herself in her office for hours, poring over her studies of the other realms for her project with Odin. She broke only for a snack, skipping dinner to continue working, then locked herself in the royal suite for the night. She threw open the doors of her armoire and surveyed her array of dresses. Just last week, Odin had arranged for the royal dressmaker to prepare her some new gowns, one of which was a gorgeous peacock blue. The king had not commented much on that particular dress, but Frigga knew someone who would appreciate its beauty. She imagined Vidar's face when she appeared in the cottage and smiled to herself with all of the cunning required for a secret rendezvous.

When she arrived in the beach cottage, quite satisfied with her appearance, her smile grew even wider when she spotted a fire on the hearth. A delicious smell wafted to her nostrils from the kitchen. A man's voice lifted in song carried down from the upper level. She had never been close enough to hear Vidar sing during any of their funerals, weddings, or celebrations. The sound wove an enchantment about her, drawing her to the base of the stairs. But she was not paying attention to where she was going and stumbled over the edge of a new blue rug in the sitting area. Though she caught herself before she fell, she knocked over a blue vase in her haste to keep her footing. The vase hit the harder floor outside the rug and shattered with a resounding crash.

The singing stopped. Heavy footsteps thundered down the stairs. Then Vidar burst into the room with his sword drawn.

"Show yourself, intruder!" he bellowed.

Fighting the urge to giggle, Frigga pressed herself into the corner by the painting, loath to reveal herself now. Vidar glanced toward the front door and, seeing it clearly locked, relaxed somewhat. But when he groaned over the broken vase, embarrassment threatened to swallow her where she stood. They had not seen each other for over two weeks, and the first thing she did was break something. But just as she reached her invisible hand into her dress pocket to activate the device and return to the palace, a sleek white cat crept out from behind the closed window curtains.

Vidar spotted the animal and smiled fondly at her. "Did you do this, Willow?"

The cat meowed and rubbed her body against Vidar as he cleaned up the mess. Then she sniffed the air delicately and began to inch toward Frigga's hiding place as if she knew someone was there.

"Dinner is in the kitchen, silly girl," Vidar laughed. "Although I might not give any to such a naughty cat."

This was too much for Frigga. She loved animals and could not bear to see the pretty cat blamed for something she had done, though she had discerned playfulness in Vidar's threat. She revealed herself at once, but Vidar was too busy sweeping up the rest of the broken pottery to notice. He deposited the pieces into a trash receptacle in the kitchen, then checked on whatever he was cooking. But Willow had seen her and ducked back behind the curtains in fright. Frigga decided to stay where she was until she figured out how to make her entrance. Vidar came back into the sitting area and stoked the fire. She watched as the light from the flames danced over his profile and muscles, suddenly filled with a desire so strong, she could not stay hidden any longer.

Visible again, the fabric of her dress shimmered and rustled as she slowly walked toward Vidar. But feeling shy and unsure of herself, she vanished just as he turned toward the sound.

He frowned. "I'm seeing things again, Willow." When the cat did not reappear, he looked around in confusion. "Willow? Where did you go, little one?"

He stood up with his hands on his hips and peered toward the spot where Frigga had hidden herself. She wondered if he had seen her after all but did not believe she was truly there.

Just as she was about to reveal herself again, the cat tore out of the curtains and ran like mad up the stairs. Vidar followed her, his face a mask of confusion. Frigga stifled a laugh and quietly eased up the stairs as well. She followed his voice as he scolded the cat. She found him sitting on the bed with Willow in his arms, petting her and crooning to her to calm down. But when the cat sensed Frigga again, she fought to get away from him, clawing him in her haste to flee. Before he could hurry after her again, Frigga gathered her courage and went visible.

"Frigga!" Vidar exclaimed, falling back onto the bed with shock. He held his hand against his chest where the cat had scratched him, but his eyes glowed as he took in every inch of her. "You look … absolutely stunning. Are you real this time?"

"If you've been hallucinating, that is not even a little bit healthy. But yes, I'm real," she laughed. "And I'm to blame for breaking your vase, not your cat."

"Oh, she's not mine," Vidar hastened to explain. "My uncle asked me to watch her for a few days. He took my aunt on a holiday."

"On a holiday? Don't they live here? In a holiday destination?" Frigga quipped.

"Yes, but they've always wanted to travel west to the mountains," he murmured as if in a trance, for just as Frigga had hoped, he could not take his eyes off her.

"Let's look at those scratches, Vidar," she suggested, slipping into the same mode as she did when tending to her sons' bumps and scrapes.

She gently pushed him backward until he obediently lay down onto the bed. She sat beside him and undid the toggles that held his tunic together, then spread open the dark blue material to look at his skin. She usually kept a little Asgardian ointment on her these days, which she applied to the raw-looking claw marks. He watched her face ravenously as she tended to him. When she finished and apologized for spooking the cat so much, he sat up and pulled her roughly into his arms, burying his face into her hair, which she had left down.

He breathed deeply of her scent and whispered, "I should have known it was really you. You always smell like vanilla and jasmine."

He pulled away enough to touch her face, his eyes flitting down to her shoulder, which she suddenly realized was partially bare due to the dress having slipped slightly. The golden glow flared in his eyes, and he impulsively kissed the exposed skin. He had never kissed her there before, and she found herself willing him to push things further. But he merely lifted his head and drew the sleeve back to where it belonged, smiling at her tenderly.

"Thank you for tending to me, my queen," he whispered as he caressed her face again. "I am beyond happy to see you. I've missed you so much."

"I've missed you too, my love," she cooed, remembering how much he enjoyed the expression.

And now that she was with Vidar again, all memory and thought of Odin fled from her mind. All she saw was the general. All she wanted was him. But as their lips met in an explosion of unfulfilled longing, Vidar did not venture below her mouth as she had hoped he would.

After just a few moments, he stopped kissing her and said, "Have you eaten yet? I think I have enough for us both."

"And for the cat as well?" she teased.

"Yes, she'll get her dinner," he chuckled. "We can talk while we eat."

He refastened his tunic, then led her back downstairs by the hand. He served the cat, who seemed to be getting used to Frigga's presence now that she could see her. Then he gave Frigga a plate of stewed vegetables and game meat, which he explained one of his crew members had shot during a wilderness expedition. The simple meal was delicious, though Frigga did not eat much of it, focused as she was on listening to him describe Berg's new house, which was almost fully framed and only slightly behind schedule.

When they moved into the sitting area, the cat curled up beside her as if finally welcoming her. Frigga told Vidar all about the Muspels' visit to Asgard, which he greatly enjoyed, including Odin's school idea to present during the next war council.

"It's a marvelous idea, it really is! But what about the tryouts?" Vidar prompted.

"So many women came, Vidar," she told him enthusiastically. "It was incredibly gratifying. We narrowed it down to forty women and started training last week. But we haven't done anything with the healers."

"And how are your dragons?"

"They're adjusting well. We've had problems with the saddles, so none of them have been ridden yet except for mine. Odin said I could ask you about it when you return for the harvest feast."

"You've done well these last few weeks," Vidar praised her. He glanced down, then looked at her intently. "And how is Odin? You've mentioned him a few times. I gather his happiness grows. And you seem happy. I'm sensing you've loved him well in my absence."

Frigga stared at her hands, feeling shy and loath to talk about such things. "I've done what you asked, Vidar. And I haven't had to imagine you."

"I don't know how to take that," Vidar admitted, pressing his hand to his brow and sweeping it back through his hair.

"Isn't it a good thing?" she suggested. "It means I can keep the two of you separate in my mind."

"It means you can keep me separate from him, yes," he acknowledged. "But can you keep him separate from me?"

"I did before we ate," she defended herself, feeling slightly resentful for having to explain. "When you kissed my shoulder."

"I remember," he murmured, his eyes glowing again and lingering where he had kissed her. "You only thought of me. You wanted more."

"I still do," she said shyly as a blush crept across her cheeks.

"So do I. Why do you think I'm keeping my distance?" he sighed.

"Because you're jealous of Odin?" she suggested softly as she scooted closer to him.

He turned his face away to stare at the fire. "It isn't just that. If I gave up my resolve now, which I'm tempted to do, I know how much it would hurt Odin because I know how much it hurts me. You were right the last time we were together. I am afraid." He turned to her suddenly and gathered her into a desperate hug. "I'm afraid I'm losing you to him."

"I am learning to love Odin again, and yes, I've been happier these last few weeks. But that hasn't changed how I feel about you," Frigga said quietly as she shifted so she could look him in the eyes. "My love for you is just as strong."

"I am relieved to hear you say that last part," he admitted.

"Didn't you already know it?"

"I am having trouble sensing what is true. Your shifting emotions and thoughts confuse me, and I fear I am willfully deceiving myself," he murmured as he took her into his arms again. "I should let you go. You are finding happiness and love with your husband."

She shook her head frantically and threw her arms around his neck. "No, Vidar, don't dismiss me again. You've already tried sending me back to Odin once, remember? It's too late for that."

"Yes, it's too late for that," Vidar choked out. "I said I should. But I cannot. All of this time away from you … I've imagined loving you almost every night since you were here last. And now that you're here again when I least expected it … Frigga, I am losing control already, and I'm not even kissing you."

"Should I return to the palace?" she asked meekly.

"No, don't go," he begged softly. "You said Odin isn't coming back for three days. Will you stay with me tonight?"

"I want to," she whispered. "But I don't want to threaten your resolve. You asked me not to push you past your limits."

"Oh Frigga, I *am* deceiving myself," he lamented. "I've gone so far past my limits in my mind, I don't know how much longer I can … If I cannot even handle … I feel it's only a matter of time before we—"

"Then I'll leave," she said sadly, pushing him away as she pulled out the transport device. "And I won't come back."

"No," he groaned in agony as he grabbed her hands and snatched the device away from her.

He kissed her suddenly, caressing her shoulders as he did so. It seemed to her he was subtly pushing the fabric off her shoulders to gain access to her skin. His touch felt far more sensual than Odin's ever had. Whereas Odin had learned her preferences over time and sometimes still charged in too quickly, Vidar seemed to instinctively know exactly when, where, and how to touch her. She felt as if he silently begged for permission to explore her further as his fingers thrummed with the heat of his desire. She wondered if this wordless communication had been forged from their strong emotional bond. Or was it a benefit of his beautiful gift? The more she focused on what his hands were doing and how close they were to where they never wandered, the more her thoughts willed him to cross that invisible threshold so she could open herself to him like a flower thirsting for rain. She knew they were on a dangerous path, from which there was no turning back, but the willpower to heed the warning in her mind was seeping from her.

"I thought you were going to leave," he murmured as he started kissing one of her now-bare shoulders and caressing the other.

"You took the device," she retorted, her breath catching in her throat as she fought to regain control. "How can I?"

He handed it back to her with a fiendish grin, his eyes flaming more than ever before as he taunted, "If that's the only reason you're still here, then go."

She smirked at him, then activated the device and vanished.

Inside the cold and silent royal suite, she tore off her dress and changed into a soft, blue nightgown she had never worn for Odin. She fluffed up her hair and sprayed herself with a touch of her favorite perfume, the same scent Vidar had commented on earlier, then surveyed herself in the mirror.

Tonight is the night, she told herself. Reuniting with Vidar and seeing how great his desire was (after Odin had treated her so distractedly yet again) had shifted her thinking. *I cannot face years on end of being taken for granted anymore. Vidar is my second mate, and I will allow this torture no longer.*

She hung up the discarded dress, then transported herself back to the cottage. Vidar sat on the settee with his head back against the cushions and his eyes shut tight as he stroked the cat, who sat curled up in his lap. When she saw the glistening tears on his face, her determination to ease his suffering locked into place. She stood by the fire so the light would show off the red in her hair and softly called his name.

He sat up with a start. When he saw her, he dropped his mouth open and shoved the cat off his lap to scramble to his feet.

"I thought you left me," he muttered as he approached, the steady golden fire building in his eyes again. "I thought I pushed it too far."

"I only left to change. That dress was too cumbersome," she informed him playfully. Then she took a deep breath. "Vidar, you are my second mate. I cannot stand to see you torture yourself over me any longer."

"I was only hurt that you could love Odin so easily, without even thinking of me," Vidar murmured as he hovered close to her without touching her. "And jealous. Definitely jealous."

"I promised to be true to you, Odin aside. But your plan has caused you more grief as you deny yourself and me to wait for something that may be years away, if it ever happens. And if you cannot even be around me or talk to me because of suppressed desire, we will gradually lose our love. We tried two of your plans. They haven't worked to curb our lust or put us back in proper boundaries." She gestured to the definition of her curves, barely hidden by the silky nightgown. "This is my plan. Let me give you all of me."

"I cannot deny how much I have longed for this," he whispered as his eyes slid over every inch of her body, flaming again as they had just before she left to change. He shut them tightly and took a deep breath. "But one of the reasons for my resolve was that I wanted you to have some commitment from me, some assurance I won't abandon you afterward."

"I know you would not, but we can commit to each other everything we are free to commit." She stepped close to him and draped her arms around his neck. "General Vidar of Asgard, will you act as my second mate? Will you love and serve only me until I release you from your oath?"

"I swear it," he promised, his voice husky with emotion and meaning as he slipped his arms around her. "What else would you ask of me, my queen?"

"To continue to keep our relationship secret until we can see a way clear to reveal it," she added. "And to be my confidante and my friend even after I share your bed."

"I pledge all of this to you on my very life," Vidar said solemnly, tightening his arms around her. "In fact, I pledge to you my very life. As I said I would when I first confessed my love, I now swear fealty to you and you alone. From this day forward, not even Odin's word will stand over yours."

"But I will not ask you to forsake any oath to him or to Asgard," she assured him. "What else would you ask of me, my beloved general?"

"Only your friendship, your confidence, your love, and your word that only Odin will have you besides me," he declared. "And to speak of our times together to no one, not even to your dragon."

"She will know," Frigga told him seriously.

He chuckled. "Then speak of it to no one but your dragon."

"I swear it," Frigga agreed. "Somehow, I think she will be the only one who understands this. And now, since we cannot legally marry, may these words bind us together even when we are apart."

"How are we going to keep this from Odin?" Vidar asked quietly as he began kissing her as he had before she left. "How will we manage to be together?"

"Let's take it moment by moment. We'll figure it out together," she whispered. "And I'll come to you whenever I can, as often as I can."

"Are you quite sure about this?" he whispered in her ear.

"Yes, without question," she whispered, a heated desperation oozing into her voice as he grew bolder with his hands and his mouth. "Oh, you are far more skilled than he is. You've taken me beyond refusal in mere seconds."

"How can you be thinking of him, even now? You're comparing me to him," Vidar accused as he aggressively pulled her body against his.

"It's hard not to," she admitted sheepishly. "It's just because it's our first time, and I've been with him many times."

Vidar winced and pulled away slightly. "I didn't need that reminder."

"I'm certainly not your first, remember?" she teased as she slipped her hands under his tunic, making him relax instantly and lean into her. "You honed your skills somewhere. Shall we see what else you can do?"

"I've never wanted to show anyone as badly as I want to show you," he murmured, tenderly leaning his forehead against hers as he lowered his hands to her lower back, anchoring his thumbs onto her hips. She could tell by the nervous energy in his fingertips exactly where he wanted to grip next, but just as she thought he would finally dare, he shifted his body weight and softly, almost shyly, said, "I hope your general can meet his queen's expectations."

"You have already exceeded them," she returned, trailing her fingers down his chest as she had wanted to so many months ago when she first visited his palace bedroom. She grinned boldly when she felt his energy building at her touch, then added, "To the victor go the spoils. Come now, take your reward."

"You are far more than that," he protested, his voice low with just a note of some lingering doubt.

The look in his eyes had grown beyond the golden glow she loved so much to a hot and steady fire, primal and almost predatory. Uncertain of what made him hesitate to take what she offered him, she slid her hands around to his lower back and pressed into him as closely as she could, letting his body heat pulse into her.

"I know how much you value me," she whispered.

Without taking her eyes from his, she unfastened his tunic again to expose his chest, then kissed his bare skin.

His ragged breathing told her they would not be talking much longer.

"A bold move, my queen," Vidar whispered hoarsely. "You have skills of your own."

"I have learned much in how to please a man, even with only one partner," she boasted.

"No more talk of him, please," Vidar pleaded, the fire in his eyes dimming slightly as he looked away.

She turned his head back to her and smiled softly, letting all of her love pour into her eyes as she caressed his bearded cheek. "Your gift should tell you where my heart lies."

"With mine," he murmured just before he smothered her mouth with his own.

The fire on the hearth slowly died as they gave in to every impulse. When a chilly darkness fell over the room, he breathlessly urged her to come upstairs with him to finish what they had started. She refused him nothing, and he thanked her with more passion and tenderness than she had ever experienced. But as they lay together gasping for air when the deed was done, she squelched the guilt and the horror threatening to choke her, lest he sense it. But he seemed to be dealing with his own devastation.

"It happened just like you said, my queen," he whispered, unable to hide the anguish in his voice. "Both of us let go of our resolve. There was no stopping it."

"No, my love," she whispered back. "I made a choice. You made a choice."

"If Odin knew what I've done, he would slay me in my sleep," he muttered.

"I thought you didn't want any more talk of him," Frigga said quietly.

"I don't," Vidar admitted. "But he is like an invisible presence I cannot escape. If he finds out—"

"He is not going to find out," she soothed him. She propped herself up on her elbow to gaze at him, smoothing his sweaty, tousled hair away from his face. "Please don't tell me you regret this. After everything we said to each other?"

"I do regret it, Frigga," he sighed, reaching out to touch her own disheveled hair. "And yet, I would do it again in a heartbeat."

"Would you like to?" she murmured seductively.

He shivered slightly and shut his eyes, a sly grin crossing his face briefly. "Yes, but not tonight. All of our promises didn't seem to make a difference in stemming the guilt of what we've done. Why does it still feel wrong?"

"Because of Odin," she answered gravely. "Because you love him and you know how this would devastate him. And so do I. I feel guilty too, but I don't regret it. I think it was worse when we deceived ourselves into thinking we weren't having an affair when we have been since—"

He groaned and flopped onto his back to stare at the ceiling. "Since we started meeting in secret."

"Maybe even before that," Frigga admitted. She reached for him and gently tugged him back to her. "We may be deceiving Odin out of necessity because you know he will not share me willingly or understand like you do, but at least we are no longer deceiving ourselves. We know what we have and where we stand."

"I suppose that's true," Vidar sighed. "I will cling to whatever honor I have left." He kissed her forehead. "I still feel guilty, but I loved every single moment with you."

She snuggled against him, reliving each sensation as she drifted off to sleep with one of his arms gripping her waist. Surprisingly, no dreams disturbed her.

When the sun lazily kissed her skin the following morning, she opened her eyes to see the space next to her empty. She panicked for a moment. Had he abandoned her after all? Would she be caught in all of her wickedness? Then the door opened and Vidar entered the room with a large plate of bread and fruit in one hand and a small pitcher of fresh milk in the other. His shy smile put her mind at ease, and she noticed how his gaze lingered longingly on what he could see of her skin.

"Thank you," she said softly as she took the plate.

"Save some of it for me," he requested as he pulled up a chair. "I went to the construction site early this morning, so I've worked up quite an appetite." He blushed slightly, then hastened to add, "For food, that is."

"Oh really?" she taunted as she set the plate down and threw aside the blankets covering her. "Perhaps I should change that."

She moved confidently toward him as he gulped, watching her with a bold and eager grin on his face.

"You're even more beautiful in the daylight," he flirted with her. "I didn't get as good a look last night."

"When do you have to be back to the site?" she asked as she scooped up her nightgown from where she had thrown it in her passion with Vidar.

She started to pull the garment over her head, but he suddenly grabbed her arm to stop her.

"I have plenty of time," he said in a low voice.

He snatched her nightgown away from her and dropped it onto the floor, grinning rakishly at her as he slid his hands down to her hips and pulled her in for a kiss.

"What about the food?" she gasped.

"Forget the food," he growled suggestively. She giggled and welcomed him back into her embrace as he added, "We'll eat it after."

But after they had finished for the second time, Frigga had lost all interest in eating, for the thought of facing Odin eventually made her feel physically ill. All she really wanted was to savor and prolong every moment with Vidar for as long as possible because she knew their time would eventually end as long as she stayed married to Odin. She sensed she had jeopardized both relationships by giving Vidar everything twice now, but she had no willpower to stop. What was left for her but to live this double life?

She watched the general proceed to eat all the food he had brought. Was he oblivious to her inner turmoil as Odin so often had been in the past? Or was he acting so ravenously to distract himself from his own feelings on the matter?

"I told my crew I needed to check on some things here, then get some supplies in the village, which is true," he told her as he polished off the last of the bread. "So I need to leave as soon as I get cleaned up. What about you?"

"I'll leave in a few minutes or they're going to start to wonder why they haven't seen me. I should make an appearance at least once," she sighed, retrieving the nightgown again.

"What will you do today?" he answered, watching her dress. "When will you return?"

"I might go for a ride alone this afternoon and join you for dinner after," she offered. Then her face fell. "Then again, perhaps I shouldn't go for a ride. The last time I did that, the staff gossiped about me meeting someone in secret."

"I remember that!" Vidar exclaimed. "I was furious."

"Were you worried?" she asked with a shy grin.

"A little," he admitted. "I knew you weren't meeting me. But I told myself there couldn't possibly be yet another man."

"I certainly hope you *never* think such a thing of me," Frigga told him seriously. But then an intrusive thought hit her like cold water to the face. She had been unfaithful *with* him, after all. What prevented him from fearing she would be unfaithful *to* him? She shook her head, not wanting to think about such things. "I do find it strange that anyone even suggested it. I managed to hide all my visits with Laufey. No one ever discovered her room or thought twice about where I might be. Why make that accusation now? Unless it's linked to when Odin was asking questions of the staff after his first peace treaty talk."

"It could be. You have to remember you're under greater scrutiny now with your programs," Vidar commented. "And when you tell the council about your newest idea, the scrutiny will increase. We will have to be very careful."

She reached out to caress his face, delighted when he closed his eyes with pleasure at her touch as she crooned, "Let's start with today, my love."

She kissed him one last time, then teleported back to the royal suite to be the queen of Asgard once again.

23

"Tell me about your day," Vidar requested as he served Frigga a small helping of cheese and bread since she had already eaten dinner at the palace.

"There's not much to tell," Frigga sighed. "I spent most of my time in my office, going over papers and daydreaming about you. I hope you got more done than I did."

"Just more framing," he said offhandedly. "I hired another worker, so things are moving faster now. When does Odin return?"

"The day after tomorrow," she answered. "I've made arrangements to stay with you until mid-morning. Then I'll come back tomorrow night, but I dare not stay until morning. And that's the last time we have to be together until you return to the palace."

"And we probably cannot be as free there," Vidar guessed. "I have a feeling the king will send me back to the South Sea after the harvest feast. My crew still has two months' worth of work to do. I wasn't supposed to stay for the whole project originally, but when I spoke with Odin a few days ago, he seemed to think—"

"A few days ago?" she gasped. "How? He didn't tell me that!"

"Why would he?" Vidar laughed. "But yes, he and I sometimes use an old communication system from our boyhood days, similar to the one Gjallar uses to send messages … though ours is audio only. No visual input."

"I have heard of that. I wonder why Asgardians stopped using those things," she wondered aloud.

"Borr outlawed them in his day. Too many security breaches," Vidar said simply. "Odin secretly kept two gadgets, one of which he gave to me, but he never reinstated the regular use of them, probably because they were Olympian tech. Perhaps someday we'll have better technology. I would love to be able to talk to you whenever I want."

"Can Odin talk to you whenever he wants?" she asked quietly.

"No, he sends me a notification that sounds like a ping, which I have to activate to receive his signal on my own gadget," Vidar explained. "And if he's too far away, it sounds garbled. It did sound like he thinks I should continue to oversee here."

"If he sends you back, when will you return to the palace?" Frigga asked.

"Before winter sets in, for certain." He winked at her. "If we can figure a way around Odin, this could be my warmest winter yet."

She blushed. "I wanted to cuddle up with you during most of the last snows."

"You did?" he asked with surprised delight. "That must have been when I was in denial that you'd fallen for me."

"There's no denial now," she whispered as she sat in his lap and kissed him everywhere she could reach.

"Do you want to go upstairs already?" he asked with surprise when she started trying to undress him.

"Yes, don't you?" she cooed. "Let's make the most of our time together!"

He lifted her up into his arms and carried her up to his bed, kissing her the whole way. They spent half of the night loving each other and could not keep their hands off each other the following morning either, which made Vidar late for an appointment at the construction site. He told her about it when they came together again that evening, laughing ruefully as he described all of the teasing for his unusual tardiness, which he had explained away as a bad bowl of soup that had made him sick.

Not knowing when they would be together again after that night, they did not talk long but stretched every moment for as long as they could until Frigga returned to the palace. Alone in her frigid and lonely marriage bed, she comforted herself with the reminder of the harvest feast in just a few days, when she would see Vidar again. But she dreaded facing Odin with the new memories of her second mate looming in her mind. Truth be told, she had entertained Vidar more times in three days than she had Odin in three weeks. And she enjoyed Vidar far more than she remembered ever enjoying Odin, although they had been happy enough before Laufey came along. With a twist of unexpected pain, she suddenly wondered if Odin's trysts with Laufey had been more enjoyable to him than loving his own queen. Was that why he had continued to go back to the giantess even though he had not loved her? Had he been as intoxicated by Laufey's love as Frigga was with Vidar's? And had he compared the two women as she had compared the two men? These thoughts were so distressing to her, she transported herself back to Vidar's bedroom in the beach cottage as the first wave of tears hit.

"Frigga?" Vidar asked sleepily when she jumped into bed with him and wrapped her arms around him. "You're back! What's wrong?"

But she could not articulate and simply sobbed into his chest.

"Did Odin come back early? No, it couldn't be. If he had, you wouldn't be here," Vidar said to himself as he tried to comfort her.

Instead of telling him her thoughts, she pleaded, "Will you still love me if we cannot be together like this again?"

"Of course I will," Vidar soothed her. "I loved you before you gave me all of you, didn't I?"

"Everything is different now," she sputtered. Then she dared to say, "Odin kept going back to Laufey, but he only used her. He never loved her."

"Is that what this is about?" Vidar asked somewhat sternly. "Frigga, I am not Odin. And I do love you. And that love was never based on your physical beauty or how you can satisfy me. I love you as a person. I love your soul."

She quieted herself, feeling whole again as she lay in the circle of his arms. "I'm afraid, Vidar. For the first time since we … He'll be home tomorrow. How can I face him?"

"I don't know. I have to face him too, knowing I reached out and took what belonged to him," Vidar murmured gloomily. "I can never go back to the way things were." He paused, then asked, "Didn't you say one of the male dragons had two mates at once? Maybe he can help us."

"We promised each other not to reveal this to anyone but my dragon and only because she already knows about you," Frigga reminded him.

"I'll be training the Valkyries, won't I?" he thought aloud. "Shouldn't I have my own dragon to train them how to maneuver in the air? And that would make it easier to fix that saddle design for Asgardians."

"I had not even considered that," she gasped.

"And if I choose him, won't he know? I've been practicing locking my mind, but I'm not as skilled as you are. And we've never had any more lessons. We've been too focused on … other things." He reached for her and kissed her possessively as he said this, then nuzzled her nose with his. "Can we agree to let me speak with him and see where that goes?"

"Yes, I agree," she said, feeling more at ease. "But you won't be able to before Odin returns. Do you mind if I speak with him first?"

"Not at all," Vidar responded. "I hate seeing you upset like this. If the dragon helps ease your mind, all the better. But you need to go back to the palace now, my queen. The nights will be long and cold without you."

"You said the same thing the last time we separated for more than a day," she laughed.

"It's even truer now," he sighed. He suddenly wrapped her up in a tight embrace and murmured, "How am I going to survive without you?"

"Only a few more days, my love," she reminded him as she stroked his hair.

"Yes, but now that I know what Odin enjoys on a regular basis, it will torture me to imagine the two of you together while we're apart," Vidar confessed.

"I'll keep myself from him for now," she promised him. "I've done it before without a second mate."

He sighed with relief and kissed her hard. "That will make my time away from you so much easier." He grinned at her suddenly. "Shall we go once more?"

"No, I do need to get back," she laughed. "Save it for next time, stallion."

"Is that a promise?" he asked playfully. When she winked at him and nodded, he hugged her one more time and told her, "I'm not a stallion, remember? There is no one for me but you."

"Do you wish it were the same for me?" she asked hesitantly.

"Of course I do," he answered without hesitation. When she started rapidly blinking to stem more tears, he kissed her forehead. "Frigga, just because I want you to myself doesn't mean I love you any less. I've had to accept that Odin came first. A year ago, I didn't think something like this was even possible. I'm thankful you can love me at all."

"Why does that sound so wrong to me?" she muttered. "You shouldn't be relegated to my leftovers."

"Is that what you've given me? Is that what this is?" he asked quietly.

"No, no," she hastened to reassure him. "In fact, before I came back just now, I realized I've given far more of myself to you than I have to Odin over the years. You somehow connected with my soul in a way he never has." She gasped suddenly. "I do believe I love you more."

A brilliant smile transformed his face, making him handsomer than ever. "Then I am content. And I still hope beyond hope for the day we can be together without lying or sneaking … or sharing. For the day you love only me."

"Only you," she whispered in wonder, revisiting her imaginations of a time and a place where she was not Queen Frigga but a common woman free to devote herself fully to the general without shame or rebuke.

At her utterance, Vidar seemed to be overwhelmed with emotion, which he poured into gently persuading her to love him in body once more. She did not want to leave afterward, but she forced herself to return to the royal suite. And early the following morning, she commanded two guards to ride hard and fast with her to the Bifröst, desperate to speak with the dragon who had balanced two mates.

A sense of dread and foreboding hovered over her. She did not know what time Odin would return or how she would act.

Is it really any different from before? she asked herself as the wind whipped about her hair and riding outfit. *I loved him in soul. I wanted him in body and experienced more than just a taste before the last few days. I was already unfaithful. And Odin did not know. I can do this. I can love two mates.*

But she doubted her silent declarations and fought with herself the whole way to the temporary dragon lair. The guards dismounted and respectfully kept their distance as she hurried inside. She went first to Idunn, who lay curled up with Brinn. The golden dragon lifted her head and approached Frigga before she even signaled her wish to speak with her.

You are in distress, my queen, Idunn thought as soon as Frigga touched her.

Do you know why? Frigga responded.

I do, Idunn affirmed. *When I probed your mind last time, I could see your desire for this Vidar rooting itself deeply in your heart. It was only a matter of time, my dear rider for life, before you actually became one with your second mate.*

Vidar wants Dwinn as his dragon, Frigga told her, hiding her consternation over the truth in the dragon's words. *And he wants me to speak with him since he has balanced two mates. I don't know how to act toward my first mate now.*

I would tell you to speak truthfully to your first mate, but having learned what I have of your culture, I know what's at stake, Idunn thought sadly. *It seems to me you do not have choices as others do. I cannot see the future, but someday, you may be forced to choose.*

I am glad you cannot see the future, Idunn, Frigga thought. *I shudder to think of losing either of the men I love. And I feel two different versions of me living within my body. One for Odin. And one for Vidar. Odin would never accept this, but Vidar does.*

Your kind is monogamous by a deeply ingrained system of values, O Queen. Though you may war within yourself now, your thoughts may shift, and your second mate may not stay content to be second, Idunn warned her. *We experience that even as polyamorous dragons. So do the Muspels. That is why King Baer wants to try your ways now. He has been hurt by this very thing.*

How do you know that? Frigga thought.

He told me, Idunn informed her. *When they first came, he spoke with me and asked me to forgive him for sending me here against my will. He explained a great many things, including how he spoke with the Salir on Muspelheim at your encouragement.*

What did he say about his experience with mates? Frigga inquired, glad to hear this news but still focused on her own dilemma.

He had three mates at once, she explained. *The first two became jealous of each other and fought for dominance. As they continued to bite and scratch each other every chance they got, he sought solace with the third. But he found her with another mate, one she had before him, whom she continued to see without telling him. The deception was more than he could bear, especially since there was no reason not to speak of it. So he sent them all away.*

Why did he tell you this, Idunn? Frigga asked.

When he asked me to watch over you and protect you, I asked why he is so drawn to you, Idunn answered. *He said that he hopes there will be a Muspel for him as wholesome and faithful as you.*

I am not faithful, Frigga contested. *I have lied to my first mate as his third mate did to him.*

I did not tell him that, Idunn said. *I advised the Muspel king to make himself worthy of the mate he desires but not to seek perfection, for he will never find it. I almost missed Brinn because of my desire for perfection.*

You are wise, Idunn, Frigga praised her. *I am glad you've found happiness with Brinn.*

Go speak with Dwinn, Idunn encouraged her. *He may have wisdom I do not.*

Frigga broke her connection with Idunn and approached Dwinn, purring as she moved. Yolann nudged him with her sleek, rust-colored head as if to urge him to speak with the queen.

What do you seek, noble one? Dwinn asked Frigga when they connected.

I have come to you with something that troubles me, Frigga thought tentatively. *And to speak to you on behalf of one who wishes to ride you.*

Someone dear to you, the crimson dragon guessed. *Another scent lingers on your skin. But it is not the scent of the king.*

No, it is not, Frigga admitted, feeling a blush steal across her cheeks as she dropped her eyes.

You have a second mate, Dwinn guessed.

I have a second mate, Frigga confirmed. *Can the other dragons guess as you have?*

They can detect his scent, but I have only guessed because of your revealed thoughts coupled with the changing color of your face, Dwinn remarked silently. *Tell me of your mate who wishes to ride me.*

He is honorable and would give his life for me, for the king, and for Asgard. He wishes to choose you as his dragon because he believes you will understand our position, Frigga informed him.

I will consider him, but only when he appears before me himself, Dwinn answered. *What is your trouble?*

I do not know how to balance two mates, she admitted. *You have done it. Will you help me? And keep my status secret?*

My experiences were not always pleasant, O Queen, Dwinn told her. *And I am a male who balanced two females, which put me at an advantage in my culture. I do not believe you will have the same advantage since you are a female balancing two males in a male-dominated society.*

Frigga snorted inwardly. *Yes, females in my culture are expected to be spotless and faithful, while the men are not always held to the same standard.*

I have no doubt, Dwinn responded. *Your position is a precarious one. That being said, I do not know how helpful I can be, but you can rest assured we Salir do not reveal secrets.*

If your first mate had chosen differently, would you have continued to share her with the dragon who hates my kind? Frigga asked.

If that arrangement had been agreeable to everyone, yes, Dwinn answered honestly. *I did not want to lose her. But I think we are all happier the way it is.*

How did you manage two mates at once? Frigga prodded.

They understood their status with me, Dwinn replied. *And it was most often my choice which of them I would mate with and when. They could request time with me or refuse me at will. But when desires were in conflict, we had troubles. It is far easier now, and I am content. But as in any relationship, communication is key. I take it your first mate does not know about your second?*

He does not, Frigga admitted, lifting her chin in defiance. *And I cannot tell him, though he has had two others besides me. He would feel betrayed. Angry. He would want me to choose. He might even force me to choose him for fear of the shame and outrage of our people.*

I understand your plight. I could not choose of my own volition either, Dwinn thought. *My first mate made the decision for me. It was a painful relief, though I do miss her. But I have found healing with my second mate. I am sorry I cannot give you more helpful advice.*

Sometimes it helps just to know someone else understands, Frigga reassured him. *I have gleaned some wisdom from your words. Thank you.*

The dragon nodded, then returned to Yolann. Frigga felt better after talking to Dwinn, though she had no real answers. All she could determine was to keep the men she loved separate in her mind. And since she could not communicate with Odin about Vidar, she would have to settle for communicating with Vidar about Odin.

As she saddled Sigurna to return to the palace, one of the guards approached with a message from Gjallar.

"The king and the princes have returned," the guard informed her. "King Odin asked of your whereabouts and requests you stay here."

"Did he say why?" Frigga asked in confusion.

"He is coming to greet you," the man replied. "The other guard and I are at your disposal until the king arrives."

Frigga bit her lip slightly as he spun around on his heel and returned to his post. She removed Sigurna's saddle and began to brush her, feeling a sickening ball of energy forming in the pit of her stomach. At least now she knew when she would see Odin and would not be surprised by his arrival. Sigurna nickered and stamped her foot, then nuzzled Frigga gently as if she sensed her consternation.

"What is it, girl?" she asked the horse. "Would you like an apple?"

Frigga fancied the horse nodded, so she wandered off in search of the barrel Gjallar kept stocked for the horses and now for the dragons. After she found it, she returned to Sigurna and fed her one of the golden treats.

"Did you bring one for Svadilfari?" Odin's voice carried to her as he dismounted from his great horse.

"I'll go get him one," she offered, smiling at him too brightly, she felt, and not quite connecting with his good eye.

She was thankful she could immediately turn her face away to follow through with her offer.

"No, he can make do without an apple." Odin had hurried to her side more quickly than she expected and stopped her with a strong but gentle hand on her arm. "I came to see you, not to watch you pamper my horse."

"I was just on my way back to the palace when the guard told me to stay," she said awkwardly, looking over Odin's shoulder at the eight-legged horse behind him. "Aren't you going to stable him?"

"No," he answered with a smirk. "I brought us a picnic lunch. We're going to the waterfalls."

Frigga allowed a smile to break over her face, but a feeling of foreboding anchored in her chest. What if he planned to try something at such a romantic spot? She forced herself to look Odin straight in his good gray eye, which she had not yet done, and saw a quizzical look there.

"I thought you would be more excited," he admitted. "What are you doing out here anyway?"

"I was talking with the dragons," she replied. "I promised you I wouldn't ride mine, so I haven't."

"What were you talking to the dragons about?" Odin asked curiously.

"So many questions, my king!" Frigga shot back with a fake but playful laugh. "Just some plans for the dragon initiative. If General Vidar is going to redesign the irscet and train the

Valkyries, he needs a dragon to ride when he returns. So I wanted to plan ahead."

"That is a fair point," Odin mused. "I'll be a little jealous if he gets a dragon too."

"I'm sure any of the dragons would be proud to bear their new king," Frigga suggested.

"Perhaps," Odin chuckled as he looked over at the resting creatures. "I rather fancy that red male."

"That's the one I spoke with about bearing Vidar as a rider," Frigga responded quickly, disguising her alarm. "Why not try my dragon's new mate? Then we can soar the currents together."

Both Idunn and Brinn lifted their heads at her words and watched the king and queen with eager eyes.

"It would seem they approve of your suggestion," Odin laughed. "But come, the waterfalls await us!"

24

Frigga sat near the edge of a rocky ledge listening to the thunderous rush of clear, cold water tumbling down into the swirling depths below. Odin lay beside her staring up at the clouds as they formed shapes against the vivid blue sky.

"Why don't we ever do anything like this anymore?" he asked with a sigh of contentment.

"I don't know," she said quietly as she stared at her hands. "I've wondered the same over the years."

"I miss moments like these," Odin admitted. "And fishing with my sons. We had the absolute best three days together. Did I tell you Loki caught the biggest fish of us all?" When she shook her head, he chuckled at the memory. "Just yesterday as twilight fell. We'll eat it for dinner tonight. I wish you had gone with us."

"You know how much I hate fishing," she muttered as she tried not to think about what she had been doing with Vidar when her son caught his prize fish.

Odin looked up at the sky again. "What fun we had," he murmured. "I'd like to go again before the weather turns cold. Would you mind?"

"As long as I have something to do," she said thoughtfully. "Perhaps you could wait until the irscet is adjusted? Then I can spend my time flying."

"I'll have to put some pressure on Vidar to figure it out then," Odin chuckled.

Suddenly, a sharp ping sounded from Odin's breast pocket.

"What's that?" Frigga asked, even though she already knew the answer.

"That's strange," Odin murmured. "He never tries to contact me unless there's an ..."

Alarm sounded in her mind as Odin trailed off with a worried look on his face.

"Who never tries to contact you?" Frigga asked innocently, dread settling over her as she imagined what emergency could have caused Vidar to initiate contact with Odin.

Before the king could answer, his pocket pinged again. He scrambled to his feet and pulled out a small metal object that looked a little like Vidar's portal device.

"What is that?" Frigga demanded as Odin pressed a button on the side to spring the lid.

"Just wait a moment, Frigga," Odin said impatiently. Then he spoke into the device. "Vidar? What's wrong?"

A garbled voice sounded. "This isn't ... been ... accident."

"It's not him!" Odin exclaimed to Frigga.

She shrugged and raised her eyebrows as if she had no idea what was happening. But inside, her stomach churned and her heart pounded.

"Where is Vidar? Who is this?" Odin shouted into the device, his grip turning his fingers white.

The voice sounded again, indiscernible.

"I need to get in better range," Odin told Frigga. "I think something has happened to Vidar."

"Go!" she urged him. "I'll meet you at the Bifröst."

Odin mounted Svadilfari faster than Frigga had ever seen and spurred the eight-legged horse onward with great haste. Not wanting to leave a mess in such a pretty spot simply because she felt frantic, she heaved the remains of their picnic over the falls, then rode Sigurna hard to catch up with Odin. When she arrived at the Bifröst, Odin had Gjallar communicating with whoever at the South Sea had tried to reach Odin on Vidar's behalf.

"What's happening?" she demanded breathlessly.

"There was an accident at the construction site," Odin informed her gravely. "I just cannot understand it. Vidar does not make these kinds of mistakes."

"Is he injured? Are the healers there tending to him?" Frigga asked worriedly.

"They're trying, but it's beyond their skill," Odin responded fretfully as he began to pace and stroke his beard as he did when trying to solve a problem. "He needs to be here in Valla, at the House." He glanced up at Frigga. "He's been in and out of consciousness, so he cannot go through the Bifröst, which is probably why they didn't contact Gjallar first."

"How did they know about that device you have?" Frigga asked reluctantly.

"Vidar told them before he passed out again," Odin answered distractedly. Unreleased tears shimmered in his good gray eye as he turned to her abruptly and stated, "Frigga, we need to prepare ourselves for the possibility that he may die."

A surge of fear and pain coursed through her so intensely, she felt as if her heart had ripped right down the middle. But she reminded herself to keep her head, for Vidar's sake.

"The dragons!" she exclaimed. "I'll ride my dragon through the Bifröst and bring him back. She's three times faster than any horse, even yours, Odin. And not limited by terrain."

"No, Frigga, it's too dangerous," Odin argued.

Gjallar had overheard. "There's no better option, my king. It's three hundred miles from here to the general. Even if I sent you through the Bifröst, it would take you hours to get him back here on Svadilfari. I fear he would not survive. Frigga's dragon could get him back to Valla in two hours at the most."

"Two hours clutched in a dragon's talons?" Odin objected. "That might kill him. And Frigga is not strong enough to hold on that long with no saddle going at that speed. It might kill *her*."

"What is his condition?" Frigga pressed. "Could we send some of the more skilled healers to him through the Bifröst?"

"That would be faster," Gjallar prompted. "It's worth trying."

Odin furrowed his brow and began pacing again.

"Odin, do you plan to just let him die?" Frigga exclaimed, frustrated by his apparent reluctance to act.

"What? No, no! I just need to think," Odin mumbled.

"The general almost electrocuted himself," Gjallar whispered to the queen. "The force catapulted him into a pile of wood and stone. He has a few severe burns and several broken ribs, but the internal bleeding is the problem."

"He needs a blood transfusion!" Frigga gasped.

Gjallar put one hand up, listening to another message coming into his communication link, a tiny device he usually kept plugged into his ear. "The healers there say his life is beginning to leave him. If a blood transfusion will save him, he needs it as soon as possible."

Frigga felt herself lock into her inner strength and will, empowering her whereas Odin seemed paralyzed.

"I can save him," she announced, her tone making it clear no arguments would be tolerated. "Gjallar, send me through the Bifröst right now, horse and all! Odin, you'd better come too. My blood might not be enough."

"Yes!" Odin exclaimed as if motivated by Frigga's determination. "Gjallar, once we're through, send for Eir and transport her as well."

The keeper of the gates hastened to obey, working the ancient controls to activate the powerful ore buried deep within the transport center. Refusing to think of anything but the urgency to get to the general, Frigga shielded her eyes from the blinding Bifröst light with one hand as she kept Sigurna calm with the other. Within moments, she found herself sitting astride her horse outside Vidar's cottage. Several men lingered outside. She threw Sigurna's reins at one of them and flew inside with Odin on her heels. Two women sat at the kitchen table.

"Where is he?" Odin demanded before anyone could speak.

"Up there," one woman blurted out as she pointed to the stairs, her face white from the shock of being face to face with the king.

Before Frigga had a chance to dash in that direction, which would have revealed she knew the cottage layout,

Odin grabbed her hand and pulled her upstairs with him. When they burst into Vidar's room, they nearly knocked over the two healers tending to the general where he lay hooked up to a fluid feed, oxygen tubes, and a heart monitor. A gray pallor had sunk into his skin where it was not bruised, and the burns on his arms looked angry and blistered. Frigga immediately blocked every memory of herself and Vidar in that room and took charge of the situation.

"Prepare the general to receive blood," she barked at the two women.

"But my queen, is this wise? You are not a healer," argued one of them even as the other hastened to obey.

"Silence! Do as I say or move aside and I will do it myself!" Frigga nearly snarled.

Still the woman hesitated, no doubt because she did not know the queen's expertise in such matters. But Frigga did not care. Her blue eyes sparked with a wild fire born of desperation. The other healer glanced over with obvious distress, pausing in her own obedience as if siding with her counterpart, who seemed frozen in time.

"Out!" Odin commanded so forcefully, the first healer blinked away sudden tears and fled from the room. The king turned to his queen and urged, "Frigga, there's no time. Do what you must."

The other healer quickly hooked up a needle and a catching vial to Frigga's arm while Frigga did the same to Odin. Frigga watched as the bright red blood pulsed out of his arm into the vial. When it was full, she smoothly pulled that one off and stuck on another as the healer did the same to Frigga. When they finally had enough blood to pump through Vidar's fluid feed, Frigga instructed the remaining healer to give it to him slowly. She swayed slightly from the effects of having her own blood pulled out of her so quickly.

The healer Odin had dismissed cautiously entered the room, carrying two glasses of water.

"Forgive me for the intrusion, my king. And for my inaction earlier, my queen," she said bravely. "If we can put that behind us, I will accept whatever discipline you deem necessary. For now, it is important that you replenish your own fluids."

"No discipline is necessary," Odin responded graciously as he reached out for a glass. He drank it quickly and wiped his mouth, then stated, "It seems you have learned from the experience."

Frigga sipped her water, eyeing the woman as she tried to deduce her level of understanding. Did she realize her inaction might have cost the general's life? But dizziness swept over her before she could address the healer. She swayed and almost dropped the glass.

Odin sprang to her side and supported her with one arm. "You should sit down, Frigga."

"She needs to lie down and elevate her feet," the healer who brought the water interjected.

Frigga frowned. "I'm not leaving this room until—"

Odin drew near her and kissed her cheek. "Frigga, please. Don't make me lose both of you in one day."

"I'm fine," she said woozily. "And you're not losing him either. Look!"

Odin turned to see what Frigga had already seen. Vidar's skin was slowly losing the deathly pallor as the blood filtered into his body.

"Inform us of any changes," Odin told the two healers, who nodded to acknowledge the order. "And I want to know the moment Eir arrives. I'm taking the queen to one of the other bedrooms."

He scooped Frigga up into his strong arms, something he had not done in an age, and carried her to another bedroom. He stood there for a moment, taking in his surroundings as if lost in memory, then gently laid her down onto the small bed.

"Vidar and I used to stay up until all hours of the night in this room when my father let me stay here in the summer," he told the queen with a strange smile. "I can tell Vidar has been doing some work. It almost looks as it once did."

"It's a pleasant cottage," Frigga murmured as she closed her eyes and willed the dizziness away.

"His family all died here," Odin stated grimly. "He has very few people left."

"Who were those people downstairs and outside?" Frigga asked.

"I didn't recognize any of the men, but I know the older woman who told us where Vidar was," Odin answered. "She married Vidar's father's younger brother. I didn't see him down there."

"The younger woman must be their daughter," Frigga commented. *Patrice,* she thought to herself.

"I suppose," Odin agreed. "I have not seen her since she was a baby, but she does favor her mother, come to think of it."

Frigga bristled slightly at the odd look on Odin's face as well as the familiarity in his tone. And remembering the woman's face when she saw the king, she had a sudden suspicion. All of the stress from the day combined with her physical state made her feel reckless and wicked.

"You told me once you had no other sons to reveal. Perhaps there is a daughter instead, my husband?" Frigga queried with a cruelly nonchalant air.

Odin immediately clenched his jaw. "I'm not certain I deserve that, Frigga. Will you think every child of a woman I once knew must be mine?"

"No," she sighed as shame flooded her. "I'm sorry. I'm not myself."

Odin dropped his good eye, which had been fierce with anger but deadened to a look of defeat. "The girl is not mine. I courted her mother briefly in my younger days, but no children came from our time together."

Frigga turned her face away. "You never told me about her."

"Try to understand, Firefly," Odin said sadly. "I never thought it necessary to speak of the women I courted before you."

"Until you were confronted with them again," Frigga stated flatly, no longer caring in the slightest about her own deception.

Odin sighed deeply. "Perhaps that is something I should change."

Frigga looked at him sharply, stunned by his comment. "You're not thinking of handing me a list, are you?"

To her surprise, he laughed. "Of course not. We'll talk more about this again. Try to rest now. I'm going downstairs to get more information about what happened."

Frigga felt a flare of resentment over Odin's old flame downstairs, but there was little she could do about it. She gazed at the ceiling for a few minutes, then shut her eyes. Tired of waiting, she lifted herself from the bed and found she felt much stronger. She made her way back to Vidar's room. The healer who had argued with her looked up from where she was monitoring the general's condition.

"My queen, I truly am sorry for my conduct earlier," she said, her voice slightly quavery. "It seems you were quite right to do this. All of his vitals are improving."

"You are forgiven," Frigga responded quietly. "And I hope you will not hold my sharp tone against me. Time was of the essence."

"Of course, my queen," the healer replied, dipping her head in deference. "My colleague has gone to speak with the king. Your skin is too pale. Would you like some fruit? If you will monitor the general, I can fetch it for you. It would do you good."

"Very well," Frigga replied, recognizing how the woman was trying to make up for her error. "Please take some to the king first."

As soon as the woman hurried out, Frigga checked the equipment, pleased to see the general's color improving and his breathing deepening. Since she was alone in the room, she tentatively reached out one hand and smoothed back his hair, which had traces of alabaster powder in it.

She leaned forward and whispered in his ear, "Don't you dare die on me now."

Then she kissed his cheek and went back to watching him sleep. The healer returned with a small plate of berries and apples, which Frigga munched on gratefully as she allowed the woman to take over.

"Have you treated the burns yet?" Eir's no-nonsense voice floated from outside the room before the head healer herself walked in, followed by the other healer and the king. When she spotted Frigga, she smiled. "Queen Frigga, you and the king have most assuredly saved the general's life. Magnificently done. I could not have done better myself."

Frigga dipped her head in acknowledgment as Odin hurried to her and Eir approached the general's bedside.

"How is he?" he asked the queen. "No, first, how are you?"

"I'm fine, and he looks better," Frigga stated.

"He needs another one," Eir spoke up suddenly.

"I thought he might," Frigga agreed. "That's why I brought Odin."

"There are other people here who can give blood," Eir reminded her.

"But the risks increase with multiple donors," Frigga protested. "He's already safely received blood from Odin and me. We took a risk since there was no time to test the compatibility. We can handle it."

"I know I can," Odin said quietly. "Are you sure about yourself, Frigga?"

"Yes, I must," Frigga said confidently.

But after the draw, she ended up confined in the smaller bedroom for the second transfusion. She could not sleep from the nausea and the dizziness, but she kept her eyes closed until it finally passed.

"Frigga?" Odin's voice in the stillness startled her. "Are you sleeping?"

"No, my king," she answered quickly as she eased herself into a sitting position.

"He's awake," Odin told her. "I thought you'd like to know. Eir says he cannot be moved safely to the House for several days."

"Does he need more blood?" Frigga asked.

"You cannot handle another draw," Odin answered sternly as the woman Frigga had guessed was Vidar's cousin bustled in with food and drink. He waved for her to give it to the queen as he said, "Eir says it is even unwise for me to do it again. What we've done has to be enough. You must eat and drink. And then you can see him."

Frigga sighed. "If he needs more, his relatives might suffice. But it would be risky."

"Eir will know," Odin reassured her. "You've done well, my queen."

He stepped out, leaving Frigga with Patrice, a pretty, dark-haired woman with hazel eyes eerily similar to Vidar's. The young woman bowed, her hands shaking as she held the water pitcher while Frigga ate the fruit and nuts on the plate.

"Thank you, my queen, for saving my cousin," she said shyly. "I am Patrice Sigurddotter. If there is ever anything I can do for you, please let me know."

"My father's name was Sigurd too," Frigga expressed with delight. She reached out and squeezed the girl's hand, which made her blush. Frigga continued, "Thank you for your own care of your cousin. The general is well respected in Valla and indispensable to Asgard. But those truths aside, there is no one the king and I hold more dear apart from our sons."

Patrice nodded, then offered the queen some water. After she drank it, Frigga made her way back to Vidar's room. Odin had directed one of the men to bring up several chairs to give the healers a break from standing. He himself sat on one drawn up close to the general's bed. Frigga approached cautiously as Odin stood and offered her the chair.

"General?" Frigga asked softly as she seated herself. "How do you fare?"

"I've … been better … my queen," he wheezed.

"It's painful for him to talk," Odin whispered to her.

But Frigga noticed how Vidar refused to meet her eyes. And she knew he struggled with something deeper than physical pain, which she imagined must be excruciating by itself.

"Eir, what herbs have you administered to ease the pain?" Frigga asked the healer.

Odin pulled her aside gently before the healer could answer. "Eir says a darkness has settled over him like it did for me. He is grieving something." He looked around him furtively. "This place is cursed. I never should have sent him here."

Frigga grabbed Odin's hand and pulled him out of the room. "Odin, when you lost your eye, he blamed himself. Foolishly. Do not make the same mistake. This place is not cursed. And you are not the cause of this any more than he was for the loss of your eye."

"Why would Vidar blame himself for my eye?" Odin asked slowly.

Frigga realized she had slipped slightly. She sighed and searched for the right words, then explained, "He was trying to help us fix our marriage. You know this. And since you damaged your eye trying to make things right between us, he took responsibility for it. Wrongly. And you were trying to help him by sending him out here. And trying to blame yourself for this horrific accident is just as wrong."

Odin peered at her, then broke into a slow grin. "I don't deserve a queen like you. I hope you know I'm quite aware of that."

She stifled a laugh, though her heart ached within her to hear him say so. Then she grew serious. "Odin, let me talk to him. Perhaps I can help him as I helped you."

He hesitated but nodded. "Very well. And I can have Gjallar send Baldur out here to ease his emotional pain."

Odin hurried downstairs while Frigga stepped back into Vidar's room.

Eir looked up as she entered. "Your Majesty, I need to confer with my colleagues. Do you mind watching over our patient? His fluid feed has only hydrating fluid flowing now. There's nothing you need to do."

"How long will you be gone?" Frigga asked.

"Can you give me an hour?" Eir answered.

"Yes, I can do that. Odin is trying to get Baldur here," Frigga informed her. "I'll try to ease his discomfort until then."

Eir nodded, then beckoned for the other women to follow her, leaving Frigga and Vidar alone in the room.

Frigga approached the bed again and looked over the injured form of her second mate. "It pains me to see you like this, my love," she whispered as she brought her head close to his.

"It pains me to be like this," he mumbled, still refusing to look at her. "What would you say to me, my queen?"

"Tell me truly," Frigga urged quietly. "Was this an accident?"

Vidar immediately raised his eyes to hers at the question. "Yes, Frigga. You have not made me so unhappy that I would wound or kill myself."

She breathed a sigh of relief. "Then what troubles you?"

"It wasn't supposed to be like this," he said slowly, each word or breath seeming to cause him additional pain. "Odin wasn't supposed to come here. To this very room, where we've—"

"Have they given you anything for the pain?" she interrupted. "Perhaps I should enter your mind and alleviate what I can."

"No, let me suffer," he groaned. "I am being punished for my wrongs. I was so careful with the wires. I don't even know how—"

"Accidents happen. People make mistakes. If you are being punished, why am I not as well?" Frigga challenged him.

"Perhaps you will be," he whispered ominously.

She drew back in spite of herself. Then she shook her head. "Do you really believe that?"

"I don't know," he sighed wearily. "I wanted to believe my love for you was pure. I wanted to believe I respected your marriage … and you, my friend … and Odin, my brother. I wanted to wait." Tears began to ooze out of his eyelids, which he kept squeezed shut as pain racked his face. "Instead, I revealed what I truly wanted when I took it. In one wild, amazing blur of the happiest days of my life. I took it, and I don't want to give it back. Even now. But having him here … And you … It's too much reality. It hurts so much, Frigga. It … hurts."

As he spoke, Frigga placed her hand on his forehead and eased into his mind, refusing to read his thoughts but searching only for the place to ease his pain. When she found it, she soothed him into a deep sleep. His body relaxed and his face smoothed out, beautiful in repose. She kept her hand on his forehead, sending soothing pulses however she could. She wished someone would do the same for her, for she blamed herself entirely for his emotional anguish. She knew the physical pain had made him somewhat delirious, but his words had wounded her to her core.

Odin came in about twenty minutes later to whisper that Baldur was on his way. Then he eased out so as not to disturb Vidar's sleep, which Frigga quietly explained she had induced since he had become distressed. When she started to grow uncomfortable, she shifted her position, which woke the general. He smiled weakly when he saw her.

"I feel a little better now," he whispered. "Did you do something to me?"

"I eased your pain a little and put you to sleep," she explained. "But I did not read your mind. Baldur will come soon and lighten your heart."

"I do not want Baldur to read my emotions," he whispered fiercely. "He must not know how I feel about you."

"How do you feel about me, Vidar?" she prodded quietly. "From the way you spoke earlier—"

"I will always love you," he murmured. "I just wish I had handled things differently … made different choices."

"We can make different choices from this day forward," Frigga offered reluctantly. "You are my second mate, and I do not wish to part from you. But if I cause you so much pain—"

"No," he wheezed out, wincing from the agony of speaking too forcefully. "Let's not speak of this now. Can you lock my mind for me? Before Baldur comes?"

"I will help you do it, but I cannot do it for you," Frigga answered.

She leaned forward and worked him through the process, then smiled as he mouthed his gratitude.

"If you leave when Baldur arrives, he won't discern the reason for any emotional distress he senses," Vidar suggested.

Frigga nodded, then checked his vitals again. The healers came back into the room quietly, allowing her to slip downstairs to find Odin, who was talking with the men who had been outside when they first arrived.

Another man had joined their number, whom Odin introduced as Sigurd, Patrice's father and Vidar's uncle. The women had gone to the village to procure food, for which Odin had insisted on paying. Eir came down and whispered something to Odin, then disappeared back upstairs again.

"What did she say?" Frigga prompted him quietly.

"She says he is much improved since you watched over him," Odin told her softly.

"Good. And what news from the palace?" Frigga asked.

"Thor and Loki are fine and send their hopes for a swift recovery," Odin answered. "It appears we will be spending the night here."

Baldur arrived soon after and ran upstairs to visit with the general. Frigga found herself wishing she could watch Baldur ease Vidar's emotions, for her son's ears always turned a pleasing pink whenever he used his gift. Though the color change embarrassed Baldur, Frigga had always found it a privilege to witness.

Vidar's relatives fixed a fine supper for everyone present, which Frigga barely noticed. But her distraction was not so great as to miss how Odin and Patrice's mother avoided speaking to one another. She had expected a familiarity, not this cold indifference, and she wondered at it. After they all left with the promise to return in the morning, Eir sent the two healers home and took turns with the royals to watch over Vidar throughout the night. His condition improved the most during Frigga's watches, which Eir brought up over an early breakfast the following morning while Baldur once again kept watch.

"You may not be a healer, O Queen, but you have the bearing of one. It must be that wholesome aura you have," Eir praised her. "Now, to update you. Judging from the imaging I could do, the internal bleeding appears to have stopped."

"What caused it?" Frigga asked.

"I thought perhaps he had punctured a lung, but not so. And his heart is fine, thankfully. But the broken ribs did damage surrounding tissues and blood vessels," Eir explained. "We've administered herbs topically and vitamins intravenously, which has helped considerably. Even the burns look better than they did."

"How long until he's back to normal?" Odin asked.

"Your Majesty, don't push him. He should only do light activity for the next six weeks," Eir advised. "He can oversee the project you have him doing in about a week. But he had better not lift even one small tool before the six weeks are over. And I doubt he'll want to do any electrical work."

"If I know Vidar, he'll be out there working again as soon as he can stand on his own two feet," Odin predicted. "He's as stubborn as I am, and he hates to be idle."

"He cannot do that," Eir warned. "If he reinjures himself or does not heal correctly, there could be permanent damage. And then he'll be no good on the battlefield. And for one such as he, whose soldiers are his life, the psychological damage … well, I shudder to think of it."

"What can we do?" Frigga asked quietly.

"Ideally, he should spend the rest of the week in the House once we can safely move him, as I mentioned to Odin yesterday," Eir stated. "And then he should not be allowed back here if he will only disregard my orders."

"I cannot do that to him," Odin contested. "He has been so proud of this project. If I hand it over to someone else and sentence him to doing nothing at the palace, I fear what *that* will do to him."

"Is there someone you trust who would watch him here and make sure he does what he's supposed to do?" Eir asked.

Odin leaned on his chin and peered intently at the queen.

Frigga drew in her breath sharply. "Oh no! Odin, that would be completely inappropriate. What would people say? And what do you expect me to do? Stay here, away from my family, laying aside my own work to babysit a man too stubborn for his own good?"

"There's no one else I trust more," Odin declared. "I could ask Baldur, but that might end in fisticuffs if Vidar decides to be contrary. I know my son. He will physically restrain the general to fulfill his task. But Vidar will listen to you. And Frigga, you have experience with caretaking. You cared for your father after a riding injury, did you not?"

Frigga crossed her arms stubbornly and glared at the king. He would never mention her care for Laufey, but she had no doubt he had thought of it. She certainly did not like being reminded of that dark time or the unpleasantness of her father's broken leg. He had been unbearable more than once, especially due to the nearness of her mother's death.

"Well?" Odin prompted. "Your father spoke fondly of how helpful you were to him, though I imagine it was not easy for you."

"I did what I had to do, Odin. You know that," Frigga retorted. "But that was my father. And I had help. What am I supposed to do if the general becomes unmanageable?"

She would like nothing better than to be with the general while he recovered, but she could not reveal that. And she wondered why Odin was pushing the idea.

"I wouldn't leave you here without help," Odin reassured her. "I'll provide you with a maid, a cook, and a squad of guards. And that will take care of how people talk."

"If you're seriously considering the queen, you'll also need a male orderly for a few days to help the general bathe and use the bathroom," Eir remarked. "You do not want the queen doing such tasks. That is the only thing I would consider inappropriate, though the entire thing seems below her social standing."

"It *is* below my social standing," Frigga stated. "And what about the harvest feast? I have only missed one since I became queen, when Thor was born. And this year, the feast falls on his birthday. I cannot miss that!"

Odin stood and came around the table to grasp his wife's shoulders. He pulled her against him and kissed her cheek from behind. "Frigga, you care about the general almost as much as I do. We cannot abandon him. Thor will have other birthdays."

"Why don't you just talk to Vidar and explain the risks? He's a grown man," Frigga huffed.

She narrowed her eyes at her husband as a thought occurred to her. Did he have another woman to entertain at the palace in her absence? And if so, why did that bother her so much? Why did her mind always leap to that?

A thud sounded from the second floor.

"Eir!" Baldur hollered from Vidar's room. "You'd better get up here!"

Eir ran up the stairs with Frigga and Odin behind her. They burst into Vidar's room to see Baldur helping the general pick himself up off the floor. It looked as though he had detached all of his equipment.

"What have you done, General?" Eir demanded angrily.

"Isn't it obvious? The same thing I would have done," Odin laughed.

"I thought I could manage," the general admitted sheepishly. "Baldur stepped into the bathroom, and I only wanted something to eat. I thought I could get it myself."

"More like you took advantage of being alone," Baldur spouted indignantly as he helped Vidar back into the bed.

"You, sir, will be confined to that bed for at least another day," Eir commanded as she began to hook his equipment back up to him. "If you want something, you need only ask."

"I don't need people waiting on me hand and foot," Vidar grumbled.

"Apparently, you do," Odin commented wryly as his mouth twitched with restrained mirth. He seemed to be the only person amused by the situation. "And while I completely sympathize with your actions, you just earned yourself a royal babysitter."

"What?" Vidar growled.

"The king is considering allowing you to recover here with the queen supervising you," Eir told him grimly.

"Whose idea was that?" Vidar demanded as his eyes darted to the queen, who kept her face placid.

"Mine," Odin barked. "Don't be a stubborn fool. You obviously cannot be trusted to do as you're told. And she's the only one you'll heed."

"The queen has better things to do than watch over me," Vidar protested. "I'll behave. It's only a few more days, isn't it?"

"You'll be on light duty for six weeks, General," Eir informed him.

"Six weeks!" he cried in dismay, wincing at the pain his outburst caused him. "What am I supposed to do for six weeks?"

"What you're told," Odin responded sternly but with a fondness that revealed his love for the general. "If you listen to the queen, who is not any happier about this arrangement than you are, I might add, perhaps you'll be released from her supervision before the six weeks are finished."

"This is not wise," Vidar retorted grumpily. "Far be it from me to disagree with the king—"

"Then don't," Odin interrupted him.

"Surely there is someone else who can do this duty," Vidar persisted. "This is beneath the queen."

"The two of you have plans to discuss anyway, do you not?" Odin reminded him. "Fixing the dragon saddle, training for the Valkyries, blueprints for the dragon enclosure?"

"Yes, but—"

"You need someone who will make sure you do not push yourself, someone you will not harm no matter how annoyed you might be," Odin explained patiently. "She has experience, and we've already established she needs your input for her projects. And you need something to focus on besides feeling sorry for yourself because you cannot do what you want."

"The king knows of what he speaks," Eir interjected.

Baldur looked from the general to the queen, a puzzled look on his face. But he remained silent.

"And how does the queen feel about this?" Vidar asked without looking at her.

"I have my reservations," she said stiffly, though not unkindly. "And I do not wish to miss the feast or Thor's birthday."

"I'll stay with him until after the feast," Eir offered. "I think I agree with the king that this is the best plan."

"Very well," Vidar sighed.

"Frigga, it's your turn to keep watch," Odin said. "We'll be downstairs if you need anything. Vidar, mind the queen. Do not try to get out of that bed again."

"Yes, my king," Vidar mumbled as he stared at his fingers, which strangely enough, had not been burned.

As soon as everyone had filed out of the room, Frigga checked over Vidar's equipment, then gingerly sat down in the chair beside his bed.

"That could not have gone better," she whispered. She grabbed one of his hands and kissed it softly. "Six whole weeks together."

"The queen is becoming a fine actress," Vidar grumbled. "You even fooled me."

"Did you think I was unhappy about this?" she asked gently. When he nodded, she kissed his cheek, then remarked, "That was only an act. We won't have complete freedom. Odin will provide staff for my stay here. But we will have plenty of time together while you recover."

"Baldur suspects something, Frigga," Vidar muttered. "Even with my mind locked. I saw that look he gave us both. We need to be more careful."

"How have we not been careful?" she asked quietly. "What more can we do?"

"I don't know," he mumbled.

"Baldur can only sense surface emotions when our minds are locked," Frigga informed him. "He might be able to tell something is there, but he's only confused. He doesn't know."

"And what about Odin? Could he be testing us again?" Vidar asked, lacing his fingers with hers absentmindedly.

"He could be," Frigga acknowledged. "But we both played our parts well. And now we just need to make sure nothing scandalous can be seen or heard for the next six weeks."

Vidar sighed. "I don't like all this deception. But I have to admit, I do like the thought of you taking care of me." He grinned at her suddenly, which made her heart flutter. He had not smiled since his accident. "I guess we don't have too much to worry about or hide since I cannot love you physically, not in this condition."

"I cannot believe you're even thinking about that," she chuckled. "No wonder Baldur senses your emotions if that's where your thoughts go when I'm around."

"Why do you think I told you it's better if you're not in the room when he's around?" he flirted.

"You are impossible," she snickered. "We should stop talking like this. You need to rest, and Odin is taking the next shift."

"Wonderful," he muttered sarcastically. "I do not like how little control I have over this."

"Would you prefer Eir?" she asked.

"Yes, but I cannot tell *him* that," Vidar stated.

"We need to return to Valla today," Frigga told him, gently patting his hand. "It will be good for you to talk to Odin before we go."

"I'll do my best, my queen," he promised.

"Sleep now," she crooned as she stroked his hair. "I won't be able to say goodbye properly before we leave."

She leaned down and gently kissed his lips, melting into him as he opened his mouth slightly to kiss her back.

"The nights will be long and cold without you," Vidar whispered when she pulled away, his eyes searching her face as if for some promise.

"I know," she returned softly. "After the harvest feast, they will be warm again."

25

Ethereal music filled the stone arena where wooden tables had been decorated in mulberry and gold, then laden with just about every delicacy known to Asgard. The annual harvest feast was the only palace event open to the commoners, and the king spared no expense to give them a smorgasbord to remember every year. People had been pouring in and out for hours, decimating the tables, which were quickly refilled. Dancing and laughter filled the rest of the arena, a completely different atmosphere than when it was used for battle training or the trials the men underwent before their rites of passage.

Frigga gracefully moved in step with her youngest son, who was becoming a fine dancer. As the music slowed to a conclusion, Loki kissed her hand before taking his place by Baldur and King Odin as Thor bowed before his mother for the next song.

"Are you having a good birthday, dear one?" Frigga asked as he swayed with her in time to the music.

"The food was amazing," Thor gushed. "But Mother, the girls will not leave me alone!"

Frigga laughed, much to Thor's chagrin. "Oh, my handsome

boy, you will have to get used to that. Someday, you might not mind so much. Baldur has the same problem."

"Loki doesn't," Thor grumped.

"That may change someday," Frigga chuckled. "Girls mature faster than boys. And boys transition at different rates. Someday, all three of you will meet someone who will take your breath away and change your life forever."

"Don't make me sick, Mother," Thor remarked, but his blue eyes shone. "Is that how it was for you and Father?"

"Of course it was," Frigga answered, though her thoughts lingered more on the general, who lay recovering in his room at the South Sea.

After the king and queen had returned to Valla to prepare for the harvest feast, Odin had confided in her his concern for the general's mental state since he had seemed listless and melancholy despite Eir's prognosis for a full recovery, provided he obeyed her orders. But matters of state had quickly turned his attention away, as they often did. Frigga had been left to arrange everything for the celebration herself while still worrying about Vidar. Odin had not noticed her preoccupation, as focused as he was on his own tasks.

But after the festivities had ended and the royal couple were alone in their chambers, Odin reached for his queen, his intentions obvious.

Frigga yawned and protested, "Odin, forgive me, but I am completely worn out from the last few days. And I'm leaving early in the morning for the South Sea."

"That's exactly why I hoped we could enjoy each other tonight," Odin contested.

"I'm just not in the mood," Frigga insisted. But when Odin turned away with a look of disappointment and rejection on his face, she felt a surge of compassion toward him. She grabbed his hand. "We've barely seen each other since Vidar's accident, my king. I will open myself to you if you wish, but—"

"No, Frigga, I've told you before … I don't want you to go through the motions or force yourself to love me," Odin said quietly as he started getting ready for bed. "Our last time together was beautiful. The memory of it is enough for now."

"Are you certain?" Frigga pressed. When he shrugged a little too casually, she took a deep breath and voiced a deep-seated fear, the one that plagued her far too often. "I half wondered if your motives to send me away were because you had someone lined up to take my place while I'm gone."

"Why must you always think that way? No one could take your place," Odin sighed, drawing near to gently hug her. "There is only you. I promised you I would never betray you again."

Frigga felt absolutely awful. "Thank you for reassuring me instead of growing angry," she murmured against his chest. "Perhaps you could visit me at the South Sea?"

He pulled away to look her in the eyes and smiled. "I will try, Firefly. I know you don't want to go. You are showing me love by doing it anyway."

"How so?" Frigga asked.

"The general is dear to me," Odin answered. "Besides you and our sons, there is no one I care for more. If anything were to happen to him, I—"

Frigga placed one hand over his mouth. "He will recover, Odin. I will make sure he obeys Eir's instructions. You will not lose your best friend."

"Thank you," Odin responded as a slight shimmer gleamed in his good eye. "Somehow, you always understand." Then he cleared his throat and asked, "Is everything prepared for your departure?"

"Yes, Mimir has agreed to take over all lessons until I return. But I did decide to take only two guards," Frigga replied.

"Only two? Why?"

"There simply isn't room for more," Frigga declared. "Not even sleeping in the stable. I think a cook, a maid, and two guards are sufficient."

"If that's what you want," Odin conceded with a shrug. "I trust your judgment. It's such a remote location, I doubt you'll have trouble. You can always send for more if you need them."

"Of course, my king," she said sweetly. "Six weeks really isn't that long."

"Tell that to Vidar," Odin chuckled. Then he grew serious. "Frigga, please do what you can to help him. He needs something to focus on."

"I am bringing plenty for him to do," Frigga assured him. "When do you think you can visit?"

"I cannot promise anything, but I will try in a few weeks," Odin offered. "I should have my prosthetic eye by then. I'll be eager for your opinion of it."

"I'm sure it will be fine," Frigga said softly as she smoothed his black hair back from his face and kissed him gently.

He smiled at her wistfully but did not push for more. Frigga felt pleased to have kept her promise to Vidar to keep herself from Odin for the time being, even while feeling guilty for having succeeded. As she drifted off to sleep, she wondered if he might try again in the morning. But an urgent matter called Odin away and kept him so long, she had to leave without saying goodbye.

She and her entourage rode out to the Bifröst, then teleported to the South Sea later than planned. She left a message with Gjallar for Odin to contact her as soon as he could. But as the palace crew settled in at Vidar's cottage, Frigga's hurt grew as the hours passed with still no word from the king. Eir had left fairly quickly, though not before leaving instructions for Frigga, which she tackled with vigor.

"What's troubling you, my queen?" Vidar finally asked as she bustled about his room.

"What makes you think I am troubled?" she asked somewhat stiffly.

Among other things, Eir had wanted Vidar kept on the fluid feed for one more day, though he no longer needed oxygen. Frigga frowned involuntarily as she replaced an empty bag of hydration fluid with a full one.

He reached out to grab her hand. "My gift isn't working quite like it was, but I know you, Frigga. Please don't try to fool me."

She sighed heavily, thankful the cook and the maid had gone to the village for food. The orderly had gone downstairs, and the guards were making adjustments in the stable. Since she knew no one would return to the room any time soon, she sat down in the chair by Vidar's bed and kissed him softly on the forehead.

"I am not supposed to burden you with my troubles, my love," she whispered. "I am here to ease yours."

He reached out to brush away a few strands of her hair that had fallen across her forehead. As soon as his fingers connected, she sensed him slip into her mind, which she had not felt the necessity to lock. She gasped and immediately rectified her mistake.

He snatched back his hand as if he had been burned again. "I saw your thoughts. I read your mind," he whispered through clenched teeth. "You're upset because Odin hasn't contacted you like you asked."

She dropped her eyes. "Are you angry with me?"

"No, I care far less about what I saw than the fact that I saw it in the first place," he replied, his eyes wide with fear. "How did I do that? Is it because of the—"

"The blood transfusion," Frigga finished for him. "You've been given a gift, Vidar. I knew this could happen, but I didn't think it would because of your age. But then, you are an Asgardian born with two gifts. And you received both my blood and Odin's."

Vidar's breath quickened slightly as he attempted to process what she had just confirmed for him, the fear in his eyes changing to wonder. "Do you mean I now have a mind gift?"

"It would seem so," she affirmed.

"Do you think I inherited any of your other gifts?" he asked slowly. "Or Odin's?"

"We'll have to experiment when you're feeling better," she told him. "It's best not to tax yourself. Whatever gifts you have now, we should keep secret, although the king needs to know. And you will have to learn how to control them."

"Will you help me?" he asked shyly, almost boyishly.

"Of course I will," Frigga replied. She kissed his forehead again as she heard the maid and the cook returning to the lower level. "Sleep now, my love. I'll see you in a little while."

"I'm sick to death of sleeping," Vidar grumped, but he obediently closed his eyes. But when a ping sounded in the room, his eyes flew open. "It's Odin! The communication device is over there in the pocket of my black tunic."

Frigga hurried to retrieve it, then handed it to Vidar.

"My king?" Vidar asked.

"How do you fare, my friend?" Odin's voice came through the device clearly this time.

"I am growing stronger," he answered. "And more restless."

"That's normal," Odin chuckled. "Is the queen there with you?"

"Yes, she just told me to sleep. Again," Vidar replied with irritation.

"You'd better listen to her," Odin warned. "Show her how to use the device. I'd like to speak with her."

Vidar showed Frigga which tiny buttons to push, then surrendered the device to her.

"It's me, Odin," Frigga spoke into the device.

"How do you fare, Firefly?" Odin asked.

Vidar turned his face away at the endearment and stared out the window.

Frigga winced, then forced a light tone. "Things are just fine here, husband."

"I'm sorry it took me so long to connect with you. I've been quite busy, but I hate that I didn't get to give you a proper goodbye," Odin continued.

"Are you able to talk now?" Frigga asked.

"Only for a little while," Odin answered. "I miss you already."

Vidar continued to stare toward the window, but she saw him clench his jaw and swallow hard.

"Odin, we're keeping Vidar from sleeping," Frigga informed him. "I'm going to go outside so we can have a little privacy. Give me a few minutes."

"Regrettably, I don't have a few minutes. Why don't I contact you tonight when things have settled down?" Odin suggested.

"Very well," Frigga sighed. "Until tonight."

She put the device back, then turned to Vidar. "Try to sleep. I have things to discuss with the servants."

He nodded and closed his eyes again, then murmured, "Do not fault the king, my queen. He has much demanding his attention. And he does miss you. I could hear it in his voice."

"How can you still be fighting for his cause?" she whispered as she drew near him again. "After everything we've shared?"

"How can you still love him after everything we've shared?" he asked somewhat defiantly. "None of this makes sense, Frigga. Let's just enjoy what we have."

Without answering, she dared to press her lips against his, delighted when he responded readily. She reluctantly pulled away to hurry back downstairs to discuss plans and schedules with the staff.

And so began a long stretch of routine as Vidar gained strength and health with the passing of every day, no longer needing the orderly after the second day of the queen's care. Her presence was like powerful medicine for him. And despite the nearness of the palace staff members, Frigga and Vidar managed to snatch some private time together, though it was not much. Odin's communications with them dwindled to almost nothing as time wore on, which grieved Frigga. But with Vidar there to comfort her, she did not allow it to affect her too much. She had far more contact with Eir, who approved Vidar's return to supervising the construction site within a week of Frigga's return. He obeyed Eir's restrictions to the letter with only a few reminders from the queen, which he playfully bucked here and there just to be ornery. At night, she worked with him to engage his mind with his new powers, which encompassed the mind gift and the ability to manipulate light. She had informed Odin of this new development during one of their rare and short conversations, and he agreed they must keep it secret at all costs.

When Odin finally arrived to visit, a little later than planned and sporting his new prosthetic eye, Frigga rushed to him and hugged him as tightly as she could, surprised by how happy she was to see him. Visibly delighted by this reception, Odin lifted her up into the air, then kissed her soundly just as Vidar came out of the cottage to greet the king.

The general dropped his eyes, then strode forward to clasp arms with the king, a welcoming smile transforming his face. Only Frigga knew how it had pained him to witness that kiss.

"Vidar, I cannot tell you how glad I am to see you up and about," Odin practically gushed. "I've meant to communicate more often than I have, but I've barely had a moment to breathe these last few weeks."

"How does your new eye feel?" Vidar asked. "You look just like yourself."

"It's uncomfortable," Odin answered with a shrug as he rubbed it. "Eir says I'll get used to it."

Vidar laughed and clapped Odin on the shoulder. "You look like Asgardian gold to me. It's good to see you, my king."

Odin turned back to Frigga. "What do you think of it?"

She cocked her head as she regarded him. "I can barely tell the difference."

"But you can," Odin contested. "You don't like it, do you?"

"Oh, I wouldn't say that," Frigga hurried to reassure him. He looked so much like his old self, she feared he had gone back to acting like his old self, especially given the lack of communication. But she did not want to tell him that. "I've just grown used to the eye patch. I'll get used to this too. They really did a fine job."

Odin stared at her with uncertainty. She found the emptiness in the prosthetic eye too much to handle and averted her gaze.

"You're just in time for our evening walk, my king," she informed him, bringing her eyes back to his face. "Won't you join us?"

"Evening walk?" Odin repeated inquisitively.

"Eir wants me to exercise without overdoing it, so we walk before dinner," Vidar explained. "The private usually goes with us, but he doesn't have to if you want to go."

When Odin agreed, Frigga hurried back inside to let the guard know he would not be needed, then returned to the men. As the three of them walked together on the beach, Vidar proudly showed off his new abilities. Frigga smiled to herself and enjoyed the way the setting sun reflected on the waves gently lapping the white sand. Neither of the men paid her much attention, but she knew they needed the time together. She walked ahead of them for a while, then stopped and turned to let them catch up with her. Her heart leaped into her throat when she saw both men staring at her. The familiar glow in Vidar's hazel eyes matched the hunger in Odin's good gray eye, but the other eye still gave her a queasy feeling.

"What's the matter?" she asked as she walked back to where they had stopped.

Odin looked at Vidar, who had quickly masked his face. Then the king told Frigga, "The light hit you as you turned. It stopped me in my tracks. Did you see it, General?"

"I must have missed it, my king," Vidar lied, but he allowed Frigga to see the look in his eyes when Odin turned his attention back to the queen.

Frigga smiled at Odin, then took his arm as they headed back and whispered, "Be kind, Odin. You'll remind the general he still has not found love."

"Or I will show him what he's missing and spur him on to find it," Odin contested quietly. "He has a lot to offer."

"I am surprised you do not wish to keep him single," she replied as softly as she could. "He serves you better unattached."

Odin chuckled. "That has crossed my mind, but I like to think I am not that selfish."

She squeezed his arm and glanced behind her. Vidar walked a few paces behind them, eyes cast down at the sand as he took several deep breaths as Eir had instructed. He lifted his eyes to hers briefly, then dropped them again. Her heart ached within her as she imagined how hard it must be for him to see her with Odin. But she turned her attention back to her husband, hoping Vidar would understand, as he always did.

The king returned to the palace right after dinner, which disappointed Frigga greatly, though she did not argue. Though Vidar seemed to be both relieved and disappointed as well, the rest of the evening passed as usual with no further discussion of Odin's visit. But once the household fell into the quiet of slumber, Frigga sneaked into Vidar's bedroom that night, then gently woke him by kissing him with all of her pent-up feelings toward him and her husband.

He sighed contentedly in his sleep, but when he opened his eyes, he seemed surprised to see her. "Frigga, what are you doing in here? Someone might catch you."

"I won't stay long," she whispered, though she longed for his embrace. "I just wanted to make sure you know how I feel about you."

"I know, my queen," he murmured as he returned her kiss with his own longing. "We should not risk anything more. Go back to bed."

"You seemed sad when we were walking on the beach," Frigga remarked, reluctant to leave him.

"I'm fine now," he reassured her. "I was feeling jealous and out of place, especially when the setting sun lit up your hair and your face. I wish I could have told you then how beautiful you looked."

"Tell me now," she urged.

"You were more stunning than the sunset," he whispered as he reached up to caress her face. "And I wanted you."

"I saw that in your eyes," she admitted. "Odin did too, but he's gone now."

"And I dare not follow my thoughts," Vidar answered. He took a deep breath, which did not seem to hurt him as much as it had. "It is hard for me to see you with Odin, but I don't doubt your love for me."

"Good," she whispered. "Don't ever. No matter where life takes us, I will always love you."

She kissed him one more time, then forced herself to return to her room. She missed Odin and her sons, but tonight, she pined for Vidar. But she knew that with his restrictions, he could not engage in the activity she wanted even if the house had been empty. She lay awake, trying not to remember their moments together as she waited for her desire for him to subside. She finally fell asleep as her old dream of Odin changing to Vidar and back again plagued her through the night.

As the last few weeks of Vidar's recovery dragged by, the dream came to her with increasing frequency. She shoved it out and did not speak of it to Vidar, focusing instead on the plans they worked on together. Though she began to look forward to returning to the palace to be reunited with her sons, any warmth she had felt toward Odin cooled as he once again fell into silence besides a few rare updates about the princes.

Finally, the day came for Eir to return to evaluate the general's progress. The healer pulled Frigga aside to praise her for her sacrifice, commenting on how Vidar's mood and physical health had drastically improved. The queen merely smiled and asked when she could return to the palace.

"Oh, as soon as you'd like," Eir encouraged with a wide smile, speaking loudly enough for Vidar to hear. "General Vidar has recovered beautifully. I am releasing him to return to full activity."

"Wonderful!" Frigga exclaimed as she turned to address the general. "Isn't that wonderful, General?"

"It is indeed!" he agreed wholeheartedly for Eir's benefit.

But by the time Frigga had informed the staff to prepare for departure and sent word to Gjallar of the time to activate the Bifröst, the general had vanished. She decided to check the stable to see if his horse was still in his stall, wondering if he had gone back to work for the day.

As soon as she entered the doors, an invisible Vidar scooped her into his arms.

"I was hoping you'd find me in here," he whispered in her ear.

"You are becoming quite skilled in your new powers," she praised him as she made herself invisible as well and hugged him fiercely.

"I'm going to miss you terribly," he murmured as he felt for her mouth with his fingers, then kissed her softly. "Do you still have my device?"

"The Bifröst one?" she clarified. When he affirmed it, she answered, "Yes, do you want it back?"

"Not yet," Vidar responded in a low, intimate voice. "I'll be here for another month. Perhaps you'll have a chance to come to me again."

"Odin mentioned wanting to take the princes fishing again before the cold weather comes. I know for a fact he's been too busy to do it," Frigga told the general. "I'll make a strong case for him to go. Wait for me to come at night."

"Until we meet again, my queen," he stated as he made himself visible.

"I know … the nights will be cold and long without me," she murmured softly as she too made herself visible. "Now you'll have to come out and bid me a formal goodbye so no one wonders what I was doing in here."

"I'll come from the house," he suggested. "I really like being invisible, you know. This might become a problem."

She chuckled and kissed his cheek, memorizing the tenderness in his eyes.

She forced herself to leave, then hurried out to inform the others, "His horse is still in there, so he must still be on the property. But I do not wish to wait any longer. We'll have to leave without bidding him goodbye."

The others nodded. One of the guards sent a signal to Gjallar. Just then, Vidar flew out of the cottage and waved at them with a huge grin on his face.

"There he is, my queen," pointed out the guard. "Everything worked out after all."

She smiled brightly at the guard. "It certainly did. I am quite eager to return home."

She mounted Sigurna and sneaked one last peek at the general. It was all she could do to hold onto that lingering vision as the South Sea vanished to her eyes and the strong pull of the Bifröst returned her to the capital city of Valla.

Odin and the princes stood waiting on the dais for her return, much to her surprise and delight. The younger princes rushed to her as soon as she dismounted from her horse.

"Mother!" Thor and Loki cried in unison as she covered their faces with kisses.

"Welcome home, Mother!" Baldur thundered as he lifted her up in a bear hug as soon as Thor and Loki moved away enough for him to gain access to her.

"Why'd you stay away for so long?" Thor demanded, pushing his way back into his mother's embrace.

"Thor, Father already explained. She couldn't leave the general," Baldur gently reminded him as a pang of mother's guilt hit Frigga so fiercely, she almost stumbled.

Loki said nothing but clung to her as if afraid to ever let her go again. In that moment, Frigga realized she could never leave her children for the life she wanted with Vidar. Before her heart broke completely, she remembered how her general served her and fought for her happiness. And she calmed herself with the knowledge that he would understand and wait for her until the timing was right. She returned her attention to her boys as they eagerly described what they had been doing in her absence.

Odin had stayed at a distance as his sons greeted their mother but finally approached her.

"Hello, Odin," Frigga said awkwardly, uncertain how his reception might be given his lack of communication.

But he smiled warmly and embraced her tightly. "How I've missed you," he murmured into her hair. "Let's return to the palace. I have much to discuss with you."

26

"What do you mean, you're leaving for four months?" Frigga cried indignantly. "We've been separated for six weeks with just one short visit and hardly any communication. And you think now is a good time to visit Svartalfheim? What about taking your sons fishing before cold weather sets in?"

"Slow down, Frigga," Odin demanded curtly. "Do you think I want to do this? I have no choices here!"

"Yes, you do," she objected. "You are the king. Send someone else!"

"Don't be ridiculous," he snapped. "This is a diplomatic mission that requires my input and guidance. And I am sorry I cannot tell you more, but you know I cannot tell you everything."

"I cannot believe how callously you are treating our marriage after all that has happened," she huffed, not caring how cruel her tone was.

"And I cannot believe how selfish you are being right now!" he shot back at her.

Before she could stop it, she blurted out, "What woman draws your gaze in the realm of the dark elves?"

"I've already told you there is no one but you!" he thundered, making her tremble. "When are you going to trust me?"

With those words, he stormed out of their chambers, leaving her with a deluge of tears that hit as soon as he was gone.

"I knew it was too good to be true!" she sobbed into her pillow.

She wished she could return to the South Sea right then and there. Vidar would comfort her. He would understand why she did not want Odin to go. Her distress had made her blind to anything but her need to stop the throbbing in her heart, an agony she did not even understand.

Four months! she thought, having no more energy for another outburst.

Her tears ebbed as she hardened her heart toward her husband and realized the benefits for her relationship with Vidar. An almost wicked determination washed over her. She had options, did she not? No longer was she King Odin's castaway. This time, she would not languish alone for nights on end, warding off loneliness and depression. She had someone else to turn to, someone who loved her the way she needed to be loved.

Four whole months! she thought again.

She eased herself off of the bed where she had collapsed and washed her face, then went in search of her sons. She spent as much time with them as possible over the next three days, speaking cordially to Odin when she crossed paths with him publicly but giving him every indication she was still miffed at him. And when they were together at night, she avoided the topic of his trip and kept a civil but withdrawn air toward him.

Finally, the night before he was scheduled to leave, he broke the stillness settling over their room after they had gone to bed for the night.

"How long will you stay angry with me?" he asked, keeping his back turned to her.

"That remains to be seen," she answered coldly as she stared into the darkness and kept her own back rigid.

"What exactly do you hope to accomplish with this hostility?" he retorted just as coldly. "This trip is happening. I had hoped for more support from you. More understanding."

"Perhaps you should have evaluated your expectations," she answered flippantly. "You were making such progress, but now? You've ruined everything."

"Four months is not that long," Odin protested in a kinder voice. "This mission is important for Asgard."

"More important than me," she mumbled. "As always."

Odin flipped himself over, and she felt as if his single eye were boring into the back of her head. "Are you listening to yourself? Do you honestly expect me to put you above all of Asgard?"

"Of course not," she muttered, desperately trying to maintain control of her emotions. "You are the Allfather. And I am only your queen. Nothing more than something pretty to display on your mantle. I'm clearly not worth your time or investment."

"How can you say that?" he demanded. "Nothing I do is good enough for you! I don't ... I don't want to do this anymore, Frigga."

He rose from the bed and grabbed his silk robe and a blanket.

"Are you sleeping somewhere else tonight?" she asked quietly as she sat up and watched him prepare to leave.

"I think it's best," he said stiffly. "I'm leaving at first light with Bragi and Trebent. How interesting that their wives have been far more supportive."

"Perhaps you should have married one of them," she said bitingly.

He whirled around to face her. But instead of throwing some nasty comment at her like she expected, he sighed heavily. "Goodnight, Frigga. I hope you'll see me off in the morning."

She did not answer but pointedly turned her back on him again, then laid herself down in their bed as if she did not care where he spent the night. She heard the door close softly, but she did not turn to look. She half hoped to feel his arms enveloping her suddenly and to hear his voice begging her to talk out their differences. But the room stayed silent, and his side of the bed grew empty and cold. She held onto her anger like a comforting anchor that kept her from giving in to her pain, most of which she had caused herself. Deep down inside, she knew her actions were unloving and that he truly could not help the timing of this mission. But the old wounds within her heart from the years she had spent like this—lonely and ignored—felt as fresh as they had when they were first carved.

She did not expect or want Odin to put her above all of Asgard, but she felt so low on his list of priorities most of the time, she questioned whether she mattered to him at all. He was far too enamored with his role as king, and though she herself had told him weeks ago they could not change who they were, she had asked him to find ways to invest in their relationship. And in her mind, he had expended some effort, then fallen right back into old habits. And it hurt far more after experiencing a taste of what could be once she had started to care again.

As her anger festered, she seriously considered refusing to see Odin off, but she could not justify shaming him in that way. And it would not be prudent for her to demonstrate any sign of insubordination before their subjects. She knew what was expected of her. And so, she took her place with her sons to wave goodbye the following morning.

Odin's good gray eye remained veiled and uncertain when he looked at her before mounting Svadilfari. As he lifted himself up onto the great horse, realization that he was truly leaving smote her, and she suddenly did not want to part from him this way. She rushed to his side and took hold of his leg. He looked down at her in surprise as she looked up at him with distress and regret across her face, for in that moment, she had seen a flash of how she would grieve if something went horribly wrong.

"Return safely, my king," she said, her voice full of meaning.

"Think better of me when I return," he answered softly as he leaned forward so only she could hear.

She merely nodded as Baldur gently pulled her back so the king could follow the two lords as they galloped off to the Bifröst, where Gjallar would send them to Svartalfheim.

"Mother, I sense you are greatly troubled," Baldur observed when the three Asgardians were no longer visible.

"I am not handling this well," she admitted.

Thor and Loki looked up at her with concern.

"I understand, Mother," Baldur reassured her. "You just returned, and now he's leaving. Four months might not be long in our lives, but sometimes even one hour can stretch on for what seems like forever."

"Like math lessons," Loki remarked dryly.

Frigga snickered at his comment, which in turn coaxed a chuckle from Loki. In seconds, they were all laughing.

"Let's cancel lessons and do something fun today!" she suggested impulsively.

"Like fishing?" Thor said hopefully.

Frigga groaned, then brightened. "Let's go riding and take a picnic lunch!"

The younger princes whooped and ran off to the kitchen, promising to pack the food themselves.

"I'm proud of you, Mother," Baldur praised her. "I've been quite worried about you."

"Oh, Baldur," she chuckled. "You shouldn't. It's my job to worry about you."

"Why?" he said with surprise. "I'm fine, though I wish General Vidar would hurry up and return to Valla."

"Isn't Colonel Vale teaching you enough?" Frigga asked lightly.

"He's doing fine, but he's just not Vidar," Baldur remarked.

Frigga noticed how he watched her closely as he said this, but she kept her mind locked and refused to feel anything toward the general at that moment. She patted Baldur's broad shoulder.

"He'll be back soon enough," she said nonchalantly.

"And so will Father," Baldur added.

"I suppose the important thing is to stay busy," Frigga sighed. "Then the time will pass quickly."

"We'll have some fun today, at least," Baldur encouraged her. "And Mother, if you ever need someone to talk to, I'm here for you."

Frigga smiled at him gratefully, then turned her attention to preparations for their outing. But the exchange worried her enough that she did not let herself even daydream about Vidar when Baldur was around.

Though the day proved to be glorious and memorable, Frigga longed for the evening. When she could finally slip away by herself to the royal chambers, she locked the door and arrayed herself as beautifully as she could. Her heart pounded as she imagined how Vidar would react when she arrived. When she felt satisfied with her appearance, she activated the device and transported herself to the cottage, choosing his bedroom as her location.

It was empty.

She listened carefully for movement or his cheerful whistle, then decided to sneak downstairs, keeping herself invisible. A fire burned on the hearth, but Vidar was nowhere to be seen. The sitting area and kitchen looked strange to her now without the maid and the cook bustling around doing their chores. Even the absence of the sleek white cat, who had returned to her own home right after the accident, made everything feel out of place. She felt as though the ghosts of memories hissed at her from unseen corners.

Just then, the cottage door swung open and Vidar stepped inside, shirtless and soaking wet. She watched, still invisible, as he grabbed a towel by the door and dried himself off. The burns on his arms were light scars now, which Frigga thought only added to his attractiveness. He shook his damp head, then checked on the fire. He walked into the kitchen and started gathering ingredients for his dinner. And with him bustling about in his own space like life had simply gone on as it had before, everything seemed right to Frigga again.

"Make enough for two," she called teasingly.

"Frigga," he breathed as he lifted his head with his back still turned. Then he whirled around and searched for her eagerly. "Are you going to let me see you?"

"Is it safe?" she asked teasingly.

"Of course," he reassured her, opening his arms wide for her. "It's just me."

She revealed herself and rushed to him, not even allowing him time to look at her despite the attention she had paid to her appearance.

"Odin has gone to Svartalfheim for four months," she told him after he kissed her.

"Four months!" he exclaimed indignantly. "What is he thinking!"

"I knew you'd understand," she said gratefully. "He said it was an important diplomatic mission."

"Did you … take care of him before he left?" Vidar asked tentatively, grimacing as he spoke.

"I haven't let him near me," she huffed. "I've been very cross with him." She sighed. "We're back to where we were before you and I came together."

"He should not neglect you so. I would not neglect you so," Vidar murmured as his eyes lingered on her form. "You look absolutely beautiful, my queen."

"Thank you," she said softly as she reached up to feel his hair. "Did you go for a swim?"

"Yes, Eir said it would be good for me," Vidar answered. "I made myself do it last night. Tonight was easier."

"I'm proud of you, my love," she whispered as she searched his eyes, pleased to see that golden flare light up in them. She pressed into him as she spoke. "When you were recovering, you said you wished you had done things differently. How do you feel about us now?"

He swallowed hard and murmured, "I think you know."

She smiled coyly. "I'd like to hear it from you. I'm not entirely certain."

Instead of answering, he pulled her against him and kissed her ardently. She sighed happily and relaxed as he expressed himself without words, though she felt her temperature rising.

Just as she thought he might pull her to the floor, he murmured, "Have I been the only one you've been with since the last time?"

"Yes," she said breathlessly. "I've kept myself from Odin as I promised."

"I have to put him out of my mind," Vidar told her. "That's the only way I can reconcile my love for you and my love for him. To separate it somehow."

"I have to do the same," she admitted. "I've wondered if I should keep coming here to see you, but I cannot stay away."

"And I need you like I need to breathe," he crooned in her ear.

At those words, she felt her soul connect powerfully with his. When Odin had spoken of his need for her, it felt like power and possession, almost oppressively so. But Vidar's confession seemed vulnerable and open, laced with a loyalty tried and true. She had no answer but to speak to him through her own wordless expression. They abandoned the meal Vidar had started to prepare and indulged in each other instead, pouring their strong bond into every caress.

Afterward, as they snuggled together in his bed, he told her, "I am so hopelessly in love with you."

"Do you still feel your cause is hopeless?" she asked in surprise.

"I only say that because I could not part from you now even if loving you meant the fall of Asgard," he proclaimed boldly.

"You love me more than Asgard?" Frigga gasped.

"Yes," he murmured as he kissed her shoulder. "Shall I finish fixing us something to eat?"

"I'm not hungry," she sighed contentedly. "You go ahead."

"I won't be long," he promised as he gently pulled away from her. "Will you be here when I get back?"

"Yes, but I might fall asleep," she giggled.

"I don't mind," he whispered as he kissed her softly. "I wish you could spend every night here until we finish Berg's beach house."

"With Odin gone, I could," she murmured sleepily.

And that is exactly what she did. During the day, she poured herself into her sons, every bit the devoted mother and proper queen. But after she locked her door at night, she eagerly stepped into her chosen role as Vidar's mate, feeling as if she were two different people. In her own mind, one version of her was married to Vidar in spirit just as the other version was to Odin legally. And her double life ceased to bother her the more she embraced it.

When Vidar and his crew finally finished the beach house, Frigga felt a profound sadness to have to say goodbye to Vidar's cozy cottage, especially because winter was just beginning to bite Valla with a permeating cold. And how she hated the cold! Vidar finally returned to the palace and took up his regular duties almost seamlessly. All talk of Solveya and Flit had long died out, though Frigga heard several maids discussing how much happier the general seemed since his return.

Busy as they were with their own projects and duties, Frigga and Vidar rarely saw each other during the day except at the training sessions he held for the Valkyries, of which she partook right alongside the healers. But she went to him in his room at night, using the device he had no need for while Odin was gone. And no one in the palace, not even Baldur, suspected that the queen spent nearly every night with the general. To all eyes concerned, they had a strictly professional and platonic relationship.

Vidar spent quite a bit of time perfecting the irscet design for Asgardian use. He had presented himself successfully before Dwinn and bonded with him faster than Frigga could have hoped. In fact, all the dragons seemed to like him, especially Idunn.

"I think it's ready," the general told the queen one night as he showed her his current prototype, which he had oiled until it gleamed. "This is where I needed to make the stirrups adjustable and closer to the dragon's body. But I made them too close last time and had to adjust them again."

"Have you tested it?" she asked eagerly.

"Not this one," he answered. "It's on my agenda for tomorrow."

Frigga leaned her head against his shoulder as she admired the shining leather and tiny gold nails of the dragon saddle. It was a masterpiece, like any project Vidar set his hand to complete.

"They'll have to be custom fit per dragon and rider," Vidar informed her. "But it shouldn't be too difficult if this one works for me."

"May I watch this time?" she asked shyly.

"Don't you have meetings all day tomorrow?" he reminded her.

She sighed. "Unfortunately, yes."

"I'll tell you tomorrow night how it goes," he offered. "And if this one works, the next step is to custom fit one for you."

"I hope it works. This is your seventh try," she lamented.

"I do lead the Seventh Corps," he chuckled as he kissed her lightly on the nose. "Maybe that's my lucky number."

She yawned suddenly. "Why am I so tired?"

"Perhaps you're overdoing it," Vidar said with concern as he laid the irscet to the side and peered at her. "You look pale."

"I'm fine," she said lightly. "Just more tired than usual."

"Do you need to sleep?" he asked kindly.

"I suppose I should," she sighed.

"In your room or mine?"

"What do you prefer?" she asked as she yawned again.

"I always prefer for you to be with me," he said in a low tone as he stroked her cheek with the back of his knuckles as he often did. "But I think you need your rest. And you'll sleep better in your own bed."

"You are so sweet and considerate, my love," she said gratefully as she kissed his cheek. "I'll stay with you tomorrow night."

"Oh, I almost forgot. Has Lord Berg mentioned he's presenting the beach house to Lady Annette in three days?" Vidar asked.

"Yes, he invited me and the princes as part of his ruse," she answered. "And he was kind enough to thank me for keeping you on task when you were hurt."

"I'm shocked Lady Annette has not figured it out yet," Vidar laughed.

"All anyone here knows is that you were building something for Odin," she reminded him. "Why would she make the connection? Berg told me he outright lied to her and said the home is mine and that I asked him to bring her out there to help me pick out furnishings."

"Clever," Vidar chuckled. "This should be quite entertaining."

27

Frigga breathed deeply of the salty sea air as she stood on the balcony of the grandest bedroom in the new beach house. Lord Berg was due to arrive any moment with Annette and Sigyn, but the queen had decided to indulge in a few moments to herself while everyone else rushed around with last-minute preparations. The noblewoman's birthday had been two days prior, during which Berg had spoiled her and showered her with small gifts in front of the entire royal court. Frigga, Vidar, the princes, and two guards had spent the night at Vidar's cottage, all part of Berg's elaborate ruse. Time would tell its success, which Frigga hoped would be as satisfying to Berg and Annette as the structure itself, for the stilted summer cottage was truly impressive, a place of relaxation and beauty even without furnishings.

Voices in the main sitting area drew Frigga out of the stillness that had settled over her.

"And where is the queen, Prince Baldur?" she heard Annette query with her usual boldness, though her tone always softened with the crown prince.

"She's—"

"Right here," Frigga laughed as she joined the group, much to the relief of her oldest son.

He had agreed to attend at Berg's personal request but expressed his discomfort over the whole thing to his mother, who had understood Baldur's concern that he or his younger brothers might somehow ruin the surprise. But Berg had laid his plans too well for that. Frigga had been thoroughly impressed with how seriously Loki and Thor had taken their own minor roles in the scheme. And here they all were for the final moment, waiting for Berg's reveal.

"Queen Frigga, this place is beautiful!" Annette gushed. "I'm so jealous!"

Lord Berg desperately tried to hide his smirk as Vidar stood taller, clearly pleased by her praise. Sigyn merely looked around her in awe.

"Perhaps you would care to see the rest of the house, my lord and ladies?" Vidar suggested. "With the queen's permission, of course."

"Of course," Frigga repeated decorously, gratified that her sons did not even snicker.

The noble family followed Vidar as everyone else filed in behind them. Though the rooms were still bare, the wholesome sea air easing its way through the open windows whispered of possibilities rich with laughter and love. When they reached the room with the balcony where Frigga had been standing, Annette sucked in her breath in a delighted gasp, touching the walls in wonder.

"You've saved the best for last, I see!" she breathed. "Queen Frigga, you have to do this room in all white with just a touch of gold!"

"Oh really? Why's that?" Berg asked innocently.

"Because this room is the best. Fit for a queen," Annette answered lightly. "I've seen so much, I've already lost track. All the bedrooms have balconies like this?"

"This is the nicest one," Vidar answered. "But there are six balconies altogether. One for each of the four bedroom suites and two attached to the living areas. Only three of the balconies look out to sea."

"General, I had no idea you had such talents," Annette told him with admiration.

"Thank you, my lady," Vidar offered with a respectful bow. "But I did have considerable help with the design."

"Is there another genius behind this architectural beauty?" Annette queried innocently.

"Your husband," the general answered lightly.

"Vidar is being modest," Berg interjected quickly when Annette glanced at him with surprise. "He is the true mastermind. You should see his blueprints for the new dragon enclosure."

"Oh?" Annette asked with interest, effectively distracted. "And when does construction on that begin?"

"It already has," Vidar answered. "We broke ground right before the first snow."

"Well, you certainly know how to keep your secrets, General," Annette quipped. "I would have thought such a thing would be a topic of palace gossip."

"We haven't announced the dragon initiative yet," Frigga reminded Annette.

"Oh, it's such a bore to keep these things to myself," Annette grumped. "When do I finally get to talk about this?"

"By spring, for certain," Frigga answered. Sensing impatience from Lord Berg over the distraction, she remarked, "It seems you approve of this place?"

"Oh yes," Annette gushed, looking around her. "I want to see the whole thing again to really take it all in. And if Berg agrees, General Vidar, you really must build one for us."

It truly was the perfect moment. And Berg seized it with all the grandeur he possessed.

"For once, I'm a step ahead of you, Annette," the nobleman announced proudly as he grabbed Annette's hand and twirled her into his arms. "He already has."

She dangled there for half of a silent beat like they were frozen in a waltz. The younger princes, who had played along beautifully so far, finally snickered into their hands. Baldur leaned against the wall in his casual way and grinned to match Frigga and Vidar, who were both fighting laughter. Sigyn stared at all their faces in confusion but giggled when Loki winked at her as if letting her in on the secret. Annette regained her footing and pushed Berg away slightly, but he only joined the others in grinning foolishly.

"Has what?" she muttered. A stubborn look crept over her face as if she did not want to believe it.

"Built this for us," Berg answered, his voice full of mirth. He got down on his knees and took her hands. "Happy birthday, Annette!"

"Are you toying with me, Berg?" the noblewoman breathed in shock.

"Would I dare?" Berg snorted.

"You absolutely would," Annette said dryly.

"In front of the queen?" Berg laughed. "I wouldn't risk my neck that much for a play at you."

Annette glanced at Frigga, who dipped her head graciously and stated, "Welcome home, Lady Annette."

"You really did this for me?" Annette squealed, looking at everyone in turn, then back at her husband, who still knelt in front of her.

"You have made me the happiest Asgardian alive in the years we've been together," Berg responded. "Make me happier still by making this place our summer home."

Frigga felt tears pricking her eyelids at the romantic moment. She dared not look at the general, especially with Baldur in the room. Instead, she focused on her friend, who did start to cry as she reached down and yanked Berg back to his feet.

"You sneaky devil, you!" she sniffed as she frantically wiped her eyes. "Lying to me? Making me think King Odin built this for the queen!"

"You can punish me by dragging me down here with you every summer," he offered with mock penance as he looked down tenderly at her tear-streaked face.

"You bet I will!" she exclaimed. "I love it here already!" Then she punched him lightly in the shoulder. "But you knew I would, you beast. Everything is perfect."

"Fit for a queen?" Berg teased.

Annette laughed, then clapped her hands excitedly and bounced on the balls of her feet. "I cannot wait to decorate this place. And throw summer parties everyone will gossip about!"

She threw her arms around her husband, murmuring something in his ear that made him laugh and blush. They seemed to have forgotten they had an audience. Frigga smiled at their joy, then gently ushered the children out to give the couple some privacy.

"Why don't we go for a walk on the beach?" Frigga suggested.

The children exchanged excited glances, then ran out of the house. Before long, they were gleefully throwing sand at each other. Baldur ran after them to calm them down but was soon sucked right into their shenanigans. Frigga and Vidar kept a safe distance from the flying sand, walking an appropriate width apart.

"That went well," Vidar remarked casually.

"It did," Frigga agreed. "I'm surprised Berg had to convince her we were in earnest."

"Everyone played their parts perfectly, especially Berg," Vidar chuckled. "When did he get so gallant and romantic?"

"If the fiercest warrior can have a soft side for the woman he loves, why not the stoic lord?" Frigga said playfully, glancing over at him as they walked.

"Truer words were never spoken, my queen," Vidar answered.

The children were far out of earshot, but he said nothing further, merely watching them with a wistful smile on his face.

"I'm surprised by how warm it is for being over a month into winter," Frigga remarked, enjoying the balmy ocean breeze.

"It doesn't get as cold here as it gets in Valla," Vidar remarked nonchalantly.

"Perhaps we should build a permanent dragon dwelling here for their winter lodgings," Frigga suggested.

"Perhaps," he murmured.

The breeze stopped, and Frigga began to feel overly warm, but she pushed it aside. "You seem so distracted, Vidar."

"Is this what it's like to have your own family?" he asked her softly, not taking his eyes off the figures ahead of them.

"Yes, among other things," Frigga answered, concerned over the sadness in his voice as she ignored a wave of nausea that washed over her. "Are you troubled, my love?"

"Do not concern yourself for me, my queen," he sighed. "Sometimes, I just wish—"

Frigga suddenly felt her vision grow black as her knees buckled. Vidar stopped what he was saying abruptly and caught her as she fell.

"Frigga, what—"

"I'm fine," she murmured as he helped her back to her feet.

Baldur had seen what had happened and came running, the children following on his heels as best as they could manage given his long stride.

"Mother, what happened?" the crown prince asked worriedly as he placed a large hand on her clammy forehead.

"I skipped breakfast," she realized aloud. "And I got overheated."

"Baldur, carry your mother to the house," Vidar instructed.

The general motioned for everyone to follow him as he jogged ahead. He grabbed a golden apple out of his saddlebag, which he polished on his tunic and handed to the queen as they entered the house. Baldur lowered Frigga down to the bare floor of the cottage as Berg and Annette rushed over to ask what had happened.

"Please stop fretting over me," Frigga requested of everyone weakly, chuckling slightly to reassure them. "I'm fine. Really."

When they all exchanged glances, she got up and slowly walked outside, holding out her hand to stop both Vidar and Baldur when they tried to follow her. She found a shaded spot and took a huge bite of the apple, expecting it to calm her queasiness. Instead, her eyes widened as she realized what was about to happen. She bent over and promptly launched the meager contents of her stomach into a nearby patch of sand. The spot was hidden from view of the house, much to her relief. Embarrassment tinged her cheeks even though no one had seen.

That's happened only one other time in my life, she thought as panic welled up inside her. *But it cannot be. No, it has to be the sun.*

She finished the apple quickly, relieved when she kept it down this time. When she stepped back into the cottage, everyone looked at her with great concern on their faces.

"You're all acting like you expect me to collapse. I told you … I'm fine!" she exclaimed. "Thank you for the apple, General. Do you happen to have any nuts?"

He relaxed his shoulders as if relieved but spoke in a rush. "I believe so. Your color is returning. That's a good sign. Wait here!"

"Yes, you should have seen your face, Mother," Thor laughed when Vidar hurried back outside. "As white as these walls."

Baldur nudged him roughly to silently tell him not to say another word.

"What?" Thor mumbled indignantly as he rubbed his shoulder.

"You might have a touch of sunstroke, my queen," Berg suggested. "You should probably spend the day resting."

Vidar came inside as the nobleman made the suggestion and nodded in agreement. He handed Frigga a small satchel of nuts as he offered, "The queen is welcome to rest at my cottage."

"That is not agreeable to me," she protested as she eagerly dug into the nuts. "Why doesn't anyone believe I'm fine?"

"I'll stay with you and keep you company, Mother," Loki offered.

"So will I," Sigyn hurried to say.

The girl smiled sweetly at Loki, but the youngest prince rolled his eyes as Thor started to chortle. Baldur hid his own grin with his hand.

"Sigyn, we have things to do," Berg said sternly. Then he picked her up when she hung her head. "We have to pick out your pretty things for your room!"

She smiled and laid her head onto her father's shoulder, though she watched Loki with her lovely blue eyes as he whispered to Thor.

"You could sit outside in a chair while we fight in the sand," Thor suggested when they finished conferring. "Then you won't be bored."

"That would be quite entertaining!" Frigga laughed. "Annette, it seems as though I will not be joining you on your shopping trip after all."

"I agree with Berg. I'd rather the queen not risk it," Annette said graciously. "Perhaps you can go with me tomorrow."

"Oh, we aren't staying," Frigga hurried to explain. "I'm supposed to try my new irscet tomorrow. Vidar finally figured out the design."

"How exciting!" Annette exclaimed.

But Berg frowned. "Your Majesty, you should not go through the Bifröst until you are stronger, let alone ride your dragon."

"We'll wait until this evening," she conceded. "I'm sure I will be fully recovered by then."

"King Odin put me in charge, Your Majesty," Berg contested. "That includes ensuring the safety and well-being of you and the princes."

Frigga bristled slightly at his statement. "What are you suggesting, Lord Berg?"

"At the very least, I think you should wait until tomorrow morning to return to Valla," Berg answered cautiously.

"Very well," she said meekly, deciding not to press the issue. "I see the wisdom in your request."

And as the group rode back to Vidar's cottage, leaving Berg and his family to their errands, she saw the wisdom even more. The shifting of her horse and the strong rays of the sun made her feel queasy again. Relief flowed over her when they arrived. Vidar set up a makeshift awning and a chair for her, then set a pitcher of water and some food beside her. He spent the rest of the afternoon playing with her sons in the sand. As she watched, she felt a pang of grief, for she knew she would never have regular moments like these with the general.

The guards did not complain about having to spend another night there, but Frigga wished they were back at the palace so she could spend the night with the general. With her sons sleeping in the third bedroom, she knew she could not risk sneaking into Vidar's room. She finally fell asleep feeling terribly lonely.

The following morning, she vomited again before breakfast but told no one, assuming it was the aftermath of the sunstroke. She did not want to miss flying with Idunn. She ate plenty of bread, nuts, and fruit for good measure, finding herself unusually hungry for once, then eagerly dragged everyone out of the cottage door when it was time to return to Valla.

Baldur took the princes back to the palace with the guard detail while Frigga and Vidar stayed at the Bifröst for Frigga's trial flight with the new irscet Vidar had left strapped on the dragon to allow the leather to stretch and settle.

Greetings, Idunn, Frigga thought excitedly when she placed her hand on the dragon. *Are you ready for our flight?*

I am most eager, O Queen, Idunn answered. *Why does your mate look so worried?*

I had a little fright at the South Sea, but I am fine now, Frigga told her.

That is good, Idunn declared silently. *I would have been most disappointed if we had to postpone this.*

Frigga smiled and patted her dragon, then mounted her and settled into the irscet.

"How does it feel?" Vidar asked.

"Perfect!" she answered excitedly. "I feel completely safe."

"I'm riding my dragon in case anything happens while you're in the air," Vidar announced.

Then he hurried off as Idunn walked out into the open space and stretched out her wings. Everything felt different with the irscet firmly in place. When the dragon launched, Frigga hovered as closely as possible to her body, relieved she did not have to clench her thighs or calves nearly as hard as she had her first time flying. Once they reached a good altitude, Frigga let out a war whoop and threw her hands in the air as Idunn soared at a downward angle. She felt as if she were one with the dragon.

"This is amazing!" Frigga screeched.

"Yes, it is!" Vidar hollered from his perch on Dwinn, who had caught up with them without her noticing.

She threw her head back and let the wind whip her curls into a mess, laughing but remembering not to swallow a huge gulp of air. Vidar and his dragon flew into position above them, then inverted. He laughed with delight when she squealed with amazement at the move.

I have never seen two people more right for each other than you two, Idunn remarked as they flew toward an outcropping of rock.

And how many Asgardian couples have you seen? Frigga laughed silently.

That does not matter, Idunn said indignantly. *King Baer told you they trust the dragons to choose their mates. We can sense things you cannot.*

And what of the king? Frigga asked seriously.

He is not wrong for you, Idunn answered. *If I were you, I would not be able to choose either.*

I feel mostly anger for Odin these days. He is never there for me, Frigga admitted. *If I were forced to choose right now, I would choose Vidar.*

The king does love you, Idunn told her. *Fiercely. If you left him, he would follow.*

You are confusing me further, my dear dragon, Frigga said teasingly.

My queen, from what I have learned of your culture, you may be forced to choose sooner rather than later, Idunn said cryptically.

What does that mean? Frigga asked.

But Idunn fell silent as they landed on the rocks. Dwinn and Vidar alighted nearby. Frigga dismounted and ran to Vidar. He swooped her up over his head as she laughed, feeling on top of the world. Out of the corner of her eye, she saw Idunn nudge Dwinn with her head. She glanced over to see the male dragon staring at her with wide eyes.

"Do you think they'll mind if I kiss you?" Vidar whispered in her ear.

"They know we're mates," she whispered back.

He grinned, then lowered his head and kissed her feverishly, growing more demanding as he deepened the kiss.

"Now *that* they might mind," she giggled, stopping his hands when they wandered.

"I've never experienced loving you outside," he groaned, pulling her against him again. "And flying makes me feel five hundred years younger. What if we go off by ourselves?"

"Where?" she laughed. "There's nothing here but rocks. You're just going to have to wait until tonight."

He sighed, visibly disappointed. "One of these days, I want to love you outside."

She smiled at him, then pulled him back to where the dragons waited. Frigga noticed Dwinn looking at her strangely again as she mounted Idunn. But she forgot all about it when they arrived at the Bifröst stables.

"It works!" she exclaimed to Gjallar when he met them. Then she turned to Vidar. "Well done, General!"

"Now we just need to fit every single Valkyrie with her own irscet," Vidar remarked.

"How many are there?" Gjallar asked.

"Eighteen, including me," Frigga answered.

"You need more dragons," Gjallar chuckled.

"We do indeed! We'll discuss that when the king returns," Frigga replied. "Have you heard from him, Gjallar?"

"Not since you asked me last," he admitted. "But I have turned my gaze on him from time to time. He has thrown himself entirely into his mission, as he often does."

"Then he is well?" Vidar asked.

"It would appear so," Gjallar affirmed. "He should return in just under a month."

"The time has flown by," Frigga remarked. "The blessing of staying busy."

Gjallar bowed as Frigga and Vidar took their leave. They took a leisurely pace toward the palace. Then Vidar brought Vasili close to Sigurna and suggested they take a detour to his parents' old trysting place.

"I know exactly what you have in mind." Frigga pushed him playfully from where she sat astride her horse. "What's gotten into you today?"

"Flying with you!" Vidar said enthusiastically. "I've never seen anything as stirring as you were with your arms stretched out, that look of rapture on your face, and your hair streaming behind you in the wind."

"You truly know how to talk to a woman, Vidar," Frigga breathed, her eyes shining as she absorbed his words.

"I don't talk to anyone else like that," he retorted as his cheeks reddened.

"I certainly hope not," she teased. Then she winked at him. "Lead the way, my good general. I shall follow."

He grinned roguishly at her, then spurred Vasili on to the willow tree by the quiet stream, which looked completely different during the day. They sat together in silence and watched the water lazily meander around several large stones. But when Vidar started kissing her, she gently stopped him, apologizing with her eyes.

"Too much risk?" he asked huskily. When she nodded, he admitted, "That just makes me want it more."

"And what if someone happened to come by here?" she argued. "I remember someone telling me we should not get careless."

"Oh, confound it all, Frigga," he whispered. "I hate that you aren't fully mine."

"But I am!" she objected. "What more haven't I given you?"

He sighed and pulled away. "What I want most."

"And what's that?" she asked as she gently brought him back into her embrace and waited for his answer.

"When we were only friends, I wanted you to love me," he explained. "But I feared what that might mean. When I knew you loved me, I wanted to express my love to you. But I feared losing control. When I tasted your lips for the first time, I wanted everything they promised me."

"But you feared that too?" she guessed.

"Yes," he affirmed. "And when we decided to become mates, as you call it, I wanted more moments and more time. And I stopped fearing anything but losing you."

"You haven't answered my question," she pointed out.

"I want us to spend the rest of our lives together, Frigga," Vidar sighed. "I want us to never be parted from each other. I want us to be free. I want to be …"

"You want to be my only mate," she finished for him when he trailed off. She wrapped her arms around her knees and stared at the gurgling stream. "I should have known you would not stay content to be second."

He remained silent. When she glanced at him, she could tell by how he clenched his jaw that her words had wounded him, perhaps even angered him. When he finally met her eyes, the grief in them took her breath away.

"Do you know what I told my dragon?" she asked. When he shook his head automatically, she continued, "I told her I would choose you if I were forced to choose."

"You did?" he breathed as wonder replaced the grief in his eyes.

"And she told me the strangest thing," Frigga mused. "She seems to think I'll be forced to choose soon."

"What do you think she meant by that?" he asked in alarm.

"I have no idea, and she didn't elaborate," Frigga admitted. "But listen to yourself. You say you fear nothing but losing me. But I know better. I heard it in your voice just now. You know what's at stake."

He dropped his head. "Almost every night, I try to think of a way to get you away from Odin without hurting him, without betraying him. When you're in my arms, I feel I could conquer all the nine realms under your banner. Not that I want to. Truthfully, I just want a quiet life with you."

"I think you'd grow bored with that, Vidar," she said honestly. "You thrive on adventure and purpose. You need your soldiers as much as they need you. You need Asgard. And Asgard needs you. Before Odin left, he accused me of being selfish, of wanting him to put me above all of Asgard. He resents me for trying to keep him from his purpose." She placed one hand over his mouth as he tried to speak. "I fear you would feel the same eventually. You would hate a quiet life with me and wish you had never left your former one."

"No," he whispered as he dropped his head to her shoulder almost in a boyish gesture. "If you were fully mine, you would hold the highest honor in my heart. You would always be first, and I would never look back."

"Be honest with yourself!" Frigga urged him. "You were never meant for anything less than what you are."

"Would you think less of me if I were only a builder and not the general over all of Odin's armies?" he pressed her.

"No, that's not what I meant," she sighed. "In fact, I have imagined myself as a common woman, devoted to you in every way and unfettered by my position. But that is not who I am."

"I would love you just as much if you were a common woman," Vidar said softly. "Your position was never the draw for me."

"What was?" she prompted, thankful to steer the conversation in another direction.

He nudged her shoulder with his. "You're fishing for compliments, my queen." When she ducked her head with a shy smile, he lifted her chin with one finger. "But I don't mind telling you as often as you need to hear it. Your beauty drew me first when I thought you were a handmaiden. But your grace and your character were what made me fall in love with you."

"My character," she whispered. "I don't know if I have much of that left."

"Don't say that," Vidar pleaded, pulling her into his arms and resting his chin on her head. They sat like that for a while. Then he stirred reluctantly and suggested, "We'd better get back to the palace."

She followed his lead, mounting Sigurna and spurring her onward, dreading the mountain of tasks awaiting her at the palace as a hovering melancholy settled in her heart. With the sheer amount of work she had to do, she knew the time until Odin's return would fly by her faster than the wind had when she flew with Idunn.

28

They should be arriving any moment, Frigga thought as she stood with her sons in the banquet hall, ready to welcome Odin back to the palace with a feast fit for the king.

She felt nervous and almost frightened to see her husband again after so much had happened. During his absence, her heart had intertwined with Vidar's with almost no obstacles. Her main worry now was how the two of them would see each other in secret with Odin around, especially since she had given Vidar back his device.

The general had ridden out to the Bifröst earlier to welcome the Svartalfheim team and escort them back to the palace for the banquet in their honor, which Frigga had spent several days perfecting.

The entire room was swathed in red and yellow silk, and the food tempted Frigga so badly, she felt she might embarrass herself by snatching something before everyone arrived. She had secretly managed the lingering effects from the sunstroke for a week or two after the beach cottage presentation, but they had long since vanished. She felt incredibly healthy lately, with an appetite to match. Baldur had dared to tease her once about her increased food intake, then backed away laughing when she scolded him. She did feel sensitive about the matter, for she was painfully aware that she had gained some extra weight, which she kept hidden with her illusions and only allowed Vidar to see. He always insisted she looked as beautiful as always when she complained about it. At least her roomier dresses still fit. Perhaps it was not as much weight as she thought. She had agonized over whether or not Odin would notice, finally deciding to keep her illusions in place for him even for when they retired privately, a moment she dreaded but knew she could not escape.

Thor and Loki both took her hands as they waited, pulling her out of her distractedness. Baldur glanced at her with concern but remained silent. He had been doing that more and more frequently, which made Frigga feel even more uneasy. But neither of them had broached the subject of his concerns.

Finally, excited voices and laughter sounded outside the hall. Then the doors burst open to reveal the king, the two noblemen, and the general. Odin had one hand on Vidar's shoulder, still laughing at whatever he had said.

He's wearing the eye patch, Frigga thought with surprise, noting how strong and tanned he looked.

Thor and Loki released their mother's hands and rushed to their father, practically jumping all over him. He lifted each boy in turn, then greeted Baldur as Frigga waited where she stood with trepidation. He slowly approached her, his own uncertainty clearly visible in his good gray eye now that the empty prosthetic did not detract from it.

"Greetings, my queen," he said somewhat stiffly.

"You've gone back to the eye patch," she observed politely.

"The prosthetic eye irritated me to no end," he explained lightly. "A member of the Svartalfheim royal court said the patch looked better anyway."

"And how do you fare, my king?" she asked respectfully, though her heart sank at his cryptic words and what she feared they meant.

"Excellently," he responded happily. "Svartalfheim was like a tropical getaway despite the work and the busyness. How have you fared?"

"I've kept busy," she answered proudly, curbing her jealousy over how much he had clearly enjoyed his trip. "The dragon initiative is almost ready to launch, though I have not had time to prepare the proposal for the university. I'm afraid it may not be ready for the spring council."

"Ah, that's fine," Odin remarked, waving one hand with a dismissive air. "There's plenty of time for that. Very good."

Frigga felt a stab of heartache, realizing their delayed project was not as important to the king as she had thought. Nor did he seem interested in what she had been doing during their time apart. As he nodded and smiled at the other Asgardians around them, she felt like an afterthought once more. But she brushed her emotions aside, knowing the banquet hall was not the place to discuss Odin's detachment. Instead, she took his proffered arm to mingle with their guests. As the festivities wore on, she felt even more ignored and left out as Odin retold the stories of his adventures to anyone who would listen. Her usual appetite faded, and she merely picked at her food.

Vidar caught her gaze once and cocked his head ever so slightly, but she lowered her eyes quickly.

"Odin, do you mind if I retire early?" she asked during a lull in conversation. "I'm quite tired."

"Of course," Odin said distractedly. "I'll have Baldur see that Thor and Loki get to bed on time."

Frigga forced a smile, then left the banquet hall with her head held high. When she reached the royal chambers, she curled up in the bed and promptly fell asleep. She was dimly aware of Odin when he came to bed, but he did not disturb her. And he left again before she awoke the next morning.

"This is worse than when he was not here," Frigga told Vidar later that day when they had a private moment after Valkyrie training.

"Do you think the way you parted makes him act so distantly?" Vidar asked.

"I actually suspect he may have met someone on Svartalfheim," she murmured, keeping her eyes down as she spoke.

"No, it couldn't be," Vidar protested, though he sounded as if he did not believe himself. "I have sensed nothing like that from him."

"Did you sense something the last two times?" she prompted.

"Yes, Frigga, I did," Vidar confirmed. "But my love for you has made it harder for me to read either of you."

"Perhaps he is just distracted by getting back into his duties here," she sighed. "Lord Berg warned me it would take longer to brief the king than last time."

"Give him time," Vidar encouraged her. "And check the wolf when you get a chance."

She nodded, smiling slightly as she always did when she thought of the little messages they left for each other in the secret compartment of the wooden figurine. She felt reluctant to leave Vidar there, but she needed to wash off the sweat and grime from her exercises, which had become slightly more difficult for her. She assumed it was the extra weight, but her ligaments seemed loose, and her muscles retained soreness longer. For the most part, she could ignore the aches as mere annoyances. After she finished washing, she grabbed a dress and found she could not quite close up the bodice. With some irritation, she chose another, pleased to find it still fit well. Then she made her way to her office to check the desk drawer, where the wolf remained hidden.

She pressed the button on the nose and released a note that read, "Ride with me tonight when Odin is closeted with Berg."

She smiled, feeling a surge of happiness to replace the misery she had been feeling. She went about the rest of her day with a spring in her step.

After dinner, she left a note for Odin in their room to let him know she had gone to practice night maneuvers with Vidar, which they would be teaching once the dragon initiative officially launched. Then she told one of the guards the same, taking another two with her for propriety. They stood watch at the Bifröst stable at her instruction, visiting with Gjallar while she and Vidar soared into the air on their dragons.

Idunn led the way to the same outcropping of rocks they had visited last time. As they cruised through the Asgardian night sky, an occasional bright star peeked through the towering black shapes looming in front of them. The two dragons wheeled away from each obstacle, needing no guidance from their riders. Whenever Idunn dipped to the right, Dwinn veered to the left and vice versa, their flight paths crisscrossing in perfect synchronized movements.

Just as the dragons had no need to communicate further, so it was for the two riders as the magnificent creatures soared past the rocks and ventured into an area they had not yet explored. A strange independent togetherness had settled over them all. As they glided on invisible currents, each dragon and rider pair moved separately in response to what was around them while remaining bound to each other in their common flight path. And every so often, a flash of an eye or a smile over some new sight far below would bring forth a camaraderie of deep contentment rooted in utter trust and the simple pleasure of those beautiful moments.

In the same way, they all seemed to sense when they had traveled far enough. Vidar reached forward to run his hand down his dragon's muscled shoulder, then made himself as small as he could between the creature's wings as Dwinn spiraled over Frigga's head. She reached up her hand just as Vidar reached down with his. Their fingers brushed for a moment as time itself seemed to freeze. But then Dwinn completed the spiral, pulling Vidar away with him, and Idunn turned to follow him back to the rocks they had left behind.

Once they landed, just as Frigga dismounted, Idunn thought, *Wait, Frigga. I must speak with you.*

What is it, Idunn? she asked impatiently. *Vidar is waiting for me, and this may be the last time I can see him privately for a while.*

Yes, I know the king has returned, Idunn answered. *It is not comfortable for me to pry. But I am greatly concerned about your condition. Have you and Vidar formed a plan?*

What do you mean, Idunn? Frigga asked. *What condition?*

Do you mean you do not know? Idunn asked in surprise. *But how could you not?*

I really do not have the slightest idea what you are talking about, Frigga said with some irritation.

Have you not wondered why your body is shifting? Idunn pressed. *Or why waves of sadness have hit you for no reason?*

Are you trying to tell me you sense some illness? Frigga demanded, suddenly feeling fearful. *Speak plainly.*

Oh, Frigga, it is no illness, Idunn chuckled within her mind. *There is another consciousness within you.*

Frigga immediately pulled away from the dragon as shock weakened her knees. Vidar had been standing by his own dragon, waiting for her to finish. But at her near collapse, he rushed to her side and caught her as she swayed.

"What's wrong?" Vidar barked worriedly.

Instead of answering him, she clutched his arm with one hand to hold herself upright and placed the other hand back onto Idunn's scaly shoulder.

You must be mistaken, Frigga told her. *I have not been able to bear children since my youngest son was born.*

Ah, that explains how you could not know, Idunn thought. *I am sorry to shock you so, O Queen, but you will be bearing a child soon. And I do not think she is the king's offspring.*

She? You can tell she is a girl? Frigga thought as her knees buckled again. Vidar held her steady as she asked Idunn, *Can you tell how old she is?*

She seems to be several months in gestation. Perhaps three or four, but I cannot say for certain, Idunn told her. *I sensed her about a month ago. I assumed you knew and would say something soon. But you have seemed somewhat careless, and I knew things might grow difficult for you with the king's return.*

How do you know these things? Frigga thought, her hands trembling.

She shook her head at Vidar as the concern in his face grew.

We know because we know, Idunn said simply. *When I first sensed her, I told Dwinn what I suspected because Vidar is his rider. My certainty has grown with each ride, especially as you have grown heavier. Soon, you should not ride me at all.*

Does Vidar know? Frigga demanded indignantly, ignoring her last few comments. *Did Dwinn tell him?*

We have not discussed it again, but I can say with certainty he would not have, Idunn reassured her. *That is not for us to reveal. You must tell him yourself.*

Now? Frigga asked in a childlike panic. Then she turned her thoughts inward without bothering to block Idunn from seeing them. *I'm pregnant. I'm pregnant! I'm having a baby girl. I'm having Vidar's baby girl!*

She started to breathe heavily as lights danced in front of her eyes.

You must calm down, Idunn thought gently. *You are frightening your daughter. I feel her distress.*

My daughter, Frigga thought with wonder as a strange joy began to emerge from the panic. *Thank you for telling me, Idunn.*

"What's going on?" Vidar demanded as soon as Frigga broke the connection. "Are you ill? What did she say?"

"Come with me," Frigga said as she grasped his hand firmly and pulled him to a more comfortable spot to sit. She took a deep breath and asked, "Tell me again … what was your only regret in loving me?"

"Taking what belongs to my best friend?" Vidar answered with uncertainty.

Frigga grimaced at his words but prompted, "No, you told me once you could not speak of your only regret. Then you said—"

"Never being a father," he finished in a low tone with downcast eyes. "That seems so long ago now. But I've come to terms with that. In fact—"

"Please don't say you don't want to be," she interrupted as she gently put her hand on his mouth. "I hope you still want to be."

"Be what?" he asked in confusion.

"A father," she squeaked as her eyes stung and watered without warning. She cleared her throat to normalize her voice. "Vidar, you're going to be a father."

His mouth dropped open as realization dawned on his face. To her shock, his eyes welled up with tears that flowed down in beautiful rivulets of clear crystal. He choked back a sob as he pressed his cheek against hers without uttering a single word, simply letting their tears mingle together.

"How can this be?" he finally whispered.

"My body must have healed somehow," she answered, feeling as if she were in a dream. "I suppose the timing was just never right the few times I've been with Odin."

"And you're quite sure about this?" Vidar pressed her. "The child is mine, not his?"

"There's no possibility the baby could be Odin's," Frigga confirmed, shaking her head emphatically. "The way of women came upon me after my last time with Odin, just before our first time."

"Is that when—"

"No, I don't think so," she interrupted. "I hadn't thought much about missing a cycle or two because I tend to be somewhat irregular anyway. But giving you blood would have likely harmed the baby, and I would be visibly pregnant if I were that far along."

"How far along are you?" he asked, his eyes shining with hope and wonder.

"It had to have been some time after you fully recovered, though it's hard to know when since I was oblivious. I only know because my dragon told me just now," Frigga answered. She gathered speed as she spoke. "She thinks three to four months gestation. That episode we thought was sunstroke at Berg's summer cottage must have been the first signs. And my increased appetite and energy now … the weight gain … by my calculations, this happened after Odin left for Svartalfheim."

"When will you have the baby?" he asked eagerly.

"Late summer," Frigga predicted. "And I'll start showing in less than a month. I can hide my appearance, but if the king so much as hugs me, he'll know. I can hide it from my sons but not from him."

Vidar drew her as closely as he could to himself. "Would he believe the child is his?"

"No, he will know the timing doesn't work," Frigga sighed.

"I hate the words coming out of my mouth, but what if you share his bed tonight and tell him the baby is his in a few weeks?" Vidar suggested grimly, his face twisting with ill-concealed disgust.

"I'm too far along! He'd never believe I started showing within a month, then had a full-sized baby three months prematurely," she contested as her voice rose slightly in panic. "He's going to know. And he'll take his rage out on you!"

"I'm not afraid for me," Vidar informed her stubbornly. "I'm worried about what he'll do to you! What if you feigned some illness and secluded yourself until after the baby is born?"

"And do what with our daughter?" Frigga asked as she started to shake.

Remembering what Idunn had said about not stressing the baby, she took several deep breaths to calm herself down as Vidar rubbed her shoulder with one hand while he gripped her hand with the other.

"We're having a baby girl?" Vidar asked tentatively as she brought herself under control. When she nodded, he exhaled a shaky breath, then offered, "I'll raise her. I'll tell Odin I got someone else pregnant who died in childbirth. I'll take the shame."

"That will never work! He'll put the pieces and the timing together," Frigga argued.

"Then let's flee!" Vidar burst out. "Somewhere Odin would never look."

"He'd have Gjallar search until he finds me," Frigga responded, her voice dropping in despair. "And then he would forcibly take me from you and possibly kill you. What would happen to our daughter then?"

"We could make it look like we fell off the dragons and died tonight," Vidar suggested slowly.

"Then Odin will seek vengeance against our dragons," Frigga informed him with a fearful shudder. "We cannot let them be punished for this. And think of all the people who would mourn us. Think of my sons!"

Vidar's shoulders slumped as if someone had stolen all of his air. "I'm out of ideas."

Frigga suddenly remembered how Odin had hidden his own wrongdoing from her. "I know what to do!" she cried, grabbing Vidar's arm with intensity. "I know exactly what to do. But Vidar, you are going to have to trust me and follow my lead. Will you do that for me?"

"Only if it doesn't put you or our daughter at risk," he agreed reluctantly. "I don't like how helpless I am in all of this. But I suppose that's the price to love a queen."

"Only when you're the king's best friend and most trusted advisor," she sighed. "If you were a commoner, you'd just be executed."

"Oh no! Frigga, you cannot do what I think you're going to do," Vidar gasped suddenly. "You wouldn't find a scapegoat and sentence an innocent man to death, would you? That is not the queen I love."

"Of course not," Frigga said indignantly. "Please trust me, my love."

"Will you at least give me some indication of what to do next?" Vidar asked, kissing her shoulder before laying his head against hers.

"I will speak with Odin privately when the opportunity presents itself," Frigga told him. "Then I will meet you in

Laufey's room for the next step, which will depend on his response. Since you might need your device now that Odin is back, just keep checking the wolf."

"Why won't you just tell me?" Vidar pleaded.

She placed her hands on his face and looked deeply into his eyes, then kissed him slowly and intimately. When she released him, she said, "Let's just spend the rest of this time rejoicing over this life we've created. No matter how she came to be, she is precious."

He tenderly placed his hand on her belly. "I love her already. What will we name her? Do you think she'll look like you?"

"We have plenty of time to name her, my love," Frigga whispered. "She might look like me, but I hope she has your eyes."

"Why? I love your eyes," Vidar murmured. "So vividly blue … like a clear and beautiful morning. And I hope she has golden curls like yours, with just a touch of red flame." He thrust his hands into her hair as he kissed her again. "Am I allowed to love you as I want to right now, my queen?"

"Not here," she breathed as longing squeezed her throat slightly.

"I meant is it safe?" he asked huskily as he rested his forehead against hers.

"For the most part," she answered. "But I will go through quite a few changes."

"I remember when my mother was pregnant with my sister," Vidar reminisced as he gently moved a stray curl away from her face. "You will still be you, no matter how much you change. I love you, Frigga. More than ever."

A sudden whirl of wind around them alerted them to the dragons, who were airing their wings to indicate they were eager to return to their enclosures for the night. Frigga and Vidar laughed together, then reluctantly separated to indulge the creatures.

When Frigga returned to her room, Odin stood waiting for her at the window.

"How did night maneuvers go?" he asked, turning toward her slightly.

"Very well!" she said brightly. "Has Berg finished briefing you?"

"We'll finish in the morning," Odin answered. "Gjallar tells me you need thirteen more dragons."

"Yes, my king," she affirmed, as she began getting ready for bed, keeping her body covered with an illusion that made her look as she was when he left for his trip. "Fourteen if you still desire to have a dragon of your own."

"I think it would be best if I do not. I cannot spare the time to consistently ride him," he replied.

"I understand," Frigga stated softly.

"Would you care to go to Muspelheim tomorrow to choose more dragons?" Odin offered as he looked out the window again.

"I would, but I have too much to do here," Frigga said with a pang of disappointment. "Would you choose them for me?"

He turned from the window and walked toward her. "You would trust me to do that?"

"Yes, of course," she said with surprise. "Odin, you've been acting very strangely since you returned. Has something happened to you?"

"Are you going to accuse me of pursuing someone on Svartalfheim?" he asked stiffly.

"I had not planned to," Frigga admitted as she sat down on her side of the bed. "Should I?"

"I would prefer that you not," he said in a clipped tone.

"Then why are you acting like this?"

"Acting like what?"

"Distant, irritated, unfriendly," she said with exasperation, emphasizing her words with her hands.

"You're imagining things," he huffed.

"You haven't touched me or showed much interest in me since you came home yesterday," Frigga pointed out.

"Still making it all about you, I see," he retorted.

"Right there! That's exactly what I mean!" she exclaimed as she stood and jabbed her finger at him. "Five months ago, you would not have said that. A year ago, you would have. You've slipped right back into your old habits, Odin."

"Have I now?" he replied with an overly innocent air. "I see you think no better of me than you did when I left."

"Perhaps it's the way you elect to treat me," Frigga retorted, folding her arms stubbornly as her heart hardened even more toward her husband.

"Perhaps you would like to find someone who treats you better," he suggested sarcastically as he walked back to the window.

"Perhaps I will!" she snapped without thinking.

"What?" he thundered, whirling around to face her with a look of such fury, she shrank back in fear.

But her anger gave her courage. "Do you think the lowly queen is so worthless that she can do no better?" she snarled. "Or perhaps you think there is no better than the great king? Perhaps I should count myself privileged to scarf up your leftovers from the ground like a dog!"

Odin stalked back over to the window and peered out as if to end the conversation, but the tension in his shoulders told her his anger burned within him. Suddenly, she realized he would have raged back at her a year ago or stormed out of the room. He had changed for the better, but she had gone right back to her biting tone and disrespect. And now she was pregnant with another man's child. Perhaps Odin was right that she had put herself and her own needs above everyone else's. Did he really deserve her scorn? How could she possibly fix the mess she had made? How could she tell him now what she had planned to tell him? In his current state of mind, he might respond quite badly. And truth be told, she needed him to procure the rest of the dragons. She decided to wait to tell him her news and rectify the situation at hand instead.

Cautiously approaching where he stood bristling with an almost electric anger, she changed her tone to one of gentle repentance. "You're right, Odin."

He looked over at her, the fierceness in his face beginning to fade. "Did I just hear you correctly?"

"I'm not above admitting when I'm wrong," she affirmed as she tentatively placed one hand on his arm. When he did not shake her off, she continued, "I have been rather selfish lately. I've been dealing with a lot and not considering you might be too."

"I'm listening," he prompted when she hesitated.

"You said once you are not my enemy," Frigga reminded

him. "But I've been viewing you as one. I've fallen back into bad habits more than you have."

He sighed deeply as his remaining anger dissipated. "And I haven't been treating you like a friend, have I?" When she did not answer, he added, "I was afraid you would reject me again when I returned. I interpreted everything you did or did not do according to that fear."

"Then how I responded would not have mattered?" she asked quietly.

"No, and I know that was not fair to you," he admitted. He peered at her closely. "Frigga, please drop the illusions."

"What do you mean?" she replied, feigning innocence.

When he merely raised an eyebrow, she did as he asked and readied herself for judgment or disappointment.

"Why do you feel the need to hide yourself from me?" he queried with hurt in his voice. "Did you think I would not accept you just because you've gained a little weight?"

"How did you know?" she asked, avoiding his eyes.

"I watched you this morning while you slept. Your illusions had faded," Odin confessed. "And Baldur warned me you've been sensitive about how much you've been eating."

She turned away from him, but he reached out to grasp her shoulders and pulled her into his arms. She stiffened, then started to cry as he held her tightly.

"Frigga, you are still just as beautiful to me," he told her. Then he lifted her chin to make her look at him. "How have I made you feel so unaccepted? I don't understand what I'm doing wrong."

"Odin, I cannot talk about this tonight. I'm tired, sore, and emotionally spent," Frigga sighed wearily. When he frowned slightly, she hurried to say, "Why don't we start over? You go to Muspelheim to choose my dragons, and I'll welcome you properly when you return."

"I can agree to that," Odin replied as he hugged her tenderly. "You'll have to tell me what to do and what to look for."

"In the morning, my king. In the morning," she pleaded.

He nodded, much to her relief. But after they slipped into bed and nestled closely together, sleep eluded her as she tried to silently communicate with her unborn daughter, wondering how to protect her and her second mate as the complications of her hidden family ate at her mind and heart.

29

"Eir, as head of the healers, you get first pick," Frigga announced, enjoying the excited buzz of conversation around her from the other Valkyries. "Then we'll let everyone else go at once."

The almost-electric anticipation of what was about to happen silenced everyone waiting in the center of the large training area of the finished dragon enclosure, a sleek and magnificent stone structure large enough to comfortably house fifty dragons. The beautiful but somewhat austere building was conveniently located within a short distance from the arena, tucked away from regular traffic. Black obsidian and soft gray dirt imported from Muspelheim brought an off-world feel that the dragons had seemed to genuinely appreciate when they had settled into their new home.

The process had not been easy. Vidar had used Frigga's descriptions of Muspelheim and some of his own ideas from Asgardian and Midgardian architecture to design the enclosure. Construction had stalled several times due to unusual weather, which led to employing every builder in Valla and the surrounding areas to complete the project. As it was, they were hard-pressed to finish the massive stone structure before Odin and the noblemen who went with him to Muspelheim had finished bringing dragons back. Those who did not fit in the overflowing stables spent more than one night loose in the training area, but the prospect of the paddocks being built kept them in nearly perfect behavior, though a few mild scuffles had broken out. The last few days had been nonstop construction, but the satisfying result brought the rest of the dragons to the finished enclosure. After a peaceful night's rest, seventeen enchanting creatures now sat at attention in the soft gray dirt, their tails curled around them as they eagerly waited to meet their new riders. Dwinn and Idunn sat slightly apart from the others, their own energy eager as they likely anticipated the joy of their fellow dragons when they too were paired.

Frigga's Fleet, Frigga thought to herself with pride and amusement, mulling over the name the people had given the group of dragons.

The air sizzled with excitement as the Valkyries murmured encouragement to Eir, who slowly approached a lovely coral female, an unusual color Frigga had not seen on a dragon until Odin brought her back. Baer had found her wandering far away from her two mates, longing for something she could not pinpoint. One of her mates, a bright orange male with enormous horns, had elected to come to Asgard with her.

Eir followed Frigga's previously given instructions to communicate with the beautiful dragon and was soon lost in telepathy, her face shining with delight over the experience. King Odin stood watching with an amused but wistful smile on his face as the rest of the healers rushed toward the dragons to look for their best matches. Vidar dashed around, taking measurements and scribbling notes to make the irscets for each riding pair.

Gjallar, his oldest son, Heimdall, and his youngest son, Hod, stood a safe distance away, enthralled by the whole process. It was somewhat strange seeing Hod there without Baldur. And Frigga suddenly wished the kind-hearted crown prince had not offered to stay at the palace to placate the younger princes, who had thrown quite the conspiratorial joint fit over being left behind. But they had seemed to move past their disappointment quickly when Baldur asked Loki to bring out the tiny gray jörmungandr creature Odin had brought home four days ago. The black-haired boy had completely fallen in love with it to the point of assuming all its care. This had delighted the king so much that he had brought home a little black snake for Thor and a wicked-looking fish for Baldur, which the greedy little jörmungandr had promptly eaten before anyone could stop it. Frigga had been oddly relieved, for she had found the fish grotesque. Though Thor and Odin had laughed uproariously, Loki had been quite distressed over what his pet had done. Baldur had immediately reassured his brother that he was not upset, as was his way of taking most things in stride and always thinking of everyone else.

He would have dearly loved this, Frigga thought as she returned her attention to the dragon pairings happening around her.

"Excuse me, Your Majesty," spoke a shy, quiet voice at her elbow.

Frigga turned to see Annette's much younger sister. "Yes, Brynhilde?"

The younger woman blinked a pair of vivid sea green eyes as she nervously played with her jet black hair. A wave of rosy pink crossed her flawless amber skin. After Annette's mother had died, her father had taken another wife—a lovely, graceful noblewoman who had passed her beauty and bearing to Brynhilde. Though the two daughters had inherited their father's eyes, only Annette had his strong personality. She took her role as oldest sister quite seriously and often grew frustrated by Brynhilde's "lack of spine," as Annette called it.

"What is it, Brynnie?" Frigga prompted fondly, using the nickname the other Valkyries had given her.

The familiarity jogged the healer out of her shyness. "I haven't been able to find the right dragon."

"Have you spoken to any of them?" Frigga asked.

"No, Your Majesty," she admitted. "I haven't mustered the courage."

Frigga had already been harboring doubts about the quiet healer, the most reserved of the Valkyries. She had given serious consideration to assigning the girl to duties on the home front if the Valkyries ever deployed. If the sweet young lady could not bring herself to speak with a dragon, how could she endure the battlefield? Suddenly, Frigga spotted the vermillion dragon curled up in a corner, away from the activity.

"Come with me," Frigga commanded as she took Brynhilde by the hand and almost yanked her over to the spot. "This dragon lost her first mate during a battle. She's accepted another mate, but she often slips into melancholy like this. Perhaps you can help her."

"Oh, the poor thing," Brynhilde murmured as she gazed with compassion at the dragon.

Frigga smiled to herself as the healer slowly approached the dragon, attempting to make the purring sound in her throat, which no one could do as well as Frigga. The creature lifted her head, then cocked it as if sensing something about the young woman. Within seconds, they were engaged in silent conversation.

The queen suddenly felt someone's eyes on her. She half expected to see Vidar watching her; instead, she saw Odin fixing her with his gaze as he absentmindedly twirled Gungnir in armband form around his fingers. He rarely wore it but always kept it on his person or at least within reach. And he had not burned her with it again. She smiled at her husband, who grinned back roguishly. Though she had promised to welcome him properly when he returned from Muspelheim, the opportunity had eluded them. Frigga had been gracious and cordial at least, and they had not argued again. But as they both returned their attention to the task at hand, a heavy sense of foreboding settled within her.

While Odin had been off assembling dragons, she and Vidar had come together twice. The general had pressed her to reveal her plan once more, then let the matter drop. Whenever she thought of the moment she must tell Odin the partial truth she had concocted, her heart would tighten with dread and fear. She had practiced what she would say and imagined how Odin would respond so many times, she had no idea how the confession would actually go. And if she had read Odin's look correctly, she would not be able to delay telling him much longer.

It has to be tonight, she concluded.

After the hubbub died down, Odin and Vidar approached the queen at the same time and wordlessly stood on either side of her. The irony did not escape her, but she pushed aside her discomfort and prepared to address her newly paired Valkyries and dragons.

She graciously smiled at each woman as her eyes took in a view she never could have imagined a year ago. Each healer stood at attention by her dragon's side, dressed in battle gear and quivering with excitement over the bonding that had already begun. The women smiled back at their queen, and the dragons regarded her with respect in their wise eyes. In that moment, her turmoil over the two men she loved faded as a pride unlike any other she had experienced welled up within her.

I have done this, she thought. *With the help of those I love. Could I have asked for more?*

Hoping the feeling would last, she stood taller and projected her voice to announce, "General Vidar and I will set up a schedule for completing your irscets, then begin training in groups of two or three. If we stay focused and committed, we can accomplish much in the next three weeks, at which time we will officially launch the dragon initiative with a flight performance for all of Asgard to witness."

The Valkyries whooped and hollered, leather clad fists in the air, as the dragons roared and arched their necks, letting loose volleys of columned fire in celebration. The flames reflected on the smooth metal of the women's breastplates even as the heat made the air shimmer and crackle in perfect harmony with the tumult. Frigga felt a deep thrill within her even as she heard both men inhale at the same time, seemingly affected by the display in the same way. And she was struck again by the similarities between the king and the general.

After the ruckus had died down, she took her husband's arm and walked with him to the royal cariole as Eir and the general followed. No banquet had been scheduled to follow, which meant Frigga could enjoy the ride back to the palace without having to think about what she needed to do once they arrived. And since all the other Valkyries had ridden their own horses or arrived in their own carioles, they could spend more time with their dragons before the guards shut down the enclosure for the evening.

Just as she closed her eyes to relax by imagining some of those bonding moments, Odin reached across Frigga to nudge Vidar, who sat beside Eir.

"Do you think we could study dragons in flight to come up with some ideas for flying carioles?" he asked with excitement.

"I don't see why not!" Vidar exclaimed.

As the two men talked about this new idea with unmatched enthusiasm, Frigga tuned them out to return to her imagining. But her thoughts soon shifted to rehearsing her confession to Odin. Eir also seemed preoccupied with her own thoughts until she suddenly addressed the queen.

"Your Majesty, I think we should have the riders spend more time with the dragons before we attempt flight," the healer suggested. "Tonight might not be enough."

"Are you suggesting we postpone?" Frigga asked warily.

"Oh no, of course not. I thought we could replace some of the on-the-ground training this week with time with the dragons," she clarified.

"That's an excellent idea," Frigga praised her.

"I agree," Odin interjected, for the men had reached a lull in their own conversation.

"Perhaps we should have gotten you a dragon after all, my king," Frigga mused, remembering his wistfulness.

"I may ride one someday, but I'm content with Svadilfari for now," Odin said lightly.

"He isn't as young as he once was, Odin," Vidar remarked.

"Perhaps not, but from what the stable guards tell me, we'll have a number of foals this spring," the king responded. "I am hopeful Sigurna will bear his replacement."

"She has already borne him eight sons and two daughters," Frigga reminded him. "Perhaps she cannot give you an eight-legged colt."

"I have my suspicions that more than one of those foals were Vasili's, though I can't prove it," Odin laughed. "There is nothing wrong with that mare … aside from her affinity for Vidar's horse."

Frigga refused to allow her face to show any reaction to that remark. In some odd way, she felt it to be a criticism of herself and wondered if Odin suspected where her heart lay once again.

"Come now, we all know some mares prefer the company of more than one stallion, King Odin," Eir chimed in, her tone teasing and affectionate. "Doesn't Svadlifari chase after other mares?"

"Indeed he does," Odin chuckled. "Perhaps the rogue deserves her fickleness."

"Should we separate her from Vasili?" Frigga suggested nonchalantly, resisting the urge to glance at Vidar.

"It's probably too late for that," Eir laughed. "At least for this season."

"If my horse has been a problem, I can certainly stable him elsewhere from now on," Vidar offered quietly.

"No, I wouldn't want to upset the mare," Odin mused. "It's best to let things take their natural course. I want her healthy and happy. An eight-legged colt will come eventually. That line has never failed before."

The conversation returned to dragons and flight, much to Frigga's relief. The odd parallels to her hidden relationship with Vidar seemed to have escaped Odin's notice, but the discussion had not only drained her but also dramatically increased her trepidation over the confession she could not escape.

After they reached the palace, Vidar left to attend to his soldiers, and Eir returned to the House of the Healers, leaving the king and queen to join their sons for dinner in the family dining room. The younger princes grilled their parents about the experience they were still sore about missing. Even Baldur seemed slightly resentful that he had not seen it as he listened to the stories his parents shared, despite his earlier insistence that hearing about it would be enough. Regardless, it was a fine evening, one Frigga greatly enjoyed, though the dread in her heart began to make her sweat as the night with Odin approached.

As soon as they were alone in their room, the king gathered her into his arms to claim the delayed welcome she had promised him. She allowed him to kiss her, but she stiffened immediately when his caress became intimate.

"What's wrong, Firefly?" Odin murmured.

"There's something I must tell you, Odin, before we take this any further," Frigga said with downcast eyes. "Something that will give you quite a shock."

He dropped his hands and took a step back as his good gray eye filled with apprehension.

"Odin, I …" she trailed off, uncertain how to start now that she was in the moment. "I don't want to tell you this, but you'll know soon enough. I cannot hide this from you much longer."

He took another step back and looked her over. "Are you … pregnant?" he asked incredulously. When she nodded fearfully, he blurted out, "But how is that possible? Why wouldn't you want to tell me … oh no …"

His last words came out like a strangled whisper as he turned his back on her, rigid and tense. One hand went to his brow and pushed back his hair while the other felt for the bedpost. He steadied himself, taking in several lungfuls of air as his knuckles turned white from gripping the slender, sculpted wood.

"Who is the father?" he growled. Then under his breath, he muttered, "There is nowhere he can hide from me."

"Please allow me to explain," she pleaded. "It's not what you think."

"Then explain!" he thundered as he whirled around.

The anger on his face and the intensity in his eye was so fierce, she instinctively took a step backward.

But she mustered her courage and began, "I was angry with you and hurt when you left for Svartalfheim. I felt unloved and unwanted like a castaway. So I disguised myself and sneaked into the city—"

He tightened his mouth into a grim line as if he could not bear to hear another word. "Who is the father?" he hissed through clenched teeth.

"I'm trying to tell you I don't know!" she burst out.

"How could you not know?" he spat back.

"If you'd stop interrupting, I'll tell you!" she cried.

"Fine. Tell me," he muttered.

"I met a vendor in the marketplace. He was attentive and charming like you used to be," she explained, ignoring his indignant snort. "I wanted to see him again, so I sneaked away the next morning to visit his little booth. After I overheard him admiring another woman to his friend, I took on an appearance like hers to see how he would react. We started talking, then he invited me to a late supper at one of the taverns."

"Oh, Frigga, how could you?" Odin groaned, grasping his hair with both hands in anguish.

"I know I should not have gone, but it felt so good to have someone express interest in me. He connected with the real me without seeing my true form." She said this with passion, for she had pulled some truth into her lie, which made it more believable. "He seduced me that very night, and I gave in willingly just to see what it would be like to be loved like that."

"And you knew nothing about him?" Odin asked flatly.

"Only that he was not from Valla and was leaving in the morning," she answered in a low voice. "Neither of us expected anything beyond those moments, so we didn't even exchange names. I had planned to never speak of it until I found out my condition."

"I don't believe you!" Odin burst out. "I think you've made up this story to protect Vidar."

Frigga stuffed down her panic and indignantly spouted, "Why do you keep suggesting that? Do you honestly think he is the only possible man who could spark my interest?

Just because my horse fancies his as well as yours, is that the only scenario you can imagine?"

Odin snorted as if the suggestion were utterly ridiculous, but Frigga could tell by how he shifted his eye away that the thought had occurred to him, which is exactly why she had brought it to the forefront. All that mattered to her in that moment was protecting Vidar, and she knew she must proceed with cunning and caution to allay her husband's suspicions. Her only comfort in her deception was that she had not actually told an outright lie in response to the accusation but had merely guided Odin away from the truth.

Is there any difference? her conscience whispered.

She silenced her inward voices and continued, "Vidar was at the South Sea when this happened. How could he possibly be the father?"

Odin's anger and pain slipped into uncertainty. He spoke more to himself than her, pacing as he did so. "That's true. He was there until the middle of winter. And you would be obviously pregnant if it had happened during his recovery. As it is, I can still barely tell. And he was in no shape to father a child anyway." He stopped abruptly and stroked his beard as he faced her again. "But he did return while I was gone. And you spent two nights in his cottage during Berg's reveal. When did you conceive?"

"Two weeks after you left," she replied defensively. "Almost a month before Vidar returned here."

"How do you know?" he demanded.

"I remember the tryst, for one," she retorted. "I also know enough about women and my own body to calculate.

Remember that episode of sunstroke I told you about? Those must have been the first signs. Ask Berg again what happened if you must. And if Vidar had fathered the child when he returned, which is insulting to both him and me to even suggest, I would not be so far along. And the two nights in the cottage? The boys were there, Odin!"

"I know that," he snapped back.

"In either case, I could have shared your bed tonight and convinced you the child was yours," Frigga pointed out. "If you ask the staff again, you'll find our conduct has befitted a queen and her general."

Odin sighed deeply. "I have to admit, despite this news, it is a relief to know I can at least trust *him*."

"Odin, please forgive me for this betrayal," she begged, though her heart smote her yet again. "I believed the healer who said I could not bear another child, which is why I thought I could risk what I've done."

"A one night tryst with some man you didn't even know," Odin accused, disgust dripping from his voice. "My own queen acting like a common harlot, which I've outlawed on Asgard. And you insinuate I drove you to it!"

She dropped her eyes and transformed her face into an expression of abject humiliation. "I await your judgment. If you plan to cast me away, please just do it now."

Odin inhaled sharply at her words and gripped his forehead in consternation as he tried to mask the agony on his face. "I should!" he exclaimed. Then his shoulders slumped. In a tone laced with sadness, he continued, "But I cannot … I cannot simply walk away from everything we've built together. Or subject you to public shaming." He suddenly strode up to her and grasped her shoulders. "You stayed beside me when I confessed my own indiscretions to you. And you haven't thrown them into my face like you could have to manipulate me into forced forgiveness."

"What are you saying?" she squeaked out.

"Perhaps … perhaps we can get through this too," he responded, his voice heavy with uncertainty. "I just need some time to work through it. And to decide what to do about your baby."

"Don't I have a say in that?" she pleaded. "I had hoped you would consider adopting this child as your own. We could tell everyone it happened right before you left."

"I … don't …" he trailed off, then took a deep breath. "Frigga, I don't think I can."

"What?" she cried in dismay. "After I've taken your sons as my own?"

"It's not the same," he hastened to say, holding his hand up to stop her from responding. "This child cannot be an heir to my throne."

"She's a girl," Frigga informed him.

"That changes nothing. Two of my sons came from different women, yes, but they still have the Asgardian royal bloodline within them."

"But—"

"No, Frigga, I will not do it," Odin declared with finality. "I will forgive you, but I cannot take in your child. And since the people cannot know what you've done, there is only one option."

"Odin, you cannot mean you would do to her what Zeus threatened to do to Baldur," she gasped.

"No, of course not," he vehemently protested. "You will have to hide your pregnancy, then give the baby to someone else to raise."

"Who?" she demanded.

"We have some time to figure that out," Odin mused. "She may have to go off-world."

"I suppose I have no choice, once again," Frigga said woundedly, her head drooping with sorrow.

"I'm sorry, Frigga," Odin said softly. "In this situation, neither of us has a choice."

She turned and woodenly walked away from him, although her mind was already spinning with her secondary plan, for she had anticipated Odin might respond this way. She had left a note in the wolf before dinner and could only hope Vidar had checked after he finished his maneuvers. Provided he had, she needed to find a way to slip away to meet him. She stuffed away the fear that he might abandon her, knowing it was rooted in what he had said earlier about stabling Vasili elsewhere and not reality. Though she consistently doubted Odin's love and mostly felt like his possession, she knew Vidar cherished her.

She dressed for bed in the suite bathroom, feeling a shame-driven vulnerability that made her not want to undress in front of her husband now that he knew she bore another man's offspring. When she returned to the main room, he had already slipped under the blankets and lay there staring up at the ceiling.

"Would you prefer I sleep elsewhere?" she asked quietly.

"I was just thinking I should," Odin admitted as he threw the blankets off and stood. "I'll use the room I used the night before I left for Svartalfheim. At least you'll be comfortable."

"That is most considerate, my king," she said humbly.

"I might not see you in the morning," he warned her as he prepared to leave. "I have a great many things to do. Perhaps I'll be in a better frame of mind tomorrow night."

When she nodded, he left. She waited for an hour to ensure he did not return, then carefully made her way to Laufey's old room as she used to before she had joined herself with Vidar.

The general had not yet arrived. She waited for what seemed an interminable time, growing fearful and impatient in her disappointment and worry over where he could be. Just as she put her hand on the doorknob to risk going to his room, he appeared. He gathered her into his arms without saying a word, seeming to sense she desperately needed comfort.

"It's been a while since we were here together," Frigga finally said after allowing him to hold her for several seconds.

"I know," he remarked as he glanced around. "It always looks the same." He lifted her chin and looked into her eyes. "I was so tired, I almost forgot to check the wolf. Now I'm wide awake. Tell me what happened."

She carefully recounted the conversation, pacing much like Odin had earlier. Vidar sat on the settee and watched, his eyes darkening.

"Now I understand why you wouldn't tell me what you were planning," he remarked when she finished. "I do not wish to surrender my daughter to someone else to raise, especially Odin." When she tried to interrupt, he held up his hand and continued, "And I cannot believe you led the king to believe you acted the role of a harlot. I don't like this at all, Frigga."

"Are you angry with me?" she whispered.

Vidar sighed heavily and looked away, clenching his jaw slightly. "A little. But I am mostly angry with him for his excuses and how he continues to treat you. He is better than this."

"What do you mean?" she asked, confused and disheartened by his words.

"The law allows for an adopted child to succeed the throne only in the absence of a closer heir," Vidar explained. "With three males ahead of her in succession, it would never have been an issue. He simply does not want to accept the child of his rival, even though he does not know who he is."

Frigga stared at him as a dull anger toward Odin throbbed in her heart, realizing Vidar was correct. She should have realized it; she knew the law. And the glaring truth that her husband was not willing to do what she had done twice pained her. Vidar reached his hand out to her, then gently pulled her onto his lap.

"I know you've only done what you thought best, my queen," he reassured her with a kinder tone.

"I knew you wouldn't like the lie I told to protect you, my love," she admitted as she nestled against him. "But it didn't occur to me you might be against allowing Odin to adopt our little girl, especially since you suggested deceiving him into thinking the child is his."

"He would not treat her equally knowing she is not his," he told her as he rested his head on top of hers. "And now that I have a chance to be a father, I could not bear to have that taken away. Promise me you won't make any more decisions about our daughter without me."

"I did formulate a plan if Odin responded this way," she said softly. "It's just a little more complicated."

"I'm listening," he whispered as he kissed her lips lightly.

"If you can get Odin to confide in you as he did with his own unfaithfulness, you could offer him your help in his dilemma," she suggested.

"And ask to adopt my own child?" Vidar chuckled. "Yes, I understand exactly what you have in mind. But you might have to be secluded here when your pregnancy becomes too difficult to hide. There are still a great many details to map out."

"I do not want to be confined to this room as Laufey was," Frigga said with a shudder. "I would go mad!"

"Why don't I suggest my cottage to the king?" Vidar offered. "Odin will not want to endure the sight of his wife swollen with another man's child. He might gladly accept that offer."

"I like that idea," she murmured. "And you can visit me there with the device."

"Every chance I get," he promised. "But you'll have to feign a sudden illness after the dragon launch."

"I can do that," she said with confidence.

"Frigga, it just occurred to me that someone will have to ride your dragon while you're away so she learns everything the other dragons learn."

"Would you?" she requested.

"I have to ride mine," he lamented. "Would you allow Odin to do it? That might make this suggestion even more tempting for him."

"Yes, as long as I can speak with her first," Frigga agreed.

He hugged her tightly with sudden emotion, then tenderly brushed his lips against her temple. "I think this will save us."

"Odin might still suspect you," Frigga warned.

"I have no doubt the thought has never truly left his mind," Vidar said warily. "He is as clever as he is suspicious. He only accepts what we've shown him because he cannot face the truth … or his own failure."

Frigga shivered. "Then you'll have to play your part perfectly."

"My beloved queen, if you can do it, then so can I," he reassured her. "In a way, we are protecting him even as we protect each other. That thought comforts me in all of this deception. It is a necessary evil."

Their conversation moved to other things, then ceased altogether as they simply held each other and became absorbed in their individual thoughts.

"Can you spend the night with me?" Vidar asked when Frigga reluctantly pulled away from him.

"I shouldn't," she sighed. "Odin probably won't return to our room, but he might. If I'm not there …"

"I understand," he said softly when she trailed off. "When will we be together again?"

"Won't I see you at Valkyrie training?" she asked playfully.

"That's not what I meant," he murmured suggestively.

He stroked her cheek, then smothered her lips with his when hers parted involuntarily. She melted into his embrace, wanting to stay there with every ounce of her being.

"Are you trying to change my mind?" she groaned when he released her.

"No, I'll let you go," he sighed. He slipped the device into her hand. "Take this, and come to me in my room when you can. I'll get it back from you somehow if I need it. I don't think Odin plans to send me anywhere anytime soon."

Vidar's prediction proved correct. Odin buried himself into his duties as king by day and long into the night, which allowed Frigga to sneak away to see Vidar several times. The king treated the queen cordially but distantly. This produced a surprising heartache in Frigga, but Vidar's attention and devotion comforted her. In public, the queen and her general maintained their professional and platonic front. But even when they could be alone together, they dared not express their love beyond occasional passionate kissing.

As the days passed, Vidar bided his time, watching and waiting for the perfect moment to coax Odin to confide in him.

30

"I could hardly wait to see you tonight, my queen!" Vidar exclaimed, rushing over to her as soon as she appeared in his room. He seemed to be bursting with suppressed excitement. "I was worried you might not come."

"Did he finally confide in you?" Frigga asked eagerly as he led her to the settee. "I saw the two of you talking in the gardens this morning, but I wasn't sure if that's what it meant."

"I'm not going to tell you about it," Vidar said with an impish grin. Before she could retort, he added, "I want you to see it for yourself."

"Show me," she murmured as she pulled him in for a kiss.

"You're distracting me," he groaned, kissing her back with intensity. "I've missed you so much. Perhaps my news can wait."

She laughed and tweaked his nose. "Oh no, you don't," she teased. "Odin took the boys night fishing. They won't be back until morning. We'll have time for that later."

"But I want you *now*," Vidar growled playfully.

A deep thrill washed over her. "I'm half tempted to give in," she sighed, shivering as he kissed along her jawline.

Odin never does this, she thought amorously as her pulse quickened with anticipation for what the general would do next.

"And the other half?" he murmured.

"I do want to know what Odin said," she admitted.

"Then I'll wait," he groaned. He took her hand and pressed it to his mouth, then to his forehead. "I'll guide you."

She entered his mind and felt his consciousness pull hers to the place the recent memory resided.

Odin frowned over the documents he perused as Vidar entered his main office.

"You sent for me, my king?" Vidar asked.

"Yes. We've started a new decade, and I need to decide which corps to bring up for duty before the spring war council next month," Odin said distractedly.

"You don't usually ask me for help with that, Odin," Vidar pointed out. "What's the dilemma?"

"The entire army served in the war with Muspelheim," Odin sighed. "And I'm afraid I've forgotten who was on duty when it started forty-nine years ago."

"General Tyr and the Second Corps," Vidar answered confidently. "Much has happened since then, but I'm surprised you've forgotten something like that."

"I've had some personal things on my mind," Odin mumbled.

"Yes, you've seemed unhappy and distracted all week," Vidar prompted gently.

"Can you not discern the reason with your gift?" Odin asked flatly.

"I haven't tried," Vidar admitted. "I've been focused on training the Valkyries. And my newer powers make it difficult sometimes."

"Try now," Odin requested with a strange light in his eye.

A surge of energy passed through Vidar as he obeyed. "You're grieving. Someone close to you has wronged you. You said it's personal. Was it me, my friend?"

"No, Vidar," he sighed. "You've always been loyal to a fault. Even though I know that, I'm ashamed to say I've thought several times that perhaps you had pursued, even dishonored, my queen."

"Why would you think such a thing?" Vidar asked in a quiet, hurt tone. "No, don't tell me. The queen is the one who has wronged you. But it cannot be. Asgard knows no other woman so virtuous and pure as the queen. She is above reproach."

"She was once," Odin declared as a pained look crossed his face. "Clearly, she has deceived you as well. I didn't think that was possible."

"I can be deceived," Vidar objected. "Especially when I don't want to believe something. And I do not wish to believe the queen has proven herself false."

"Not false," Odin corrected. "She succumbed to the seduction of a mysterious commoner in a moment of weakness."

As the king spoke, Vidar cast an illusion of utter shock across his visage. "I … I cannot believe that!" he stammered.

"She told me herself. And she's asked me to forgive her," Odin stated. "You know I haven't always been true to her. How could I not forgive her? How could I subject her to public condemnation when she treated me with kindness and grace? Especially when I drove her to it."

Odin's voice broke as he said this, and he dropped his head into his hands.

"You drove her to it?" Vidar repeated questioningly.

"Yes," Odin affirmed as he quickly mastered his emotions. His voice became strong once more. "I've neglected her and treated her ill."

"Is that going to change?" Vidar asked innocently. "Can you repair the damage you've done to each other?"

"I don't know, Vidar," Odin sighed. "I've not experienced grief like this before. And there is a complication I cannot ignore."

"What complication?" Vidar asked.

"Would you care to walk with me in the gardens?" Odin asked abruptly, gesturing for Vidar to follow him. "I cannot risk anyone overhearing."

"Of course, my king," Vidar said graciously.

As the two of them walked side by side, a deep sadness seemed to drip from the king's posture. He silently trudged on as if focused only on willing his feet to take one more step. Vidar's head drooped slightly from a strong sense of guilt over causing such pain to his friend.

When they reached the garden paths, Odin stopped, turned to Vidar, and grasped his shoulder. "My dearest and truest friend, you cannot tell anyone what I'm about to tell you."

"I swear it," Vidar promised. "I have kept your other secrets."

"Frigga is pregnant by the man who seduced her," Odin stated without emotion.

"No!" Vidar gasped, allowing his face to whiten with dismay. "What are you going to do?"

"She can hide her belly as it grows, but we cannot hide a living child," Odin said as they began walking again. "And she did not ask the man's name or where he was from. Purposely, I think. She thought I would execute him if I found out."

"Would you have?" Vidar asked quietly.

"I do not know," Odin replied wearily as he started down the path toward the golden apple grove. "The political implications would have been great. But it matters not. At least I will have no blood on my hands over this. Regardless, I have not found a solution for her."

"Why do you not take the baby as your own as she did for your sons?" Vidar suggested.

"I cannot bear to have the offspring of this knave as an heir even though she is the daughter of my beloved queen," Odin admitted.

"The baby is a girl?" Vidar asked.

"Frigga says she is," Odin confirmed.

"You have three male heirs, Odin," Vidar reminded him. "She would not ascend to the throne. Perhaps you should reconsider."

"No, I cannot!" Odin snapped. His shoulders slumped again as his face fell in defeat and shame. "I know I'm being boorish and selfish. Frigga has more heart and love than I've ever had."

"But Odin, if you separate her from her baby, it would break her mentally," Vidar pointed out. "For that very reason."

"What do you suggest I do?" Odin erupted in exasperation. "This is one of the hardest things I've ever had to face. Stop trying to persuade me to adopt the child."

"Is there someone you could ask?" Vidar prompted gently. "Someone who has always wanted a child, perhaps?"

"I have tried and tried to think of someone, but who can I trust?" Odin admitted with frustration. "I told Frigga we might have to take the child off-world, but I do fear that would destroy them both."

"What if … No, I cannot ask." Vidar lowered his voice into uncertain silence.

"If you know of someone, speak up," the king commanded.

"Odin, you know I've been unlucky in love," Vidar began. "Whatever Jillian did not break in me, Solveya did."

"And you know both of those situations were your own fault," Odin said, although not unkindly. "Do not give up hope."

"I already have," Vidar admitted sadly. "I cannot see myself ever marrying now. But I have always wanted to be a father, especially seeing you with your fine sons. Perhaps I could take the child as my own?"

Odin turned to peer at him intently as he spoke, stopping them both in the middle of the path again.

He laughed suddenly. "Vidar, you always did want to do everything I did. When we were young, you eyed or courted the sister or cousin of almost every woman whose company I sought. Then you joined the military because I did." His jesting tone grew serious. "And you've not left my side for centuries, protecting my throne and my family as if they were your own. I would grant you this request if it were up to me. But the queen must decide. I will approach her about it."

Vidar's face transformed into an enormous grin. "I hope she will look favorably upon my request. But please, Odin, would you permit me to ask her myself?"

"Wouldn't it be better for me to prepare her?" Odin contested.

"No, my king, I have my own words I would say," Vidar answered. "I've come to know her quite well, as you already know. I do not wish to manipulate her, but I believe I can speak to her in a way that would tug at her heartstrings."

"Very well," the king agreed. "We will meet in the pavilion immediately after breakfast. I will take her out there as if for a walk. Join us quickly though."

"I will," Vidar promised.

Odin clapped him on the shoulder as they walked inside. "Already, my heart is lighter, my friend. You could be saving my marriage, which I believe you have tried to do in the past, though I would not listen."

Frigga eased out of Vidar's mind and looked at him thoughtfully. "I could feel your feelings too, Vidar, as if they were my own. Guilt mingled with pride when Odin praised you, anger when he pointed out how you've shadowed him. Then guilt and pride when he praised you again. Joy when he suggested the three of us talk. And no small amount of cunning throughout."

Vidar looked at her with uncertainty. "Are you unhappy with how I played my part? Or for some other reason? I cannot tell."

Frigga regarded him thoughtfully, then decided to confront him with the worry that plagued her. "All this time, have you only pursued me because you want what the king has?"

His mouth dropped open and his face looked so distressed, she immediately interpreted the look as confirmation. She stood abruptly, crossed to the other side of the room, and hugged herself with her arms.

He followed her immediately. "No, Frigga! Please do not start doubting my love for you." He took her hand and pressed it to his forehead again. "Search my memories. All of them."

She hesitated, but since she desperately needed reassurance, she eased back into his mind and did exactly as he suggested. She skipped his childhood and transition years but watched a few of his battles and even dared to touch the memories of some of the women he had entertained, though she did not look too far into them, painful as it was. She saw herself through his eyes as well as all of his pent-up love and desire for centuries. And she noted the marked difference between his emotions during his previous escapades and his memories with her. When she simply could not handle any more, she broke the connection.

Completely speechless, she stood there gaping at him as he smiled knowingly, though still with some uncertainty. He had seen everything she had.

"Vidar, I'm stunned," she breathed.

"No, you are stunning," he corrected softly. "Your eyes shine with such light."

She blushed and looked away, overwhelmed by the emotion in his eyes, what she had seen in his mind, and what she felt in her own heart. He stroked her cheek with his knuckles, then kissed her hungrily. She trembled against him but surrendered to him gladly.

He broke away suddenly, grinning like a child. "I was going to wait, but this seems like the perfect time."

"For what?" she asked breathlessly.

"I have a gift for you, my queen," Vidar answered. "I can't give it to you until the dragon launch, but I want to show you tonight so I can explain what it means to me."

Frigga raised an eyebrow at him in confusion. He kissed her cheek and vanished, then returned seconds later with a small metal box.

"I commissioned these after we paired the dragons and Valkyries," Vidar informed her as he opened the lid to reveal a jumble of silver and gemstone pendants. "I picked them up yesterday."

"What are they?" Frigga asked curiously, still feeling confused and wondering what the jewelry had to do with her.

"Whenever a trainee joins the Valiants, we initiate him into service with a task, a ceremony, and a small gift," Vidar explained. "I wanted to do the same for the Valkyries. The task is the flight performance, which will include the ceremony. These are the gifts." He set the box down to pull out one of the pieces, which he held out to Frigga. "They're designed to be worn around the neck with a silver chain but could easily be turned into brooches."

Frigga gingerly took the jewelry from him and nestled it in the palm of her hand. "It's so delicate and beautiful," she breathed as she carefully fingered the elaborate construction. Thin strands of silver wire had been twisted into the shape of a gnarled tree then wrapped onto an outer ring. The roots were bare, but small chips of a lovely red stone flecked with tiny gold sparkles enhanced the nine branches. "Is this supposed to be Yggdrisil?"

Vidar nodded, looking pleased. "I chose a gemstone for each one that corresponds with one of the nine realms. I just need to decide which two Valkyries will get each color."

"Is this one mine?" she asked.

"No, that one represents Asgard. One of the Vanaheim ones is for you," Vidar answered. He then handed her a pendant studded with smooth gemstones of soothing, translucent purple. "I thought I'd let you choose who gets the other."

"Brynhilde," Frigga responded without hesitation.

"That's two down," Vidar chuckled. "Sixteen to go."

"Eir should get one of the Asgard ones," Frigga suggested.

"I agree," Vidar replied. "I might ask you for your opinion on the others. But there is one more I haven't shown you."

"For Odin?"

"No, for the leader of the Valkyries."

"I get two?" Frigga queried gleefully, feeling like a girl again.

"You get two," Vidar confirmed playfully. He drew out a pendant made from gemstones of nine different colors interwoven into the exact same design. The effect was mesmerizing. "I wanted to show you before I officially give this to you at the ceremony. It is a professional gift, but only you and I will know what it means."

"And what does it mean?" she whispered, looking up at him from examining the breathtaking pendant he still held.

"That no matter where we go in the nine realms, we will somehow find our way back to each other," he murmured. "Day to day, night to night, onward till our paths unite."

"That's incredibly romantic, Vidar," Frigga sighed, wishing their paths never had to separate again. "Perhaps you should add poetry to your list of hidden skills."

"Perhaps," he conceded, his voice low and intimate. "But only with you."

Frigga gently set aside the three pendants, then reached for Vidar. She could no longer resist him the way she resisted Odin, nor did she want to do so. Probing Vidar's memories coupled with seeing the gift he had designed for her had linked her soul even closer to his. She had never felt so assured of Odin's love as she did of Vidar's in the moments of passion that ensued. The resulting effect was so powerful, everything she had felt toward Odin while watching him in Vidar's memories vanished. And the desire to run away with the general and never look back hit her with an intensity for which she was not prepared.

"No, don't say it, Frigga," Vidar stopped her just as she was about to speak. "I already know. I can feel your thoughts stronger than I ever have."

"I wonder why," she mused. "Could probing your mind have forged an even greater bond between us?"

"I think so," Vidar affirmed. "I do feel closer to you, even more than usual when you share my bed."

"Why don't you want me to say what I was thinking?" she queried innocently.

"Because you were right the night you told me about your condition," Vidar answered. "The king would chase us wherever we went. Gjallar cannot find me, but he will find you. I won't put you and our daughter at risk for what I want most. There is always a cost to pay in the end."

"But what about all those times you've told me you would try to find a way for us?" she pleaded. "You yourself said, 'Onward till our paths unite.' I want you to find a way."

"I will, Frigga. I promise you that," Vidar responded huskily. "The timing just isn't right. Think of Odin and your sons."

"I'm usually the one thinking of my sons, but I do not wish to think of Odin," she replied indignantly. "You've completely swept me away."

He kissed her tenderly. "Now that you know how strong my love is for you, cling to that. I still believe we'll be free someday."

"Something has shifted, Vidar," Frigga told him. "I think you've become my first mate."

He chuckled shyly. "I love hearing you say things like that. Will you stay here with me tonight?"

"I wish I could," she sighed. "I can stay a little while longer, but Odin is coming back early in the morning. And we both need our rest for tomorrow."

He held her tightly until she finally extracted herself from his arms and returned to her room to prepare for bed. She fell asleep quickly and had no awareness of when Odin returned. But when she woke up the following morning, the king sat beside her, watching her sleep. She smiled at him groggily.

"When did you get back?" she murmured.

"I didn't look at the time, but the sun hadn't risen yet," he replied. "You didn't even stir."

"Did you enjoy yourselves?"

"Yes, we did," Odin said contentedly. "Thor caught the biggest fish this time. I had to curb his bragging a bit."

"That sounds like Thor," she laughed.

"I told them they could sleep in today. I doubt any of them will show up to breakfast. You don't even have to do your usual lessons if you don't want to," Odin told her. "Although I did tell Thor and Loki to report to Mimir at the usual time."

"Thank you, Odin," Frigga sighed with relief. "I have been slowing down."

"I've been meaning to ask how you've been feeling," he asked with a touch of tenderness.

The compassion she had felt for him the night before returned in a fierce rush. "It's easier than it was with the twins and the one we lost. I just hope I can manage the performance with the Valkyries."

"Are you certain that's wise?" Odin objected. "I don't think you should."

"And what excuse would I give?"

"I may have a few ideas," Odin mused. "But let's not discuss it now. I thought perhaps we could have breakfast together, then go for a leisurely morning walk."

"In the gardens?" she asked eagerly.

"Of course," he said softly. He reached out and cupped her cheek. "I'm still working through everything, but I have missed you."

She placed her hand over his and closed her eyes, lacking the energy to hide the turmoil she felt. "I appreciate how respectful you've been toward me, my king."

"Shall we go then?" Odin said somewhat stiffly.

He slipped his hand away, then got out of the bed to prepare for the day. She wondered what she had said that had caused him to close up like that. But as she followed suit, she realized she had not returned the sentiment he had offered.

"Odin?" she spoke tentatively. When he looked at her questioningly, she said, "I have missed you. I just thought it was important to mention how I've noticed your efforts to treat me with more kindness."

"I understand," he responded simply.

But when he said nothing further, she sighed to herself and finished her morning preparations in silence. Over breakfast, they conversed only about casual things of little importance. As they walked the garden paths after they finished eating, she knew he was watching for the general to appear. But she refused to allow herself to look as they drew near the pavilion. So great was her concentration to not reveal she knew he would be joining them, she jumped when his voice sounded a cheerful good morning. Odin snorted with amusement at her reaction, then returned his friend's greeting.

"How fares the king and queen?" Vidar asked, bowing slightly. "It is a beautiful morning!"

"It is indeed," Odin replied, matching the general's cheerfulness. "What brings you out here, Vidar?"

"I would seek an audience with the queen," Vidar answered confidently.

"Regarding what?" she asked. "Could it not have waited until Valkyrie training?"

"No, my queen," Vidar replied. "I would speak with you regarding a private matter that I am quite certain you would not care for anyone to overhear."

She straightened her shoulders and raised an eyebrow at the king, who looked obviously uncomfortable. "Odin, why are you squirming like a caterpillar in a bird's beak? And why do I get the feeling you two have conspired against me?"

"Frigga, please do not overreact," Odin sheepishly exhorted her. "I told him about your condition."

"Why would you do that?" she whispered fiercely. "You told me no one could know, but you've told the *general*?"

"My queen, may I speak?" Vidar interjected. When she turned her angry gaze on him, he dipped his head respectfully and said, "I understand why you've done what you've done. I don't condone it, but I am guilty of grievous relationship mistakes myself. I'm not here to cast judgment but to present a solution that might help all three of us."

Frigga cocked her head even as she allowed herself to bristle at his words. "I will hear your proposal."

"My queen, I have long desired to be a father, but I'm afraid my prospects have dwindled to nothing," Vidar stated.

"Nonsense, General," Frigga retorted. "I have seen the way the noblewomen behave around you. One of them would surely—"

"Forgive me for interrupting, my queen," Vidar interjected. "But I have been too wounded to consider such things of late. If you would allow me to adopt your child as my own, it would solve your problems and soothe my heartache."

"How would giving my daughter into your care solve my problems?" she asked slowly.

"I currently reside at the palace," Vidar pointed out. "If I adopt her, you would see her far more often than if you surrendered her to another. And since the two of you wish to keep this secret, you would not have to explain anything to anyone else."

"Frigga, you know he can be trusted," Odin chimed in. "You could even care for her yourself when Vidar is gone."

"You would allow her near your own sons?" she asked somewhat bitingly.

"I only said she could not be an heir to my throne," Odin protested. "Vidar is providing us with an excellent solution. I think we should take him up on it."

"I do not expect an answer now, my queen," Vidar hastened to add. "But I would like to add that if you accept my offer,

I will make my beach cottage available to you for the seclusion you will need when the time comes to deliver your child."

Odin glanced at him in surprise, but Frigga demanded, "If I leave Valla, who will ride my dragon while the other Valkyries train?"

"You should not ride your dragon as your condition progresses, my queen," Vidar informed her. "And that will be difficult to explain if you stay here. At the beach cottage, you will have more privacy and freedom to move about. And you're already familiar with it from caring for me there."

"You haven't answered my question," Frigga prompted.

"I could ride your dragon, Frigga," Odin interjected before Vidar could answer. "If she would allow me, that is."

"You would have to communicate telepathically with her to ride her, Odin," Frigga warned. "I thought you needed to protect your mind."

"I think it's been long enough," he said with a shrug. "I could try one ride to see how we both handle it."

"I am willing to consider your offer, Vidar, though I am not ready to give a final decision," Frigga said with resignation. She turned to the king again. "Are you willing to ride her today, Odin?" When he nodded eagerly, she said, "Then let's start there. And if it goes well, we can discuss this further. I have other concerns, including how this will affect my sons."

"Why don't you put together a list?" Odin suggested. "Like you did when you planned the self-defense program."

"I'll work on that this afternoon," Frigga agreed.

"Vidar, is your schedule open right now?" Odin asked. When he nodded, the king continued, "Why don't you accompany me to ride Frigga's dragon?"

"Have you forgotten me?" Frigga asked somewhat indignantly. "I need to speak with her first."

"Oh, of course," Odin reassured her. "You may come as well."

"I am not asking your permission, my king. My fate should not be decided without me," Frigga added, feeling her temper rise.

"You're not exactly in a position to be making demands, are you, Frigga?" Odin said quietly.

She opened her mouth to retort, but Vidar spoke first in a gently rebuking tone. "Odin, that was not helpful. The queen is right. My offer stands only with her approval. I will not take her child against her will."

"I have no intention of deciding her fate without her," Odin protested. "But we do have limited options. It merely did not occur to me that she should be present when I attempt to ride her dragon."

Vidar dipped his head respectfully, then clapped his fist to his chest twice. "I will go on ahead and meet you at the enclosure. You'll need to use my irscet until I can make yours."

"Thank you, Vidar," Odin acknowledged. "We'll follow after we finish our walk."

The king held his arm out to Frigga. She nodded at the general, then took her husband's arm, not even allowing a backward glance at the man whose love she cherished. Odin remained silent as they walked through the gardens, where signs of spring were just beginning to burst forth. Daffodils raised their lovely yellow heads to the sun and the fat leaf buds dotting the trees. Frigga breathed in a lungful of fresh air, her heart lightened by Odin's encouragement for her to consider Vidar's proposal.

"Are you alright?" Odin asked with sudden concern.

"I'm just taking it all in," Frigga replied in a light tone. "This winter was hard for me."

"I need to ask you something, Frigga," Odin said as he stopped abruptly.

Frigga stiffened as she faced him. "Yes, my king?"

"Did you do this because you believed I was secretly entertaining another woman again?" he asked.

"That may have factored into it," Frigga admitted. "But not fully. Most of it was how unloved and neglected I've felt. I wanted to be valued and cherished. But it did not turn out the way I expected at all."

"Of course it didn't," he scoffed. He grimaced at his own response, then continued in a gentler tone, "Frigga, a man who would take advantage of an emotionally wounded woman and seduce her after one meal together is not honorable. Men like that do not respect women but only use them for their own needs, often employing manipulative tactics and even acting romantic and chivalrous. He may have made you feel valued, but he deceived you and treated you as if you had none."

For a moment, Frigga's heart stopped, forgetting they were talking about her imaginary seducer and not Vidar. But remembering what she had seen in Vidar's mind, she pushed aside her anxiety.

"And what about you, Odin?" she asked.

"What about me?" he asked warily. When she stared at him in silence, he answered, "Yes, Frigga, I know how those men think because I was once one of them."

"You told me you had only entertained the mothers of your sons," she accused. "I never fully believed that. You made it clear to me that Patrice's mother succumbed to your charms. I had hoped perhaps there were no others."

"I meant in the context of our marriage," Odin admitted. "Sadly, there were many others before you. And her. Please do not think I purposely deceived you. If you had asked me, I would have told you honestly of my wretched past."

"When you wandered with Zeus?"

Odin grimaced as if the memories were painful for him, almost as if he felt disgusted. "Yes, but not only with Zeus. I'm ashamed to say I introduced Vidar to that life as well. The general and I were not exemplary in our behavior toward women when we were young. In different ways, we have both suffered because of our choices. And the women we loved and left have surely suffered as well."

"I'm not going to ask again about the women you've entertained," she declared, turning her face away from him, her heart aching equally over both of the men she loved. "I no longer want to know."

He dropped his head. "Why do you think I controlled myself with you when we were courting?" Without waiting for an answer, he rushed on to say, "I respected you, Frigga. I've always respected you. And your value to me is beyond measure."

"Then why do you neglect me and wound me with your words and indifference?" she asked honestly, without accusation in her tone. "Don't you understand how you have made me feel?"

"I'm starting to," Odin sighed. "I now know what it's like to be betrayed by the person I trusted most."

She winced and turned away to continue walking.

He grabbed her arm. "Frigga, I don't know how we're going to get through this. But I want to try. I truly do want to understand."

"Can we discuss this another time?" Frigga begged. "The general awaits us at the dragon enclosure. And I do not wish to cry the entire way there."

Odin dropped his hand from her arm and nodded, his expression disappointed and resigned. "Very well. Can you ride or should we take the cariole?"

"I can ride a little while longer. I'd like to while I'm still able," she answered. "It's not far, after all."

But by the time they reached the enclosure, she regretted her decision. Her ligaments felt stretched, and her joints ached from the ride. When she dismounted, she twisted the wrong way and felt something tear in her lower abdomen. She hid her pain, thankful when the sharp stabbing began to fade. Then she hurried as quickly as she could to greet Idunn. She filled her dragon in on everything that had happened, then asked if Odin could stand in as a rider for the duration of her pregnancy and recovery.

He must ask me himself, Idunn insisted gravely. *It is our way.*

"Odin, she desires to speak with you," Frigga said aloud. But silently, she pleaded, *Please do not tell him the baby is Vidar's.*

That is for you to reveal, not for me, Idunn answered as Odin cautiously approached. *But if it makes you feel more secure, you may listen to our first interaction.*

I did not know that was possible, Frigga gasped internally.

Keep your hand where it is and your mind closed to all but listening, the dragon responded. *And tell him to lock his mind to probing from either of us.*

Frigga obeyed, then told her husband, "She wants me to listen to your first interaction. You'll have to ask permission to ride her yourself."

Odin nodded, then placed his hand between the creature's eyes. *Greetings, majestic one,* he thought. *I have long desired to speak with you.*

I know why you have not, Idunn answered kindly. *And I will expend my energy so you may reserve your own.*

Do you know of our dilemma? the king asked.

I do, Idunn confirmed. *I am the one who first sensed the child and told the queen of her existence.*

Then you know who the child's father is? Odin asked tentatively.

I know what the queen knows, Idunn repeated. *And we will leave it at that. I hold her secrets in confidence, as I will your own secrets should you choose to reveal them. Very rarely will a dragon meddle, for we believe each soul must search to find the right path. But we will give wisdom when asked.*

Then let me ask two things of you, noble one, the king responded. *First, do you believe the queen and I can heal from this and bring back what once was?*

Heal you both must, Idunn replied. *But you cannot and should not bring back what once was. The past serves as a lesson only. Focus instead on moving forward. Focus on growth.*

I will heed your words, wise one, Odin stated, though he furrowed his brow as if discouraged by her admonition.

I am Idunn, the dragon informed him.

I know of your culture and am honored you trust me with your name, the king thought, immediately brightening. *And though I have many names, to you I am simply Odin.*

I also know of your culture. And it is my honor to call my new king by his name, Idunn replied. *But what of your second question?*

May I ride you during Frigga's absence? he requested.

That would be an even greater honor, she said simply. *We will speak again, and I will protect your mind each time we do.*

Odin thanked her, then withdrew his hand.

Frigga kept hers on the dragon long enough to say, *Thank you, Idunn. I am sorry I doubted you even slightly.*

At the signal from Odin, Vidar strapped his irscet onto Idunn's back, making adjustments where he could. The apparatus fit Odin surprisingly well. In a matter of minutes, Idunn launched into the air, bearing Odin as she soared the heights.

When the duo became a faraway speck, Vidar turned to Frigga. "This is going to work. I just know it."

She turned to smile at him, but before she could respond, a searing pain shot through where she had felt the tear in her abdomen.

"I need to sit down," she gasped, grabbing at him.

"What's wrong?" Vidar asked, his face immediately drawn with worry and fear.

Since no one was close enough to witness anything, he scooped her up and carried her back inside the enclosure. He set her down gently onto the cold benches built into the stone wall near the entrance. One of the guards on duty rushed from somewhere in the back of the building to assist Vidar.

As she bent over and groaned, Vidar pushed the guard back. "I'll attend to the queen. Send for a healer!"

"No!" Frigga burst out. "I'm alright. I don't need a healer. I just need to catch my breath." When Vidar looked at her with uncertainty, she begged, "Let me catch my breath!"

"Back to your post," Vidar commanded the guard.

The man began to obey but cast several furtive glances toward the queen as she began massaging her abdomen to ease the dull ache and throbbing that pulsed on the right side below her belly button.

Frigga narrowed her eyes at him. "Avert your eyes, Private!"

"Apologies, my queen," the guard responded immediately. "If you need privacy, the bunkhouse is empty."

"Yes, I think I've pulled something," Frigga informed him. "I'd like to check."

"Of course, my queen," the private said. "General, what are your orders?"

"I will escort the queen," Vidar answered in a clipped tone. "Notify me immediately when the king returns."

Frigga stood, then gripped her abdomen as the ache increased with the movement. "I cannot walk," she gasped. "General, I'm afraid I need your assistance once more."

"Please allow me to send for a healer, Your Majesty," the guard pleaded as his face twisted with genuine concern.

"I will consider that once I have examined myself," Frigga replied, wincing as Vidar lifted her up again. "I do not wish to cause any more alarm than necessary."

"Stand by, Private," Vidar commanded. As he carefully carried Frigga to the bunkhouse, he whispered, "Is it the baby? Did I hurt you last night?"

"I don't think so," she murmured. "But we cannot involve the healers. I have to take care of whatever it is by myself."

Vidar fell silent. After he set her down inside the bunkhouse bathroom so she could look in the mirror at her belly, he stood guard outside. She pulled up her dress and carefully examined the spot. A large, deep purple bruise had already formed on her soft flesh. Judging from the location and color, the tear was just under the skin, but too much movement made the area feel like blood still pooled underneath the surface. And she did not have her healing kit with her.

She poked her head out of the bathroom door. "Vidar, would you get some Asgardian ointment from the medicine locker?"

He hurried to obey and returned quickly bearing a small jar of the sweet-smelling, sticky jelly. She shut the door and massaged the healing concoction into the spot, sighing with relief as it began to work. She checked for signs of miscarriage, then grabbed the jar of ointment and walked out on her own.

"I tore something just under my skin when I dismounted earlier," she informed Vidar as she handed him the jar to return it to its proper place. "The ointment is helping a lot. But I won't be able to ride or fight until it's healed."

"What about the baby?" Vidar asked as worry creased his brow.

"She should be fine," Frigga reassured him. "I have no signs of miscarriage."

"I would like to know for sure," Vidar pressed her. "There has to be a healer we can trust. You cannot deliver the baby by yourself anyway."

"Vidar, no one else can know," she protested. "How could I explain my unfaithfulness to a healer?"

"How will you be able to tell if the baby is safe and healthy?" Vidar insisted anxiously.

"I should be able to feel her move soon. And this episode could actually play into our plans. It will be easier to feign an illness now."

"I don't like this!" he exclaimed, grasping his hair in frustration. He turned suddenly and snapped his fingers. "Patrice!"

"What about her?" Frigga asked warily.

"She's been studying with the healers at the South Sea for several years," Vidar informed her. "She is nowhere near Eir's level, but she has access to some equipment and could help you monitor everything."

"Then why didn't she nurse you back to health instead of me?" Frigga grumped as jealousy sparked in her heart.

"It was never presented as an option," Vidar answered. "And I wouldn't have listened to her. Odin knew that."

"Or perhaps it was because he seduced your aunt before your uncle came along," Frigga mused.

"Why are you bringing that up? Her mother's past relationship with Odin has nothing to do with Patrice," Vidar said somewhat defensively. "It sounds like you don't like her much."

"She's fine," Frigga sighed. "I envy her freedom and familiarity with you. That's all."

"She is my cousin, Frigga," Vidar stated flatly. "We have always been close, but there is nothing to be jealous of. I trust her, and I think she would help us. She's followed me like a duckling since she was a youth. Besides, you know how much she admires you. You spent a little time together while I was recovering. Didn't she tell you to ask if you needed anything?"

"Yes, but—"

"Did she also tell you she wants to be a Valkyrie some-day?" he interrupted eagerly. "We could use that to our advantage."

"What would we tell her?" Frigga argued, ignoring this latest tidbit of news and feeling decidedly uncomfortable with how Vidar was pushing his cousin as their solution.

"The truth?" Vidar suggested.

"No, we cannot!" Frigga exclaimed, horrified by the thought. "She would never accept us!"

"She would not want to see me executed, whether she agrees with us or not," Vidar argued. "We could tell her we secretly married. The argument could be made that we did in a way."

"We made each other promises, but that was no wedding," she contested.

He leaned down and nuzzled her nose. "Would you like one?"

She sighed heavily. "I often feel I'm more married to you than to Odin, but this seems foolish. We're grasping at straws to legitimize our relationship when we know absolutely no one on Asgard would ever sanction it, including your cousin."

"I think we could persuade her," Vidar insisted.

"I'd prefer she not be involved," Frigga pleaded quietly.

"I'm not giving up just yet. Maybe Odin will have an idea," Vidar responded. "He would not want you to give birth alone either."

"We'll speak of that later. We'd better go back," she told him. "The king may have returned by now."

But when they entered the main enclosure area, Odin had not yet returned. Frigga assured the guard that her injury was minor and did not require a healer, much to his relief. Vidar went out to watch for Odin, but Frigga opted to sit inside and wait, knowing she should not strain herself.

"What a rush!" Odin exclaimed when he finally returned. "I might not give you back your dragon, Frigga!"

She frowned even as she met Idunn's wise and laughing eyes. She could tell her dragon had also enjoyed the flight. "That's not part of the agreement."

"I know," he laughed. "But I sure did enjoy that. And I feel just fine."

"Well, I don't," Frigga declared. "I'm afraid I injured myself. I cannot ride. Or fight."

"What happened?" Odin asked, his face sobering instantly.

"I'll show you at the palace," Frigga told him. "The injury is in a delicate location."

"Can you walk?" Odin asked. "The palace isn't far."

"I shouldn't," she admitted.

"I can ride back to the palace and send the cariole back for the queen," Vidar offered.

"A guard can do that," Odin responded. "We three have important matters to discuss."

"First, I must explain to my dragon what happened and why I cannot ride her," Frigga interjected. "Odin, can you ride her for next week's performance?"

"Gladly!" he blurted out happily. "Although Svadilfari might turn green with envy if he hears how much I loved that."

"Now we can fly together, my king," Vidar said excitedly. "Until the queen has recovered, that is."

Frigga rolled her eyes playfully, even though she did not like the situation. But knowing this part was no one's fault, she dutifully approached Idunn.

After briefly conversing with her, she returned to the men. "My dragon understands the situation."

"Let's talk outside," Odin suggested, eyeing the guard who acted as if he were trying not to listen. "Private, take the dragon back to her paddock and get someone else to man your post, then fetch the cariole for the queen. Bring back three more guards. We will wait outside."

As the guard hastened to obey, Odin helped Frigga walk outside while the general followed. She clutched her belly as it began to ache again.

"I'm overdoing it," she informed the two men. "But my dragon said the baby is fine. No permanent harm done."

"How does she know?" Odin asked with concern.

"She can sense her consciousness and any distress she might feel," Frigga explained. "She sent soothing pulses to the baby just in case, but she is certain she was not affected by my injury."

"What exactly happened?" Odin pressed. "Can you give me some indication of what's wrong?"

"I tore something under my skin in my lower abdomen when I dismounted. The bleeding formed a hematoma," Frigga explained. "It's rather ugly, but it looks worse than it is. Asgardian ointment will heal it with a little time. But no more riding or fighting for me."

"Very well. This could play into our plans quite well. Now, be honest. How do you feel about staying in Vidar's cottage at the South Sea?" Odin asked. "Away from all of us."

"I do like it there," she stated. "It's remote without being isolated. I would miss everyone, but I would prefer it to being confined to one room in the palace. Do you think you and the boys could visit me?"

"That might be possible with a little clever planning," Odin mused, stroking his black beard with one hand. "What other concerns do you have? We've solved the dragon problem."

"You asked me to write a list," Frigga reminded him. "I said I'd do it this afternoon."

"We have time to spare now," Odin prompted. "Let's just discuss whatever is in the forefront of your mind."

"Well … I'm concerned about lessons for the princes, how we could manage visits, how they'll handle my absence for such a long time, what I'll do with myself, who will keep my projects moving forward, how we'll explain this, who will stay with me in the cottage, and how and when I'll give birth," she listed.

Odin let out a low whistle. "Sounds like you've made your list. That's quite a bit."

"I can answer two of those," Vidar finally spoke up. "Vale and I will take over training the Valkyries for now.

You wouldn't be able to do it from here either. And you can work uninterrupted on your university proposal for the war council while you're staying at the cottage."

"How do you know about that?" Odin asked, too casually.

"She told me about it during one of our training sessions," Vidar answered nonchalantly. "I'm sorry if I spoke out of turn, but I think it's a marvelous idea. The two of you make an incredible team when you work together."

Odin grinned and winked at Frigga, who smiled back at him. And for a moment, it was as if they had both forgotten the circumstances they discussed. Vidar shifted his body weight, and Frigga became instantly aware of how painful the scene was for him.

Odin's eye clouded over just as quickly. "I can answer another. The princes will be far more upset to find out their mother was impregnated by some stranger than to think you've fallen ill and need to seclude yourself in a milder climate."

Frigga dropped her eyes at his terse words.

But the king continued, "Mimir and Baldur can take over lessons. And as long as you have the strength to maintain your current illusion, I can provide a small staff for you at the cottage as well as arrange for occasional visits."

"And if my strength fails? What then?" Frigga asked nervously.

"Then you'll have to stay in whatever room you choose for your own until you've regained your strength," Odin stated.

"My king, I think she should have a healer attending her," Vidar suggested tentatively. "Especially after what happened today."

"We cannot subject the queen to the risk of exposure or gossip," Odin said, shaking his head.

"My cousin Patrice might help her without revealing anything," Vidar contested gently, ignoring Frigga as she narrowed her eyes at him. "She has been studying to be a healer and has access to equipment and medicine."

"People would not understand why I would choose a novice to care for the queen during her illness," Odin pointed out. "And you said she might help her. How can we risk that she might not?" He paused, then asked, "Is there something we can do for her? Something she desires?"

Frigga felt the decision slip away from her in that moment and decided to grasp at whatever control she had left. "Vidar says she wants to be a Valkyrie someday."

The general grinned with a cunning glint in his eyes. "Yes, after she completes her internship next year. And as far as why you would choose her, perhaps you can say the queen's condition is not dangerous enough for quarantine but such that she needs daily care. Eir would not be available for that. Nor any of the other Valkyries. And perhaps we can say the queen is most comfortable with Patrice, of the options left. And quite honestly, it could count toward my cousin's internship, which would appeal to her. And if you pay her enough, it would help with her continued education. In fact, if the queen agrees to all of this, I would help cover the expenses as well."

Odin clapped him enthusiastically on the shoulder. "Brilliant, Vidar!"

"But what would we tell her? And what about when it comes time for me to deliver?" Frigga demanded, not yet ready to give in completely. "The staff will know if they stay."

"Would Patrice be willing to do the work required?" Odin asked Vidar. "Can she manage a household?"

"I can ask her if she's willing," Vidar answered. "She is domestically skilled, for certain."

"What if we hired local servants just for daytime work?" Odin suggested to Frigga.

"If you arranged it so no one stayed there at night but Patrice, you could send the other staff on errands if you go into labor during the day," Vidar added.

"I suppose," Frigga admitted, imagining opportunities to be alone with Vidar.

"What about security?" Odin asked.

"One guard who can sleep in a stable bunk?" Frigga suggested, much more open to the idea in spite of herself.

"I'd prefer two," Odin declared.

"So would I," Vidar agreed. "There's room."

"We still have two problems," Frigga commented lightly. "We'll have to tell Patrice why I'm pregnant. And how do we explain Vidar's adopting a baby around the same time as my seclusion? You know how people love a scandal. They might actually suggest the ludicrous idea that …" Frigga allowed herself to look uncomfortably embarrassed. "I cannot even speak it out loud, it's so ridiculous. But people make assumptions and fill in the blanks all the time. We need an explanation for where she came from."

Vidar and Odin exchanged puzzled looks.

"Are you accepting my offer, my queen?" Vidar asked.

"If we can solve those last two problems, then yes," Frigga affirmed.

Odin's posture instantly relaxed, and Vidar's face transformed into a rapturous smile as he expressed his thanks.

"Let's ride together," Odin suggested as the guard returned with the cariole. "I want this decided so we can execute whatever plans we make."

The king instructed the first guard to return to his post and two of the new guards to take the horses they had ridden to the enclosure back to the royal stables. The last guard climbed into the driver's seat for the short ride back to the palace.

"Any ideas, Vidar?" Odin asked as he and the general helped Frigga into the cariole together.

"I'll speak with Patrice about the queen's condition and be as delicate as possible," Vidar offered.

"I want to be there when you do," Frigga said with resignation.

"I would strongly suggest you stay hidden," Vidar urged. "It will be hard for her to accept. She greatly admires you, my queen."

"Perhaps I should be there," Odin suggested.

"You'll only frighten her into compliance, my king," Vidar told him. "We need to be certain she won't betray our secret. If she seems like she might, the queen can probe her mind and change her memories."

"I would prefer not to do that," Frigga objected. "We do not yet understand the damage that could potentially cause in the future. And I despise even having that ability. My forefathers used it far too often in Vanaheim's past."

"I agree with Frigga," Odin declared. "Asgardian royals have also abused that gift. It is good that mind powers have diminished greatly over time. The more you learn about your new abilities, Vidar, the better you will understand how dangerous they are."

"Of course," Vidar acknowledged. "But it is an option."

"When would you speak to her?" Odin asked.

"I'll go with the queen to get her settled," Vidar offered. "I'll handle Patrice then. Perhaps the day after the dragon launch?"

"That's good timing," Frigga agreed. "Then I won't miss the performance."

"That solves that problem, provided Patrice cooperates," Vidar remarked. "If she doesn't, though I think she will, we can try another novice healer who wants to be a Valkyrie."

"It's risky," Odin mused. "But it very well may be what needs to happen. Now, what about explaining to Asgard where the baby came from after you've adopted her?"

"The only thing I can think of is to claim I got someone pregnant who died in childbirth," Vidar admitted.

"That's too convenient," Frigga protested. "People would not believe it. They would make terrible assumptions or assume you lied to protect your queen."

"I've got an idea!" Odin exclaimed. "My mother told a story long ago of a servant girl who left her baby in a basket at the home of a wealthy family with no children. Could Patrice leave the baby at someone's door? And you could happen upon the scene and offer to take her?"

"And what if that family won't give her up?" Vidar asked warily.

"Then the problem is no longer yours," Odin quipped. "Or mine."

Frigga glared at him, her heart turning to stone at his attempted levity.

"I'm afraid I have my heart set on adopting this baby girl," Vidar confessed. "I've already started to love her. Besides, I've offered financial help in this. Why should I expend my own resources for nothing in return?"

"Then leave the baby at the palace doors," Odin amended. "I'll arrange for one of the princes to find her while you keep watch. Come into the palace casually, find us hovered over the baby, and make your offer then."

"Wouldn't a destitute mother be more likely to leave her child with the healers?" Frigga asked quietly.

"There's my queen!" Odin praised her, the cunning spark of his youth flaring in his good eye. "It would be far easier to execute this plan at the House. Frigga could do it herself—in her disguise, of course—so the baby is safe during this entire charade. It will all have to be done with witnesses, while people believe the queen is still at the South Sea. And Frigga, you'll have to use your gifts to be seen several times before she is born, visibly *not* pregnant."

"This plan could work," Frigga remarked, feeling her heart break within her as a thought occurred to her.

"Why do you sound so sad?" Odin asked.

"Because I won't be able to nurse her," Frigga answered quietly.

"Actually, you could," Odin said brightly. "Vidar can make a show of finding a wet nurse for the child. If you return to the palace quickly enough, you could take another disguise and be the wet nurse. If most of your feedings are done in secret, no one need know."

"Where would I feed her in secret?" Frigga asked.

"I'm sure you remember the place I will never set foot in again," Odin said with a slight shudder.

"I remember," she said quietly with downcast eyes. "But are you sure you want the general to know about it? He may have to bring the baby to me there."

"He already knows about Loki's mother, though not about the room," Odin informed her.

Frigga looked up at Odin. "What does he know about Loki's mother?"

"Very little," Vidar interjected. "Does it matter? If nothing else, it shows I can keep a secret."

Odin cleared his throat nervously. "If you want to nurse her, Frigga, then that's what you'll have to do."

"And how will we explain why I've disappeared when the baby needs to nurse?" Frigga asked.

"You both know how to go invisible and cast illusions," Odin reminded her. "You'll figure something out. I'm certain of that."

"I think we've got a plan," Vidar announced triumphantly with gleaming eyes.

Despite her growing worry that something might go wrong, Frigga smiled at his delight over their joint performance. "Yes, General, we do. I hope you're ready to be a father."

31

Frigga watched with breathless ecstasy as all nineteen dragons whirled, soared, and darted through the air, bearing their riders with obvious delight. She wished with all of her might that she could be up there with them instead of sitting in the royal box, but Odin seemed to be doing a fine job in her place. The people packed into the arena stands seemed to share her fascination with the performance, and Frigga's heart swelled with pride over the success of her project—her baby.

My baby, she thought with rapture as she involuntarily put one hand over the slight swell of her stomach, which she always kept hidden from everyone but Vidar and Odin.

"Are you unwell, my queen?" one of the guards asked, the same who had been present when she injured herself at the dragon enclosure a week prior.

Baldur looked at her with immediate concern, but Thor and Loki were too entranced by the dragons in the air to notice.

"I'm fine," she gulped, making her breathing sound shallow as illusionary beads of sweat appeared on her brow. "I wish to see the rest of the show."

"Please let me know if you feel faint, Your Majesty," the guard insisted. "It would not do for all of Asgard to see you collapse."

That is exactly what they need to see, Frigga thought as she dismissed the guard's plea and Baldur's agreement with a wave of her hand.

The dragons landed, and the riders bowed to thunderous applause, their new Valkyrie pendants catching the sunlight now and again. Frigga fingered her own, sliding her thumb over the multi-colored stones. Odin, who was wearing the Vanaheim design in her honor, gestured to the queen to honor her involvement. She dipped her head in acknowledgment, grasping the rainbow pendant again to steady herself as the Asgardians cheered and roared their approval. Loki and Thor looked up at their mother with shining eyes.

"Mother, why are you so pale?" Loki asked with sudden dismay.

"You look terrible!" Thor exclaimed.

"Just a few more moments," she gasped as she let go of the miniature Yggdrasil at her throat to clutch at her illusionary stomach.

"Mother, please," Baldur whispered. "Everyone is watching!"

"Which is why I cannot ..."

But she didn't finish her sentence. As she pitched forward, Baldur sprang into action to hold her up before she fell. From the arena floor, Odin gestured for his son to escort the queen out of sight. She could hear the king dismissing the crowds as Baldur helped her to a private area. Even from where she doubled over and moaned in pain, she heard the worried murmur of the people as they poured out of the arena.

"Baldur, give me some space!" she gasped as he hovered over her.

Thor and Loki stayed a safe distance away, whispering to each other with frightened faces. Frigga hated deceiving her sons and causing them worry, but she knew she had no other option. The guard urged her to allow him to send for Eir, but Odin joined them before she had to answer.

"Take charge of the princes," Odin instructed the guard.

"I just need to sleep," Frigga said, slurring her words slightly.

"This is the third time, Frigga," Odin said in the guard's hearing as he was leaving with the princes. "I want you examined."

He lifted her up into his arms and carried her to the palace. He took her straight to their royal suite and lowered her onto the bed.

"That was all part of the act, wasn't it?" Odin asked with genuine concern.

"Yes, Odin, I'm perfectly fine," Frigga answered. She smiled as she felt a strange flutter in her abdomen. "I think I just felt the baby move."

His face twisted slightly, and she guessed he wished the child was his own.

"Everyone will expect you to call for Eir," Frigga warned him. "She may come on her own when she settles her dragon. She saw my act."

"I've already thought of that," Odin admitted. "We'll need her cooperation to make this more believable."

"But how?" Frigga questioned. "If she examines me, she'll know I'm pregnant. But if we can deceive her into thinking it's something else …"

"It would help your story be more believable, as I've already stated," Odin finished for her. "So what could we make it look like?"

"Stomach ulcers? An infection of the gut?" Frigga suggested. "That would fit with everything that's happened. But how will we convince her to let Patrice attend to me?"

"I think she will. She let you attend to Vidar, after all. But she would want to check on you from time to time. That's the only problem I foresee," Odin mused. "Perhaps the two of us together should just change her memory, though I would prefer not to do that."

"No, there's too much risk to your mind," Frigga protested. "I won't allow you to harm yourself over this. If she runs any tests, I can change the imaging or results she sees. And since she also believes I cannot have children, pregnancy may not occur to her."

A knock sounded at their door. Odin opened it to reveal two guards and the healer Eir, just as Frigga had predicted.

"When were you going to tell me about these issues you've been having, my queen?" the healer asked in her no-nonsense tone. "I think you have something more serious than that hematoma."

"It's nothing, Eir," Frigga said casually. "I only told you about that because you wanted to know why I wasn't riding. It's almost healed."

"I ran into General Vidar on the way here," Eir replied. "He says you had an episode of sunstroke at the South Sea. But sunstroke does not linger this long."

"What does?" Frigga asked, widening her eyes as if alarmed.

"After what I saw today and what the guard witnessed when you injured yourself a week ago, I've become quite concerned," Eir answered. "Have you experienced nausea and vomiting with your abdominal pain?"

Frigga dropped her eyes. "From time to time. As well as other problems I'd rather not discuss, if you catch my meaning."

"Did you eat anything unusual? Vidar said he had problems with a meal he ate some time ago. He's concerned whatever contaminated his food may have crept into yours when you stayed there for Lord Berg's reveal," Eir suggested.

"You're not suggesting foul play, are you?" Odin interjected. "Is someone poisoning the queen?"

"I wouldn't rule out the possibility, but I wouldn't publicize that either," Eir remarked. "It's possible the contaminant is natural. Especially since Vidar also had problems."

"And why have you drawn that conclusion?" Odin pried.

"I've not drawn any conclusions yet. But anyone who would poison the general and the queen would also target the entire royal family, in my opinion," Eir pointed out.

"Let's not panic and start spinning wild tales about espionage and intrigue," Frigga scoffed, silently wondering why Odin had brought up foul play. "But if the food was contaminated, wouldn't the princes and the guards staying at the cottage have fallen ill as well? And wouldn't I have fully recovered by now?"

"Not necessarily," Eir answered. "They may have all been in better health. The general was compromised by his accident when he had his episode. And in your case, heightened stress can weaken the immune system and irritate an existing condition."

"Then I should take some herbs for gut health," Frigga said confidently.

"Forgive me, my queen, but if you've had a gut infection for this long, it will not be a quick fix. Herbs are not enough," Eir contested. "You also need a good, long rest. And healing foods."

"How would you know for sure if that's the problem?" Odin queried. "Is it life-threatening?"

"At this point, no," Eir confirmed. "How often are you experiencing symptoms, my queen?"

"Not often. Very sporadically, I would say," Frigga answered.

"I could do imaging of her gut, but unless she has lesions, ulcers, or an obstruction, I won't see anything," Eir admitted. "I could also test her blood or collect a st—"

"Please no," Frigga interrupted. "I don't see a need for all of this. I know I don't have an obstruction. It seems clear to me it's a lingering gut infection."

"I agree, but just in case it is poison or something more serious, I think it's best for you to stay at the House of the Healers," Eir told her. She turned to Odin. "If she doesn't improve under treatment, then we'll know what steps to take."

"I'm not spending any more time at the House," Frigga protested. "I've had my fill of that place."

"Whatever will I do with you stubborn royals?" Eir sighed with exasperation. "The stress of palace life will most likely continue to exacerbate the issue and lead to long-term problems."

"What if she took a holiday?" Odin suggested tentatively. "Somewhere safe and hidden."

"That is an excellent suggestion, especially if someone is trying to poison her, though I cannot imagine who would do such a thing," Eir said thoughtfully. "Wherever she goes, she needs protection and care. I could possibly spare one of my assistants."

"I don't think that's necessary," Frigga interjected. "A holiday sounds wonderful, but I have so many things to do here. And what about my sons?"

"Even mothers should take a holiday from time to time," Eir admonished her gently. "You have done so much for so long, my queen. I believe you need this. And I want you to rest, not continue to worry about your responsibilities. Others can carry the load for a while."

"I agree," Odin said as he stroked his full black beard with one hand. "Especially with arranging for protection and care. I will tighten up security here and look into the possibility of a plot against the royal family. These things do happen, after all."

"That would be prudent, but keep it quiet as much as you can. You don't want to throw the kingdom into an upheaval," Eir warned. "Meanwhile, I will provide instructions for treating a gut infection."

"Eir, this is terribly embarrassing," Frigga spoke up. "I would prefer no details be shared about this."

"I would not do anything to make you uncomfortable, my queen," Eir said indignantly. "Prepare an official statement like we did with the king. And I'll sign off on it. Stay wherever you decide to go as long as you need. And I will choose a healer to look after you."

"Why do I need a healer?" Frigga protested.

"I am sure the king would agree it's better for someone trained to stay with you," Eir answered. "Especially if you have another blackout."

"Then I would prefer to choose my own healer. Someone I know from the healers who are not training as Valkyries," Frigga offered reluctantly.

"Who?" Eir prompted.

"General Vidar's cousin Patrice," Frigga answered. "If she is willing and available, that is."

"I remember her. I've heard she is doing quite well in her studies. Are you thinking of staying at the South Sea?" Eir asked.

"Yes, I find it incredibly relaxing there," Frigga replied. "It's remote but not too isolated. Odin, what do you think?"

"It would be quite convenient to have you there as opposed to the northern borders or the mountains to the west, if you cannot stay here," Odin answered slowly. "I do not want you to be confined to the House either."

"Do you think this wise, O King?" Eir interjected. "The South Sea is where she fell ill the first time. What if the contaminant is still there? It could even be in the water."

Frigga looked at Odin in consternation, stumped by this concern. He winked at her slightly, then responded, "I will arrange for purified water as well as careful inspection of food and all preparation areas."

"Very well. I'll agree to this on one condition," Eir asserted. "Patrice reports directly to me. And if the queen worsens, I am to be notified immediately. Do you agree?"

Frigga nodded. "I suppose I'd better start preparing to leave."

"The king and I will ready everything," Eir offered. "Right now, I want you to take a nap."

Frigga sighed gratefully. A nap sounded wonderful.

"I'll be along shortly, Eir," Odin told her. After she left, he turned to Frigga with a cunning glint of excitement in his eye. "She played right into our hands!"

"It was almost too easy," Frigga agreed, eyeing Odin with some suspicion. "Did you talk to her beforehand and decide not to tell me?"

"Of course not," Odin harrumphed. "The general's conversation with her was perfectly timed and well executed. And you were marvelous!" He paused and gave her a warning look. "Just don't get too skilled at deception, Frigga. I don't ever want to have to do this again. For either of us."

"Neither do I," Frigga agreed with a slight shudder. "Do you think you could have Eir speak with Patrice first about caring for me? Before Vidar tells her the real reason? And it might be best if people don't know where I am staying. I don't want any unexpected visitors."

"I was going to suggest that myself. I'm surprised you didn't notice, but Eir actually gave me an idea for a poisoning plot," Odin mused. "Why didn't I think of it before?"

"I did notice," Frigga admitted. "But don't you think that would be distressing to the people and complicated for us?"

"Not if we do it right," Odin reassured her. "But let's not speak of that now. You'd better obey Eir and take that nap. I'll arrange for you to leave with Vidar tonight. You've already packed most of your things?"

"Yes, I've been stashing everything in the old storeroom under the palace just as you instructed," Frigga replied. "What's left, I'll need to keep with me for the journey."

"Very good. I'll have the two guards we chose start loading those throughout the day," Odin informed her. "We don't want to draw attention or arouse suspicion."

He kissed her forehead, then strode from the room. Frigga sank into her bed and slept soundly, unaware of anything until Odin returned. He gently woke her to update her on all of the arrangements.

"Eir spoke with Patrice through Gjallar's link. And I persuaded Vidar there's no need to tell her the real reason for your seclusion until you're closer to delivery," Odin remarked. "By then, she might be more open to keeping quiet."

"What will we tell her then?" Frigga asked. "Will I have any privacy at all?"

"She'll stay as often as she can, but she won't be there all the time, at least not at first. We're going to spread a few rumors that someone has tried to poison you, which we'll also make a show of trying to squelch," Odin informed her. When Frigga tried to argue, he held up a hand and continued, "It will explain why you're hiding your location and not taking an entourage of palace staff. When you're seen in the village at the South Sea, make it look accidental. Perhaps even act worried with people who spot you and ask them not to reveal your whereabouts."

"Won't people check Vidar's cottage?" Frigga asked.

"Lord Berg and I are going to make it look like you're staying at his summer home," Odin answered with a self-satisfied grin.

"You've brought him into this now?" she gasped.

"Only into the suspected poisoning plot. I'll increase the guard here and let it leak that we are having the food tested. As soon as the baby is born, Vidar will take the disguise of a rogue assassin, whom we will pretend to capture and interrogate. I'm thinking we can have him fake his death in his prison cell after you return … before we can try him, of course."

"This plan continues to get more complicated," Frigga sighed. "Why is that even necessary?"

"Because people might still speculate about why you had a lengthy illness, especially when a baby shows up at the House," Odin answered. "Like you said yourself, people love scandals. And it was too easy with Eir. I'm concerned she might interfere again. We might need to add yet another layer to our deception."

"What does that mean?"

"I'll explain when I have it worked out in my own mind. All you need to do is your part," Odin said firmly, using the tone he used when he was finished with a discussion. "Vidar and I will handle everything else."

"Such great lengths to hide my wrongdoing," Frigga muttered. "I don't deserve the effort you're making."

Odin fell silent. Then he spoke gently, "I didn't deserve what you did for me either. And if I could bring myself to accept this baby, none of it would be necessary. I've tried a few times, but I just cannot."

Frigga looked away. "It's too late for that anyway."

"Yes, it is," Odin agreed. "But I have to admit, there is an exciting element to this." He stood. "You and Vidar leave in an hour."

"Through the Bifröst?"

"No, that's too risky. I've told Gjallar just enough to ensure he protects your privacy and location, but there are too many eyes at Asgard's gates," Odin stated as he handed her a threadbare cook's uniform. "We're smuggling you out of here on a farmer's wagon with your belongings. You'll be in disguise."

"Vidar too?" Frigga asked, shaking the dress out and looking it over as a strange excitement filled her.

"Yes, but without illusions. Physical disguises only, lest the guards realize Vidar's new gifts," Odin informed her. "And I don't want you to have to do anything more than hide your condition."

Frigga nodded as the excitement quelled and a quaking fear filled her. Knowing she was leaving the palace for months on end hit her with a staggering reality. Would her children suffer without her? Would she grow mad from loneliness during the long separation?

"Odin, I have to see the boys!" she burst out.

"Now? I'm bringing them out to you next month," he protested.

"Yes, now," she insisted. "Bring them here while I finish packing the last of my things."

"And what do you intend to tell them?" Odin inquired intently. "I've already explained everything."

"Surely, you don't mean everything," Frigga scoffed.

"I told them that you are unwell and have to go on holiday to recover," Odin clarified. "If they hear the rumors of the poison plot, I will deal with that then. What else do you need to say?"

"I only want to say goodbye to my children, Odin," Frigga answered testily. "Is that asking too much?"

Odin looked as if he intended to argue. But he finally nodded and left the room. Frigga hurriedly dressed in the worn uniform, then began gathering the rest of her belongings, struck by how empty her drawers and closets appeared. She soon lost herself in her task, visibly jumping when Odin opened the door and ushered all three boys into the room.

She sank down onto the bed and silently reached out for her sons to embrace her all at once, carefully avoiding any contact with her belly. One by one, they reluctantly released her and stepped back. The boys had understood when she had helped Vidar recover; would they understand now?

"How long will you be gone?" Loki asked, his bright green eyes dulling to a sad gray.

The boy held his chin and shoulders high, but his lower lip trembled ever so slightly, betraying his feelings. Thor stood beside him with his arms crossed, staring at the floor.

"It could be a long time, Loki. Several months at least," Frigga answered, desperately trying to control her own emotions. "Remember, Healer Eir and your father are sending me on holiday to get better."

"How sick are you?" Thor finally asked, raising his fierce blue eyes to meet hers. "Are you going to die?"

Baldur knelt before his younger brothers and put one large hand onto each of their shoulders. "Father wouldn't let anything happen to Mother. He's doing this for her. And we must all do our parts."

"I have no plans to die," Frigga added. "Not when I have all of you to live for. And your father will bring you to visit me whenever he can arrange it."

"What if he's busy?" Loki asked her, trying not to look at his father. "Who will bring us if he can't?"

"I'm old enough," Baldur boasted.

"We can talk about that later," Odin spoke up. "Your mother does not need to worry about such things right now. Only that you will see each other as often as we can manage it. Right now, you must say your goodbyes so she can finish what she needs to do before she leaves."

One by one, the boys hugged their mother again and whispered their well wishes and love. Frigga fought to maintain control, but her eyes welled up with tears despite her best efforts.

"It's okay to feel, Mother," Thor reminded her softly, reaching out to touch a tear that had escaped.

"Are you letting yourself feel, Thor?" she asked gently. "You seem angry."

He dropped his eyes. "That's just my sadness wearing a disguise like you are."

Odin glanced at his son with a sudden look of realization as if seeing himself in the boy's words.

"That was wise beyond your years, my son," Frigga told him.

Thor looked to his father, puffing his chest out slightly with pride. Odin acknowledged him with a nod, and a silent message seemed to pass between them. Something that had not yet occurred to Frigga hit her with a jolt. Could her absence become an opportunity for the boys to bond with their father?

How hard it is to let go, she thought sadly, hugging them one last time before they all filed out of the room.

After they had gone, Odin turned to her. "Our sons remind me of what we stand to lose if we don't find a way to get through this. I'd like to think you see it that way too."

Frigga raised her chin and gritted her teeth, hating the reminder of how much her choices had cost thus far. But knowing he was right, she declared, "That is why I accepted Baldur and Loki as my own in the first place."

Odin winced. "I deserved that." In an uncharacteristic show of emotion, he suddenly rushed to her, taking her hands into his. "Is there any hope for us, Frigga? Please tell me there's still hope."

She had no idea how to answer. She could not deny that she still loved Odin in some way, but her heart had chosen Vidar … yearned for him, in fact. And she knew she would not stay with the king if it were not for her sons and her people. But her circumstances were what they were. Did she really have any other options? And now, an unborn child had complicated things further. But since Frigga's nature was not one to wallow in despair, she raised her eyes to her husband's face and reached out one hand to tenderly cup his whiskered cheek.

"There is always hope, Odin," she replied simply.

He covered her hand with his own and tightly shut his good eye. A single tear squeezed out, and he abruptly stood. "When you're ready, meet Vidar at the stables. He will take you on horseback to where the guards are waiting with the wagon."

Frigga reached out for him, suddenly unwilling to part from him. Odin pulled her to her feet and folded her into his strong embrace, resting his head on hers briefly before releasing her. Just as quickly, he was gone. She gripped the handles on her remaining valises, then hid herself to walk down to the stables. She found Vidar and Vasili hidden in darkness behind the building. She revealed herself, fully aware of how her pain showed in her eyes.

"How do you fare, my queen?" Vidar asked gravely.

She wordlessly shook her head, grieved by the wounded look on his face. But she knew she could not speak, even to reassure him that what he most likely sensed did not mean she no longer loved him. She allowed the general to lift her onto the horse, then leaned against him when he mounted and spurred Vasili into a careful trot. She cloaked herself with invisibility again, focusing on the rhythmic movement of the magnificent stallion in an effort to soothe herself.

Finally, Vidar stopped near a section of the wild and wooded wilderness where Asgardian men went to complete their rites of passage. A hidden guard dressed in one of Vidar's spare uniforms stepped from the foliage and took Vasili's reins. No other guards or wagons were visible in the growing dark.

"What are we doing?" Frigga asked in confusion as Vidar helped her dismount.

"The other guards are waiting further in with the wagon," Vidar answered. He turned to the first guard, who had already mounted the stallion. "Stay under cover of darkness as much as you can. Your king does not wish our movements to be known."

"I'll keep to the countryside as much as possible," the guard responded briskly. "Take care of our queen, General."

Vidar bowed his head slightly and clapped his fist to his chest twice. The guard did the same, then rode Vasili in great haste back to the palace.

"Is this part of the plan?" Frigga asked when they were alone.

"Yes, anyone who sees him must believe I am returning from whatever errand I just went on," Vidar answered. "And Vasili won't go in there, so we would have had to walk from here even if I hadn't needed an alibi."

"Why wouldn't Vasili have gone in there?" Frigga asked, eyeing the trees fearfully.

"There are many dark creatures living in the wilderness," Vidar replied, reaching for her hand. "Don't be afraid. I will protect you." He stopped, and his face twisted again with some inner pain. "I will always protect you. To the death."

She pulled him toward her before he could lead her into the forest. "Wait, Vidar. You're going to visit me, aren't you?"

"How could I stay away?" he asked lightly, looking down at her tenderly.

Then he pulled her into a desperate embrace, his eyes filled with sudden grief. Almost without pause, he kissed her as if it would be their last moment together.

"You are acting so strangely," she murmured when he let her go.

"So are you," he whispered. "I know you don't want to leave. And it isn't just your sons you grieve. I feel your pain as if it were my own. I fear all of this will eventually come to an end and I might never see you again."

"You must not say such things," she admonished him. "Whatever happens, my heart will always belong to you."

"But not your will," he said sadly. "Your heart might choose me, but your will chooses him."

Shocked at how closely his thoughts mirrored her own, she allowed frustration to take hold and blurted out, "What choices do either of us have besides the ones we've already made? This was never what I wanted."

She buried her face in her hands as all of the pent-up stress released in great, gasping sobs. In the same manner as Vidar had said he could feel her pain, she felt his distress over her reaction keenly as she began to sink toward the ground, her heart squeezing her from the agony of her emotional duress. He held her up as if doing so kept him from collapsing himself.

"I'm sorry, Frigga," he choked out. "I'm so sorry that I've caused you this much pain."

"Please don't, Vidar," she pleaded as she clutched at him. "We cannot go back. Only forward. We have our daughter to think of now."

"You're right," he breathed. "I will know what it is to be a father because of you. Nothing can take that away from me. And no regret can live in me as long as that joy. I am content."

"Content?" Frigga pressed him. "I fear I will never be content but always divided. Caught between two men … two loves … two lives."

"No, Frigga," Vidar protested, holding her gaze intently with his own. "I too am divided, caught between two loves and two lives. Someday, we will both be whole again. I know this as deeply as I know my love for you and for our child."

Unable to speak yet again, Frigga allowed the comfort of Vidar's arms to wash over her until her heartbeat slowed to normal and her tears stopped. The small spark of hope she had experienced at Vidar's reassurance spread warmly through her heart, dispelling some of her anguish.

Suddenly, the babe leaped in her womb as if rejoicing in the closeness of her father.

Vidar pulled away and searched Frigga's face, his eyes filling with wonder. "Was that …"

"You felt her too?" Frigga asked shyly.

He nodded eagerly and spread the palm of his hand over her growing abdomen. "Her beginning might be less than ideal, but there is life growing here, Frigga. She gives me hope, just as you always have. No matter where our paths lead, mine will forever be linked to yours and now to hers."

"Day to day, night to night," Frigga began, reaching up to take hold of the rainbow Valkyrie pendant she rarely took off since Vidar had given it to her at the dragon launch.

"Onward till our paths unite," Vidar finished, closing his hand over hers that held the pendant. "My love for you both will never die even if I do. Death can only delay a love such as ours and only for a little while."

"Why do you speak of death, Vidar?" Frigga rebuked him, trembling within her at some sense of foreboding she did not understand.

"Only because it is a part of life," he answered solemnly. "And new life is before us."

"Then let us speak only of life," she pleaded softly. "She gives me hope too, as her father always has. Whatever partings we may face in the future, I will hold to that hope. Perhaps we will find a way to be together without causing pain to anyone else."

"I've never wished pain on anyone else, least of all you. Least of all Odin," Vidar lamented. "Nonetheless, I have brought it. That is a burden I must carry, but your love and trust in me make even that weight easier to bear."

"Is this regret I hear, my love?" she asked tentatively, the deep sorrow below the surface of her emotions threatening to overtake her yet again.

"You have asked me this before, my queen. My answer is the same," Vidar responded gently. "I wish I had followed a more honorable path, but I would not part from either of you for all the nine realms."

The baby kicked against Vidar's hand at this utterance. He bent over to kiss the spot, the closest he could get to his unborn daughter.

"She knows her father's voice," Frigga murmured lovingly, keeping her own hand near where the growing child had settled. "She is still now. I think she is comforted by your presence, as am I."

He stood and kissed Frigga's cheeks where they glistened from her tears, then whispered, "You will both be in my presence again. But for now, we must go."

She nodded, then took one last look at the twinkling lights of the palace off in the distance where she knew her other children must be winding down for the evening by now. As she turned to follow Vidar into the wilderness, a new chapter seemed to be unfolding before her. And though she had no idea what the unwritten pages of her life's story might contain, she somehow knew all of the glorious mess that had led her to this point would eventually fall away to reveal something beautifully crafted, something she could only begin to imagine. And that thought gave her a fresh surge of courage as she took one more step after the last one, gracefully moving onward.

ACKNOWLEDGMENTS

Many thanks to all the people who were part of making this book a reality. I wish I could name every single one of you, but since this book has been in the making for two years, there are just too many to count or list. But know that your involvement and efforts are valued and appreciated:

Dawn Lewis, for being the first to read the very raw rough draft and encouraging me to continue to develop it. Jacob Brein, Katy Ford, Ariana Meinking, and Jeremy Meinking for many incredibly helpful plot hashing sessions. Katy, you brought about the birth of the Valkyries because of this comment late one night: "Frigga just needs something else to focus on."

Both D'Anne Frazier and Jennifer Z. Marshall, for professional editing skills and incredible developmental insight, which have brought this book to an even better depth. Ariana Meinking, for bringing together the cover concept. Nick Zelinger, for his excellence and professionalism in producing yet another beautiful cover and interior layout. Both Jacob Brein and Veronica Yager, for being invaluable assets to my production team.

Kyanna Almanza, Amala Anand, Matt Anderson, April Aragon, Megan Austin, Nico Bamford, Shumane Bailey, Tina Baker, Brigid Bielak, Kenyon Bradley, Amanda Branch, Jacob Brein, Shawna Brenden, Sarah Brenner, Ollie Capperilli, Geneva Cazares, Kathy Chatel, Lori Christian, Pete Christian, Marissa Cleveland, Jordan Collman, Angela Creamer, Mary Cornell, Edward Dieball, Luis Duran, Carol

Fleske, Ashley Foote, D'Anne Frazier, Esther Frazier, Lillian Frazier, Rachel Frazier, Ariel Frengal, Sylvia Greene, Bruce Goldberg, Rayne Hall, Cambri Holden, Rita Hotchkiss, Kevin Jarbo, Ryan Jarbo, Maggie Hyatt, Emma Kennedy, Sarah Ketter, Daniel Kuehn, Autumn LaFountaine, Nancy Mandeville, Annette Mankin, Gilles Marchal, Kaitlynn Meach, Ariana Meinking, Jeremy Meinking, Sandy Thomas Meinking, Felicia Mize, Alyssa Montgomery, Melanie Muschanow, Tami Palmer, Mark Peer-lee, LaDonna Plew, Kyla Pohl, Jennie Price, Muffy Roberts, Jaymes Rosalez, Michelle Ross, Sarah Scherer, Laurence Sims, Dameon Spurgeon, Damian Starr, Chastity Sullins, Amber Sullivan, Cheyenne Tommaney, Becky Thomson, Jason Tippner, Pam Torivio, Christie Treen, Janelle Trujillo, Lance Tucker, Stacy Valverde, Nicholas White, Chloe Whitney, Je Wright, and Elizabeth Vance for reading scenes, for listening while I read aloud, or for offering opinions, expertise, and/or wisdom, whether derived from philosophy or experience. And as many as I was able to list, there are countless others who have come in and out of my life that have told me their stories or shared things with me that have inspired me. Thank you to all of you!

A pawtastic shout-out to all the pack members at the Great Wolf Lodge who put up with my oddities and ways of zooming everywhere for the better part of a year. How can so many people be "the best?" I cannot possibly name every single person who impacted me, but you all did in one way or another. Thanks for keeping me sane and making my time at the Lodge the best working environment I have ever had. You are all aces in my book!

And finally, a huge thank you to all my amazing backers from Kickstarter for helping me fund the publishing of this book:

Kenny Agostino
Russell Allen
Jamie Anderson
Matty Beniers
Bryce Bennett
Kevin Bickner
Maame Biney
Giorgia Birkeland
Aaron Blunck
Kevin Bolger
Brittany Bowe
Megan Bozek
Kenyon Bradley
Amanda Branch
Peny Campbell
Melayne Cohen
Darin & Tracy Elgersma

Kathy Filardo
Floatnetics
Melissa Fuentez
Michel Goossen
Allison Harvey
John Meinking
Steve & Sandy Meinking
Felicia Mize
Owens
Peer-Lee
Sharon Pettit
Jennifer Poole
Damian Starr
Becky Thomson
Alisha VanderVos
Kay Wolfe

Frigga, Odin, and Vidar will return in

TO LOVE A ROOK

Sign up for the newsletter for even more content and updates.

jennifermeinking.com

lokiofmidgard.com

email: ladymeinking@gmail.com

facebook.com/authorjennifermeinking

instagram.com/jennifermeinking

twitter.com/jenmeinking

pinterest.com/jennifermeinkingauthor